MW01138553

ON THE BORDER

Debra Walden Davis

READER'S COMMENTS

Debra Walden Davis' first novel, *Almost Home*, is great. Her second, *Whispers*, is greater. *On the Border*, third in her stand-alone series, is the greatest read so far. Her plots provide the chills and thrills that will keep suspense fans on the edge of their seats. Her characters are memorable and likely to pop up in the "next" story. This reader has a thing for Rick Hadley, described as 'tall and whatever'. If Elle Wyatt doesn't want him, I'll take him—especially to 'The Shed'. Do what ya can for me, Deb.

Sharolynne Barth, *The Dreamin' Tree*

Debra Walden Davis ... I read *Almost Home* 2-3 chapters at a time to make it last longer. It wasn't natural to me but I'm glad I read it that way. It was like you were telling me the story over coffee every day. Made it pretty special.

Pat Berndt Mccollum
Florida

Reading *Almost Home* was like reading about your life—not a work of fiction. Then came *Whispers*, and again I was on the edge of my seat. I've read a lot of 'who-done-its', yours ranks at the top for keeping me captive till the end.

Karen Evans Eckert
Arkansas

Write on! The stories are captivating, well-written and held my attention throughout. I am impressed with your writing skills and style.

Joe Skaggs
Arkansas

All rights reserved.
© 2020 by Debra Walden Davis

This book is a work of fiction. The characters, places and events are the
product of the author's imagination except as noted below. Any
resemblance to actual events, locales or persons living or dead is entirely
coincidental.

Actual places:
<u>Springfield, Missouri:</u>
Bambino's Café
Crosstown Barbeque
Mojo Pie Salon
Billiards of Springfield
Blue Room Comedy Club
The Moxie
Gailey's Breakfast Café
Casper's
Dublin's Pass
Harmony House
St. Agnes Cathedral Adoration Chapel
<u>Battlefield, Missouri</u>
Fabbiano's Auto
<u>Nixa, Missouri</u>
Piccolo's
<u>Poplar Bluff, Missouri</u>
The Rodgers Theatre
<u>Talent, Oregon</u>
The Grotto
<u>Astoria, Illinois</u>
State Street Grill
<u>Mackinaw, Illinois</u>
Tea Room at the Depot
Actual events:
<u>Harry Connick, Jr. Concerts</u>
Atlanta, GA (2007)
St, Louis, MO (2008)
<u>The Winter's Tale</u>
Oregon Shakespeare Festival
Ashland, OR (2006)
Actual persons:
Heather Heinrichs
Anthony Fabbiano
Springfield's Three Missing Women:
Stacy McCall, Suzie Streeter, Sherill Levitt
Fay Rawley
Ralph Manley

Printed by Kindle Direct Publishing
Available from: kdp.amazon.com and other retail outlets.

Cover art by BespokeBookCovers.com
peter@bespokebookcovers.com

This book may not be reproduced in whole or in part by
photocopy or any other means, without permission.

ISBN: 9781696018067

Songs Quoted in *On the Border*

"The Right Thing to Do", composer Carly Simon

"Walkin' Through the Park", composer Muddy Waters

"Let Them Talk", composer Sonny Thompson

"Marie Laveau", composers Baxter Taylor/Shel Silverstein

"You Can Sleep While I Drive", composer Melissa Etheridge

"Addicted", composer Cheryl Wheeler

"Ain't Too Proud to Beg", composers Norman Whitfield/Edward Holland

"Hush", composer Joe South

"Help!", composers John Lennon/Paul McCartney

"I Am a Rock", composer Paul Simon

"It's Five O'Clock Somewhere", composers Jim Brown/Don Rollins

"Something to Be Said", Shelby Lynne

"How to Handle a Woman", composers Alan Jay Lerner/Frederick Loewe

"California Dreamin'", composers Michelle Phillips/John Phillips

"Kiss", composers Lionel Newman/Haven Gillespie

"Margaritaville", composer Jimmy Buffett

"You Can't Talk Me into Loving You", composer Will Tucker

"All Around the World", composer Titus Turner

"Legend in Your Own Time", composer Carly Simon

"Revelation Road", composer Shelby Lynne

"The Thief", composer Shelby Lynne

"Lie", composers Brad Ramsey/Jason Peter Massey/Ruben Estevez

"Need You Now", composers Hillary Scott/Charles Kelley/Dave Haywood/Josh Kear

"If Two Wrongs Don't Make a Right", composers Eric and Wendell Erdman

"Sadie, Sadie", composers Jule Styne/Bob Merrill

"Woman", composer Bernard Webb (pseudonym for Paul McCartney)

"Wichita Lineman", Composer Jimmy Webb

For Hal Davidson
Thanks for guiding me through the maze.

In loving memory of
Brad Moses Justice Skiles
and
William Webster Walden

I'm out on the border
I'm walkin' the line
Don't tell me 'bout your law and order
I'm trying to change this water to wine"

From the song, "On the Border"
by
Glenn Frey, Don Henley, Bernie Leadon

· 1 ·

Missouri State Senator Claire Nelson Hutsell turned on the outside light and opened one of the French doors that led to her deck. It was 7:30 P.M., and the freezing rain predicted by southwest Missouri meteorologists had finally arrived.

Ice. Dangerous if one was out on the road, but from where she stood, the frozen water glistening on the trees in her back yard was beautiful.

She started to push the door shut when her dog barked and shot through the opening.

"Chewy, get back here!"

The Beagle/Corgi mix didn't stop until he'd reached the end of the stone walkway at the entrance to the greenhouse. He began growling.

"Chewy, it's probably just an animal trying to get out of the weather. C'mon, it's too cold to be out." The growling continued. "Chewy. Come."

When her command went unheeded, Senator Hutsell went with the word she knew would get her dog to return no matter what had captured his attention.

"Treat."

Instead of turning on his heels and double-timing it to the house, Chewy began running along the glass walls of the greenhouse. He replaced his growling with aggressive barking. The motion sensing lights around the structure illuminated the area. The senator saw a figure move inside the building. From its size and shape she realized it wasn't a shelter-seeking critter that had invaded her greenhouse.

Always leery of putting her name and address on the airwaves in today's political environment, she called her son, former Greene County Deputy and St. Louis Detective, John Hutsell.

"John, there's someone in the greenhouse. It's probably one of the homeless men from the camp across the field at back of the estate. Chewy's going nuts, and I can't get him back inside."

"Mom, don't you dare go out there; you hear me?"

"Yes, John. And don't you dare get on the road in that red sports car of yours."

"I'll call Rick, and we'll be there as soon as we can."

"Tell him to drive safely."

"Yes, Mom."

Rick Hadley pulled his four-wheel drive Silverado into the driveway leading to the Senator's home just outside Springfield, Missouri. His partner, John Hutsell, sat in the passenger seat.

"Just park in front of the garage door," Hutsell said. Then in his cell, "We're here, Mom. Where are you?"

"The kitchen."

"Stay there. I'll use my key to the mudroom."

"Got it," she replied. "Oh, John?"

"Yes."

"Remember to walk like a penguin . . .." Hutsell allowed a half smile and waited for his mother's safety-tip punch line, ". . . *not* like an Egyptian."

"I don't hear Chewy barking," Hutsell said, once inside.

"He gave up and is warming himself by the heating vent in the bathroom. Maybe the guy left."

"Rick and I will check it out."

The two private detectives were at the French doors when Senator Hutsell said, "Warm coffee cake when you boys return."

Her son looked over his shoulder and caught his mother's eye. She smiled and said, "Yes, John, it's almond apricot. "

"Thank goodness. 'Blueberry is so overdone these days,' " he teased, cabbaging his cousin Elle Wyatt's comment from when the two were teens.

He looked at his partner. "Long before you arrived on the scene, Hadley," he said. "It was the night of a bake sale at our high school, the day after Elle had passed her driver's test. Aunt Jean was in the passenger seat of her SUV; Mom and I were in the back. Elle stuck the key into the ignition, then turned to Jean, and out of the blue, said, 'Blueberry is so overdone these days.' "

Hadley laughed. "That's my girl; she is partial to peach, though."

"And blackberries," said Claire Hutsell. "She'll have you picking them this summer, Rick."

"Whatever her heart desires, ma'am," Hadley replied with a smile.

John and Rick headed toward the greenhouse. The motion lights soon came on. Hutsell stopped at the entrance and looked at Hadley. Rick nodded his readiness. John opened the door and eased inside. Once he was satisfied the main room was clear, he used the door frame to the annex as cover and peered inside. He soon spied the partial outline of a body behind a potting bench.

"Come on out," he said.

There was no reply.

"There's two of us, and we're armed."

Still no response. Hutsell motioned the intruder's position to his partner. Hadley moved along the outside glass wall. Another motion sensor light came to life, startling the person inside. Rick could now see a petite woman crouched between tables. She turned her head in his direction. He hadn't seen that kind of fear since his days with the Shannon County, Tennessee, Sheriff's Department. She glanced at the side entrance, then back at Hadley. As she tried to gauge her chance of escape, Hutsell spoke again.

"Nobody wants to hurt you, but we will use force if necessary."

Rick made his way to the side entrance and slightly opened the door.

"It's a woman, and she's holding a trowel," he told his partner.

"You need to drop the weapon," Hutsell said. "We're coming in."

Hutsell moved to where he could see the intruder. She was hunched down. She dropped the gardening tool without meeting his eyes.

"Put your hands where I can see them," he said.

Still looking down, she complied by placing her hands on either side of her head, palms outward.

"Get to your feet," he instructed. When she didn't move, he took a step toward her. She immediately rolled into a fetal position and covered her head with her hands. His trained eyes took in the scene. She was alone, and he could see no other weapons at hand.

"Looks clear," Hutsell said to Rick. Then to the woman, "I'm going to help you to your feet."

He was a step away when she kicked out. The potting bench crashed to the concrete floor. Hutsell took a step back.

"Everything okay?" Hadley asked.

"She's a fighter."

"Dang. Guess it's time for the police, then," Hadley said in hopes she would feel her chances would be better with them than with the authorities.

Hutsell followed with, "Yeah, I hate to get them, but . . .."

"Don't. I'll come out."

The woman rose to her feet. She slowly turned, and lifted her head enough that John Hutsell could see her face.

"Damn," he said.

· 3 ·

John Hutsell and Rick Hadley studied the woman standing in front of them.

"What's your name?" Hutsell asked.

The woman remained silent.

The two men took a few steps back and talked in hushed voices.

"How old do you think she is?" Hadley asked.

"Eighteen . . . nineteen, maybe," Hutsell said. "You got your medical bag in the truck?"

"Yep."

Hutsell tried again to engage the young woman in conversation, "How'd you get hurt?"

Still no response.

"What do you think?" he asked Hadley. "Beating or car accident?"

Hadley surveyed the bruises and abrasions on the woman's face.

"Could be both," he said. "Look at the color of her bruises, John. They're too old to be the result of a car accident due to tonight's icy roads. But there's fresh blood around the cuts and abrasions."

"Yeah, I see what you mean," Hutsell said "Call Elle on your way to the truck. Our visitor's going to need a change of clothes." He turned so his back was to the woman. "But first, I'm going to step outside and call my mom. She doesn't need to be a witness to this."

"In other words, plausible deniability. I hate the political climate these days."

"Yeah, you never know who's going to take an innocent act of kindness and turn it into something it's not."

Rick Hadley had first-hand knowledge of how easily damage could be done. Years ago, he'd been home from college for the summer when a lawyer in Shannon County, Tennessee, set out to discredit Rick and a former girlfriend in favor of his peeping-tom client. The man had insinuated that Rick had fathered a child with his client's victim. The lawyer topped off the story by 'suggesting' that Rick had abandoned Kerry Donlan, forcing her to abort the child—none of which was true.

Hutsell returned after completing his call. He took a step in the young woman's direction. She backed away causing him to stop.

"What's your name?" he asked for a second time.

"Amber," she said.

"Okay Amber, let's head to the house." He moved aside so she could pass in front of him. "We'll be in the den," he said as they walked by Rick.

Hadley remained behind and called Elle Wyatt. He explained the situation and ended by saying, "Now Wyatt, I know you're great behind the wheel and all, but . . . .."

"Yeah, I know. I kind of like you, too, Hadley," she said. "See you in a few."

Rick put his phone in his pocket and went to get his medical bag.

Amber was sitting on a blanket covering the sofa when Rick entered the den. As he advanced toward her, she used her feet and arms to push herself farther into the sofa.

"Don't touch me."

"Amber, he's a licensed EMT. He knows what he's doing," Hutsell said.

"I don't care."

Amber climbed over the sofa's arm to put distance between her and Hadley. She was attempting to crawl backwards across an end table when her eyes rolled back in her head. She fell to the floor, taking a ceramic planter with her. Being supine increased the blood flow to her brain and allowed a return to consciousness. She picked up a piece of the broken pot and held it out as a weapon. Realizing how futile an act it was, she positioned it above her wrist instead. She looked at Rick and repeated, "Don't touch me."

"Amber, you're making this way harder than it needs to be," Hutsell said.

"I don't want 'him' to touch me."

"Lost your touch there, Hadley?" Elle Wyatt asked as she entered the room with a bag on her arm. Then, to the woman on the floor, "He's an Eagle Scout for crying out loud. He wouldn't know the first thing about doing you any harm." She winked at Rick and asked, "So, what's 'wrong' with him?"

"He's a man."

Elle looked up and down Hadley's six-foot-four frame and smiled.

"That, he is," she said. She placed the bag on the floor. "But you need medical attention, so what's it going to be?"

"You can do it," Amber replied.

"I'm not the medical professional here, he is," Elle said.

The woman looked at Elle. "Please, don't let him—them— touch me," she begged with wide, innocent eyes.

Elle looked at Rick for guidance when a soft voice came from the hall.

"You can call Jenise."

Elle's eyes immediately went to her cousin. With the exception of Amber, his mother's suggestion would affect him more than anyone else in the room. He was sitting with his elbow propped up on the arm of the chair. His thumb was under his chin for support, while his index finger lay against his cheek. "John?" she asked, wanting his approval before she made the call.

Hutsell rose to his feet. "Yeah, go ahead," he said, and walked out of the room.

Rick gave Elle a questioning look. "Later," she mouthed.

· 4 ·

The Senator saw the lights of Jenise Alexander's Cherokee as it turned off a farm road and onto her estate. She walked into the kitchen. Her son was staring blankly out the window over the sink.

"John?"

"Yes."

"She's here," she said. "Elle told her to wait, with the doors locked, until you arrived to safely escort her inside."

"Okay," he said.

John Hutsell set down his coffee cup, picked up his coat and headed for the mudroom door. His hand was on the knob when his mother spoke again.

"John, we needed someone we could trust."

He did a half turn and looked in his mother's eyes.

"I know, Mom," he said. "It'll be all right."

The Cherokee's driver watched as John Hutsell made his way to her car. The vehicle's headlights kept him from seeing her until he was standing outside the SUV's door. The window lowered. Her hair was shorter and lighter than the last time he'd seen her.

"Hello, Jenise," he said.

"John."

"Ready when you are."

She raised the window and turned off the ignition. He heard a click and opened her door.

"It's slick," he said and offered his arm to steady her as she climbed out of the vehicle. She chose to exit without his assistance.

"Thanks for coming, Jenise," Claire said as she took Alexander's coat.

"Not a problem, Mrs. Hutsell. Where's the patient?"

"I'll take you to her," John said.

Rick Hadley was leaning against the door frame when his partner approached, followed by a woman he gauged to be a few years younger than John. Her face was unreadable.

Hutsell looked at Hadley and said, "I'll make introductions later."

Rick stepped aside so Alexander could enter the room. Elle and Jenise acknowledged each other with a nod.

"Rick and I will be in the great room if you need us," John said, knowing his cousin was capable of handling anything Amber could dish out.

"Amber, this lady is an emergency room nurse—and a friend—so play nice," said Elle Wyatt.

Alexander examined her patient and provided treatment for the woman's external injuries. She picked up her medical bag and told the young woman to try to get some rest. She then made her way to the great room to discuss the woman's condition with Hadley and Hutsell. John was standing to the right of a free-standing fireplace when she entered. Chewy was lying nearby, and perked up as she walked in.

"She's running a fever and experiencing pain in her lower abdomen and back," she said. "I escorted her to the bathroom and positioned myself so she couldn't flush when finished. Her urine was dark in color, accompanied with a strong odor. Not sure, but blood may have been present."

Rick Hadley, carrying two cups of coffee, arrived in time to hear her comments.

"You thinking UTI?" he asked as he offered Alexander one of the cups.

"UTI?" John said.

"Urinary tract infection," Jenise answered without looking in John's direction. She accepted the cup, and continued with her assessment. "Her pain is located in the lower abdomen as opposed to the upper portion, which is an indicator, but there could be other causes."

Rick stuck out his hand. "Rick Hadley," he said, introducing himself.

"Jenise Alexander," she replied, and shook his hand.

"I'm sorry," John said at his failure to introduce the two. "Jenise, Rick and I partner Gambit Investigations." He turned to Rick and took the second cup of coffee. "Jenise and I met when I was with the Greene County Sheriff's Department. Jenise is an emergency room nurse at Melcher Memorial South."

Rick glanced at her left hand, no wedding ring. "Miss Alexander."

"In addition to being a good investigator, Rick's also an EMT," John added.

Jenise looked at John and said, "Elle informed me of Mr. Hadley's credentials." Alexander turned her attention back to Rick. "She also told me about your suspicions concerning the timing of the woman's injuries. I concur; her bruises are over a week old, while the cuts and abrasions are recent."

"Did she offer any explanations?" Rick asked.

"She said the car she was in slid on the ice and ended up in a ditch."

"Were there any other passengers?" John asked.

"She wouldn't say."

"Doesn't add up," John said. "If you've been hurt in an accident, you seek help, not hide from it. And she doesn't have a purse, so no identification."

"I asked her a series of questions she couldn't—or wouldn't—answer, such as 'what town are we in' and 'what day is it.' " Alexander sipped her coffee. "She's presenting as malnourished; she's inappropriately dressed; no explanation of old scars. Gentlemen, she's got a barcode tattoo on her inner arm."

"She could be a victim of sex trafficking," Rick said.

Alexander nodded.

"Sounds like a 'branding' tattoo," Hutsell added. "Saw several during my time with the St. Louis PD."

John Hutsell looked from Alexander to Hadley and said, "We need to proceed very carefully from here on out. I don't want my mom involved."

"Understood," Rick said.

At that moment, Chewy jumped up, ran to the French doors and started barking. John took Jenise's arm and ushered her to the den's entrance. Rick followed and found Elle peeking between the drapes as the lights to the north side of the greenhouse came on. He

11

caught her eye. She moved her head up and down, confirming the presence of a second trespasser.

The exchange did not go unnoticed by the young woman reclining on the sofa. She shot to a sitting position.

"Don't let them take me," she pleaded, looking every bit a scared little girl. Her eyes went to Rick and then John. "I'll do anything you want—both of you—anything!"

The two detectives exchanged glances and went into action. John headed to the French doors as Rick motioned Alexander and her patient to the space between the bookshelf and a perpendicular wall. He doused the room's lights. He withdrew his weapon from his ankle holster and stood guard where he could see both inside and outside the room.

"What's going on?" Claire Hutsell asked her son from the kitchen.

"With me, Mom, now!

Shielding his mother from view, he steered her past the den to the adjacent bathroom.

"What about everyone else?" she asked.

"Rick has it under control. Now go!"

John made a side trip to the kitchen to get his parka before heading outside.

· 5 ·

The Hutsell Estate had two wings; each branched off the great room at a forty-five-degree angle. From Rick Hadley's vantage point, he could see all four points of entry: the French doors to the courtyard, the sliding glass doors of the den, its window, and the hall leading to the southeast door of the garage.

Elle Wyatt was stationed at the glass doors that opened onto a deck. Rick knew from experience that John's blue-eyed blonde cousin could handle herself in an intruder situation. Pity those who underestimated her, he thought, for they would find themselves on the wrong end of a stick. It was one of the reasons he found her so attractive.

A weak Amber was crouched down with Jenise Alexander in a corner of the room with a bookcase providing cover, while Senator Hutsell was in the next room. Hadley whispered for all to set cell phones to silent and then he waited. Sooner or later there would be a clue, one signaling danger or one signifying all was clear.

John Hutsell slipped quietly onto the lanai and made his way to the greenhouse. He was tracking a dancing light moving toward a road east of the estate when he realized the person responsible for the night's second incursion was now in retreat.

The light suddenly stopped moving. Hutsell eased ahead until he was close enough to see a still burning flashlight lying at the bottom of a small ravine. He was cautious in his approach, stopping every few steps to listen for sounds of the whereabouts of the light's owner. He heard a branch snap and a grunt. Hutsell picked up the flashlight and rounded a cedar in time to see a figure use a tree limb to pull himself up an incline. He followed, but was slowed by the slick terrain. He crested a small ridge and saw the red taillights of a waiting vehicle. Hutsell fired his weapon in the air. If the intruder was contemplating a return visit, he'd definitely think twice before setting foot on the Hutsell Estate again. He watched the man duck and jump into the passenger seat of a small recovery vehicle. John heard the door slam and the sound of tires spinning on ice. The tires finally gained traction and the truck took off. John scanned the fleeing vehicle for details that might help identify it at a later time. The truck disappeared. Hutsell pulled out his cell, and called his partner.

"Just missed him. He's cleared the farm road and is well on his way to Hwy FF," he said. "How are things on your end?"

"Copacetic."

"We've got a big problem, Rick."

"Which idiom you want, John? 'First rodeo' or 'falling off a turnip truck' "? Rick said referring to their experience and abilities.

"This involves my mother, Rick," John said, stressing the seriousness of this particular situation.

And Jenise Alexander, thought Hadley.

"Then get your butt back here so we can make a game plan."

Rick Hadley took a chair across from John Hutsell. An almond apricot coffeecake sat on the table between them. Claire Hutsell was making a fresh pot of coffee while the two men discussed the situation.

"Our latest visitor managed to track Amber to the greenhouse," John said. "The ice was soft enough in a few places to allow for imprints. No need looking for the car Amber was riding in. A recovery vehicle just towed it off. They've got to have connections to get a tow truck as fast as they did. You know tow companies are backed up tonight. We saw at least four vehicles in the ditch on our way here."

"Either that or they have deep pocketbooks. Question is, will they continue to look for her or high tail it out of the county?" Rick asked. "On one hand they might assume the authorities have been called, cut their losses and run. But on the other . . .."

"It depends on how well indoctrinated Amber is. How much they think she'll give up."

"She's already told Elle she won't talk to the police," Rick said. "We can't just dump her on the street. We could put her up in a motel, but those chasing her might have informants scattered

14

around town. There's also the possibility they'll be staking out the city's homeless shelters."

"Well, she can't stay here, or anywhere associated with the Senator," John said, with reference to his mother. "Which means even the Gambit Building is out."

"Wish we knew of a safe house," Rick said. "One in a rural setting, where neighbors wouldn't be tracking the comings and goings of its occupants."

"Well we don't have time to consult a real estate agent, Rick."

"Maybe you do," Claire Hutsell said. "John, do you know Carine Velardi?"

"I've seen her signs around town."

"Her ex-husband buys and flips houses. When renovations are complete, she acts as his broker. He might have one that's not quite ready to go on the market." She carried the coffee carafe to the table and refilled their cups. "The house would be vacant and utilities would be hooked up and in his name."

"Can you trust her?" John asked.

"Remember when you and Rick were working the Anniversary Killer case in St. Louis? You called and said a guy in Shannon County, Tennessee wasn't playing by the rules."

"Yeah. You persuaded Missouri's AG to contact the Tennessee Attorney General, and we got a warrant."

"I helped her with a similar situation two years ago. We can trust her," she said, matter-of-factly.

"What about her ex?"

"The situation involved their daughter's former boyfriend. He's no longer a problem. They were both very appreciative of the low-key manner in which everything was handled. I'm confident the Velardis will work with us."

"Carine Velardi and Jean are good friends," Elle said of her adoptive mother/aunt as she entered the room. "Carine recommends Wyatt Interiors to her clients, and Jean suggests Velardi Real Estate to friends and colleagues." Elle took a mug from a cabinet and walked to the table. Her aunt Claire filled her cup. "What's going on that we need the Velardis?"

John relayed the key points of the conversation as Elle cut the coffeecake. She placed a slice on a small plate and sat down next to Rick.

"Rick, have you got one of our burner phones in your truck?" John asked.

"Sure do. I'll get it."

Hadley slipped on his coat and headed for the mudroom and the outside door beyond.

"How's it going in there?" John asked his cousin.

"Well, you made some points in chasing the guy off and a few more by not calling the sheriff's department. She's actually dozed off a couple of times but jumps every time her head drops. Jenise has a calming effect on Amber—partially because she's a nurse but also because of Jenise's nature. Jenise is the whole package—Florence Nightingale, Mother Teresa and Princess Diana—rolled into one."

Rick walked back into the kitchen in time to hear Elle's description of Jenise Alexander. He placed the ghost phone on the table. He gently squeezed Elle's shoulder on the way to his chair.

"By the way, Amber is now wearing the clothes I brought from home. Hers are in a bag inside the hall closet. I figured they'd end up either in Rick's lab or that of the highway patrol."

Claire Hutsell put a paper containing Velardi's number on the table.

John picked up the phone and handed it to Elle.

"You want to do the honors since you are acquainted with her?" he asked.

"Sure."

"Ms. Velardi won't recognize the number so you may have to leave a message," John said. He checked the clock on the wall: 11:05 P.M. "She may not answer at all."

"I'll just keep calling till she does."

·6·

Carine Velardi's ex-husband was more than willing to help Senator Claire Nelson Hutsell's son. Cid Velardi credited the senator with his freedom. If she hadn't intervened on his daughter's behalf, Cid would probably be serving time in an Oklahoma prison for assault. He was happy to provide a ranch style home on a rural route east of Clever, Missouri, at the disposal of John Hutsell—no questions asked.

With Amber and Jenise in the back seat of Alexander's Cherokee, John Hutsell drove the vehicle to Velardi's ten-acre property. Hutsell drove by way of Wilson's Creek National Battlefield to the rural town of Clever, some twelve miles southwest of his mother's home near the city of Battlefield. He backed into the driveway that led to the detached garage and put the vehicle in park. He checked the time: 12:30 A.M. While he waited for Ms. Velardi to arrive with the key, he mentally went over the plan he and Rick had devised while sitting at his mother's dining table.

The home was vacant, so the first step was to obtain the bare necessities for setting up house. Rick and Elle were now shopping in a 24-hour discount department store. Rick's list included one full and three twin air mattresses with built-in pumps, a fold-in-half table and four chairs. Elle was responsible for food and personal care items. She would also pick up a few pieces of clothing as she made her way from the grocery section to health and beauty. Thanks to Elle, they had cash on hand.

For most of her thirty-three years Elle hadn't been the responsible type, so their Grandpa Nelson had put Jean in charge of Elle's finances – a position Jean would hold for two more years. As a result, Elle had always kept large sums of cash at the ready. Throughout her adult life, Elle had often taken to the road when life started to close in—running, the family called it. Use of cash was her way of keeping Jean from tracking her moves through credit cards. A year ago, Elle had been on the edge and had put herself in several life and death situations. In the past ten months, she had drastically turned things around—especially after she'd let Rick Hadley become a part of her life.

Step two would be to contact a doctor they could trust. Amber had a fever—an indication her body was likely fighting an infection. They needed a prescription for antibiotics. Jenise Alexander had provided an answer by suggesting they call a physician who volunteered at Rita's Rose, a Springfield clinic for low-income families and the homeless. Jenise donated her time at the clinic as well and felt that Dr. Timothy Shulman would help. As soon as they were settled inside the house, Jenise would make the call.

Their next move would depend upon Amber. From their law enforcement experience, both John and Rick believed that Amber was a victim of sex-trafficking. They knew victims were distrustful of authorities and in many cases loyal to their captors. Amber didn't fit the latter as she had more or less asked for asylum. The question was, would she cooperate so those responsible could be located and eventually prosecuted. John knew sex trafficking was a problem in southwest Missouri from his days with the Greene County Sheriff's Department and recent headlines. So far, the only crime that could be proved was trespassing on the part of Amber. If, and when, he discovered anything substantial, he would pass it on to law enforcement.

Headlights appeared on the lane leading to the driveway where Hutsell and his charges sat. John exited the Cherokee and moved so the car's driver would see him and stop before reaching the Cherokee. The vehicle pulled in and parked. The window went down. An attractive blonde woman sat at the wheel. Hutsell guessed her to be in her late forties.

"Ms. Velardi?"

"Yes."

"I'm John Hutsell."

"I recognize you from media reports," she said of the national attention John had garnered in helping to solve Springfield's Cross Timber Murder five years ago and the Anniversary Killer Case last year in St. Louis. "Here's the key," she said as she handed him an envelope through the open window. "Internet is available. The password's in there, too. Cid said the house is yours for as long as you need it."

"I appreciate it."

"Not a problem. If Cid or I can be of further assistance, don't hesitate to let us know."

"Will do. Good evening."

Once Velardi was out of sight, John returned to the Cherokee.

"Amber, the ground is extremely slick. For your safety, will you let me assist you inside?" he asked.

The young woman nodded. Progress, thought Hutsell.

With key in hand, John Hutsell escorted Amber to the home's entrance. Jenise Alexander followed. The front door opened into the living room. There was an arched entryway in front and off to the right that led to the kitchen. They moved past a wall to a hallway on the left.

There was little furniture, so the trio made their way down the hall to the full bath where Amber could sit on the toilet lid. Jenise stood in the hall and called Dr. Shulman. When the doctor agreed to make a house call, she handed her cell to John so he could relay driving instructions. John then checked out the rest of the house. There were two small bedrooms across from the bathroom. One housed Velardi's renovation equipment. Next to the bathroom was the master bedroom with an adjoining bath. He chose this room to set up two of the twin air mattresses. One for Amber and one for whomever would sit with her.

Rick and Elle pulled up in the driveway at twelve-forty in separate vehicles. Elle carried several plastic bags inside, passing John on his way outside to help Rick. She entered the kitchen and was thankful it had been high on Cid Velardi's list of rooms to renovate. She deposited the bags on a small island, took a few steps to the oven and set it to preheat. It wouldn't be long until the frozen pizzas would be ready. Not the best fare, but they would have to do. Rick soon arrived with a coffee maker, flatware and dinnerware. John followed with pans, a skillet and linens. He spied the pizza boxes and gave his cousin a look.

"C'mon, John," she said. "You've had worse. Think stakeout in St. Louis."

19

"In St. Louis I could lay my hands on bar-b-que for a stakeout."

Elle held up one of the boxes like she was in a commercial.

"The crust is stuffed" she said.

"I'm not impressed," Hutsell replied.

"With me or DiGiornos?"

Rick smiled and from behind John's back mouthed, "I'm impressed with you."

While John and Rick inflated mattresses, Jenise sat in the bathroom as Amber showered. When done, Amber exited the shower, dried off and donned flannel pajamas and warm socks. Jenise handed her a new toothbrush and watched as the young woman slowly took it and walked to the sink. Amber stared at her image in the mirror before turning on the water to brush her teeth. A few minutes later the two women made their way to the master bedroom where Amber was greeted with a bed, linens and a comforter. A sheet had been attached to a curtain rod above the window with a second bed positioned below. A folding chair leaned against a wall.

"Either one," Rick said to Amber. "Your choice."

Amber chose the bed closest to the door.

He unfolded the chair for Jenise and said, "Make yourselves comfortable ladies. I'll see about dinner."

Jenise took Amber's temperature in order to have an accurate reading for the doctor.

"Still the same," she said. "A hundred and two."

Rick returned and said dinner would have to wait, the doctor had arrived.

Dr. Shulman joined John, Rick and Elle in the kitchen after he had examined his patient.

"The closest all-night pharmacy is in Nixa. I can make the call now, if you'd like," he said to the group.

"That would be fine," John said.

"What name would you like me to use?"

"Amber Lawrence," John said.

Dr. Shulman walked into the living room and placed the call. Elle was spooning chicken soup into a bowl when he returned.

"I'd like to run some tests, but Amber refuses to go to the clinic tomorrow. With all the regulations concerning non-profits, I can't just hand carry specimens in."

"Doctor, we are in the process of setting up a private forensics lab in Springfield. We already have several pieces of equipment. I might be able to run the tests for you," Rick said. "What do you need?"

"To check for the presence of E. coli and staphylococcus in her urine. I'd also like to screen for STDs. Some can be detected in a urine sample, but others require a blood test."

"I can perform those for you."

"Here are specimen containers for Jenise to collect samples," Shulman said as he placed them on the table. "She has my personal number. Contact me when you have results."

John Hutsell walked over and extended his hand. "Thank you, Doctor," he said.

The two men clasped hands. John released his grip, Dr. Shulman did not. He held on and said. "Mr. Hutsell, I know you have to handle this situation in a way that protects your mother, but I'm counting on you to make sure the same considerations apply to Jenise."

"Yes, sir," John said.

John Hutsell stood on the porch, watched Shulman's SUV drive off and wondered how much the doctor knew of his private history from over five years ago.

Elle Wyatt entered the master bedroom carrying a bed tray with a bowl of chicken soup and a cup filled with cranberry tea. She handed it to Amber and sat down on the air mattress under the window.

"Rick's on his way to Nixa to get antibiotics. It will take a while with the icy conditions even though his truck is four-wheel drive."

"I remember seeing him in a national news report about The Anniversary Killer. That was about a year ago, wasn't it?" Jenise asked.

"Yes. Rick was a deputy sheriff in Shannon County, Tennessee, at the time. He had a couple of unsolved murders

21

related to a case John and his St. Louis partner had picked up on Valentine's Day."

"I had no idea he was so tall," Jenise said.

Elle smiled. "Yeah, it comes in handy when he's chasing the bad guy. He can see over the crowd."

"He seems pretty enamored with you."

"'Enamored'," Elle repeated. She shook her head and smiled. "Keep talking like that, and you'll increase your status in his eyes. He believes if a person has a good vocabulary, he or she won't feel the need to cuss. A good vocabulary never stopped me from pulling out a four-letter word here and there, though."

"How long have you two been together?" Jenise asked.

"He and John left law enforcement and opened Gambit Investigations in May of last year. We were good friends for several months. In early August things started to change. It wasn't until the end of September . . . ." Elle Wyatt paused, remembering the memory.

"The incident in Tennessee?"

"Yeah. He figured out what was happening before it even took place. He was there before the blood on the carpet was dry." Elle gave Amber a look of caution that said, *this guy is important to me, and you better not cause him a moment's grief.* She slowly looked back at Jenise and added, "Even then I continued to push him away."

"What changed your mind?"

Elle laughed. "A conversation with his mother. And that my dear friend, is a different story for a different time." Elle stood and stretched her arms over her head. "What about you? You still seeing Kyle?"

"Yes . . . ."

"But . . .?" Elle asked.

"He's my best friend. He's always—always been there for me. Kyle would do anything I asked without question."

"Best friend? Sounds like Rick and me last summer. Maybe you should have a talk with Kyle's mother," Elle said, only half-joking.

Amber moved the tray to the floor and lay down on the make-shift bed.

"I'll sit with her," Elle said to Jenise. "Why don't you go have some dinner? There's pizza in the kitchen."

Jenise rose to her feet and picked up her bag. "Think I'll head out. I'm scheduled to work at the clinic tomorrow."

"Good to see you again, Jenise."

"Yeah . . . well we do travel in different circles now," said Jenise, her tone somewhat sarcastic.

The change in Alexander's voice did not go unnoticed by Amber.

John Hutsell was drinking coffee at the kitchen window when Jenise Alexander walked through the entry.

"How's it going—?" He stopped midsentence when he realized it wasn't his cousin Elle in the room with him. He quickly recovered and asked, "How is Amber doing?"

"She's finished eating and is resting comfortably," Alexander said as she picked up an empty plastic bag and placed blood and urine samples inside.

"You hungry?" he asked. "There's pizza and—."

Jenise interrupted. "Nothing." She slipped into her coat. "What's next?" she asked.

"Tomorrow, Rick will run tests on the samples at the forensics lab he's setting up on Boonville. He's already got the equipment needed for rape kit analyses. He'll scan for STDs in addition to DNA."

Alexander sat a paper on the counter. "Here's Dr. Shulman's number."

"I'll give it and the samples to Rick," he said. "We're hoping Amber will begin to trust us enough to answer a few questions. As you know from your training, sex-trafficking is big business in southwest Missouri with I-44 being a major east-west corridor."

"Yes." She held out her hand. "May I have my key?"

John Hutsell reached in his pocket, pulled out Jenise's key and dropped it in her outstretched hand. It was warm to the touch. She dipped her head at the memory of another time he'd put a key in her hand.

Hutsell grabbed his parka, putting it on as he walked to the sliding glass door. "This way," he said. "I moved the Cherokee to the back of the house."

23

He accompanied her outside. As she keyed entrance he said, "Thanks for your help tonight."

"Anything for your mother."

As Jenise began the turn to open the door, she lost her footing on the ice. John reached up and with both hands grabbed the Cherokee's roof rack, pressing his body against hers and the car door for support. She regained her balance and twisted so they were no longer face to face. When her hand was tightly on the door handle, John stepped back. She got in, closed the door and drove away.

John waited until Jenise's vehicle was out of sight and then walked inside.

"She's the most dangerous kind of woman there is, isn't she John?" said his cousin, who'd witnessed their near fall and how it had been avoided.

"And what kind of woman is that, Elle?" he asked.

"The kind you can fall in love with."

Rick Hadley walked in the kitchen with Amber's meds in time to hear the conversation. John Hutsell looked in Rick's direction, set his jaw and walked past him on his way out. Rick looked at Elle.

"Anything I need to be concerned about?" he asked.

"Don't think so," she answered. "You know Rick, extended family members used to say I was the unlikely Nelson cousin to have kids. To them, John is the last hope for the Leland Nelson line to continue. Watching him tonight, I'm thinking they need to adjust their thinking."

Rick allowed a slight grin.

"Reel it in, Mister Hadley. Don't go getting your hopes up," she said.

Elle was lying next to Rick Hadley on the double air mattress as she thought about the woman who, in the summer of 2013, most assumed would become Mrs. John Hutsell. Sure, John could be a son-of-a-bitch at times, but did he enjoy chasing the bad guy so much that he was willing to put Jenise Alexander at emotional risk? Or did he agree to call her tonight because a small part of him wanted to see her again?

John Aaron Hutsell was master at keeping his private life private. The only woman he'd ever dated for any length of time had been Jenise—and by no means had he been celibate since then.

From the time they could walk, Grandma Nelson'd had Elle and John dancing together. As a result, Elle had seen countless women slip him their number after seeing him on the dance floor.

Elle discounted the idea that John would entertain the thought of picking up where he and Jenise had left off. If anything, he was more aloof since his return to Springfield than he'd ever been. Still, anything was possible, she thought. No one would have guessed five months ago she would've stopped running through men like they were last week's news, and yet, here she was, lying in the familiar curve of Rick Hadley's body. She nudged him with her elbow.

"You awake?" she asked.

"Am now."

"Your phone done charging?"

Rick picked up his cell. "Yes."

"Play me a lullaby."

Rick tapped the screen a few times, set his phone down and put his arms around Elle as the music began.

"There's nothin' you can do to turn me away . . .."

Carly at her finest, thought Elle.

Jenise Alexander pulled to the side of the road two miles into her drive home. She checked the time on the dash, then brought out her cell and began composing a text. Even though it was 3:35 A.M., she felt the recipient would still be awake.

"Leaving now. I'll see you at the clinic at ten."

"Okay. If you need anything, let me know," came Kyle Jeffries' response.

Kyle David Jeffries, executive director of Rita's Rose, knew John Hutsell had reopened a wound when he'd agreed to have Elle Wyatt place a call to Jenise at 9:15 P.M. Jeffries career depended on his ability to accurately read people, and there was no doubt in his mind Wyatt wouldn't have made the call without Hutsell's approval. Scars take time to heal, and for the one Hutsell was responsible for, five and a half years wasn't long enough. Jeffries

25

was a man who met things head-on, and he understood the underlying meaning of Jenise's message—she would rather he not be at her apartment when she returned home. He put on his winter coat, gloves, and cuffed stocking cap. He locked the door to Jenise's small apartment before heading to his own. On the way, he hoped Jenise would find enough peace for a few hours of sleep before she walked through the clinic's doors at 10:00 A.M.

Amber seemed to be feeling better the next morning. Thanks to the ibuprofen Dr. Shulman had prescribed, her fever was down. She had just finished a poached egg for breakfast when John Hutsell and Rick Hadley entered the room.

"Amber, feel up to a little conversation?" Hutsell asked.

Amber looked at Elle, who had been her with since she'd awakened. Elle walked over, picked up the bed tray, handed it to her cousin and asked, "John, would you and Rick give Amber and me a few minutes?"

"Sure," John said.

When they were alone, Elle sat on the mattress under the window.

"Is Amber your real name?" she asked.

"You don't like Amber? How about Casey or Brandi or Chrystal? I've answered to all those and more."

"So why did you choose the name Amber last night instead of one of the others?"

"I'm not sure what my *real* name is—if I ever had one. But I do know what an Amber Alert is. I figure at one time I was one of them. So, why not use Amber? It's better than using one of the names they gave me."

"Who are they?" Elle said.

"What's it to you?" Amber asked.

"Do you know who those men in the next room are?"

"You said last night they used be in law enforcement. But you weren't, were you?"

"John's my cousin and Rick's—."

"Your lover," interrupted Amber.

"Among other things," Elle said.

Amber gave a sardonic smile, "You don't shock easy."

"Just not interested in playing games," Elle replied. "They are private investigators and they are good at what they do. What they are about to do is offer you a way out of the life you're in."

"How do they know what kind of life I'm 'in'?"

"They've investigated sex-trafficking cases before."

"Does their help include talking to police?"

"I won't lie to you; they hope at some point you will."

"What is it with you?" Amber asked. "You're different from them and the lady last night."

"Different experiences."

"Such as?"

"Similar to yours in some ways. I was eleven years old when a man forced me down night after night and raped me. When I tried to stop him, he shot me, killed my mother and himself. Any other questions?"

Amber took a moment before she spoke again. "How do they 'want' to help me?"

"Let's call them back and find out."

Elle stood, walked to the hall and called for John and Rick to return.

Each man carried a chair into the room. They positioned them between the two beds, closer to the unoccupied bed than the one Amber was settled in. Since both Hutsell and Hadley wanted to pose as non-threatening, the chairs were arranged in a semicircle rather than linear.

"Amber wants to know how you intend to help her," Elle said.

John Hutsell leaned back in his chair and placed his hands on his upper thighs, his arms flared.

"Amber, we need a foundation from which to start. The more you can tell us, the better we can assist you," he said.

"Don't tell me that's all you want—to assist me. Last night that lady over there and the nurse talked about a famous case you solved, *John*. I think you're just looking for another headline."

"I don't like headlines. The more recognizable I am, the less effective I become. You don't have any money so there's no financial gain. My satisfaction comes in the apprehension. I like the look on the face of a son-of-a-bitch when he realizes he's been beat."

"So, that's what gets you off, huh?" she asked.

28

"Yeah, it is."

Amber turned her attention to Rick Hadley. "What about you?" she asked.

Hadley smiled. "I've been described as 'The Boy Scout' of the partnership."

And there it was; good cop, bad cop. Elle smiled.

"She says you're pretty smart?"

"Her name is Elle, and I am good at putting clues together, So, what do you think Amber? Willing to chance it?"

"Can you guarantee you'll keep them from finding me?"

"Amber, there are no guarantees in this business. But, take some time, weigh your options and let us know what you decide," said Hutsell.

"What other *options* do I have, *John*?" she asked. "It's either you or the street."

"Pretty much," Hutsell answered.

"You got a TV?"

"You want to watch TV?"

"Yeah."

"Anything in particular?"

"The Simpsons."

"Why the Simpsons?"

"Bart always stood up to the grownups," Amber said.

"We'll see what we can do."

For the next hour Amber gave an account of her early life. She didn't know her given name. She remembered her mother and grandfather. Her grandfather called her Boo Bear, her mother called her Kid, as in "Get your ass over here, Kid," which meant that Amber was going to get a beating. She didn't know what part of the country she was from. She'd been told so many different stories, she didn't know which one to believe—if any. She did have some memories—some distinct, some hazy.

Her grandfather had given her a pink teddy bear with two hearts on its tummy. He'd told her the two hearts were because he loved her "double more than anyone else." She remembered being with her grandfather in a park. They sat on a bench in front of a pond and watched the ducks swim. He'd let her play on the playground until she wore herself out. Her grandfather wouldn't let her drink from the fountain because the water was 'nasty,' so he would bring bottled water on their trips.

One day Amber recalled seeing a princess in the park. She knew it was a princess because she had a crown. It was a cold day, and the princess was wearing a long red, heavy coat. It had slits instead of sleeves. The princess had one big glove that she put both her hands in. Amber'd said, "Grandpa, she's so pretty." The princess overheard and bent down. Amber asked if she could touch the princess' coat and was granted permission. She took off a glove and ran her hand on the princess' shoulder. The coat was softer than Amber's teddy bear.

Sometimes her grandfather took her to a different playground. It was near a lake. He had a little fishing pole he'd bring along especially for her. The two would fish, then have a lunch of sandwiches and potatoes chips. Grandpa would watch as she climbed the steps of a fort and went down the slide.

What Amber recalled of her mother wasn't pretty. The woman was scary and mean. Other people called her Sissy. She remembered the last day she'd seen her mom. Amber awoke early, and with her mother still in bed, she'd gone to the living room and played with the doll her grandfather had given her the day before. Her mom finally got up. She entered the living room, went to the couch and told Amber to get a box of cereal. While her mom ate cereal from the box, Amber sat on the floor and brushed her doll's hair. It wasn't long before her mother said, "Get your ass over here, Kid." Amber did as she was told. Her mom grabbed Amber's chin and squeezed really hard. "Look at me," her mother demanded. Amber recalled the sores on her mom's face and smeared mascara under her eyes just before her mother hit her. A knock at the door saved Amber from a second blow.

A friend of her mom's came inside. The two whispered to each other, occasionally looking at Amber. They stopped talking and her mother moved her head up and down. She told Amber to get her jacket. They were going on a drive.

Amber vividly remembered that day—after all it was the day her life had ended. The three got in a man's car and drove for a long time. They finally pulled off the road where there was a big waterfall. Her mother took her hand and they walked on a path.

They stopped where she had full view of the waterfall. Her mother told her to sit down on a step and wait. Amber was holding her pink teddy bear, watching people on a bridge when her mom's friend came up and said, "Your mom told me to come and get you. It's time to go back home." When they'd reached the car, Amber realized it was a different car than the one that had brought them to the waterfall. Amber'd asked, "Where's my mom?" The man said her mom was getting something to eat, and they were going to drive over and pick her up. Amber got in the back seat. The man belted her in and left. Another man got in the car and drove away. It wasn't long until he stopped, reached in the back seat, grabbed her teddy bear, said "You won't be needing this anymore." and flung it out of the window. Amber never saw her mother, her mother's friend, nor her grandfather again. The man took her to an old house, and that's when the real nightmare began.

Rick Hadley stood. "Amber, let's take a break. We've got enough to get started. Ducks, ponds, princesses, and waterfalls. And all of these places are within a day's drive of each other, so that helps," he said. "We'll get a computer out here, fine-tune your descriptions, and start looking at images."

Hutsell rose and said, "Rick and I are going to bring in a colleague. Her name is Erin. She's around thirty-five and a licensed PI."

"What's she like?" asked Elle.

"Well dear cousin, in a lot of ways, she reminds me of you. She's smart, and I wouldn't want to meet up with her if I was 'Walkin' Thru the Park' in the dark."

Elle Wyatt smiled. "You mean 'she may cut you; she may shoot you, too'?"

Rick smiled and caught Elle's eye. "Go ahead, show off," he said.

"Muddy Waters. Late fifties."

Hutsell shook his head and looked from his cousin to his partner. "Ready to get started, Rick?"

Hadley nodded. On their way out the door, Amber asked, "How can you afford all this?"

Elle wanted to say, "John's a trust-fund baby" but kept her mouth shut.

"Financially, I'm in a position to do what I want," Hutsell said.

"That good, huh?" Amber asked.

"Isn't it time for your meds?" Hutsell said. He held out his hand. "Elle, if you would."

Elle tossed him the bottle containing Amber's antibiotics. He handed it to Amber.

"How'd you come up with Lawrence?" she asked about the name on the bottle.

"Needed a last name. Lawrence is the name of a neighboring county. It was either that or Greene. Amber Greene just didn't sound right."

"I like Lawrence," she said.

More progress, he thought as he followed Hadley down the hall.

Amber picked up a bottle of water and took her antibiotics. She stood and said, "I have to go to the bathroom."

As she passed, Elle spoke, "I know there's a good chance you're setting up those two men, who at this very moment are trying to come up with a way to keep you safe. So Amber, know this; where they might hesitate, I won't."

Amber walked into the bathroom and recalled last night's "before the blood on the carpet was dry" comment. She didn't doubt Elle Wyatt for one minute. There are people in this world who act and ask questions later. Amber wondered if Elle Wyatt would bother to ask questions at all.

·8·

Jenise Alexander finally gave up on getting any sleep and rolled out of bed at 7:10 A.M. She'd been a fool to send Kyle Jeffries on his way last night. If he'd been there, he would've wrapped his arms around her and held her till dawn. He wouldn't have asked any questions; he would have just given her what she'd needed at the time. And what she'd needed was to feel loved. Besides John Hutsell and herself, Kyle was the only person who knew the whole story about the summer of 2013.

'Wonderful,' 'giving,' 'gracious,' 'smart,' 'self-assured,' were all words she'd heard others employ to describe Kyle. She'd used them herself when answering the question, "What's he really like?"

She did love him, but it wasn't the same. If only there had never been a John Hutsell. If only she had paid attention to detail. If only . . ..

Jenise poured herself a cup of coffee and walked to the sliding glass door that led to a small patio. The ice from last night was already beginning to melt. Every few seconds, a water drop would fall from a break in the guttering overhead.

Welcome to the Missouri Ozarks. If you don't like the weather, wait five minutes; it'll change.

Maybe she should just go ahead and get the day started— after all, it was a Saturday, and therefore a busy day at the clinic. Might as well get in the shower, get dressed, and get going. She might even stop and get a couple of boxes of donuts, including one with raspberry filling, for Kyle's secretary and right arm, Brett Gilson.

Jenise headed for the shower. *Make it hot and set the setting to its highest level.*

The shower did help. The heat and pressure relaxed her muscles. Jenise wrapped a towel around her and went to work styling her hair. She liked her pixie cut even though it required more attention than the long, straight hair she'd had for most of her life. But that was just fine—she wasn't a kid anymore. She'd sacrificed versatility for a more modern style. Gone were the quick ponytails, French braids, and updos. But that was just fine, too. Nobody was pulling the pins away so her hair would fall down and . . ..

She placed her hands on the sink's rim and looked at her reflection in the mirror. *Why didn't you just say no last night?*

Jenise carried a mug of coffee to her vehicle. At least she didn't have to scrape windows. The freezing rain had stopped long before she'd driven home. She turned on the ignition and streamed Harry Connick, Jr.'s *Oh, My NOLA* CD. A love for jazz was something she and John had shared.

"Let them talk if they want to," Connick sang. Jenise closed her eyes and remembered John's arms around her as they'd danced to the song years ago. Sure, things had changed, but it was Connick's next line that had taken on a whole new meaning since then. "Baby, talk don't bother me."

And why would it bother you, John? You weren't around when the 'talk' started.

Jenise put the car in drive and drove to Rita's Rose, stopping to get donuts on the way.

John Hutsell took Rick's Silverado into Springfield. He stopped off at his loft apartment to shower. He trimmed his beard to the length Elle called a "nice looking stubble." He donned an off-white Henley, then layered it with a Prussian blue chambray shirt. Clean jeans, his black Wesco boots and parka got him out the door. With his laptop under his arm, he was soon keying in the security code for Gambit Investigations on Boonville.

Hutsell pulled a paper from his bottom left drawer and stuck it in his computer case before checking his messages. Leaning forward, elbows on his desk, he returned a few calls then sat back and placed one.

"Jay, John Hutsell."

"John, how in the world are you?" said Missouri State Trooper, Jay Randall.

"Pretty good. Yourself?"

"Can't complain. Wouldn't do any good if I did." Randall chuckled. "What ya got going?"

"Got a case that needs a woman's touch," Hutsell said. "Wondered if I could get Erin's number from you, see if she's available."

"She's right here. Hold on, I'll get her."

Hutsell heard Randall's muffled voice, "Hey Marie, you got a live one." Hutsell shook his head and smiled.

"This is Erin Laveau. How may I help you?"

"Hi, Erin. John Hutsell. I heard Jay in the background. Is he still causing you grief?"

"Yeah, and I don't see it changing anytime soon," she said. "He loves the look he gets when he tells people his significant other is Marie Laveau."

"Well, you could marry him. Instead of Erin Marie Laveau you'd be Erin Marie Randall."

Laveau huffed. "Wouldn't give him the satisfaction of changing my name to his."

Hutsell laughed. "Erin, you available to help with a case Gambit's working on?"

"Does this request come with compensation?"

"Yes ma'am, it does."

"By all means then, let's talk."

"Your location the same?" he asked.

"Yep, still working out of the basement. Come on over."

John Hutsell pulled into the driveway of the home Laveau and Randall shared north of Interstate-44. He'd always liked the house, though his tastes ran more towards the older homes in Springfield's Phelps Grove division. He stood on the stoop, admiring the natural thin stones accenting the gray siding. The door was of etched glass set in burgundy-stained mahogany with sidelites on either side. Jay Randall opened the door before Hutsell had a chance to ring the bell.

"Good to see you John," Randall said. "Erin's downstairs. Would you like a cup of coffee?"

"No thanks. It was a long night, and I'm about 'coffeed' out."
"What's the nature of the case you're investigating?"

"Sex trafficking," Hutsell answered.

"Hard cases to work. Multiple jurisdictions."

"City, county, state, federal, international. It's a mess," Hutsell agreed from the view of law enforcement officers.

"The task force out of Joplin's making a dent. Government agencies and communities are stepping up educational efforts. Awareness is the key," Randall said.

"Yep," agreed Hutsell. "I think Erin would be perfect in this situation."

"Well, she can do anything she puts her mind to," Randall said with a smile. "She's tough."

"She'd have to be to put up with the likes of you for—what is it now, six years?" Hutsell joked.

"Pretty much," Randall said. Hutsell started down the stairs. "Holler on your way out, John."

"Will do."

John Hutsell made his way to the basement office of Erin Laveau. She rose from her desk and pointed to one of two upholstered chairs in the room. After Hutsell settled in one, she took the other.

"What's going on?" she asked.

"Ran across a young woman last night who's a victim of sex-trafficking. After an accident on icy roads, she managed to escape her captors. She's probably eighteen and not willing to talk to law enforcement. Rick and I didn't want to chance taking her to a shelter. That would be the first place they'd look for her. Besides, last night the shelters would've been at capacity."

"Why do you say, 'probably eighteen'? Is she that uncooperative?" Laveau asked.

"Erin, there's very little she knows for sure—not even her name," Hutsell answered. "Her best guess is that she was around five or six when she was abducted."

For the next ten minutes, John Hutsell told about the events of the previous night and what he knew of Amber's background. He ended by saying, "Elle's been a big help and will continue to be, but Rick and I both feel we need a professional—one who's female—from here on out."

"Are we talking about a glorified babysitting job?"

"We need to provide 24-hour protection, but we also need a good investigator. Erin, there's a good chance we'll end up on the road in search of Amber's real identity and the circumstances surrounding her kidnapping. And of course, we'll pass along what we find to law enforcement," Hutsell said. "So, what do you think? Sound like something you'd be interested in?"

Erin took a moment before answering. "Okay, John. I'm interested. Now, let's talk money."

"Your going rate plus expenses."

"Deal. When do I start?"

"As soon as you pack a bag and get to the safe house," he answered. "You can relieve Elle, and she can run some errands for us. Have you met Rick Hadley?"

Davis

Walden

Debra

"Briefly, at the opening of Gambit Investigations. He is pretty. My sister's hoping I'll run into him, so I can invite him to Jay's first big cookout this year."

"Rick's off the market. He chased Elle till he caught her," Hutsell said with a smile.

Laveau grinned. "Never met Elle either, but from what I've heard, she's not one to allow herself to be 'caught.' "

"Yeah, well I guess, after what happened in Tennessee, she had a change of heart."

"She had the guts to do what needed to be done, John. One thing's for sure, the Tennessee incident put the word out—'don't mess with a Nelson cousin'."

"One positive thing," Hutsell said, "people in Springfield don't judge her as harshly as they used to. Hell, a year ago, I was one of them. Hadley's the one who set my butt straight. The guy is good. And he's a lot more diplomatic than I am. You'll like him."

Laveau picked up a notepad and pen, then handed them to Hutsell. "Write down the directions. It usually takes about thirty minutes to drive to Clever. How are the roads between here and there?"

"Not bad. Thawing has begun. Of course, they'll start freezing over again when the sun goes down." Hutsell stood. "I've got a few things to take care of, so I'll see you later today. I included Rick and Elle's cell numbers, as well as my own," he said as he handed her the paper.

Laveau took a business card from the holder on her desk, turned it over and wrote her personal cell number on the back.

"Okay, John. See ya when I see ya."

Hutsell headed upstairs and found Jay Randall sitting in front of the fireplace, reading a book. Randall saw Hutsell enter the living area. He slid in a book mark, set the book on the coffee table, and stood.

"Good one?" Hutsell asked of the book.

"Yeah. *Silent Joe*, by T. Jefferson Parker. Mom finally sold the big home, too much to keep up. She downsized her library. Erin and I were the happy recipients. Mom said I'd like Parker, and she was right." He changed the subject. "So, what's the verdict?"

"Erin's signing on with Gambit Investigations for the time being. She's getting things together now. I'll let her fill you in on the details," Hutsell said.

Jay Randall looked out of the corner of his eye at the top of the stairs. When he saw they were alone, he pulled a business card from his shirt pocket and handed it to John Hutsell.

"Erin already gave me a card."

"Not like this one, she didn't," Randall said.

Hutsell took the card. The background was chili red with a graphic scarlet skull. Erin MARIE Laveau was printed about one-fourth the way down, with titles and qualifications underneath: Private Investigator, Voodoo Queen, Swamp Witch, Disapearer of Men, Hairdresser.

Hutsell smiled. "It's a wonder she hasn't killed you yet." he said as he put the card in his hip pocket.

"Did you see the voodoo doll with my name on it?" Randall asked.

"Nope."

"She probably put it away before you got here," Randall said. "Ah, life with that woman is good."

·10·

John Hutsell drove to the south side of Springfield and pulled into the parking lot of Safety-Net; a local company run by Michelle Thomas. The bottom floor of the business condominium held a reception area and two offices. Another office and a break room occupied the second floor. Chelle Thomas's name was on the door to the right, and Greg Baptiste's office was on the left. The receptionist's cubicle was in between. John, Elle, Greg, and Chelle had thirteen years of Catholic education under their belts. They often referred to themselves as The Four Musketeers. John and Elle would be standing next to Greg and Chelle as they took their vows in six months.

Before he went inside, Hutsell ordered enough pasta, salad, and toasted ravioli from Bambino's to feed five people for two meals. He then exited Rick's truck and walked through Safety-Net's door.

Ashley Freeland, looked up and smiled.

"Hello, Mr. Hutsell. Mr. Baptiste is in with Ms. Thomas at the moment. She has an appointment in ten minutes so he will be out soon."

"Thanks, Ashley," Hutsell said as he sat down and checked his phone for messages. The situation outside Clever was quiet. Amber was sleeping while Rick and Elle discussed princesses. They were anxious to get their hands on John's computer so they could assemble a series of images for Amber to view. Rick was glad to hear Erin would be arriving soon and that she was bringing a computer with her.

Chelle's office door opened and Hutsell stood as Greg Baptiste entered the reception room.

"Social call?" Baptiste asked upon seeing his best friend.

"Not today," Hutsell answered. "You got a few minutes?"

"Sure," Baptiste said. He put his arm out for Hutsell to take the lead. Once inside his office, Baptiste asked, "What's going on?"

"Mom had a trespasser last night. First thought was a homeless man but that wasn't the case. Greg, we've got a sex-trafficking victim in a safe house near Clever recuperating from a urinary tract infection. We got her on antibiotics last night, and as soon as I get back, Rick's going to the lab and run tests for pathogens and STDs."

"How do you know she has a urinary tract infection, and how did you get a prescription in the middle of the night?"

"She wouldn't let Rick near her, so Elle called Jenise. Jenise came out, examined the woman, and then called in a doctor."

Baptiste's left eyebrow raised ever so slightly at the mention of Jenise Alexander. One would have to be looking for Greg's reaction to have actually seen it.

Hutsell told Amber's story a second time and ended by asking, "We want to find out who Amber really is and where she's from, which means Erin and I will likely take to the road. Rick is involved in setting up the forensics lab and—."

"You want to know if I'm available to handle Gambit's cases while you're gone."

"You really should just go to work for Gambit full-time you know," Hutsell said.

"Chelle and I have been discussing it," Baptiste said. "Problem is, John, I left the Secret Service to come home and convince her to marry me. She finally said yes, and we want to start a family. She doesn't object to my chartering business. She knows how much I love flying, and she'd never ask me to give it up, but I can't start galivanting all over the country again and be gone for days at a time."

"You won't have to. I'll take the out-of-town cases and if need be, I'll hire a another operative. Erin Laveau has signed on for this one. Who knows, maybe she has a future at Gambit."

"Erin's got good connections, John," Baptiste said.

"Don't we all?" John asked with a smile. "And she *can* handle herself. Back in 2013, I was with her and Jay at Earharts. She'd gone to the restroom, and on her way back, a guy stood and blocked her way. I started to get up when Jay put his hand on my arm. 'She can handle it,' he said. And she did. She grabbed the guy's arm, twisted it behind him, put her foot on his ass, and shoved him face-down on a table. His friend started to make noise. Jay and I flashed our badges, and they couldn't get out of there fast enough."

Baptiste laughed, "Okay John, I'll talk to Chelle tonight and let you know tomorrow."

"Good enough," Hutsell said.

Outside Hutsell checked his watch: 1:10 P.M. He started the Silverado and headed for Bambino's near the MSU campus. The shortest path took him past Rita's Rose. There was a chance that Jenise's Cherokee would be in the parking lot, but Hutsell didn't entertain the thought of taking an alternate route. Reliving the past was something he wasn't interested in. It was over and done—accept it and go on. He had a job to do, and he'd become a master at isolating himself from distractions. A man chose the best route to get from one place to another and took it—nothing more, nothing less.

John Hutsell walked into the safe house carrying Bambino's take-out. Erin Leveau and Elle Wyatt were sitting at the table with Laveau's computer in front of them.

"How's it going?" he asked.

"Making progress," Elle answered. "Amber's princess is not of the winged or Disney variety, so I'm thinking maybe from literature."

"I'll be right back," Hutsell said. "I need to get my computer from the truck."

Elle checked on Amber while Erin moved her computer to the counter. Elle returned with Amber's empty lunch tray at the same time John walked through the side door.

"Is Rick at the lab?" he asked as he unloaded his laptop case and placed its contents on the counter.

"On his way," Elle said. "Once Erin arrived, he felt comfortable enough to take my car and head to Springfield."

"How's Amber doing?"

"She's feeling better. The lime Jell-O was a big hit."

Hutsell picked up the paper he'd brought from his office and said, "I need to talk with Amber. Erin, will you come with me?"

"Sure thing."

Hutsell and Laveau walked down the hall and into the master bedroom.

"I hear you're feeling better," Hutsell said. Amber nodded. "The doctor needs a few lab tests run so he can determine exactly what health issues you are facing and if further treatment is necessary. My partner can do them, but we need your permission to release the results to the doctor. I'm going to read the entire release form to you. Stop me if you have any questions."

When he finished reading, he asked if she understood what she was signing.

"Yes, but what name do I sign?"

He handed her a pen. "Amber Lawrence is fine."

Amber signed the paper and handed it and the pen to Hutsell.

"Let us know if you need anything."

Amber nodded a second time and the two detectives left the room.

Elle had lunch laid out when they returned. Hutsell handed the paper and pen to Laveau.

"Erin, will you please sign on the witness line?"

"Sure."

John pulled out his cell and dialed Rick Hadley.

"We've got her signature. Go ahead and run the tests," he said into the phone, then disconnected the call.

Elle skimmed the paper as Erin and John filled their plates.

Damn, this is going to come back and bite you in the ass, John.

"We should know about possible STDs shortly," Hutsell said. "But it will be several hours for DNA results. Glad we don't have to rely on outside labs anymore."

"When did you get your own forensic lab?" Laveau asked as she dipped toasted ravioli in marinara sauce.

"Getting," Hutsell said. "We're in the process of setting it up. It's not open for outside business yet."

"Going to be a cash cow for you, John."

"For the Nelson/Wyatt Group it will be," he said.

"Ah, I see. So Elle, have you turned into an entrepreneur?" Laveau asked.

"No. The Nelson/Wyatt Group comprises Pat and Jean, along with the Senator," Elle said with a smile. "I don't want to work that hard. I dabble at the sewing machine for Jean's interior design business and what interests me, but other than that, I'm a free agent."

Hutsell changed the topic of conversation. "Now that you're fully engulfed in the case, what are your thoughts?" he asked Laveau.

"I think you're wise to concentrate on finding Amber's true identity at this stage," she said. "Good way to establish trust—

which will be a long time coming. I do think she respects Elle on some level. And that's a start."

Hutsell looked at his cousin.

"Don't worry, John," Elle said. "I've got your back. And once Amber realizes the full implication of that form, you're going to be glad I do."

"Part of doing business," he said.

Once the table was cleared, Hutsell and Laveau set up their computers. Elle stored leftovers in the refrigerator.

John's cell rang. "It's Rick," he said before answering. The two women listened to the one-sided conversation. "I'm not surprised. Anything else?" While Hadley talked, Hutsell put the signed form in his computer case. "Hold on a sec," he told Rick. Then to Elle and Erin, "Amber's got chlamydia. Rick's contacted the doctor. He said she'll be okay if she takes all her antibiotics."

"Could be a lot worse," Erin commented.

"Sounds good," Hutsell said into his phone. "We've got two computers here, but it wouldn't hurt to have another." He paused for Hadley's comments. "Okay, and Rick, would you mind picking up a portable DVD player and several *Simpsons* DVDs before heading back?"

"*The Simpsons*?" Laveau said, once John had disconnected the call.

"The only request Amber's made," Hutsell said. "Definitely an avenue to pursue where background is concerned—how did she come across the show? The way she talked about Bart Simpson, I got the feeling she was older than six when she was watching it. Were Amber and other victims allowed to watch it on TV? Was it a favorite show of a sex-trafficker?"

"And if she was allowed to watch TV," Laveau added, "what other shows did she see? Any local programs could help pinpoint locations where Amber might have been held."

"Which means we can contact law enforcement and maybe develop new leads," Hutsell said. "So, let's get this show back on the road."

Amber appeared at the kitchen entrance. "Can I have some more Sprite?"

"Sure," Elle said. She caught John's eye as she walked to the refrigerator. "What?" she said. He shook his head. "You know

45

Sprite's standard fare for what ails you. I know a couple of times you faked being sick just so Grandma Nelson would let you have a can."

"Don't go telling tales out of school, Elle," he said, then sheepishly asked, "You got an extra?"

"Head's up," she said before she tossed him a can. "I'll text Rick to bring more."

"Amber, what can you remember about the waterfall?" Hutsell asked as he pulled the tab on the can.

"It was big."

"Most all would be from a child's perspective," Hutsell said. "Was there anything about it that set it apart from other waterfalls?"

Laveau stood and said, "Have a seat, Amber." She pulled her keys from her pocket. "I've got a couple of lawn chairs in the car. I'll be right back."

"It had a bridge about halfway down. I saw people walking across it and wanted to ask my mom if we could walk on it, too. I never did because I thought it would make her mad."

Hutsell typed "U.S. waterfalls with bridges" into the search bar. When results popped up, he clicked "images."

"That's it!" Amber shouted. John and Elle looked at each other.

"Amber, that's just the first picture. Why don't you look at a few more before you decide?" said Hutsell.

"Fine. But that's it."

There was a problem with Hutsell's suggestion as most of the images on the screen were of the same waterfall. There were a few other photos, but the bridges were always in the wrong place. They were either at the top or bottom of a waterfall and Amber insisted it was in the middle. Hutsell tried a different browser but got the same results.

"It can't be this easy," he mumbled as Erin unfolded one of the chairs.

Elle spoke up. "Where is it, John?"

"The Columbia River Gorge in Oregon," he said. "Multnomah Falls."

Hutsell limited his search to images of Multnomah Falls. After scrolling several rows down, Amber said, "Wait. Go back."

"Did you see something?" Hutsell asked.

"That path," she said, pointing to the middle of the screen. "I think that's where I was sitting."

"Okay, let's look at some more," Hutsell said.

The group continued viewing more photos. Most of the pictures were from the same reference point. Hutsell clicked on "show more images" and kept scrolling until one photo made him stop. Amber rose to her feet and left the room.

"Damn," Hutsell said.

"At least one of them isn't a pink teddy bear," Elle said as she stared at the photo of two stuffed animals sitting nearby a plaque showing the heights of the upper and lower falls. Multnomah Falls was in the background. She got up and headed to the master bedroom.

Amber shoved the mattress underneath the window to the center of the room. She pulled the window covering aside and stared into the front yard. Elle entered the room, walked over, and stood beside the young woman.

"I don't care what he says," Amber said. "That's the place."

"And that's what they're going with for now," Elle replied.

"Elle, Rick's here," Hutsell yelled from the living room. "Is it okay for him to come to the bedroom?"

Elle gave Amber a questioning look. The young woman nodded.

"Yes," called out Elle.

Rick Hadley entered with two bags. "Didn't know which ones you've seen, so I started with season one," he said as he unloaded a DVD player and several boxed sets.

"Did you get The *Simpsons* movie?" Elle asked.

Rick pulled out the last DVD and tossed it to her. "Wouldn't deprive you of the opportunity to engage in a little trivia."

"Amber, a few miles up the road is the city of Springfield, Missouri. *The Simpsons* is set in Springfield, but there are a lot of 'Springfields' throughout the US. Which Springfield is it? To promote the movie, a competition was held to see which 'Springfield' would host the premiere."

"What's a premiere?"

"The first time a movie is shown in public," Elle said. "Cities that entered made a video explaining why their Springfield would be the best choice. We lost, which is really too bad. The movie opens with a concert on Lake Springfield, and we really do have a Lake Springfield."

"Everything's ready to go when you are," Hadley said after he'd set up the DVD player. "Come over, and I'll show you how it works."

With Amber settled in, watching the first episode, Hadley stepped to the hallway and motioned for Elle to follow. "You want to go help with the princess search. You've got more experience in that field than I do."

"Did they tell you about the last picture Amber saw?" He nodded. "She shouldn't be alone right now."

"Go on. I'll sit with her," he said as he hugged Elle.

"You smell good," she said.

"Grabbed a shower and some clean clothes while I was in town."

"Have you had lunch?"

"No. John said he'd take care of it. Would you mind dishing it up for me?"

Elle Wyatt smiled. "Rick Hadley, you know this means you're going to owe me?"

"That's fine with me," he said. "I like the way you collect a debt."

Elle picked up the bed tray and returned with Rick's lunch.

"Enjoy," she said.

"I believe you forgot to curtsey." he teased.

"Keep digging that hole, Hadley."

Elle Wyatt turned and left the room.

Laveau was browsing an array of princess images while Elle put the six-pack of Sprite that Rick had brought in the refrigerator.

"Where's John?"

"Taking a walk," Laveau said. "None of these pictures resemble the princess Amber described from her childhood. Let's try a new search. How about winter princesses?" Elle was leaning on the counter, trying to come up with an additional search term when Laveau said, "Still nothing."

"Try winter queens," Elle suggested.

A few moments later, Erin asked, "Ever heard of Elizabeth Stuart?"

"Doesn't sound familiar."

"She was the daughter of England's King James I and granddaughter of Mary Queen of Scots. She married Frederick V, Prince Palatine of the Rhine, on Valentine's Day in 1613. Both were sixteen at the time. They eventually became King and Queen of Bohemia when Protestant Bohemians overthrew Ferdinand II, their Catholic king. Elizabeth and Frederick were in power for only a year before Ferdinand was able to reclaim the throne. Elizabeth and her family fled Prague—she was pregnant at the time—and settled at The Hague. She is known as the Winter Queen, as she was only on the throne for one winter."

"Hold on a minute," Elle said. "Let me check for literary references?"

Elle sat down at John's computer as he walked in the door.

Laveau stood and headed to the refrigerator for a bottle of water. "Anything for you, Elle?" she asked. Elle shook her head. "John?"

"No. Think I'll make a fresh pot of coffee."

"The Winter Queen is mentioned in several novels but not in any plays that I can find," Elle said.

She sat back in her chair and folded her arms. She was in deep thought as John walked to the coffee maker. He emptied into the sink what was left from breakfast and set about making a fresh pot.

"Winter, exiled pregnant queen, Bohemia. It sounds so familiar. What am I missing, John?" Elle asked her cousin.

"If Grandma Nelson was still alive, she could tell you," he said.

"Seems like something from high school."

John shut the lid of the coffee maker and pressed start. He turned to face his cousin, "Okay, The Winter Queen is from what period, the Elizabethan, right?"

Elle nodded and a few moments later John caught a familiar look in Elle's eyes. "Watch closely Erin. Elle just hit warp drive."

Hutsell walked to the glass doors that led to the small back porch.

"You know this house has a storm shelter," he said. "The entrance is out there to the left."

"Do you know when this place was built?" Laveau asked.

"Maybe the 1940s," he answered. "But it's been remodeled several times. When I get some down time, I think I'll start looking for a house. Always been in lofts and apartments—didn't know how long I'd be at any one job. I'm my own boss now, and the business is doing well. It's time."

"You want a country setting?"

"No, I like the Phelps Grove area in Springfield. Many of the homes were built in mid-1900. They have a lot of character. Mature trees, great landscaping, well kept."

"You're not interested in building your own home on the Hutsell Estate?"

"There's room. Grandpa Nelson acquired a lot of acreage back in the day. The Senator has a beautiful home, as do Jean and Pat. And Elle loves her Usonian style home on the grounds of the Wyatt Estate . . . ."

"But . . .?"

"Maybe it goes back to my childhood. Grandpa and Grandma Nelson lived in Phelps Grove before he hit it big. As far back as I can remember he was a contractor. He got in on the ground floor when the music theatre business took off in Branson in the 1990s. When people would ask him what his secret to success was, he'd say, 'Right time, right place and faith enough to take the leap.' Anyway, I spent a lot of time in Phelps Grove in my 'formative' years."

"Got it," Elle said. Hutsell and Laveau walked back to the table. "Shakespeare's *The Winter Tale*. Leontes, the king of Sicila mistakenly thinks his pregnant wife, Hermione, is carrying his friend's child instead of his and banishes her. The friend was the King of Bohemia."

"Did Shakespeare base it on Elizabeth Stuart's life?" John asked.

"No, on *Pandosto*, a story by Robert Greene. But look at this," she said. "An example of Hermione's costume from *The Winter's Tale*."

The image was an artist's rendering of Hermione's entrance in the first scene. The costume included a red velvet cloak and a head piece that encircled the Winter Queen's head. "Usually you see a crown sitting on top of the head, but if the 'princess' Amber saw wore something like this, she might have seen it as a crown."

"What about the 'glove' thing?" John asked.

"Muffs were in fashion at the time," Elle said. "Could have been an accessory added by the costume department, or the actress playing the part might have had her own." She started typing again.

"Want coffee, Elle?" John said.

"No, but you might see about Rick."

Hutsell went down the hall and stood at the bedroom door.

"How's she doing?" he whispered to his partner.

"Sleeping. You guys making any headway?"

"Elle's got a lead on the 'princess'. Possibly a character from Shakespeare's, *The Winter Tale*."

Rick smiled and shook his head.

"I know," Hutsell said. "She's come a long way in a year."

"Do I smell fresh coffee?"

"Yes. You want a cup?"

"Yeah, but if it's okay, will you sit with Amber while I get it? I really need to stretch these legs."

"Sure."

Rick walked into the kitchen and poured himself a cup of coffee.

"I hear you're about to break this case wide open, Wyatt."

"Funny, Hadley."

"Give me the high points," he said.

"I'm busy," she replied.

"Guess it's up to you Erin. Fill me in."

Erin Laveau gave Hadley an update. She had just finished when Elle said, "Pay dirt."

"What you got?" Rick asked.

"Oregon Shakespeare Festival. *The Winter's Tale* opened on February 24, 2006 in Ashland, Oregon."

Erin pulled out her phone, tapped the screen and said, "What is the driving time from Ashland, Oregon, to Multnomah Falls?"

"There is light traffic to Multnomah Falls, so it should take four hours and fifty-seven minutes," came the reply.

Elle continued working at John's computer. Rick had downed half his cup when she said, "Take a look at Ashland's Lithia Park."

Erin and Rick moved to where they could see the screen.

"Ducks swimming on a pond," Erin said.

"And it's a short walk from the park to the Shakespeare Festival grounds," Elle added.

"Is there a lake nearby?" Rick asked.

Elle typed in the key words. Results were quick to appear. "Emigrant Lake," she said. She hit a few more keys and images popped up on the screen. "And there is a playground."

"I better get John," Rick said.

Elle pulled Amber's meds out of her pocket and tossed them to Rick. He went to the refrigerator, brought out a bottle of water, and made his way to the bedroom. He stuck his head in the door. Hutsell was staring out the bedroom window at the setting sun. He turned around when his partner whispered his name. Rick motioned him to the hall.

"We've got some search results you need to look at," he whispered.

Amber stirred. "What's going on?" she asked from inside the room. Hadley walked in the room, and Hutsell headed toward the kitchen. It was too early to get her hopes up, so he decided the time was right to discuss her test results. He handed her the water bottle and sat in the chair.

"How long since you took your last dose of antibiotics?"

"Right after you left."

He opened the pill bottle and tapped out the correct dosage in his palm. He handed the pills and bottle of water to Amber. Rick waited till she'd downed her meds before he spoke again.

"Amber, I've got the results on the samples taken last night." She looked at him. "You have a second infection, but the good news is the antibiotics you are taking should take care of it also."

"What is it?"

"Chlamydia. It's a bacterial infection transmitted through sexual contact," he said. "How are you feeling?"

"Good."

"Ready to watch some more of *The Simpsons*?"

"What's going on in the kitchen?"

"Multnomah Falls is in Oregon. They're trying to narrow down what part of Oregon you might be from. So, you ready to start up the DVD player again? How far did you get into Season One?"

"Fell asleep on the second one."

Amber was watching episode two when Elle Wyatt appeared at the doorway.

"You got a minute, Hadley?"

"Sure," he said and walked into the hall.

"I'm going to head home to shower and change," she said.

"Will you be coming back tonight?"

She smiled. "Yes. I can sit with Amber while you professional gumshoes do your thing. You need me to pick up anything?"

"No, but you might see if Amber needs something."

Elle stepped inside the bedroom.

"Amber, I'm heading out for a while. Is there anything you'd like me to get while I'm in town?"

"Something I can put my hair back with."

"Got it. See you in a few hours."

Elle stepped back into the hallway. Rick put his arms around her and pulled her close.

"It's starting to ice up again, so take it slow, okay?"

"Yes."

"Which route are you taking?"

"I'll go by way of Republic to pick up hair ties for Amber."

"Text me when you get there and again before you start back, please?"

"Will that make you happy?"

"It's a start." He smiled and kissed her. He watched her disappear into the kitchen.

·12·

Dear God, how am I going to tell him?

Jenise was in her Cherokee outside the building that housed the studio apartment she had lived in five and a half years ago, reliving the night everything had changed.

She remembered sitting at her kitchen bar late on July 12, 2013 with her hand clamped tightly over her mouth staring at the results.

Maybe it's a false positive.

She'd picked up the package and scanned the back. Expiration date: January 2015. The contents were good for another year and a half.

Jenise had closed her eyes and thought of the night John had returned from Benton County, Arkansas, where he'd gone to pick up and escort a prisoner back to Greene County. His schedule with the Greene County Sheriff's Department and hers in the emergency room at Melcher Memorial South had kept them apart for nearly a week. John had dropped off the prisoner, completed the necessary paperwork, and driven non-stop to her studio apartment. He'd walked through the door, pulled her close, and whispered, "God, I've missed you." Even now, the memory was so vivid, she could almost feel the warmth of his breath on her ear. He'd then kissed her, stealing her breath as he slightly inhaled. She'd slipped her hand into his and led him to the bed.

A few weeks later, Jenise had detected a tenderness in her breasts but had thought nothing of it. It had been two days since a violent patient had struck her hard enough to send her to the floor, so it was no surprise she might have some bruises. Then, Jenise's period hadn't started on time—which was strange, as she was on the pill, and her cycle was regular as clockwork. She was sure she hadn't missed taking a pill; it was part of her nightly ritual. Just to make sure, she'd checked the pack anyway. All slots were empty.

So why did the stick on the counter in front of her show the word, "Pregnant"?

Jenise had mentally started down the list of items that interfered with the effectiveness of birth control pills when number two made her drop her head in acceptance. She'd then wrapped her arms around her abdomen, cradling the embryo that was developing inside her.

Dear God, how am I going to tell him?

Twenty minutes later, Jenise had changed into her night shirt and had been sitting on the edge of her bed when thoughts of her friend Caitlin surfaced. Caitlin'd been in the same situation four months earlier. When Caitlin had told Trevor, her live-in boyfriend of eight months, she was pregnant, he'd turned on her.

"Damn it, Caitlin! How did you get pregnant?"

"No form of birth control is one hundred percent," Caitlin'd reminded him.

"You did this on purpose, didn't you? You're trying to trap me into marriage."

"You were there! How could I trap you?"

"You didn't want to take the pill so we had to *make do* with other types—less effective types—of birth control."

"My doctor said I shouldn't take the pill. What else could we have done?"

"Are you sure it's mine?"

Caitlin had been speechless at Trevor's suggestion and had turned her back on him.

"What about Brad? He's still in love with you. Get him to marry you."

At that point Caitlin had walked out of the apartment and shown up at Jenise's door. That night, her friend had slept in the bed while she had taken the sofa. The next morning, Jenise had exited the shower and found Caitlin in a fetal position on the floor.

"Caitlin, what's wrong?"

Her friend raised her hand and offered her cell phone.

"I've packed my things and moved in with Dustin. I left money on the counter for an abortion. From here on out, you're on your own."

Jenise had closed her eyes trying to shut out thoughts of Trevor's words. She'd risen to her feet, walked to the bathroom, and looked at herself in the mirror.

Dear God, how am I going to tell him?

Jenise had met John for dinner at Crosstown Barbecue three days later. He was still on duty, and the restaurant was only five minutes from the Greene County Sheriff's Department. They'd engaged in small talk, with John doing most of the talking. He paid the bill and walked her to her car.

"Everything all right?" he'd asked. "You seem preoccupied."

She'd looked in his eyes. It wasn't the right time or the right place, and she still didn't have the words.

He'd pulled a spare apartment key off its chain and handed it to her. "Go to my place. I'll be there as soon as I get off duty."

She'd nodded and driven to his loft ten minutes away. She'd climbed the stairs, dropped his key on the table by the front door, and made her way to his bedroom. Jenise took off her shoes, slid under the covers and waited for John to come home. Four hours later, he walked in the bedroom and lay down beside her. He spooned his body to hers.

"You going to tell me what's going on?" he asked.

"I don't know how."

"Start at the beginning."

"The third week in June, I was taking antibiotics because of a sinus infection," she began. "You went to Arkansas to get a prisoner early the next week. It had been a while since we'd seen each other, and when you got home the first thing . . .." She hadn't finished the sentence.

"I remember," he said.

"John, I wasn't thinking, I should have realized . . .." she'd paused.

"Realized what, Jenise?"

"Antibiotics decrease the effectiveness of the pill. I'm late. I took a home test last Friday and this morning I went to my doctor's office. I'm pregnant, John."

Jenise remembered starring at the wall waiting for him to respond.

"Jenise, there was always a chance this could happen. We're adults. We knew what we were doing, and we knew the risks. It'll be okay."

Jenise had soaked up his words, thankful his reaction was the opposite of Trevor's. John had spent most of the night with his arms around her, but he never spoke again until her cell's alarm went off for work the next day.

Jenise sat in her car, five and a half years later, and remembered the uncertainty of his words, and how she'd lain next to him all night and wondered what he was thinking.

It'll be okay.

What does that mean, John? Will we get married and try and make a go of it? Or does it mean, 'I'll support you and the baby financially'. Or could it mean, 'You can get an abortion."

"Dear God, help me," she said out loud. "Because I still didn't know the answer."

·13·

Elle Wyatt returned to the Clever house several hours later and found John and Erin clearing the table of paper plates from dinner. She deposited a couple of plastic bags on the floor near the kitchen's entry.

"Anything new?" she asked.

John moved his computer from the counter to the table and motioned her over. He tapped the keyboard, lighting up the screen.

"What do you think?"

There were two photos, side-by-side on the monitor. On the left was a photo of a young child, with an age-enhanced version on the right. Elle felt like she was looking into the face of the woman they knew as Amber Lawrence.

"Damn John, I don't believe it," said Elle. "What's her name?"

"Marissa Baylor. She was six years old when she went missing on May 21, 2006 at Multnomah Falls."

"Next move?"

"We've got Chelle looking up Baylor's family background."

"If there're any social media pictures, she'll find them," said Elle.

"Erin's found a few newspaper articles. The FBI was called in early on. It was one of the first cases the agency's CARD west coast team investigated."

"CARD?"

"Child Abduction Rapid Deployment. The unit was established in October of 2005. It's composed of several teams with seasoned investigators experienced in crimes against children."

"When you going to tell her?"

"After we have more details," he said. "I'll contact Multnomah County in the morning, and Greg's going to get in touch with his contacts at the federal level."

"Have you eaten, Elle?" asked Erin.

"No, Rick had a late lunch so I thought I'd wait and have dinner with him."

"Amber hasn't eaten either," said Erin.

"I'll take her the items she requested and see how they both feel about dinner," she said and grabbed one of the bags on her way out.

Elle Wyatt entered the master bedroom and found Rick texting on his phone and Amber watching *The Simpsons*. She sat the bag on the floor next to Amber's bed.

"There's an assortment of scrunchies, hair ties, and barrettes," she said. "Knock yourself out."

Amber paused the video. She pulled out the items and headed to the bathroom.

Rick Hadley finished texting and put his phone in his pocket.

"We just got invited to Tennessee for mom's sixtieth birthday," he said.

"When is it?"

"Saturday, March ninth."

"Travel dates?"

"We can discuss it later," he said. Rick stood and stuck his hands in his pockets. He leaned down and took a deep breath. "And there it is. The smell after a forest rain."

"Thanks to a particular bottle of body wash that found its way into my stocking last Christmas," she said.

"Santa's got great taste."

"I don't think Santa had a thing to do with," she said. "Personally, I think it was an inside job."

Rick smiled and kissed the top of her head. Amber emerged from the bathroom with her hair pulled back and held in place by a pink scrunchie.

"You ready for dinner, Amber?" asked Elle.

"Yes. But can I eat in the kitchen?"

"Sure; I'll call you when it's ready." Elle disappeared out the door.

"Amber requested to have dinner in here," she told John and Erin. "You two want to store your computers while I get it ready?"

Elle opened a can of condensed vegetable beef soup. She poured it and a corresponding amount of water into a saucepan.

Ten minutes later, Amber sat down to a bowl of soup and saltine crackers.

"Applesauce for dessert," Elle said as she sat down at the table. "I'll be heading to the grocery store tomorrow. Thought I'd pick up some yogurt since it's an all-around good food. Is there any flavor you prefer over others?"

"What happened in Tennessee?"

Silence. Then John stood up with enough force and speed that his chair banged against the wall. Amber jumped. All eyes followed as John pulled from his pocket the card Jay Randall had given him and tossed it on the table. Erin immediately recognized it.

"There's about to be 'another man done gone,' all right," she said.

Elle picked up the card. She was smiling from ear to ear as she read Erin's qualifications out loud. Rick started chuckling before she was through.

"What's so funny?" said Amber.

"Marie Laveau was a voodoo practitioner in New Orleans in the 1800s," Erin explained. "There's a song loosely based on her that my dad used to play all the time. My mother wanted to name me Erin, and the only way Dad would agree is if Marie was my middle name. My 'gentleman friend' had cards made up as a joke."

"What's voodoo?" asked Amber.

"Voodoo is actually a religion," said. Erin "It originated in Africa and was brought by slaves to the West. Myths abound largely due to fear from colonial times, and later Hollywood depictions that it was black magic in movies and television. The song, 'Marie Laveau' by Bobby Bare, humorously capitalized on these myths."

"Considering the song's lyrics, the card is pretty funny," said Elle.

"I know," agreed Erin. "The truth is Dad and I had a good time singing and dancing to it when I was a kid. And . . . I have been known to dress up like her on Halloween."

"Did Jay go as Handsome Jack?" asked Elle.

Erin smiled. "I told him he might pass for Marie's one-eyed snake, but he could never pull off Handsome Jack."

"I don't get it," said Amber.

"Before the night's out," said Elle, "I'll pull up a video of the song, and you will."

After eating, Amber, accompanied by Erin, started for the bedroom. She was a step away from exiting the kitchen when she stopped and looked over her shoulder.

"Strawberry."

Everyone understood the implication. Amber had just apologized.

It had been a long and stressful day. After showering, Amber quickly fell asleep. Erin made her way back to the kitchen where Elle was cleaning up after a late dinner with Rick.

"You'll have to wait till tomorrow to play 'Marie Laveau' for Amber," said Erin. "She's conked out. Where are John and Rick?"

Elle pointed to the sliding glass door. "They stepped outside for a few minutes."

Erin walked across the room and looked at Gambit's partners as they talked. Elle followed suit.

"How long have you known John?" asked Elle.

"Since 2011. I was a dispatcher with the Greene County Sheriff's Department when he became a deputy. He was only twenty-six at the time, and a lot of people felt the only reason he got the job was because he was the son of State Senator Claire Nelson Hutsell. He proved them wrong, though."

"Yeah," agreed Elle. "The Cross-Timbers Murder Case made him a household name. He really hated that episode of *Murder in the Fifty* on the True Crime Investigations Channel."

"I know, but it was great PR for the department," said Erin. "Jay's a Missouri State Trooper. He and John met at a law enforcement seminar in Jefferson City and became fast friends. Jay stopped by the department one day in January 2013. My shift had just ended. I'd collected my left-over lunch from the refrigerator in the break room and was on my way out when he rounded a corner and bumped into me. He apologized and followed me to the exit. Just before we got there, he quickly maneuvered around me. He opened the door and did the 'ma'am' thing."

Elle smiled. "Yeah, Rick was a Shannon County, Tennessee, deputy when I met him, and he did the same thing. They are quick on their feet."

"Law enforcement showing courtesy and respect," said Erin with a smile. "Anyway, Jay walked me to my car, and I drove home. I found out later that he'd gone back inside and asked John who I was. Next thing you know, Jay and I are on a double date with John and Jenise Alexander."

"Jenise was here last night helping with Amber," said Elle.

Erin turned and looked at Elle. "How'd that go?"

"Definitely strained. He walked her to her car. She slipped on the ice, and he caught her. I felt like I was watching author Lee Child's Jack Reacher. You familiar with Reacher?"

"Yes," said Erin. "Reacher never walks away with the girl, he just walks."

"And walks . . . and walks . . . ." Both women smiled. "Everyone thinks John left Springfield because of the notoriety after solving the Cross Timbers case, but I always thought there was more to it."

"Yeah, I know what you mean. People, especially women, were asking, 'What happened between John and Jenise?' My standard answer was, 'Don't know and wouldn't tell you if I did.'"

"People knew better than to ask me," said Elle.

Erin smiled. "I don't doubt that."

John Hutsell and Rick Hadley were still talking when Erin and Elle walked away from the back door.

"Nice move with the business card," said Rick.

"Needed a diversion," said John. He looked up in the night sky. "No light pollution out here."

"You ever seen the Aurora Borealis?"

"No, have you?"

"Yep, when Dad was stationed at Fort Richardson in Alaska. Unbelievable sight."

"I'll make it someday," said John, then changed the subject. "Looks like Erin and I will be taking a trip to Oregon. Greg's agreed to fill in while I'm gone."

"Did you two discuss the possibility of him signing on with Gambit full-time?"

"Yeah. He's not too keen on anything that will take him out of town any more than he already is with his chartering service. But he has agreed to help out for now," said Hutsell. "We've got a meeting Wednesday with the Brentwood Insurance Group about a fraud case and you never know when Carver D'Orsay will call. He's our top client. Where he's concerned, we need to have someone available at the drop of the hat. And you've got your hands full with setting up the lab."

"There's no clear-cut deadline on the lab, John. It can play second fiddle for a while."

"I know, but the sooner we get it going, the better we can meet our client's needs—especially D'Orsey's."

"Can't argue there," said Hadley. "Erin's taking the first shift with Amber tonight, right?"

"Yes. Go ahead and get some sleep. I'll work at the computer, then handle the second shift."

The two men headed to the door.

"Wake me when it's time for me to take over," Hadley said.

Elle and Erin were sitting at the table when the two men stepped inside. Rick moved behind Elle's chair and touched his fingers to the back of her neck. She immediately shrugged her shoulders and pulled away.

"Damn, Hadley. Your hands are cold as ice. Just for that, no Girl Scout Cookies for you."

Elle stood, walked over to the kitchen's inside entry and retrieved the bag she'd left earlier.

"Thin Mints?" asked Rick.

"And Peanut Butter Patties."

"You are a cruel woman, Elle Wyatt," he moaned as he watched Erin open a box of cookies.

"I'm going to bed," said Elle. She stopped at the doorway and looked over her shoulder at Rick. "You coming?"

Rick grabbed two of the Peanut Butter Patties. "Yes, ma'am," he said and followed her down the hall. He had just closed the door to the small bedroom when Elle pulled off her thermal crew-necked shirt.

"I can't stand this bra for one more minute," she said.

Rick laughed. "Did you bring your flannel pjs?"

"They're sitting in an overnight bag on my bed at home."

He grinned. "Guess I'm all you've got for warmth tonight."

"It's the least you can do, cookie-stealer."

He smiled. "Do you know how hard I'm fighting right now not to do an impression of the Cookie Monster?"

"Oh shut up, take off your shirt and get over here."

They were spooned together when Elle said, "Know what I miss?"

"I think I do."

Rick reached above his head and picked up his charging cell phone. He tapped the screen a few times and Elle soon heard the comforting voice of Cheryl Wheeler.

"I never get tired of these songs," she said of the playlist she'd given him on the day after they'd met.

"You know my favorite?" he asked.

"Hard to choose one from that list."

"Not for me."

Elle had never been comfortable with intimacy in terms of touch and words, so he knew he was taking a chance when he picked up his phone and selected a song by Lee Roy Parnell. He felt her body tense as the first notes of the song's acoustic guitar came through the small speaker. Parnell's voice followed. "I've heard the talk in this little town. 'Bout all the heartache you've been through."

Elle closed her eyes as Parnell continued to sing.

Rick knew Elle put up a good front, but inside, she was still struggling. So much so, that whenever he tried to tell her how he felt, she always stopped him. So, he lay beside her and waited till he knew she was sleeping, then whispered, "I love you, Elle Wyatt."

Sunday morning in Clever found John still sleeping as the rest of the crew had breakfast. The sun was out, and there were still a few patches of ice left from Friday night. Elle was beginning to feel a little stir crazy and wondered if Amber was experiencing the same. The temperature was barely above freezing, so she headed to the spare room for her coat and gloves.

"Amber, I'm going to take a short walk around the property. You want to go?"

"My coat's not here."

"It wasn't a winter coat," Elle said about the jacket Rick had taken to the lab along with Amber's other items of clothing. Elle stood and went into the living area. She picked up a few shopping bags she'd deposited Friday night and carried them to the kitchen. She pulled a black hooded parka from one of the bags. "Try this on for size."

Amber put it on.

"How does it feel?" asked Elle.

"Good."

Elle pulled gloves from a second bag and handed them to Amber. "So, how 'bout it? You want to get out of here for a few minutes?"

"Can I put on real clothes first?"

Elle nodded yes. Amber started down the hallway for the clothes Elle had given her Friday night.

"Those clothes are really too big on you," Elle said and held out the second bag. "I think these will be a better fit. John's still sleeping, so you can change in the big bathroom."

Outside, the two women took a path walking along the tree-lined perimeter of the lot the house stood on. When they reached the one-car garage, Amber stopped. She put her hands on the window of a side door, shielding it from the sun's glare and peered inside.

"What's it like having a boyfriend?" she asked.

"Mmm . . . boyfriend. When I think of the word boyfriend, I think of being in high school and the conversations of most of the girls on campus. They were either talking about 'their boyfriends' or who they wanted as one. It was like they were defining who they were by who they were with." Elle smirked before continuing. "I kind of like the term Erin used yesterday; 'gentleman friend'." Although, in no way could I be described as Rick's 'lady friend'."

Amber pulled back from the door. "Why?"

"It's got an old-fashioned connotation—the fairer sex, the gentler sex." She laughed. "I don't fit that mold."

"You've got a lot of rules about words," said Amber.

"Yeah, guess I do. It's just that I don't like labels, although bitch has actually been a good descriptor of me at times."

Elle started walking again. Amber fell into step.

"You two gonna get married?"

"You're getting kind of personal, there," said Elle.

"Do you trust him?"

"It took a long time, but yeah I do. He's a good man."

"What about the other guy?"

"John's my cousin, and he's pulled me out of more scrapes than I care to remember," said Elle. "John's a fixer. He wants to set things right in the world. He's made a small dent. He's focused, and he gets things done. He just can't fix it all."

Their path had taken them around the house. Elle pointed to the two chairs on the small concrete porch outside the front door. They walked over and sat down.

"You like to read, Amber?"

"I'm not very good at it. Haven't had much schooling."

"What kind of schooling have you had?" asked Elle.

"I had a friend once. We were the same age. Her mom and her mom's helper taught us a lot of things. I lived in a farm house close to them for a while."

"How did you know it was a farm house?" asked Elle.

"In the summer there were lots of rows of corn along the road between my friend's house and the one I lived in.

Elle was about to ask a follow-up question when she spotted a car on the road leading to the house.

"Let's get inside," she said and hurried Amber through the door.

Elle moved to the front window. She pulled the sheet aside and called out, "Rick, we've got company."

Rick Hadley walked into the main room.

"It looks like Greg," she said. "I'll get John." Then to Amber, "Let's go to the bedroom, and I'll show you the video I told you about last night."

Rick Hadley opened the front door and motioned Greg Baptiste inside. The two men were engaged in small talk when John Hutsell entered the room. He was wearing a long-sleeve gray T-shirt and combing his short brown hair with his fingers.

"Sleeping on the job, are ya, John?"

"Not all of us are as lucky as you and roll out of bed looking like Jesse Williams on the set of Grey's Anatomy," said John.

"John, I've told you before. I don't look like Jesse Williams—Jesse Williams looks like me."

Erin Laveau was leaning against the kitchen door frame observing the scene, when Baptiste pulled a 5x7 manila envelope out of his inside coat pocket.

"Chelle ran these off this morning," he said.

"Come on in the kitchen, and let's have a look," said John.

Rick and Erin made eye contact and shrugged their shoulders in ignorance of what was in the envelope.

Baptiste pulled out three photos and handed them to Hutsell. John looked at each one, then passed them to Laveau and Hadley.

"Where did you find these?" asked Hadley.

"Chelle found them on a Facebook page set up by Mark Baylor's niece eight years ago. She sent the link to John late last night, and he asked if Chelle would print three of the pictures for Amber."

"Mark Baylor?" asked Rick.

"Amber's grandfather," said John.

Erin logged onto her computer. "What's the page title?"

"'Find Marissa Baylor'," said Baptiste. "It's similar to the page for Springfield's Three Missing Women."

"How long has it been now? Twenty-seven years?" asked Laveau of the famous Springfield case.

"In June," answered Baptiste.

"Someone want to fill me in?" said Rick.

"Stacy McCall and Suzie Streeter graduated from Kickapoo High School the night before they went missing. They left a graduation party in Battlefield in the early hours of June seventh, 1992, to spend the night in Springfield at the home of Sherill Levitt, Streeter's mother," said Hutsell. "Police were called in the next morning after friends of the girls and McCall's mother could not locate the three after finding their personal belongings abandoned in Levitt's home."

"The case gained national attention and has appeared on true crime channels," added Laveau.

Hadley recalled a similar program he'd seen a year ago about Hutsell and the Cross Timbers Murder Case. Hadley knew many in Springfield felt that John's 'celebrity' status had prompted him to leave southwest Missouri soon after the case had been solved. Whatever the reason, Hutsell had eventually landed in St. Louis, where he'd caught a stalking case a year ago. Hutsell suspected the stalker might have been active in other states and sent out a nationwide bulletin. The MO of the St. Louis suspect was the same as a person wanted in a Tennessee murder case Rick had worked for five years. Rick had traveled to Missouri, and along with Hutsell, and his partner, Trish Rankin, had solved what came to be known as The Anniversary Killer Case.

Erin Laveau interrupted his thoughts. "The Baylor page is up if you want to see it, Rick."

"Pictures. Links to law enforcement agencies," he said as he viewed the 'About' section. "When was the last entry on the timeline?"

"Christmas," said Laveau. "A picture of a Christmas present under the tree. The name tag says Marissa."

"John, what are your thoughts? When do you want to inform Amber?" said Hadley.

"Now that we have something we can put in her hand, I'm ready when you are."

"Okay, let's bring her in," replied Hadley.

Rick Hadley walked down the hall and into the master bedroom. Elle was sitting in the chair, and Amber was lounging on the bed. She was holding Elle's phone and watching a couple as they acted out the song "Marie Laveau" on YouTube.

"I get it now," she said when the video ended. She handed the phone back to its owner.

Rick moved to the side of the bed and crouched down.

"Amber, we've got some search results to share with you. Are you ready?"

Amber looked at Elle. Elle nodded.

"Okay," she said.

Rick held out his hand to assist Amber in getting up, but she didn't take it. He moved to the hallway and stepped aside for Amber and Elle to go ahead of him. Amber entered the kitchen and looked in turn into the faces of John Hutsell, Erin Laveau, and a man she'd never seen.

"Amber, meet Greg Baptiste. He's been helping in the search to find your true identity," John said.

Greg nodded and said, "Amber."

She nodded back.

Hutsell motioned to an empty chair in front of a computer. "Have a seat."

Amber sat down. Hutsell tapped the space bar and the screen lit up. The poster from the missing children's website came into view. Amber brought her hand up and covered the lower portion of her face. John allowed a few moments before speaking again.

"Marissa Baylor was six years old when she went missing from Multnomah Falls on May 21, 2006. The photo on the left was taken at a picnic at Emigrant Lake in Oregon a month before. The one on the right is the same photo, aged-enhanced, to show what Marissa might look like today."

"It's me, isn't it?"

"We think so and here's why."

John moved the computer back and laid out the first photo. It was a picture of smiling Marissa Baylor sitting on a blue-flowered sofa. She held a children's book in her lap. Next to her sat a pink teddy bear with two hearts on its chest. She picked up the photo, studied it and then clutched it to her chest. She closed her eyes and dropped her head.

69

"Would you like to see another picture?" asked John.

Amber looked up at him and nodded. He placed a second picture on the table. Marissa Baylor was standing on the bank of Emigrant Lake with a pink Minnie Mouse fishing rod in her hands. She was wearing a man's cap and Snoopy sunglasses. Her grandfather stood behind her with his arms around her, showing her how to use the reel. Still clutching the first picture with her left hand, Amber used her right to pick up the second.

"Is he still alive?"

"Yes," answered John. "His name is Mark Baylor. He's fifty-six years old and lives in Talent, Oregon. Talent is about twelve miles from Emigrant Lake and about six miles from the city of Ashland. Ashland is important for two reasons."

Amber took her eyes off the second picture and looked up at John Hutsell. He put the last photo on the table.

"This was taken at Ashland's Lithia Park in October, 2005."

The photo was of Mark Baylor holding a smiling Marissa. Behind them were ducks swimming on a pond. The five other people in the room watched as Amber studied the last photo. Her eyes moved from her grandfather's face, to her own and then to the ducks in the background. They then moved back to her grandfather.

"Do you think he still misses me?"

"Yes," answered John. "And let me show you why."

John nodded at Erin and she turned her computer around.

"Are you familiar with Facebook?" he asked.

"No."

"It's what is known as a social network. People have their own 'page' where they share pictures and experiences with friends and family. Here is an example of one."

Laveau tapped her keyboard. "This is the Facebook page of a friend of mine," she said. "She lives in another state, so we don't see each other very often. But we keep up with what's going on in our lives by what are called posts. This post shows a view of her backyard after a big snow last month."

Laveau paused to allow Amber time to view the screen. A few moments later Amber looked from the monitor to Laveau, signaling she was ready to move on.

"We know your grandfather still thinks about you because he and his niece set up this page asking for help in finding you," Laveau said. She scrolled to the most recent entry. "This picture was posted a month and a half ago on Christmas Day." She let Amber take in the post. "He still buys you a present every year on your birthday—November eighth—and another every Christmas."

Laveau spent a few minutes showing Amber how to navigate the page, then handed her the mouse. When Amber was done, she picked up the three pictures and headed to the bedroom.

"I'm not comfortable with her being alone right now," said Rick.

He was halfway down the hall when Elle caught up with him.

"Let me," she said.

"Rick stepped aside to let Elle pass, then stationed himself outside the room.

Elle sat down on the bed under the window. "Hard to decide, huh?" she asked.

"What do you mean?"

"What name to use?" Amber continued to stare at the picture of her Grandfather holding her. "Do you know my name?" asked Elle.

"Elle Wyatt."

"Yes . . . but that's not the name I was born with." Amber finally looked up. "The name on my birth certificate is Elaine Stafford. My parents divorced when I was a toddler. My mom and I lived alone till I was ten. She got married again—I told you about her husband's midnight trips. Elaine Stafford no longer exists. She died the same night my mother did."

Rick Hadley had known Elle's history before he'd met her, but this was the first time he'd actually heard her talk about it.

"My biological father didn't want me. My last name was changed to Wyatt when my aunt and uncle adopted me. I had a friend at my new school named Michelle. She came up with the names, Elle and Chelle." Elle paused for a few moments before speaking again. "What was the name your friend called you?"

"Maddie."

"Was Maddie a good fit?"

"Yeah. For a while I almost felt like a regular person," said Amber. "Marissa . . . Maddie . . . Amber . . . ?"

"Or some other name."

"You know . . . it's like you said about Elaine Stafford . . . Marissa and Maddie are dead. I know now I was an Amber Alert kid. Amber's the name I chose two days ago. It's the name I'm going to keep." Amber put the pictures under her pillow and slid under the covers. "Miss Wyatt, I'm tired, and I've got a lot to think about. Can I be alone for a while?"

Rick moved to where he was visible to Elle. She looked at him for approval. He gave it with a nod.

"Call me if you need anything," she said and walked into the hallway.

Rick took her hand and led her to the end of the hall. He put his arms around her and, in his mind, repeated the words he'd spoken the previous night after Elle had fallen asleep.

· 15 ·

On his way to the kitchen, Rick Hadley nodded at Erin Laveau as she talked to Jay Randall on her cell. He found John and Greg in conference as John prepared a ham and cheese omelet for his breakfast. Rick poured himself a cup of coffee and joined his two friends at the table. He waited till Erin walked in before relaying the conversation between Elle and Amber.

"Elle's sitting in the hallway," he said. "She needs a little time to herself right now, too."

"I've never known Elle to open up like that," said John.

Diverting the conversation away from Elle, Rick said, "The important take away from this is that Amber's name choice is a move forward for her."

"True," said John. "But we need to proceed with caution. This is the 'third' Amber we've seen. She's gone from cowering victim to hostile teen and now a hint of receptiveness. She's lived a life where she's had to say or do anything to survive."

"Point being, John, she *is* a survivor," said Rick.

"Now, I see why you two are so good together," said Erin.

"Yeah," said Greg. "Go-for-the-jugular Hutsell and Mic-drop Hadley reeling him in."

"Mic-drop Hadley?" asked Rick.

"Yeah, it's how Elle described you to Chelle shortly after you two met," said Greg.

Rick smiled and shook his head.

"What's the next step?" asked Erin.

"Wait for responses from the inquiries we've sent to law enforcement in Oregon and at the federal level," said John. "Then lay the situation out for Amber and see if she wants to go to Oregon. Who knows, she may say, 'No thanks.'"

"And if she does?" said Erin.

73

"Amber has known from the beginning one of our goals is to gain information to identify and apprehend sex-traffickers. If she chooses to walk away, we'll do what we can with what we've got, then pass on what we learn."

"In other words, her family and law enforcement will know she has been found," Rick said, "But it's Amber's decision if she wants to pursue a relationship with her grandfather or not."

"Rick, if she decides to go to Oregon, how soon till she's well enough to travel?" John asked.

"Tuesday."

Elle entered the room. Rick rose to his feet and offered his chair.

"She's going to need clothes," said Erin.

"Sounds like a shopping trip is in order," said Elle. "Erin, how about it? We can be in Springfield Tuesday morning when the stores open."

Laveau smiled and said, "Let me check with my boss."

"Have at it, ladies," said John. "Whether she decides to go to Oregon or not, she's going to need clothing and shoes. I'll get some cash for you tomorrow."

"I've got cash," Elle said.

"Elle, Gambit Investigations does pro bono work several times a year," John said. "We got it."

Elle nodded and checked her watch.

"I'm headed to town for supplies," she said. "Why don't you guys start making a list of what we need, while I get my coat."

"You cooking dinner," asked Rick.

"I could, but I'm thinking barbecue."

"And tomorrow?"

"Okay, Hadley, what are you wanting?"

"Fried chicken and mashed potatoes."

"You willing to mash potatoes?" said Elle.

"Yes, ma'am."

"Add potato masher to the list," she said.

Elle went down the hall and returned to the kitchen with her coat and bag. She was almost out the door when Rick called out, "Hold on a minute and I'll go with you."

She gave him one of her 'looks.'

74

"What?" he feigned ignorance. "It's just that you're kind of stingy when it comes to sharing Girl Scout Cookies."

"So, you're going to get your own?"

"I'm going to clean them out on Thin Mints and put them in the freezer."

Rick and Elle headed for her car. She tossed him her key on the way.

"First stop, Girl Scout Cookies," she said once they were belted in.

"Nope," he said. "First stop, my place."

"Should have known you had an ulterior motive."

Rick Hadley reached over and squeezed her hand. "But 'my intentions are true'," he said, quoting a song from the playlist they'd fallen asleep to the night before.

Elle pulled up the song he'd referred to—a Melissa Etheridge song Trisha Yearwood had covered in the mid-nineties. After the second chorus, she said, "Sometimes I wish we could take off and drive like the people in the song—just get in the car and go wherever we want, no particular destination, no timeline."

"We can."

Elle looked at him.

"Return trip from Tennessee after Mom's birthday," he said.

Elle pulled up her phone, tapped the screen, and said, "Where should I go on my next vacation?" The third result was the from the *Washington Post.* "Here we go," she said. "Vacation Finder: Where should you travel in 2019?" She followed the link, "Pick one, 'set parameters' or 'roll the dice.' "

"Bookmark it. The Monday after Mom's birthday, we'll get in the truck and 'roll the dice.' "

They were a few miles from M Highway when she said, "Take the road to Battlefield."

"Any particular reason?"

"My place is closer."

· 16 ·

Jenise Alexander and Kyle Jeffries attended Sunday mass at 9:00 A.M. in Springfield. Senator Claire Nelson Hutsell was also in attendance. The two women nodded at each other across the aisle.

After Mass, the couple headed to the home of Kyle's parents just outside Nixa for Sunday dinner. Both Kyle and Jenise were noticeably quiet throughout the afternoon, though neither one of his parents spoke to him about it. They had raised their son to be independent and were never ones to interfere. Kyle had a good head on his shoulders. If he felt the need to talk, he would.

Kyle walked Jenise into her apartment that evening. She took off her coat and hung it on the coat rack by the door. She reached for his and realized he was still wearing it. He made sure he had her full attention before he spoke.

"Jenise, I've never wanted to replace him. There's no replacing a first love." He reached up and gently moved her bangs aside. "I've always known John Hutsell was unfinished business. You still have questions. One way or another, for your own sake, you need to find the answers."

He took a step back and saw a tear on her cheek. He wiped it away with his fingers. "No matter what, I'll always be your best friend and I'll always be here if you need me."

"You always have been," she said.

He turned to go. At the door he asked, "Your next volunteer date is Thursday, right?"

"Yes."

"See you then," he said, then walked into the night.

Jenise leaned against her closed door, hugged herself and remembered the first time Kyle had held her through the night—August 22, 2013. She'd tried all that day to get hold of John. He was in Wichita, Kansas, working the Cross Timbers case, and all

76

her calls and texts had gone unanswered. By the time he showed up the next night, it was too late.

She saw John sporadically for the next several months. He solved the case in early October. A week later, he told her he'd resigned from the Greene County Sheriff's Department and was moving to Columbia, Missouri, with no explanation as to why. A friend of Kyle's at the Sheriff's Department had told him about John's resignation and acceptance of a position in Columbia. That night, Kyle knocked on her door. It was the second night he'd spent with his arms around her.

Jenise went to her bedroom and changed into her night clothes. She set her alarm for 5:00 A.M., and turned out the light. Jenise knew Kyle was right. She'd been going through the motions for five and a half years, pretending the summer and fall of 2013 were over and done. She thought again about John's words when she'd told him they were going to have a child.

"It'll be all right, Jenise."

Well, it hadn't been. In fact, nothing had been right since. And seeing him Friday night had brought it all back to the surface.

Jenise got up, hit the lamp switch and sat down at her computer. She clicked on her media player and looked at the playlists. Her eyes landed on the name of a singer/songwriter John had introduced her to in the spring of 2013. It had been over a year since she'd last played any of the songs.

John and Jenise had attended a Hutsell/Wyatt family gathering in March of that year. John's cousin, Elle Wyatt had been seated next to Jenise at the dinner table. Like most people in Springfield, Jenise was aware of Elle's reputation as the wayward Nelson grandchild. So, she wasn't surprised that Elle kept mostly to herself that afternoon. After the meal, everyone but Elle had gathered in the great room of the Hutsell Estate. Elle had skipped out and gone to the covered lanai instead. On her way back from the bathroom, Jenise stepped through the lanai's entry and asked if she could join Elle. Elle removed her earbuds and said, "It's a free country."

Trying to find a suitable topic of discussion was a challenge until Jenise recalled Grandma Nelson's performing arts influence on John and suspected Elle'd had the same experiences.

"You like Harry Connick, Jr.?"

"Saw him in concert in Atlanta with Grandma Nelson and John in June 2007."

"I saw him at The Fox in St. Louis with my mom. December 2008."

"Talk about a man who can do it all . . .."

"I know what you mean," said Jenise. "My mom still has a crush on him. The moment she saw him two-stepping with Sandra Bullock in *Hope Floats,* she was a goner."

"Yeah, but his character was a little far-fetched," Elle commented.

"What do you mean?"

"Never known a guy who was that good. Never will. Guys like that don't exist."

"John's a pretty good guy," said Jenise.

"Well . . . at least he can dance."

"That I can," said John from the entryway. "Jenise, you ready to head out?"

"Yes. Nice talking with you Elle."

"Yeah."

On the way home, John had told her that if she really wanted to understand Elle, she should listen to Cheryl Wheeler, that Elle played her music all the time.

"Cheryl Wheeler?"

"She's a folk singer/songwriter. Her songs have been recorded by various artists from groups like Peter, Paul, and Mary to Bette Midler. Country singer Suzy Bogguss had a big hit with "Aces" in the early nineties."

"I'm not familiar with it."

"It's about a falling out between friends. Most of Elle's friends have distanced themselves. Chelle Thomas from high school is one who's stayed around. The only other two friends I know of are Shellie Matheson and Cal Davies. She met them a couple of years ago in a therapy group for sexual assault victims. Shellie's the one who introduced her to Wheeler."

Jenise had checked out Wheeler on YouTube and had been so impressed she'd ordered a couple of the artist's CDs online. Then, after August 2013, several songs began hitting closer to home, and Jenise found herself listening to Wheeler almost every night.

She clicked on Wheeler's name, then scrolled to the last song on the list—the one that had perfectly described her failing relationship with John later that year. Talk about songs hitting home. This one knocked her to her knees every time. Jenise had finally decided that was a good thing because tears brought release. Soon, Wheeler's voice and songs were Jenise's chosen form of therapy.

"She says she feels like she's addicted to a real bad thing . . . always sitting, waiting wondering if the phone will ring . . .," Wheeler sang.

John's words came back to haunt her.

"It'll be all right, Jenise."

Jenise keyed up her email account and selected a folder she hadn't been able to bring herself to delete. She opened a six-year-old message from Erin Laveau and clicked on the attachment. A photo of her and John slow-dancing appeared on the monitor.

Jenise stared at the image.

"Liar," she whispered.

For the love of God . . . it didn't make sense that a part of her still wanted him.

Once an addict, always an addict.

As Wheeler sang in the background, she begged God for the millionth time to tell her why John had left. God remained silent.

"She says she feels like she's addicted to a real bad thing . . .."

·17·

Results from Hutsell and Baptiste's inquiries came in Monday morning. By 11:00 A.M., Gambit's three investigators were ready to update Amber with what they'd learned since the previous day. They requested Elle Wyatt also be in attendance at the meeting. She was leaning against the kitchen counter as Amber took a seat at the table.

"Amber, we have some more information for you," said John Hutsell. "It concerns your mother."

"What about her?" she said with contempt about the woman who had given her birth.

"Her name was Kristina Baylor Revelle. She had several arrests for drug possession. Most notably for methamphetamine. She died of an overdose in 2011 at the age of thirty-eight. I have a mug shot if you would like to see it."

Amber took a few moments before nodding her head. She watched Hutsell as he turned his computer around. She moved her eyes from Hutsell to the monitor and into the face of her mother—sores and all.

"That's her," she said without effect.

"The dark circles under her eyes and the lesions you spoke of may have actually been due to her drug use," said Hutsell.

"Anything else?" asked a stoic Amber.

"Your mother's friend on the day you went missing was Devin Zimbeck. He's serving a twelve-year sentence in an Oregon state prison for the production and distribution of methamphetamine," Hutsell said. "As for the investigation into your disappearance, one of the FBI's Child Abduction Rapid Deployment teams was notified within five hours after you were reported missing. Both the state of Oregon and the FBI exhausted what few leads there were. The FBI offered a ten-thousand-dollar reward for information leading to your recovery. It was matched by an Oregon businessman."

"Did they think my mother or her friend had anything to do with it?"

"Mr. Baptiste was a member of the Secret Service for ten years. A former colleague is now with the FBI. Mr. Baptiste contacted him late Saturday night and he agreed to research the case. According to him, the story given by your mother and Zimbeck was suspect. The FBI just didn't have enough evidence to charge either one."

John Hutsell gave an almost imperceptible nod to his partner. Rick Hadley adjusted his chair so he was facing Amber.

"Amber, we know this is a lot to take in. You're facing some big decisions about what happens next. When you look at your options—."

Amber cut him off. "I'm not talking to the police," she said. "I've seen too many of them take money and look the other way before they disappeared behind closed doors for their turn with one of us."

"Nobody here is going to force you to do anything you don't want to do," said Rick. "We just want you to know that since you are of age and have expressed a distrust with some members of law enforcement, if you decide you want to go to Oregon, we will help you get there."

"Why?"

"Because we choose to"

Amber looked at Elle.

"Hell Amber, I can't tell you any more than I already have," said Elle. "You're finally free to make your own decisions. What happens from here on out is up to you."

"When do I have to decide?"

"You'll be physically ready to travel tomorrow," Rick said.

"So, what *are* my 'options'?"

Rick leaned forward in his chair, placed his elbows on his upper legs and clasped his hands between his knees.

"There are several shelters in Springfield that provide assistance to victims of violent crime in terms of temporary housing, counseling, and advocacy."

"Can they get me to Oregon if I decide that's what I want?"

"They may be able to help," Rick said.

"What other choices do I have?"

"We can take you to Springfield, where you can open the door, step out, and head in any direction you want." Rick leaned back in his chair. "Whatever you decide, we will provide you with basic essentials such as clothing and enough money to get through the week."

"And if I want you to take me to Oregon?"

"John and Erin will drive you to Talent, where you can reunite with your grandfather, if you so wish," said Rick. "If not, your options once in Oregon are the same as they are here."

"No strings?" she asked.

"No strings. But there is one thing you need to know. We will be letting the proper authorities know that you are no longer missing. The people who worked so hard to find you need to know, because, believe me, they haven't forgotten you. Your case is still open. They deserve to be able to close it."

"How will they know you're telling the truth?"

John Hutsell slowly rose to his feet.

Elle Wyatt took a deep breath. *Here it comes.* She understood the reasons why Gambit Investigations needed the signed release, but that didn't mean she was happy with what her cousin was about to say.

"Amber, you remember the paper you signed giving permission to run the tests needed for a diagnosis?" Amber didn't answer "One of the items on the form was for the analysis of a rape kit. The doctor wanted to check for STDs that might not show up in blood or urine. Results of such tests include the DNA of the man who raped you last Friday as well as your own. If you will recall, included in that form was permission to release the findings to medical care providers and authorities, if and when it was determined the results might help solve a crime."

Amber jumped to her feet. "You tricked me," she said through clenched teeth.

"No Amber. You've known from the beginning what my motivation was. As for the release form. I read every word to you and asked if you understood what you were signing before I handed you the pen," Hutsell reminded her. "You can do whatever you want. You don't have to talk to, or meet with anybody. But the people who searched for you from the beginning and the grandfather who still mourns you, will have proof you are alive. That's it, end of story."

Amber stormed out of the room. Elle made a move to follow. Her cousin rounded the table and met her at the kitchen's exit.

"Elle, it's Rick's job to handle this."

She turned to face Rick.

"Your job, Hadley?" she asked. Elle stepped aside "You are good," she said as he passed. "I should know . . . I've seen you in action before."

Elle Wyatt pulled her car key out of her jeans pocket and walked out the side door. Rick Hadley left the kitchen and went to the master bedroom.

Erin Laveau arched her left eyebrow but didn't say a word.

John Hutsell headed to the coffee pot. "Elle will be fine," he said. "Eventually she'll come to terms with the situation because Rick Hadley is not only good, he's genuine. And by God, nobody knows that better than Elle Wyatt."

"*Is* Hadley that good?" Laveau asked.

"Yeah, he is," John said. "I watched him gain the confidence of a woman intent on suicide. He convinced her to change her mind— she even agreed to help catch a killer—all in the space of one afternoon. His compassion is real, and he's successful at conveying it to victims."

Amber lay on the air mattress that had been provided by the private investigators and wondered what to do. They had told her that what happened next, where she was concerned, was up to her––that it was her decision. Well, except for one very important item.

Her DNA. The problem was she felt like she was being held captive all over again. "Tell everyone you've been 'found' or we'll do it for you—your decision." Some decision.

Rick Hadley showed up a few minutes later and sat down on the floor. He brought his legs up, placed his elbows on his knees parallel to his chest, and interlocked his fingers.

"Amber?"

She turned her head and refused to look at him.

"Why did you give us so much detailed information Saturday morning?"

She didn't answer.

"You didn't have to," he said.

Still refusing to look at him. "Yeah, I could have—should have lied."

"But you didn't," he said. "You could have derailed this investigation numerous times."

No response.

Hadley continued, "Everything you've done—everything you've said, indicates you want to 'be found.' And even more important, to know if there's someone out there who not only misses you, but loves you."

Silence.

"Amber, as much as we'd like to, we, as human beings, can't control everything we start. There are just too many variables that enter into any given situation. You might not have realized it at the time, but you chose this journey. It would be nice if all we had to consider is how this will affect you, John, and me, but for various reasons we cannot."

Rick Hadley rose to his feet and said, "Erin will be in shortly to sit with you."

He was almost out the door when she spoke.

"Whose lives in the big house?" she asked.

Rick turned to face her.

"That person knew I was there a long time before you and *John* showed up. And it took even more time before Miss Wyatt and the nurse got there. All of you made sure I never saw that person. Why?"

"If it wasn't for that person," said Hadley, "You would be in the Greene County Jail or back with the men you escaped from."

"You know Rick, you, and John can't control everything you start either," she said, throwing his words back in his face. "I could cause a lot of trouble, if I wanted to."

"And therein lies the reason for your signature on a piece of paper," Hadley said.

·18·

Elle Wyatt walked into Chelle Thomas's office and plopped in a chair.

Chelle looked at her and laughed. "Who's done what now?"

"Both of them."

"Okay, we've got the who. Now, the what."

"They're using her," said Elle.

"By her, do you mean Marissa Baylor?"

"She wants to go by Amber."

"Okay, how are they using Amber?"

"Her DNA. They know she wants nothing to do with law enforcement, but they're going to release her DNA anyway."

"Did they give a reason?"

"To close a case."

"Do they have the men who abducted Amber and forced her to be a sex slave for twelve years?" asked Chelle.

"No."

"Then the case can't be closed. Cross that reason off the list. Next."

"Okay, okay. So they can give her grandfather and those who worked on the case closure . . . I guess."

"No such thing as closure, Elle."

"You know what I mean."

"Yes, I do. And you, *Ms*. Wyatt, know what I mean"

Elle remained silent.

"Can you think of another missing child case Rick worked?" Chelle asked.

Elle knew Chelle was referring to her second cousin's little girl.

"Yes," she said reluctantly.

"Did he do so behind the scenes?"

85

"You know he did."

"Were those responsible brought to justice?"

Elle nodded.

"And in the end, were the victims and their families grateful?"

Elle knew Chelle was right and knowing her best friend as she did, said, "So, you going to quote 'it' again?"

Chelle pulled a silver cuff bracelet off her arm and tossed it to Elle. Elle studied the bracelet's twist wire design.

"Native American?" she asked.

"Got it in Albuquerque a couple of weeks ago. Look inside."

Elle held the bracelet up so she could see the inscription. *God grant me the serenity to . . ..*

"You need it right now more than I do," Chelle said. "In fact, keep it. They've got a website. I'll get another one." She smiled. "We are 'twins' after all. Elle and Chelle ride again."

Elle looked at the five-foot-eleven woman with rich golden-brown skin standing before her.

"True," she said, "if it wasn't for the chickenpox scar on my forehead, people wouldn't be able to tell us apart."

Elle's cell signaled a message had been received.

"It's from him, isn't it?" Chelle asked.

"He wants me to meet him at the pavilion."

Chelle Thomas laughed so hard she grabbed her sides and doubled over. "Give it up, Elle; you haven't got a prayer."

Elle Wyatt drove her Cadillac down the Wyatt Estate driveway. She pulled around the main house and parked under the carport of the what was the estate's former guest house. It belonged to her now, part of her inheritance from Grandpa Nelson. She exited the car and pocketed the key. She looked over to the pavilion and saw Rick's truck parked nearby.

Elle made her way to the structure and paused at the building's main entrance. She took a breath and pulled open the door. Rick Hadley was sitting at a nearby table. He clicked the remote control in his hand, set it on the table, and stood. The sound of drums filled the room. Cymbals soon joined in.

Elle finally gave up a smile with the song's first line. "I know you want to leave me . . . but I refuse to let you go . . .." He held

86

out his arms. She placed her right hand in his as the chorus started. "Ain't too proud to beg, sweet darlin' . . .."

Rick led her in a West Coast Swing around the pavilion's dance floor. The song ended and she asked, "Who taught you how to dance?"

"Some person who promised to fry me up some chicken today."

He walked to the table, picked up the remote and clicked off the sound system.

"Must be a hell of a woman," she said.

He stuck his hands in the pockets of his jeans, looked around the room and said, "Evidently."

Elle raised up on her toes and kissed him. "Guess we better be heading out."

"Guess so . . .." They kissed a second time. "Potatoes *are* waiting to be mashed."

Rick's hands were still in his pockets when Elle unbuttoned his plain blue shirt. She pulled out the shirt tail, as well as that of the white tee underneath.

"You *are* the master of mashed potatoes," she said.

Elle slipped her hands inside his tee. The conversation continued with slight interruptions as they kissed and Elle's hands roamed.

"I've got to put the remote in the office . . . and return the key to Pat."

"Then you better . . . get started."

She picked up the pavilion key from the table and stuck it in her right hip pocket.

"Elle, as much as I'd like—."

"One more dance, Hadley" she said, matter-of- factly.

Rick picked up the remote, made a few clicks and the big screen came to life. A man and woman gracefully skated around an ice rink to a Manhattan Transfer recording.

Rick pulled Elle into his arms once more. He placed his leg inside hers and with his hand firmly at the small of her back, led her in a soft, slow dance.

"You are unbelievable," she said, as Alan Paul began singing.

"Well, it helps that Pat likes me and handed over the key," he teased.

"Yeah, but you're not going to get *that* key unless you sing, too."

"A dance and a song? You drive a hard bargain, Ms. Wyatt."

"It's part of my charm."

Rick picked up the lyrics in the second chorus. The song ended and Rick reached in her hip pocket and retrieved the key.

"Things will get back to normal after tomorrow," he said.

"I know," she replied. "Control issues, again."

"Elle, you know why we had no choice about the release form, right?"

"You always have a choice," she said.

"If John and I were the only people to consider, it would be a different story. But, Jenise and Dr. Shulman also went out on a limb Friday night," he said. "And what about the investors in Gambit and the forensics lab?"

"The Nelson/Wyatt Group: Pat, Jean, and Claire," she said. He hugged her one last time. "I'll wait for you at the gate," she said in his ear. Elle broke the embrace. "I'll lead, you follow."

Rick nodded and picked up the remote. He was on his way to the pavilion's office when Elle stopped at the exit. She glanced at the bracelet on her wrist and said, "It's just that I know how she feels."

"I know you do. It's not going to be smooth sailing for her, but it will get better. If I don't believe that, then I'm in the wrong business."

"You're in the right business," she said.

Elle opened the door and walked out.

Pat Wyatt was watching a cable TV sports program in his family room when Rick entered.

"How'd it go?"

Rick laid the key on the coffee table and gave a thumbs up. He turned to go.

"Rick?"

Rick stopped and looked at the man who had adopted Elle twenty-two years ago.

"Yes, sir."

"Remember . . .."

Rick smiled and waited for the rest of the Red Green quote he knew was coming.

"I'm pulling for ya."

"Yes sir," he said for a second time.

·19·

It had been three and a half days since the young woman who now called herself Amber Lawrence had sought shelter in Senator Claire Nelson Hutsell's greenhouse. In that time, she had learned her true identity and that local, state, and federal law-enforcement officials had pulled out all the stops to find her after she'd gone missing.

By Tuesday morning, she'd decided to let John and Rick foot the bill a little longer. She agreed to the Oregon trip, mainly because it would get her out of Missouri. She'd been transported several times through this area, often passing the 'Big Arch' up the road in the process. She'd read the signs and knew that I-44 was a favorite highway of sex-traffickers. They had a vast network, and she didn't want to take a chance that they were out looking to reclaim her.

Amber knew John would use the time driving to Oregon to glean information from her. She was contemplating whether or not she should give him what he wanted. In the end, she decided to cooperate to a certain extent if it could save other children from being taken. But John had to understand that the minute there was any talk of bringing law enforcement in, she would shut down. She would talk to him but not to 'them'.

After breakfast and a shower, Amber followed John Hutsell, Elle Wyatt and Erin Laveau outside to Elle's Cadillac. Cousins Wyatt and Hutsell sat in the front, Laveau and Amber in the back. Elle allowed the Caddy to warm up a few moments before putting it in gear and heading on their shopping trip to Springfield. On the way, Amber's companions made suggestions on what she would need concerning clothing and accessories for her new life.

Elle dropped John off at a car rental agency on South Campbell before heading to Battlefield Mall. She pulled the Cadillac into the southside parking lot a little after 10:00 A.M. She had just driven into a space close to the entrance when Laveau's phone signaled a message from Jay Randall.

"Can you talk?"

"Yes, give me a few moments," Laveau typed. She turned toward Elle. "It's Jay. I need to make a call."

"We'll sit here till you're ready to go inside," Elle replied.

Laveau stepped out of the warm car into the cold air and placed the call. Three minutes later she re-entered the Caddy.

"Jay has some documents needing my signature before I head out of State," she said. "His mother set up an irrevocable trust with me as trustee last year. She needs my signature to proceed with the sale of some farm equipment. Would it be possible to meet with him about 2:30 at Applebee's on North Glenstone for lunch? Jay and I can sit in a different section from you and Amber."

"Fine by me," said Elle.

The three women visited several boutiques in the mall, featuring styles for teens and young women. Amber was trying on clothes in the third store when Elle asked Erin if Jay Randall would be in uniform when they met for lunch.

"Unfortunately, yes. We'll need to let Amber know before he shows up, or she'll think we're pulling a fast one."

Elle checked her watch. "We need to be heading that way soon," she said. "But first, I want to get Amber a few pieces of luggage."

In the parking lot, Elle keyed open the trunk. Amber and Erin got inside the car while Elle placed Gambit Investigations' purchases inside the suitcase. The Caddy had just pulled onto South Glenstone when Laveau turned and addressed the situation.

"Amber, it's important that you know that the man I am going to meet is a Missouri State Trooper." Elle saw Amber's immediate change of expression in the rearview mirror as Laveau continued, "When we enter the restaurant, you and Elle will request seating on the southside. I will remain in the waiting area till he arrives. He and I will sit on the north side. After lunch, he will leave, and I will join you and Elle. You can watch him drive off before we head outside."

"It's always something with you guys, isn't it?" Amber said.

"So goes life," Elle said. "Plan all you want, but wrenches get thrown into the mix all the time. Don't make more of this than it is, okay?"

Amber didn't engage. Instead, she held onto her few negotiating cards—the biggest one being the identity of the person in the 'big house'.

Soon after Amber and Elle were seated in a booth, a Missouri State Trooper patrol car backed into a street-side parking space across from the restaurant's entrance. Trooper Jay Randall stepped inside and removed his hat. Erin Laveau joined him, and the hostess led them to a booth on the north side.

Three bites into her Chicken Wonton Stir Fry Amber said, "This looks better in the picture than it really is."

"What would you like to have instead?" Elle said.

"Just a regular hamburger and fries."

Elle signaled for the waiter. He made his way to their table and said, "How may I help you?"

"My friend doesn't really care for her dish. Would you bring her a hamburger with fries?"

"Yes, ma'am."

Thirty minutes later, Laveau and Randall parted company at the door and Erin walked over and sat down next to Elle.

"Business is now out of the way," she said. "Ready to head back when you are."

Elle asked for the check. When it arrived, she placed on the table several of the bills John had given her that morning.

"I need to get gas before we leave town," she said.

"There's a station next door," Laveau said. "You won't even have to get out on Glenstone."

The three women stood and made their way to the car. Elle pulled to an outside pump, put the car in park and shut off the ignition.

Erin said, "I'll pump it, since the tank is on the passenger's side."

As she took Elle's credit card, a man in the next lane stepped into view. Amber careful slid down onto the floor board.

"That's one of them," she whispered.

"From Friday night?" asked Laveau.

"Yes."

"Cover yourself with the blanket," Elle said of the throw she carried in her car.

"You sure?" Laveau asked Amber.

"Look at his earrings," answered Amber. "The one hanging down is an arrow and there's a round one on the inside of his ear."

A second man emerged from the vehicle, exchanged a few words with his companion and walked toward the station's convenience store.

"What did the other guy look like?" Laveau asked.

"Real long forehead—like it takes up almost half his face," Amber said from underneath the blanket. "Hair is turning gray and combed back. He likes to wrap different colored leather strings around his left wrist."

"Call John," said Laveau. "I'll start filling the tank, then go inside and get a better look at the friend."

John Hutsell answered on the second ring.

"What's going on?"

"You're on Speaker. We're getting gas on North Glenstone, just south of I-44. Amber says the guys filling up in the next lane are the ones she escaped from."

"She sure?"

"One of them has two earrings. She described both to a tee."

"Make and model?"

"Just a minute," said Elle. She exited her Cadillac, clicked off the nozzle trigger and returned the nozzle to the pump. Back inside the car, she said, "A silver Hyundai Elantra."

"Not the same one from Friday night," he said.

"Erin followed one of them inside." Elle looked in the rearview mirror. "She's on her way back to the car now."

"Can you get the plate number?"

"We'll follow them and get it."

"Elle, just long enough to get the number and see what direction they take, you hear?"

"Yes, John." Hutsell heard the passenger door shut. "Here's Erin."

"Amber's description of the second guy checks out," said Laveau as Elle pulled out and got behind the Elantra.

"He wants the license number," interrupted Elle.

Erin rattled off the Missouri plate's combination of six letters and numbers.

"Got it," said Hutsell.

"They're turning onto I-44 East."

"Elle, take I-44 West and head back here."

Elle put on her blinker for the turn.

"John," Erin said, "Jay's on duty."

"Give me descriptions of the men, and I'll get in touch with him."

As Erin talked, Elle checked traffic, saw it was clear, then eased onto I-44 West. "It's safe, Amber," she said. "We're going in the opposite direction from the Elantra. You can sit up now."

John disconnected the call.

"What happens next?" Amber asked.

"My guess is the Highway Patrol will get an 'anonymous tip' about possible sex-traffickers on I-44," Leveau said. "They'll find a reason to pull the car over and get the men's identities. The vehicle will probably remain under surveillance for as long as it's in Missouri."

"And me?"

"We continue as planned and head to Oregon in the morning. Unless . . .?"

"No," Amber said.

John Hutsell had been sitting in his office at Gambit Investigations on North Boonville when Erin Laveau's call came. After getting descriptions of Amber's captors, he dialed Jay Randall and learned that the trooper was on his way to Lebanon, Missouri, via I-44 East. John explained the situation.

"Where are you now?" Hutsell asked.

"Just passed Strafford. I'll pull off at the Northview Exit and get behind them. With all the distractions from cell phones, sooner or later, they'll do something that will be considered 'reckless driving.' "

"Hard-ass Trooper Jay Randal."

"He pops into view when he needs to," Jay said. "Talk to you later."

Hutsell then called his partner at Gambit's lab.

"Any new evidence from Amber's clothes?"

"Some hairs, fibers. And John, you aren't going to believe this?" Rick Hadley said. "We've got blood from the knee of her jeans that's not hers."

"Well, Rick, there's a chance we may soon have an identity to go with that blood."

"'Splain," said Rick, using a *I Love Lucy* line, Hutsell and his former partner, St. Louis Detective Trish Rankin, often quoted.

"Elle pulled into a gas station on North Glenstone where Amber identified two other customers as her captors from Friday night," Hutsell said. "We've got descriptions—car and individual––as well as the tag number. Jay's on I-44 East and will hopefully have them under surveillance before too long."

"Where are the girls?"

"On I-44 West, on their way back to Clever."

"Good," said a relieved Hadley. "I'll finish up here and head that way. What about you? Any change in plans with this new development?"

"No, the sooner I get to Oregon, the sooner I can confront Zimbeck. I know it's a long shot, but I want to find a sex-trafficking link between here and there. Not much we can do in Oregon, but if we get the right information, with our connections in Missouri, we just might make a dent."

"May be on the verge with this new info," Hadley said. "When do you plan to arrive in Clever?"

"I've rented the SUV and picked up what I need from home for the trip, so just as soon as I close things down here, I'll be on my way."

"Dinner?"

"Oh, hell," John said, "what haven't we had?"

"Why don't I get Qdoba on the way out of town?"

"Good idea," said John. "See you at the safe house."

Rick pulled up Elle's cell number and tapped the dial icon.

"How's it going Buttercup?" he said.

"You're on speaker Hadley," Elle said, her tone flat.

"Buttercup?" questioned Erin in a soft voice.

Hadley heard Laveau and said, "Yeah, I can usually get by with using it once a month before she lowers the boom . . . if the eye roll just wasn't so darn cute . . .."

"Yeah, yeah, yeah . . . so what you want Hadley?" said Elle.

"I'm picking up Qdoba for tonight. I know what you want but is there anything special Erin and Amber would like?"

"It's all good," said Erin.

"What's Qdoba?" Amber said.

"Mexican," Erin said.

"Tacos," Amber said.

"Got it," Rick said. "See you ladies soon."

After dinner, Elle announced she was going to her place to wash and dry Amber's new clothes, so they'd be fresh for the trip. Rick Hadley accompanied her to the Wyatt Estate. He carried the loaded suitcase inside to the small laundry room. As Elle cut off tags and sorted the clothes, Rick made his way to the living area and her media player. Elle was loading the washer when she heard his music selection. She paused and smiled just before Rick peeked around the corner and did a Groucho Marx bit with his eyebrows. She lowered the washer's lid.

"It's true you know," he said. She gently bit her lip to keep from laughing. "You turn me on, I'm a radio," Rick said, repeating the title of the Joni Mitchell song Gail Davies was singing.

Elle shook her head. "To quote the 'one in the turban,' 'You're incorrigible.' "

"Incorrigible; hopeless, incurable. When it comes to you Ms. Wyatt—heavy on the Ms.—you bet I am. Now hush and pretend it's Sunday afternoon and raining." He nodded in the direction of the bedroom.

"Thank God, your mother raised you right," she said of his knowledge of movies and songs. 'If she hadn't, I wouldn't have given you a second look."

"Na na na na na na na," he sang. "Now, I believe I said 'Hush.' "

"Yes sir, Mr. Royal."

Elle was folding Amber's clothes in the utility room when she heard Rick's phone ring. He soon appeared in the entry.

"John wants to know when we'll be back. He says we've had enough time for 'whatever,' and it would be nice if Erin could spend the night at home with Jay."

"Just need to put these in the suitcase, and I'm ready."

Rick put his phone to his ear and said, "We're on our way."

Erin saw the lights of Rick's Silverado as he pulled into the driveway of the Clever house. She passed Rick and Elle on her way out, saying, "See you in the morning."

Rick stopped at the refrigerator and grabbed a bottle of water. He held it up. "Elle?" She shook her head and said, "Juice, please." He tossed her a small bottle of cran-apple juice and sat down across the table from John.

"How's Amber?" he asked.

"Okay, I think. She was pretty anxious for a while. Then Jay called saying her captors had crossed the state line into Illinois. After that, she relaxed somewhat. She's watching DVDs now."

"What's the full report?"

"Jay pulled onto I-44 from the Northview ramp and followed the Elantra from a safe distance. He feels that the driver was aware of him soon after, as he dropped his speed and stayed with the speed limit. The driver did great until Conway, where he swerved into the passing lane and quickly back again. Jay pulled him over."

"The driver is forty-two-year-old Trey Burleson. He has an Illinois CDL. Said he and his friend—the one with the earrings— had been in Tulsa last week. A cousin had driven them to Springfield, where they stayed with relatives until today. They rented the car Saturday morning so they would not be dependent on family and could come and go as they pleased. They started for Jacksonville, Illinois, this afternoon."

"And the friend?" asked Rick.

"Jay didn't have a reason to check his ID, so nothing on him. He did run a check on Burleson. He has a 2009 conviction for domestic abuse in East St. Louis. I showed his mugshot to Amber. She said he looked like one of the guys, but he seemed too young. Makes sense, the picture was ten years old."

"Anything else?"

"The Patrol kept track of them all the way to St. Louis till they crossed into Illinois. As a professional courtesy, Illinois State Troopers took over and reported the two stopped in Jacksonville for the night."

"Any plans to check on them tonight and in the morning?"

"Illinois troopers were willing to do periodic drive-bys, but no surveillance, so I called Trish. She got in touch with Joe Kleeman––you remember him?"

"One of the detectives from your former St. Louis squad," Rick said.

"Yep, two years ago, Kleeman worked a kidnapping case; a thirteen-year-old girl was being groomed online. Her mother had tried desperately to stop the correspondence, but the guy found ways through her friends to continue contact. She agreed to a meeting where she was abducted. She had been his sex slave for two weeks when Kleeman caught up with her captor. Knowing he was caught; the guy stabbed her multiple times before killing himself. She died in Kleeman's arms. Her last words were, "Tell my mom I'm sorry." Kleeman's got the next few days off. He's on his way to Jacksonville now to do surveillance."

Elle stood. "Gentlemen, I'm going to take Amber's suitcase to the bedroom. I guess you need me to sleep in there tonight, since Erin's in Springfield?"

"Yeah, thanks Elle," John said. "Rick, you can go on to bed. I'm going to be on the computer for a while."

"Night," Rick said.

John Hutsell typed, "Homes for sale, Phelps Grove Division, Springfield, MO" in the search bar and hit enter. A few homes caught his eye. The realtor listed for the second property was Carine Velardi. He clicked on the contact button and composed a message, "Ms. Velardi, I plan to be out of town for a few weeks. I am interested in purchasing a home in the Phelps Grove area and will contact you concerning available properties upon my return. On another note, my partner Rick Hadley will drop the key to the Clever house at your office tomorrow. Again, thank you for your assistance. John Hutsell."

·20·

Wednesday morning found Elle in the kitchen while Rick and John started packing up supplies. She had just placed bacon in a skillet when her cousin entered with the folded double air mattress from the spare room.

"John, would it be okay if I took Amber to my stylist this morning?"

"Have you talked with Amber about this?"

"No. Thought I'd get your okay first. It won't take more than a half hour. Just a trim and maybe some layering."

"Can you get her in early? We need to get on the road. I'd really like to make it to Aurora, Colorado, tonight."

"You'll pick up an hour due to a change in time zones. Let me call my stylist and see if she will come in early."

"If you can get her in by eight, okay," John said. "But check with Amber first. She may not—."

"I will," Elle interrupted. "Don't let the bacon burn."

Elle stepped into the living room and placed the call.

"Heather, I promise a big tip if you can—."

"Come in early. What's the urgency?"

"A young woman. From the conversations you and I have had, I know you'll peg the situation once you begin working with her. She's got long dark hair. Needs a trim, maybe some layering."

"You wouldn't ask if it wasn't important. Okay. I'll meet you at the shop at 7:45."

"Thanks. I'll call if there's a change in plans—but you'll still get paid."

"You're a hot mess Elle Wyatt."

Elle walked into the bedroom as Amber emerged from the bathroom after a shower.

"Amber, I've got an appointment to have my hair trimmed this morning. Would you like to have it instead?"

"Can she make mine look like yours?"

"Yeah, she can add some soft layers if you want."

"Okay.

"You finish packing while I get breakfast on the table. We need to be out of here in twenty minutes."

Elle returned to the kitchen and found John whipping eggs.

"We're a go," she said. "Scoot over, I need to get the biscuits out of the oven."

Rick Hadley entered and said, "Jay and Erin just pulled in the driveway. Looks like everything is on schedule."

"Hardly," said John. "Elle's taking Amber to get her hair styled."

Rick looked at Elle.

"We'll be done by 8:15," she said, "so do your part, Hadley, and get the butter and jelly out of the fridge."

"You going to come back and help me put this place back the way we found it?" Rick asked with a smile.

Elle leaned in and whispered in his ear, "Leave one of the mattresses aired up and you've got a deal."

John overheard. "Oh brother."

Erin accompanied Elle and Amber on the drive to Mojo Pie Salon in Springfield. Elle pulled into Starbucks on the way and ordered an iced Venti blonde roast Americano, with extra cream and three Splenda, for Heather.

"Miss Wyatt, can't you go to Oregon with us?" Amber asked as they waited in the drive-thru. "You said you don't work, why can't you go?"

"It's Elle, and I do have some obligations."

"You don't want to be away from him, do you?"

"The truth, Amber?" She paused. "Hell, I don't know what I want."

"I don't either."

"What about you Erin?" asked Elle. "Do you know what you want?"

"Right now," Erin said, "I'm doing what I want. I live with the man I love and I'm doing the job I trained for."

"Right now?"

"Life throws curves," Erin said. "Who knows about tomorrow? None of us even knew each other until a few days ago."

The conversation ended as Elle eased up to the window and exchanged cash for her order. All three women remained silent on the five-minute drive to the salon.

Elle watched Heather layer Amber's hair, as Erin paged through a magazine.

"What do you think, Erin?" Elle said. "Has she got a chance?"

"Where were you this time last year?"

"Missing in action."

"Well, you aren't anymore. Yeah, she's got a chance."

Heather finished and walked Amber to the waiting area.

Elle looked at the young woman and, for the first time, didn't see a waif.

Yeah, she's got a chance.

"I'm going to schedule an appointment," Elle said to Erin and Amber. "I'll meet you two outside in a few minutes."

The outside door closed. "I saw it," Heather said of Amber's tattoo. "Any chance of getting those responsible?"

"John's working on it."

"Hope they end up on the bad side of a real-life Quentin Tarantino movie."

Elle handed her stylist several bills.

"Way too much," said Heather.

"Worth every penny."

John Hutsell was standing by a Nissan Rogue when Elle walked into the parking lot. Amber and Erin were already seated inside the vehicle.

"Rick's almost got things packed at the house. He said you don't need to go back—that he'll serve you leftovers for lunch at his place."

"See you in a few weeks," Elle said.

Elle waved at Erin and Amber as John got into the vehicle. She watched as they pulled out onto the main road, then got in her Caddy and drove to Gambit Investigations. She parked in the back of the building, ascended the outside stairs to the second floor, and used her key to enter Rick's loft. After showering, Elle wrapped herself in a towel and made her way to the wardrobe in his bedroom. She looked inside and smiled at the starched and pressed shirts that came in only two colors. White or blue. He never wore anything else. She pulled a white one off its hanger. Elle removed the towel and slipped into his shirt. On her way to the bed, she caught a glimpse of herself in the dresser mirror.

I don't need you or your damn shirt.

That's what she'd said in Tennessee after she'd ripped off his shirt and thrown it in his face—the shirt he'd helped her into because hers had been taken into evidence.

Elle turned away, walked to Rick's bed, and sat down. She composed a text.

"I'm in your bed. Come home."

"On my way."

Rick carried perishables from the Clever house into his loft and stored them in the refrigerator. He made his way to his bedroom and found Elle sleeping. He disrobed and slid in next to her. She stirred.

"Go back to sleep," he whispered.

Rick had just dozed off when his cell sounded. He quickly grabbed his phone to silence the call and saw that it was John on the other end. He answered and said, "Just a minute." He slid out of bed and walked into the living room. "What's going on?"

"Burleson and his friend are in East St. Louis, Illinois. They've just returned the rental. Joe got the license number of the car that picked them up. There's no way to get an Illinois warrant for the rental, but with the promise of double their daily rate, he convinced the rental agency not to clean the car until after we got a look. Get your butt on the road, Rick."

"Address?"

"Texting it with Kleeman's number."

"Will be in touch."

Rick Hadley got dressed, made his way to the far side of his bed and kneeled down.

"Elle?"

She opened her eyes. "It was John, wasn't it?"

"Yes. I've got to go to St. Louis. I don't know how long I'll be gone. There's food in the fridge when you wake up."

Elle looked into his blue eyes. There was a part of her that wanted to say, "Hurry back" but those words showed a commitment she wasn't willing to admit to.

"Okay," she said.

He leaned in and lightly kissed her forehead. Her hand reached for his arm, but stopped midway. Rick noticed the cancelled gesture.

"Scoot over," he said.

"Don't you have to go?"

He smiled. "Just do it, Wyatt."

He crawled in next to her and put his arms around her.

"Eggplant parmigiana tonight?" he asked.

"You think you'll be back before Piccolo's closes?"

"Who said anything about Piccolo's? Mom gave you a recipe, right?"

Elle smiled. Classic Hadley. Thank God he didn't expect any more than what she could give.

"Grandma Reale's from the old country?"

"That's the one."

"Here or my place?" she asked.

"Here."

"Text when you're on your way back to Springfield."

"Yes, ma'am." He got out of bed and placed the safe house key on the night stand. "Will you return this to Ms. Velardi?"

"Yes."

Out on Boonville, he thought back on Elle's attempt to reach out and touch him. He wondered if she realized how far she'd come in five months. Only lately, had she become comfortable with his loving touch. Maybe one day, she'd be able to touch him the same way. But if not, that was okay. Some people didn't understand why he wanted to be with her. They'd warned him early on that she was emotionally unavailable. The truth was, he knew her in ways they didn't. And what if they were right? It didn't matter. He knew he'd love her for as long as she'd let him.

·21·

Amber sat in the back seat of the Nissan and thought about John Hutsell's comment about catching bad guys.

"He's rich you know?" she said.

"Who is?"

"The man who paid for me Friday night. I was sleeping with three other girls when they pulled me out of bed. One of them said, 'She'll pass for fourteen.' "

John waited to see if Amber would continue.

"We were on our way back from the rich man's house when we crashed into the ditch."

"Does he live close to where you crashed?"

"I think so. We had to go through a gate and past some other houses to get to his."

"Can you describe his house?"

"Brick. It had three garages in the back. The guy in the mugshot you showed me took me in the back way and then downstairs to the basement. When the rich guy was done, we left."

"Amber, what do you want to happen to him?" asked John.

"I don't want anyone else to have to play a fourteen-year-old girl in that basement ever again. And right now, I don't want to talk anymore."

Rick Hadley pulled his Silverado into the parking lot of the car rental agency and found Joe Kleeman snoozing in his vehicle. He tapped the window and brought the St. Louis detective back to life. Kleeman opened the door and stepped out.

"Hello, Hadley. Long time, no see."

"Been a year."

"You ready to go inside?" Kleeman asked. Rick nodded. Kleeman placed his hand on the door handle and paused. "Crazy bastards let me put police tape around the car to 'preserve the evidence'." He laughed. "Everyone wants to be on *Criminal Minds* these days."

Rick smiled. "Whatever works."

Both men knew the evidence Rick collected would probably never end up in court, as the chain of evidence would be suspect. But, from the standpoint of Gambit Investigations, what they found could point them to further leads and identifications. From there, law enforcement might be able to obtain warrants to gain evidence that would be admissible.

When done, the two men gathered outside near Rick's truck.

"My partner's working on the car that picked up Burleson and his friend," Kleeman said. "Will pass on what he finds. By the way, I did get a few shots of the two guys on my phone. I'll send them to you before I start home. Are you heading up the investigation in Springfield since John's on his way to Oregon?"

"Yes. But I'll have help. John's friend, Greg Baptiste will be assisting."

"Former secret service guy from *Murder in the Fifty* segment?"

"Yeah." Hadley smiled.

"Well, tell Hut-one, Hut-two Hutsell hello when you see him," Kleeman said, using John Hutsell's high school name that had been divulged in the program.

"I'll use your exact words." Rick got in his truck. "Thanks, Joe."

"Just get the bastards."

·22·

Rick stopped for lunch in St. Clair, Missouri. He was about to call Elle to say he was on his way home, but decided on another call first. His friend picked up on the third ring.

"Well, if it isn't everyone's favorite gumshoe," Lieutenant Colonel Todd Jayson said.

"Nah, I believe that moniker belongs to my partner," Rick said.

"Don't be modest Rick," Jayson joked, "you're the one oozing with personality. Who handles all Gambit's PR?"

"Well, John hates the limelight. Besides every time he's in the media, people are drawing lines to his mother. I don't much care for it myself, but you know the saying."

"Yeah, it's a lousy job, but someone's got to do it," Jayson said with a laugh. "Besides, your pretty face looks good on camera."

"Yeah . . . well . . . moving right along. I'm in St. Clair, and thought I'd stop by Fort Wood on my way back to Springfield, if you and Natalie don't have any plans."

"You won't even have to come on base. Cooper's got a basketball game at the high school in Waynesville."

"I didn't think he was in high school yet."

"He's not. He plays with the Armed Services YMCA Youth Basketball League. His game starts at six. You can make it in plenty of time. Coop and Caroline would love to see their 'Uncle Rick'."

"I'll text when I hit the parking lot."

"How long can you stay?"

"I'll stay for the game, then I've got to head to Springfield," Rick said. "I kind of made a big deal about dinner tonight, and I don't want to disappoint."

"She got you on a short leash?"

"She's got me right where I want to be."

Jayson laughed again. "See you in Waynesville."

Rick disconnected and brought up Elle's number. After five rings, it went to voice mail.

"I'm going to a basketball game in Waynesville. Todd Jayson's son is playing. I should be in Springfield about 8:30. I could go by Garbo's and get the house salad if you'd like. Let me know."

Elle replied with a text forty-five minutes later. "I'm at the grocery store. I'll stop by Garbo's while I'm out. Beer or wine?"

Rick pulled off on the next exit ramp to text back. "Grandma Reale would say wine, but I prefer a cold beer."

"Got it."

"See you soon."

She sent a thumbs up emoji.

Rick called John to give him an update.

John picked up and said, "You're on speaker."

"A car showed up at the rental agency and picked up our suspects. Luis Mendoza will be checking out the car sometime today. Evidently our guys felt they were no longer being followed as they made no attempt to wipe the rental clean. Got several good prints and hairs—they even left their McDonald's cups. John, these guys are low totem. They're making stupid mistakes."

"Yeah, I know. If they hadn't taken a chance on icy roads, they wouldn't have ended up in a ditch. Not only did they lose Amber, but it put them in need of another vehicle, which has now left not only a paper trail, but an evidentiary one, too."

"Think they were free-lancing?"

"I've considered it. I'll call you once we get settled tonight. It will be late."

"Talk to you then."

Rick Hadley texted his friend when he arrived at Waynesville High School. A few minutes later Jayson met him at the entrance to the gymnasium. Their move to shake hands quickly turned into a Man Hug. Caroline Jayson saw Rick walking with her father and jumped down from the bleachers. She ran into her 'Uncle' Rick's arms. He carried her to where her mother was sitting.

"Hi, Natalie," said Rick.

"You made it just in time," she said. "As soon as they sweep the floor, Cooper's team will begin warming up.

"Mommy, can I have some popcorn?" asked Caroline.

"Sure." Natalie got up to go to the concession stand but Rick beat her to her feet.

"My treat," he said, and took Caroline's hand.

The teams were well matched, with Cooper's team taking the honors. Both teams had left the floor when Rick asked Jayson," You got a few minutes?"

"Yep." Jayson leaned over and told his wife he'd meet her and the kids outside.

"What's going on?" he asked as they stood beside the family's SUV.

"You're eligible for retirement this year, right?" Rick said.

"Yeah, twenty years, come June."

"Have you decided if you're going to take it, or are you going to stay in a while longer?"

"Already completed the paper work. We were due for another transfer. Natalie and I talked about it. You know what life is like as a military brat, Rick. We got to experience life in many places most kids never even get to visit. But Cooper's entering high school next year, and it would be nice if we didn't have to uproot him during those four years."

"Yeah, that's what my folks did. It was nice to finish high school in the same school I started," Rick said. "You going to head to Texas where your parents live?"

"No. We're thinking of staying around here. Waynesville's got a large veteran community and the Commissary and Exchange are close by." He nudged Rick. "You like Missouri, right? Or are you just hanging around because of a certain woman?"

"Elle's a big reason I'm in Springfield, but I do like my job and working with John."

"Well if headlines are any indication, Gambit Investigations is a highly successful agency," Jayson said. He paused before continuing. "How's she doing Rick? What's it been, five months now?"

"Yep. There are times when she retreats and the best thing to do is let her have time to herself. But for the most part, she is doing well. Gambit's working on a sex-trafficking case, and she was instrumental in identifying the part of the country where the victim's from. Once we had the place, it was easy to find the victim's identity."

"You two thinking of tying the knot?"

"No. That's a subject that doesn't enter the equation. There's no way Elle would even consider it right now—if ever."

"So where does that put you?"

"Like I told you earlier; right where I want to be. I've never known anyone like her. I'm happy. Life is good."

"And thoughts of a family?"

"No thoughts, Todd. I accept it as a part of being with her," Rick said. "Besides I've got Coop and Caroline, what more do I need?"

Natalie walked up with two kids in tow. "Well, they love you," she said.

"You looked good out there, Coop," said Rick. "You're a team player for sure. Your coach has got to love that."

"Yeah, a few of the other guys have some height on me, so I concentrate on getting the ball to them when they're open. But I am working on those three-pointers."

"Wish I had more time to spend with you guys, but I've got to get on the road," Rick said. "I've got home-cooked eggplant parmigiana waiting on me."

"Someone sure thinks a lot of you," Natalie said.

"And I want to keep it that way."

"When do we get to meet her, Rick?"

"Maybe when my partner gets back from Oregon. We'll see."

"Uncle Rick, do you have a girlfriend?" Caroline asked.

Rick kneeled down and said, "Yep, and she's smart and almost as pretty as you."

"You got a picture?"

"Sure do." Rick brought out his phone and tapped the gallery icon. He scrolled down till he found the one he was looking for. "This is us at a party last year. She made the dress she has on."

"She has blond hair just like me," Caroline said. "She can stay in my room if you guys want to spend the night."

"I'll tell her about your invitation. Now give me a big hug."

Caroline hugged Rick and told him bye.

"Okay kids, climb aboard," Todd said. "After all, it is a school night."

Rick Hadley laughed.

"What's so funny?" Jayson asked.

"'It's a school night,'" Hadley said, "straight out of Parenting 101."

Jayson smiled back. "Well, *it* is."

Rick parked beside Elle's Cadillac and climbed the stairs to his loft. He walked inside and found Elle with her hair up and oven mitts on both hands.

"It's about time," she said without looking up.

Rick deposited his keys in the catch-all by the door. He turned away, took his cell from his pocket and tapped the camera icon. He waited till she was pulling a tray of toasted garlic bread out of the oven before he took the picture.

"You are so much dead meat, Hadley."

"Well *you* are the picture of domestic bliss—and I do mean picture."

"That was an improvident move, buddy."

"Oh yeah, pull out the big words."

"I can give you a few four-letter ones to go along with it."

"Like 'Help! I need somebody. Help! Not just anybody. Help! You know I need someone.' "

She turned around so he wouldn't see her laughing, but her body heaved up and down, giving her away. Still smiling, Elle faced him, pulled off the mitts and threw them at him.

"Dinner is served," she said.

With left-overs stored in the fridge, and the dishwasher going, Rick and Elle walked to his sofa.

Rick was about to put his feet on the coffee table when he noticed three DVD movies spread out in front of him. Emotionally unavailable Elle Wyatt. Not true. The proof was right in front of him. Robert Mitchum—*Out of the Past, Angel Face,* and *Macao*.

"I've got a couple of four-letter words for you," he said. "Come. Here." He put his hands on her waist, lay down and pulled her on top of him. "Mitchum can wait."

John Hutsell had made reservations at a hotel off I-70 in Aurora, Colorado. He had kept an eye on the weather and listened to road-condition reports throughout the trip. On the way, they had encountered wet conditions of the melting snow variety. It would have been nice, if they could have flown to Oregon, but Amber didn't have an ID. Something they would look into once they arrived.

Hutsell pulled the Nissan into the hotel's circle drive, went in, and returned with card keys to two side-by-side rooms. He motioned for Erin to roll down her window.

"The restaurant closes in about twenty minutes, so let's go eat, and unload the suitcases after."

"Okay," said Erin.

After dinner, they carried their luggage upstairs. Hutsell saw the women safely inside their room before going into his own. He deposited his suitcase on a stand, sat down on the bed, and called Rick Hadley.

"Let it go," Elle whispered.

"It's John, I can't." Rick slipped out from under her, sat up and answered the call.

Elle lay on the sofa a few minutes. The call might take some time, so she stood and picked up the last DVD on the coffee table.

"Mitchum and I are going to the bedroom," she said. "Join us when you can."

Rick nodded and returned to his phone call. "Sounds like Amber is willing to provide information a little at a time."

"Yes," John said. "I'm trying to rack my brain in terms of who this 'rich guy' is. I talked to Mom earlier, and she's putting thought into identifying him, too. Have you heard anything more from Kleeman?"

"We have a name for the second guy," Rick said. "Twenty-four-year-old Layne Kastner. No criminal record. Burleson and Kastner used a ride-service app to get from the car rental agency to Kastner's apartment in Kirkwood."

"Kirkwood's a good location. Easy access to I-270—which connects to other freeway systems including I-44."

"Kleeman will continue to work from his end in his spare time. I'll hit the lab tomorrow, and maybe Amber will be even more forth-coming. Things are starting to come together, John."

"Still early. But you could be right. We are working on three fronts now. Talk to you tomorrow."

Rick walked into the bedroom. "How's Bob treating you?"

"Bob can do no wrong, but Brad Dexter just hit my Drop-Dead List. He told Gloria Grahame diamonds cheapen a woman."

"You want a diamond, Elle? All you gotta do is ask," he said with a smile.

She reached to the floor, picked up her shoe, pulled a Jane Russell and threw it at him. He ducked and laughed.

"Shut up, Hadley," she said.

Amber got up at 2:30 A.M. to go to the restroom. She bumped into Erin Laveau's bed on her way back to her own.

"Everything all right?" Laveau asked.

"Yes."

Amber got back into bed. A few minutes later, she spoke out in the dark. "I know one thing I want," she said, referring to the conversation with Elle Wyatt and Laveau that had taken place in Starbuck's drive-thru.

"What's that?"

"I want to get a real education, but not in a school. I have nothing in common with those people."

"Have you had any schooling?" Laveau asked.

"About three years, but not like in a classroom or anything like that. But it all ended four years ago."

"What happened?"

"I think I was ten years old when a man bought me in the town with the big arch." Amber said.

"St. Louis?"

"Yeah. He took me to a farm house a long way away. The day after we got there, a woman came to see me. She reminded me of the guy from Sunday. You know, John's friend."

"Greg Baptiste?"

"Yeah."

"In what way did she remind you of Greg?"

"The color of his skin."

"You mean brown?"

"Yeah."

"Greg's bi-racial. His mom was black, and his dad, Hispanic."

"What's Hispanic?"

"Hispanic refers to someone from a Spanish-speaking country, usually from South America. A Hispanic person isn't always from another country, but their ancestors at least were."

"I know where South America is," Amber said. "The woman was my teacher."

"Do you remember her name?"

"Miss Evonne. She had a daughter who was my friend. Miss Evonne taught us a lot. We even got to use computers. Miss Evonne was in a wheelchair a lot of the time. There was a lady who took care of Miss Evonne and her daughter. The lady's name was Teena. She was black and really nice to me. Miss Evonne was married to the man who bought me."

"What was his name?"

"Tate," said Amber.

"Was that his first name or last name?"

"First. I think. I lived in a different house with another man. He called him Tate, too."

"Were you safe while you lived there?"

"Do you mean, was I raped when I was there?"

"Yes, but also safe in other ways."

"It was better than any other place I'd been. I wasn't being moved around all the time, and I didn't get beat up a lot, but yeah, Tate and his friend made me have sex with them, while I lived there."

"Amber—."

"Look, Miss Laveau, I know you're going to tell all this to John, and that's all right, but I'm done for the night, okay?"

"Sure," Laveau said and waited a few moments before continuing. "Concerning your desire to get an education, most communities have literacy classes where adults learn to read and write well enough so they can go on to take what are known as GED classes. From there, many choose to go to college."

"GED?"

"Depending on where you are and what you want to accomplish, it stands for General Educational Development or General Equivalency Degree. What it means is that you can take classes and pass tests to get what amounts to a high school diploma."

"Does it cost a lot?"

"Some communities offer free courses and you can also take them online. Financial aid is often available. I went that route myself."

"You didn't go to high school?"

"I did till I was sixteen, when I started to get in trouble."

"Did they kick you out?"

"A couple of times for fighting. My best friend had grown up as a girl, but never felt like one. When she was fifteen, she decided to start gender transitioning, which means she began to look and dress as a boy. She changed her name from Maura to Sawyer. Sawyer got bullied a lot. The school did very little to stop it, so when kids started beating up on him, I started beating up on them."

"John told Elle you were good at that kind of stuff."

Erin laughed. "Elle is, too."

"Yeah, that's what he said. Would you teach me how to be like that?"

"I'll show you one move in the morning, and more once we get to Oregon. Now, what do you say we get some sleep. John will be knocking on the door at the crack of dawn."

·24·

Rick Hadley heard his phone ring as he stepped out of the shower.

"Elle, will you get that? It could be important."

"Okay." Elle reached over to the shelf on his headboard and picked up his phone. "Elle Wyatt for Rick Hadley. How may I help you?"

"This is Detective Joe Kleeman in St. Louis, and it's urgent that I speak with Rick Hadley."

"Just a moment Detective Kleeman." Elle hit the mute button and walked to the bathroom door. "It's Detective Kleeman from St. Louis. He says it's urgent."

Rick wrapped himself in a towel. He took his phone and headed toward the desk in his bedroom.

"What's going on Joe?"

"Trey Burleson is dead. His body was found this morning by a homeless man behind a dumpster at a truck stop in Bridgeton. Bullet to the back of the head."

"What about Kastner?"

"Bridgeton Police are holding him for questioning. I'm on my way there now."

"Any news reports yet?"

"Just a mention of a found body," said Kleeman. "I'll keep you informed."

"Thanks, Joe."

Elle started to ask about the call, but Rick held up his index finger and immediately dialed his partner. John Hutsell picked up on the first ring.

"Just getting ready to call you. We've had breakfast, and will be loading the SUV soon."

Rick relayed the new developments from St. Louis.

"The guy made one too many mistakes, Rick."

"Yeah. Wonder what Kastner's role is in all this."

"Hopefully Kleeman will find out soon," John said. "On another front, Amber's continuing to provide more information. In addition to the 'rich guy' she told us about yesterday, she had a discussion with Erin in the middle of the night. There was a three-year span when Amber wasn't passed from place to place—where she had a friend, and even got a bit of schooling. She said she lived in a farm house. Don't know where, or why she even thought it was a farm house. Maybe she can shed some light on the Burleson/Kastner situation. Just need to proceed with caution."

"Hope so. I'm about to head to the lab. Should have something to report later today."

"We'll be staying in West Wendover, Nevada, tonight. Be in Medford, Oregon, late tomorrow," Hutsell said. "No plans to contact Mark Baylor just yet. We need official confirmation of Amber's identity first. Good thing we've got DNA to prove Amber is Marissa Baylor, because when you think about the memories she told us . . .."

"I know. She could be an imposter." said Rick. "Though there are easier ways to be 'found' than in the greenhouse of a Missouri state senator on an icy night. I submitted her DNA to several genetic genealogy sites on Saturday. Maybe we'll get a hit soon."

"Call the Multnomah Falls Sheriff's Department. If Mark Baylor submitted his DNA to a genetic geology site, they might be able to speed up the process. Grease the wheels of the site's lab if you have to."

"Will do. I'll call when there's more to report."

Rick set his phone down and went to his wardrobe. As he dressed, he told Elle about Amber's middle-of-the-night disclosure.

"Oh damn, Rick," she said. "She told me part of that story Sunday morning just before I saw the car coming toward the house. I hurried her inside. Turned out it was Greg, but then John showed Amber the pictures, and I forgot all about it."

"What do you remember?"

"The only other thing she said, besides what she told Erin, was the name she went by then: Maddie, and there were rows of corn along the road in the summer between the farm house and her friend's house."

"I heard the conversation from the hall about the name Maddie," he said. "So, John already knows that part.

"I'm sorry, Rick."

"Don't be." Rick walked over and sat down on the bed next to Elle. "Look at it this way; the farm house was fresh news to Erin and John, which means Amber knows you didn't drop everything and run to one of us with the information. You were the first to carve out a relationship with her. Now she's beginning to open up to Erin and John. She's known from the beginning that John wants to get those responsible. Amber is helping with the investigation now, and I think it has a lot to do with that conversation."

"You know what I like about you, Rick Hadley?"

Rick stood, took Elle's hand and helped her to her feet. He pulled her close.

"I'm optimistic, cheerful, and a student of music history," he said with a smile.

"Yeah. You rock me, Amadeus," she said. "All good qualities, but the fact that you're always clean shaven really trips my trigger."

"Hold that thought until tonight," he said and lightly kissed her on the lips.

"Oh, come on Hadley. You can do better than that. Put some tongue into it."

·25·

Kyle Jeffries sat in his office at Rita's Rose and thought about the past week. If nothing else, John Hutsell had forced him to come to terms with what was missing in his relationship with Jenise Alexander. He knew she loved him, but he was *in* love with her. Funny how the addition of a little two-letter word made all the difference in the world.

He reminded himself why he'd made the decision to walk away; he could no longer act as a crutch for Jenise—or even worse—as a surrogate for John Hutsell. In the long run, he knew his resolution was best for both of them.

His thoughts were interrupted when Brett Gilson knocked on his open door.

"Hope your morning is off to a good start," she said. "Got the final two confirmations from hair stylists this morning for 'Free Stylin' Day' during Spring Break."

"March 11, right?"

"Yes," Gilson said. "Oh, last minute change: Dr. Sahota and Dr. Shulman changed shifts, so Shulman is our doctor today. See you in the vestibule for the morning prayer."

"Thanks, Brett."

Fifteen minutes later, Sister Belina led staff and volunteers in prayer in front of a painting of St. Rita of Cascia holding a crucifix with one hand and clutching red roses to her chest with the other.

Once in the examining room Dr. Shulman asked Jenise if she had any information on how the Amber Lawrence case was progressing.

"I haven't had contact with anyone from that night—and probably won't. I know I was called only because of the location where she was found. Any other place, and they would have called someone else.

"Jenise, I know Friday night was hard—."

"It was a long time ago. I'm fine."

But she wasn't. And as a result, she had an appointment with a therapist on Tuesday.

26

Elle received a message from Chelle Thomas just as she turned on her signal to pull into Karai Ramen and Handroll on West Republic Road.

"I'm here."

Elle pulled alongside Chelle's black Cadillac. The two friends fell into step and made their way to the restaurant's entrance. Elle held the door open for Chelle to enter first.

"New fragrance, Elle?" Chelle said.

"Well, that's a disapproving look. You don't like it?"

"A little masculine for my tastes."

Elle laughed. "It's Rick's body wash, if that makes you feel any better."

"I thought he made sure you had your own. You know, the forest-rain thing."

"That bottle was empty."

"How is—what was it Cal called him—tall and whatever?"

"Well, with Rick's eye and hair color, dark didn't fit," Elle said. "Anyway, he described himself as optimistic and cheerful this morning, so I guess he's doing fine."

Chelle smiled. "How many nights have you two spent together this past week? Why don't you just go ahead and move in together?"

"You know I like my space, Chelle," Elle said at her friend's teasing. "Things are fine just the way they are; thank you very much."

The two women placed their orders.

"How're wedding plans coming?" Elle asked.

"Got the permit for the wedding parade Tuesday. Waiting on confirmation from the band."

"Do you know how glad Rick is that you and Greg decided on a New Orleans wedding?"

"Flowered shirts notwithstanding, The Bahamas was Greg's half-sister's choice, not mine."

"Where did she and Seth get married?"

"They skipped a big wedding and eloped to Niagara Falls," Chelle said, putting on a big smile. "You know, I can see you doing the same thing."

"Funny lady today, Chelle."

"Not the Niagara Falls bit, but the eloping part," Chelle said as their orders arrived.

After paying their checks, the two walked outside to their cars. Elle had been subdued since Chelle's eloping comment. Feeling that she'd overstepped, Chelle apologized.

"I'm sorry; he loves you, Elle. I just wish—."

"Yeah, I know. Everybody just wishes . . .." Elle paused. "I know he deserves more . . .."

"He's happy and that's what matters."

"Maybe he is for now. But sooner or later . . .."

"Don't go borrowing trouble, Elle."

"Who needs to borrow?" Elle keyed open her car.

"Damn me and my big mouth," said Chelle.

"Don't worry about it. Good intentions and all that," Elle said. "Talk to you later."

Chelle watched her friend drive away. Normally it was quid pro quo when the two friends were together, but it wasn't today. Something's up, Chelle thought.

Elle drove onto the Wyatt Estate and pulled into the circle driveway in front of her home. She went inside, packed a bag with enough clothes for several days, and returned to her car.

From his kitchen window, Pat Wyatt watched his adopted daughter load her Cadillac. The last time she'd done this was five months ago. She'd ended up in Tennessee where she'd cheated death a second time. As she drove to the gate, he bowed his head and whispered the Irish blessing for travelers, "May the road rise up to meet you . . .."

Around Rock Springs, Wyoming, Amber asked John Hutsell what was going to happen once they got to Oregon.

"Several things," said Hutsell. "Before we even think about contacting your grandfather, we need to 'officially' confirm your identity."

"Why?"

"Remember when you asked me how law enforcement would know we were telling the truth about your identity?" Amber nodded. "You were right in your thinking. If we just show up without any corroborating evidence, who's to say we would be believed? Imagine a person looking for a free ride. She comes across your grandfather's Facebook page. From there, she reads articles about your abduction and watches all the videos she can find, until she feels comfortable enough to impersonate you as an eighteen-year-old woman. Mark Baylor will welcome her into his home and people all over the country will send money to help 'Marissa Baylor' get off to a new beginning."

"I never thought of it like that."

"How about this for a start," Hutsell said. "When we get to Medford, we tour the area—visit the places you remember. Seeing them might help you decide what *you* want to happen next."

Laveau said, "You know Amber, we could also go online and look for nearby places of interest."

"Could we at least drive by my grandfather's house?"

"Sure," said John.

"What do you know about him?" asked Amber.

"Not much other than he's an electrician," said John. "He doesn't work for a specific company, but contracts out to businesses and individuals. His wife, your grandmother, passed away when you were two. He never remarried. His niece, who helped set up the Facebook page you saw, is fourteen years older than you. She is your first cousin, once removed."

"Like you and Miss Wyatt?"

"Elle and I are first cousins. Her mom and my mom were sisters. If Elle had any children, they would be my first cousins, once removed."

"Does that mean my mother had a sister?"

"No, your mom was Mark Baylor's only child. The woman who has helped him look for you all these years is your grandmother's brother's daughter. She was first cousin to your mother."

"That's a lot to keep straight."

"Yeah, it is," said John. He leaned forward in the seat and slowly tilted his head left and then right. "Erin, you want to drive for a while. My shoulder's acting up."

"What's wrong with your shoulder?" asked Amber.

"Bursitis."

Laveau laughed and said. "Well, what do you know, 'old man.' You aren't the perfect male specimen after all. Wait till the women in Springfield hear this."

Hutsell knew Laveau was going for a little levity and played along.

"I don't believe press agent is one of your duties, 'Marie.' "

"Jay just forgot to put it on my business card along with my other qualifications. I can have new ones printed up if you'd like."

"Oh, brother," said Hutsell.

At 3:10 P.M., Rick messaged Elle. She had just gassed up and was opening a bottle of water when his text arrived.

"Steak okay for tonight? Say around 7:30?"

"Not tonight. I'm halfway to Memphis. Won't be back for a few days."

Rick understood. Elle was dealing with something she didn't want to share. And he knew questioning her would only make her pull away further. So instead of asking her to text when she got to Memphis safely, he typed, "Send video of BB King's Blues Club All Star Band."

"Will do."

Rick knew he'd wait for the video to arrive before going to bed. At least he'd know she was safely in Memphis before he went to sleep.

Rick Hadley was still at the lab when Detective Joe Kleeman called at 5:30.

"That Kastner is one punk son-of-a-bitch," he said right off the bat. "He's like that Sergeant Schultz on those reruns of *Hogan's Heroes*—'I see nothing. I know nothing.' "

"Did you get a crack at him?"

"No, but I apprised Bridgeton detective Jarrod Clarke of the situation from our end. Kastner said he didn't know Burleson very well. Clarke told him word was they were real tight traveling buddies. Visiting the 'in-laws and all' from Tulsa and Springfield. 'Don't know what you're talking about' he said. So, Clarke threw the pic I took of the two of them on the table. Then asked if they hadn't shared a special night in Jacksonville, Illinois, on Wednesday. That really pushed his little prick homophobe button. He jumped to his feet and shouted, 'I'm ain't no homosexual!' "

Rick heard a familiar female voice. "Is that Trish in the background?"

"Yeah. She loves giving me shit. If she wasn't hooked up with Fenske, I'd think she was gunning for me." Kleeman gave a big laugh.

"Trish Rankin and Gabe Fenske are dating?"

"Yep. Think it started soon after the Juliette Case."

Rick shook his head at the name Kleeman had given to the Anniversary Killer Case before the news media got wind of it.

"Anyway, a second Bridgeton detective jumped in and asked, 'Wasn't Burleson your sugar daddy?' to which Kastner said hell no. 'Then who pays for your apartment and car—you don't have any visible means of support.' Jerk wad said a friend gave him money. Clarke asked, 'What's *his* name.' 'It's a her,' he said. Damn Hadley, you should've seen him."

"Did they get the name of his benefactor?"

"Yeah, Brenda Sidemore. A wealthy fifty-four-year-old woman in Wildwood. According to both of them, Kastner and her son were druggies in high school. Kastner got clean four years ago and tried to help her son kick the shit. Kid died of an overdose in a crack house, and mom 'adopted' Kastner."

"Do you believe her?"

"Hell no. She's about as smooth as a two-dollar whore. And I'll bet she didn't come into money through any legal means."

"When and where was the last time Kastner saw Burleson?"

"A Kirkwood sports bar about ten last night," said Kleeman. "Not much more I can do, Rick. Everything's out of my jurisdiction. Copies of all reports are going to the state guys. Occasionally, two and two do make four, but I'm not holding my breath."

"Thanks, Joe."

"Not a problem. Later."

Before he left for the evening, Hadley sent John Hutsell an email. He attached a report of his findings from evidence collected from the rental car.

Rick closed up shop and walked to his truck. He turned on the ignition and checked the time. Elle was probably getting ready for her evening on Beale Street. The All Stars wouldn't take the stage until 8:00. Rather than spend the evening alone, he drove the few blocks to Billiards of Springfield on East St. Louis Street, and parked in the side parking lot.

"Hey Rick, long time, no see," the bartender said as Rick took a seat at the bar. "Will Elle be joining you?"

"She's out of town. How's the competition tonight?"

"Andy's here. You two are a good match."

"Yep, but first on the agenda is dinner."

"Hamburger, fries, and draft beer?"

"You got it."

Rick was in the middle of game three when John's call came. He handed his cue to his opponent's girlfriend and told her good luck. As he walked away, the girlfriend asked, "Think he and my sister would hit it off?"

"He's taken," was the reply. "Elle Wyatt."

"Really? He doesn't strike me as the 'wild girl' type."

Rick sat down in a booth between the pool hall and adjoining Blue Room Comedy Club for some privacy before answering his phone.

"What you know?" asked Hutsell.

"Quite a bit." Rick relayed his conversation with Kleeman and followed with, "I sent the lab report on the tests I ran today, so check your email. And Multnomah County says Mark Baylor and his niece, Susanne Lechay, have both submitted DNA with signed permission for its use in the search for Marissa Baylor."

"So, there's paternal and maternal DNA available."

"Yes. And they did go ahead with a request to a couple of genealogy sites for expediency in the comparison of Amber's DNA with that of Baylor and Lechay. How about on your end?"

"Amber gave us more detail on 'Mr. Rich.' We've got his physical description and more specifics about his home. It's in a gated community, and I'm thinking Carine Velardi might be able to help pinpoint the property."

"If you get a name, we can always do the 'discarded cup routine' to compare his DNA to that from Amber's rape kit. You know John, the chances are good he's got chlamydia. Problem is it's known as the 'silent disease,' because half the men that get it don't know they're infected—even a higher percentage for women."

"How long before symptoms show up?"

"Usually one to three weeks after exposure."

"Wonder if he's married?"

"Well, he's not using condoms, so he's going to pass it on to whomever."

"I'm going to check with news reports on Burleson before I go to bed. Touch base with you in the morning."

"Say John, did you know Trish and Gabe are dating?"

Hutsell laughed. "It's about time. He made no secret he was interested. Some people thought she wouldn't go out with him because he lost a leg in Afghanistan. She could have cared less. She was only hesitant because he's seven years younger."

"Nothing wrong with that."

"That's what I told her."

"One more thing. Elle said Amber told her there were corn fields between her friend's house and the farm house she stayed in."

"Anything else my cousin *forgot* to mention?"

"No. Amber told her just before she saw a car approach Sunday morning. Elle didn't know it was Greg at the time and hurried Amber inside. The next thing, Amber's looking at pictures and Facebook pages. It slipped Elle's mind."

"Damn."

"Don't John. We asked for her help in this. She's not a detective. Yet, she's the one who found the 'winter queen' tie in. She's the one who connected with Amber initially by opening up in ways even you found hard to believe."

"'Mic-drop Hadley' reels my butt in again. Damn good thing I saw your potential."

"Ain't it though," said Rick. Then on a serious note, "It cost her, John. She took off for Memphis this afternoon."

"Are you worried? Do you want to go after her?"

"No. The quickest way to get her to shut down is to invade the space she's carving out for herself."

"Elle's thirty-three, and for the first time since she was eleven-years-old, she seems happy," said John. "What am I missing, Rick?"

"'Seems happy,' John. Happy's a word she has no faith in." Rick's cell vibrated in his hand. "Gotta go. She just sent a message."

"Night."

Rick tapped the video's play button. He listened to the entire song and then typed, "Thanks." He waited a few moments in case there was a reply. None came.

Rick Hadley carried a six-pack of beer into his apartment. He took one bottle by the neck and set the rest in the refrigerator. He walked over to his computer and brought it to life. There were a lot of songs about Memphis, but he wanted the one by the man whose music Elle described as 'love with an edge.'

Rick knew Elle needed time. But it didn't keep him from wanting to go after her. So, he clicked on a song and let Buddy Miller go for him.

27

Friday morning, John Hutsell viewed news reports of Trey Burleson's murder. After breakfast, he told Amber of Burleson's death.

"He's the one who took me to the rich man's place."

"Wait a minute," said Hutsell. "Kastner didn't go with you?"

"No. He was there when the older guy chose me, but he didn't go with us."

Hutsell and Laveau looked at each other. Amber saw the exchange.

"What?" she asked.

"Not sure yet," said Hutsell. "Amber, there was blood on your clothes from that night that isn't yours. Do you know who it belongs to?"

"Burleson. From the accident."

"Why don't you two finish packing," said Hutsell. "I'll get my things and meet you back here in a little bit."

He returned to his room and dialed Joe Kleeman.

"Joe, do you know if Bridgeton PD got a warrant for Kastner's cell phone records?"

"Yeah, they did."

"Any chance you could get hold of them?"

"I'll check, but copies of everything are with the state guys. Your trooper friend, Randall, may be able to get his hands on them before I could."

"Right. Thanks."

Hutsell placed a second call and made the same request and added, "Jay, Burleson might have been acting on his own Friday night. He took a big chance getting out on the ice. I'm thinking Mr. Rich made an order, but the big guys said no go due to road conditions. Burleson may have seen it as an opportunity to get some pocket money, disregarded orders and filled the request on his own."

"Which resulted in the loss of a vehicle and a high-dollar commodity."

"Yep. And if so, Kastner might not have wanted to be on the short end, so he informed on Burleson. Those in charge, not knowing where Amber was, didn't want to set off any alarms in southwest Missouri, so they decided to wait and take care of him in St. Louis."

"If Kastner was informing on Burleson, then they know about the stop in Conway and the 'escort' we gave them."

"Exactly. How did he communicate with them? I'm willing to bet his contact is Brenda Sidemore in Wildwood. We'll need her phone records, too."

"Thanks for the 'anonymous' tip. I'll be in touch," said Randall. "By the way, how's Marie?"

"Good. She's teaching Amber some self-defense moves."

"You know when she was a sophomore, she used Title IX to make her high school allow a girl's wrestling team?"

Hutsell laughed. "Didn't see that coming, did they? Bet she could've taken half the boys team."

"Ask her about her wrestling 'uniform.' "

"You didn't?"

"Yeah, I did," said Randall. "Talk to you soon."

Before her relationship with Rick Hadley had picked up steam, Elle Wyatt's go-to person had been Cal Davies. She'd met Cal in a therapy group for sexual abuse victims eight years ago. It was in this very hotel last September that Cal had tried to convince her that Rick Hadley was the real deal. She'd ignored Cal and, instead of going to New Orleans as planned, changed her mind and headed farther into Tennessee.

Right now, she didn't want to talk to Cal . . . or to Chelle. The only thing she knew for certain was that she didn't want to put any more distance between her and Springfield, Missouri.

Elle looked at herself in the mirror.

"He loves you, Elle."

She turned away from her image, closed her eyes, and lowered her head.

Best friend. Lover. Both labels she was willing to acknowledge about the man from Tennessee. But in love—no. So, Elle Wyatt lied to herself, said she missed her best friend, and headed back to Springfield.

Elle drove straight to Gambit Investigations and went up the stairs to her best friend/lover's loft. She climbed into Rick's bed and sent the same text she always did when he wasn't home.

"I'm in your bed. Come home."

Rick was processing a crime scene for Carver D'Orsey when her text arrived. He read it and wondered why she'd changed her mind and come home early. Either something was very right or something was very wrong.

"I'm in Bolivar. I'll be there as soon as I can."

Elle rolled over to Rick's side of the king-sized bed, placed her head on his pillow, took a deep breath, and fell asleep.

It was late afternoon when Rick Hadley passed the Springfield city limit sign. He drove straight to the lab and stored the evidence he'd gathered in a locker. He got back in his truck and traveled five blocks north, pulled to the rear of the Gambit Investigations building and parked next to Elle's Cadillac. He took the stairs two at a time. Rick made his way to the bedroom and found Elle right where she said she'd be. She was lying on her side, face toward the door. She appeared to be resting comfortably. He crouched down by the bed and watched the rise and fall of her body as she breathed. He gently touched her hand. She stirred.

"Not only are you in my bed, but you've taken up residence on my side."

"Rick . . .."

"Yes."

Rick moved his hand from hers. Elle's eyes opened and quickly closed. Her arms came up, her hands close to her face. In shaky, nervous motions, her fingers closed into lose fists, then opened again. Her hands finally settled. Her arms hid her face, her palms cradled her head.

"Elle, what's wrong?"

Her arms came down, then crossed tightly over her chest. Her body slowly moved back and forth.

"Elle, talk to me."

Elle raised her head and looked in Rick's direction. There was a distant look in her eyes. It was almost like she wasn't seeing him.

"The wall is falling. Poetry's not stopping it."

Rick tried to make sense of her words as her eyes changed. He felt as if they were now begging for him—pleading with him to do something—to make *it* stop. He got in bed and held her.

"I'm here Elle. I won't let go."

"Don't talk of love . . . don't disturb its slumber . . .."

Rick recognized the words and finally understood. She was loosely quoting a song. He went over the lyrics in his head, then asked, "When was the last time you cried?"

" ' . . . a rock feels no pain . . . an island never cries.' "

"Then I'll cry for you."

·28·

Elle wiped the fog away from the bathroom mirror as Rick cooked breakfast. She'd slept through most of yesterday evening and on into the night. She didn't seem anxious this morning, so Rick felt that the rest had been what she needed. His favorite upbeat playlist could be heard in the background. A sudden smile crossed his lips, causing him to sneak into his bedroom. He took a package from the top shelf of his wardrobe and, on his way back to the kitchen, saw Elle towel-drying her hair in the bathroom. He quickly unwrapped a new shirt and put it on. He walked to the media player and waited for a song to finish before clicking on, "It's Five O'Clock Somewhere."

Rick took the bacon from the skillet and laid it on paper towels. He moved to the wall outside the bathroom and waited for a certain lyric: "At a moment like this, I can't help but wonder what would Jimmy Buffett do."

Rick, now wearing a tropical shirt, leaned around the door frame and, along with Buffett, answered the question, "Funny you should ask, Alan."

Rick had expected Elle to laugh, as she always did at one of his song antics, but she didn't.

Elle turned away from him and said, "Take it off." She wrapped her arms around her waist, leaned against the vanity and slowly slid to the floor.

Rick pulled off the unbuttoned shirt and rushed into the bathroom. "Elle, I'm sorry." She couldn't hear him; she was too busy trying to get a breath.

Rick kneeled on the floor next to her. He didn't touch her. "Elle, deep, slow breaths. One . . . two . . . three . . . ." He repeated the words till her breathing slowed. "Are your meds in your purse?" Elle shook her head from side to side. "Are you still taking them?" She shook her head no. "Can I call Sarah?" Elle's head moved up and down.

Rick went to the night stand and picked up Elle's phone. He searched her contacts until he found Sarah Bennett. He dialed the number. Bennett's answering service picked up. He explained the situation and was assured Bennett would receive the message as soon as she could be reached. He gave his cell number before hanging up.

Rick grabbed the shirt off the floor and shoved it into a drawer. He hurried to the media player and exchanged one playlist for another. Back in the bathroom, he found Elle's breathing was near normal. "Elle?" She nodded. "You want to move to the bed?" She nodded again. Rick helped Elle to her feet. She was lying on the bed when she heard Shelby Lynne's voice from the living room.

"There's something to be said about Airstreams," Lynne sang.

She looked at Rick and mouthed, "Thank you." Elle shut out everything except for Lynne's voice. "I want me a big ol' Cadillac. To haul all the demons and dreams . . .."

Rick's phone rang. He picked it up and moved to the doorway. Rick listened to Bennet's instructions, then walked over to the bed and crouched down so his face was even with Elle's. He held his phone against his chest.

"Elle," he gently said. "Sarah has contacted Dr. Chandra. He says you need to go to The Fillan Center and get your meds straightened out."

Elle nodded.

Rick stood and told Bennett that Elle had agreed to be admitted to Melcher Memorial's psychiatric ward.

"Rick, think with your head and not your heart. Don't blame yourself for this," said Bennett.

He turned around and whispered, "It was a stupid move."

"No, it wasn't. It brought something to the surface, and hopefully this will be the trigger for her to deal with the underlying cause of her fear. Dr. Chandra will see her tomorrow on his morning rounds, and I will stop by Monday after my last appointment."

Rick drove Elle to The Fillan Center. He watched her disappear with the registration clerk behind the intake room door. The clerk returned fifteen minutes later and handed Rick the drawstring from Elle's coat along with other personal belongings.

"Can I see her one more time?"

"No sir. I'm sorry. Dr. Chandra has requested Ms. Wyatt be placed in Ward B. Visiting hours are from 7:00 to 8:30 P.M."

Rick returned to his truck and called Pat Wyatt.

"Jean and I will be right there."

"Pat, they won't let you see her till seven tonight."

There was a pause while Pat told his wife they couldn't visit their daughter till that evening.

Rick heard Jean Wyatt ask, "What if she won't see us?"

"If that's what she wants, we have to accept it," said Pat. "Rick will keep us informed." Then to Rick, "I knew something was up when she left Thursday afternoon. I'm thankful she was with you when it happened."

Rick Hadley remembered what had precipitated Elle's anxiety attack and recalled Sarah Bennett's last words. He hoped she was right.

John Hutsell and company had rolled into Medford, Oregon, late the previous night. Amber's interactions with Hutsell and Laveau had been subdued on the last leg of their trip. Both Hutsell and Erin Laveau had been respectful of her silence.

The three were eating breakfast in a hotel suite while they discussed plans for the day.

"Amber, where's the first place you'd like to visit?" asked Laveau.

"I want to see the ducks—but we need to bring our own water."

"Okay. Any particular kind?"

"My grandpa used to take me in a store before we went and let me pick the water I wanted. There was one kind that was different from the rest. It was a kind of a square bottle and had flowers on it."

"Fiji," said Laveau. "Shouldn't be a problem."

Hutsell's phone vibrated in his pocket, indicating a message had been received. It was from Rick Hadley. "Call me."

135

Hutsell stood, excused himself, and walked to his bedroom. He dialed Hadley.

"What's going on?"

"Elle's in the Fillan Center."

"What happened?"

"She came home yesterday afternoon," said Rick. "I was in Bolivar for Carver, so she waited for me at my place. She told me everything was crashing in on her. She calmed down and then this morning she had a panic attack. John, she hasn't been taking her meds. I called Sarah—who contacted Dr. Chandra. He wanted her where her meds could be regulated."

"Hard to believe Elle would agree to being admitted to Fillan."

"Sarah thinks it's a good sign," said Rick, "but, here's the thing; I've already lost several hours in the lab, and Carver wants results as soon as possible. I'd like to call Lieutenant Colonel Todd Jayson to come and assist. He teaches forensic science at Fort Wood, and I know he's got the day off. Okay by you?"

"Do what you have to do," said Hutsell. "Greg's got the Brentwood Insurance case, so we've got that covered. How are Pat and Jean taking all this?"

"As you might expect. Jean overthinks, Pat uses a level head."

"Okay. Keep me posted."

"Talk to you when I can."

Hutsell returned to his breakfast.

"Was that about the two guys?" asked Amber.

"No. A family matter."

"Is Miss Wyatt oaky?"

"Rick Hadley's with her—what could be wrong?" he said, side-stepping the issue. "So, what else is on your agenda today?"

"Emigrant Lake and a drive by Mark Baylor's place," said Laveau. "When do you want to head out, John?"

He smiled. "As soon as you ladies make yourselves presentable."

"Careful, Hutsell. There's two of us and only one of you."

Hutsell saw a small smile cross Amber's face and was reminded again of the asset Erin Marie Laveau was to this case.

Amber finished eating and went to take a shower. Hutsell used the time to fill Laveau in on the situation in Springfield.

"This isn't the first time Elle's been in the Fillan Center. Jean more or less forced her to go six years ago. Elle's never been one to admit she has a problem."

"She can't admit a weakness, John. If she does, that means she's vulnerable—that she can be hurt. To her, being on anti-depressants and anxiety meds means she's not in control."

"I didn't see this coming," he said. "Did you see anything?"

"A few things caught my attention. Rick Hadley's the kind of man most woman would kill for, yet Elle keeps him at bay. Then she floundered a bit when Amber asked if the reason she wasn't coming to Oregon was because she didn't want to be away from Rick. This past week she was with him almost constantly. Maybe she liked it a little too much, and that's why she went to Memphis. And another thing—her brand of humor. It's designed to mask, and her mask started slipping when she opened up to Amber. Just supposition, mind you."

"Damn, Erin. Hut-one . . . hut-two . . . Hutsell."

"Your talents lie elsewhere, John. Mr. Rich doesn't have a snowball's chance in hell. And Zimbeck . . . he thinks life is bad now; well, he has no clue it's about to get worse. He thinks he's in the clear concerning Marissa Baylor. Hell, he's evaded Multnomah County and the FBI for twelve years, why wouldn't he? When do you plan to meet with him?"

"Carver D'Orsey's setting something up with Zimbeck's lawyer. After all, is it better to talk to me or the FBI? He and I can make a 'deal'—trade my silence for information concerning the sex-trafficking network. But hey, I'm not the only one who knows the truth about Marissa Baylor's abduction, and I can't be responsible for other 'anonymous' sources who might wish to place a call."

Erin smiled and said, "Yeah, I'm familiar with the term some of you law enforcement guys use."

"Plausible deniability," said Hutsell. "Gotta love it."

Rick sat in his truck in the Fillan Center parking lot and made another call.

"Todd, I hate to ask, but Elle's in the hospital and I've got a deadline. Is there any way you can come to Springfield for the day and help run some tests?"

"Just let me clear it with Natalie."

Rick waited and wondered how he could get Elle's favorite music to her. Any personal items were discouraged—mainly because they tended to go 'missing.' Maybe Sarah could help by making music part of Elle's therapy. Why not? Therapists liked to give 'homework' all the time.

"Rick?'

"Yes."

"Natalie says okay. She's been wanting to take the kids to The Wonders of Wildlife so she's going to make a weekend of it. She's booking a hotel room now. She'll drop me at your lab before checking in and then off to the museum and aquarium."

"Thanks, Todd, I can't—."

"Don't worry," Jayson teased, "you'll get the opportunity to make good. Our anniversary is coming up, and Natalie and I want a down-home and personal celebration, so to speak. You can take Cooper and Caroline to Silver Dollar City, while we enjoy a little R&R in a cottage on Table Rock Lake."

"Just tell me when."

"You know I will," said Jayson. "I'll call you when we hit Strafford."

Rick disconnected the call and did a search on his phone for MP3 players. He then ran by a discount store and picked up a small model with a long battery life. If they wouldn't let her have one, he'd smuggle one in. To deprive Elle of music was a cruel move, and he didn't care whose toes he had to step on.

After loading Elle's favorite artists and a playlist she'd made years ago onto the MP3 player, Rick drove to the lab and started running tests on the evidence he had collected the day before.

Jayson showed up and got to work. Rick struggled at trying to explain the situation about Elle without revealing too much of her condition. Jayson interrupted with a line he'd heard Rick Hadley say many times, "If and when . . .."

After the first tests were run, Jayson continued working in the lab while Rick began compiling results in the office. Rick made a lunch run around 1:00. The two men were heading back to work when Rick's cell rang. It was the Multnomah County's Sheriff's Department.

"Mr. Hadley, this is Deputy Mitch Brenner. We have confirmation of Marissa Baylor's identity."

"You must have that special touch Deputy; her DNA was submitted only a week ago."

"Well, let's just say the company was taken with the idea of positive law enforcement comments on their web site."

"My partner, our associate, and Marissa Baylor arrived in Medford last night."

"Has she decided if she wants to meet with her grandfather yet?" said Brenner.

"No, but when they were discussing visiting the places she remembered, she asked if they could drive by his home. So she's definitely thinking about it. However, she's still adamant about not talking to law enforcement. It's a sad situation."

"Rarely do child abduction cases have a happy ending from a law enforcement point of view, but thanks to you guys, people around here are pretty happy right now."

"Will you be able to keep a lid on everything for a few days— give Mark Baylor time to prepare for the media onslaught?"

"The order's been given—nothing from the department until an official announcement. I'm heading to Talent this afternoon to meet with Mr. Baylor. He'll know his granddaughter's alive by the end of the day." Brenner paused, continued, "You know I checked you guys out."

"I'd expect nothing less," said Rick.

"Pretty impressive. You're sure you and your partner don't want some recognition on this?"

"We're sure. John likes to work behind the scene as much as possible."

"Yeah, I get it. For a private investigator, anonymity's the word. But—and this is just a hunch, mind you—I wouldn't be surprised if your partner doesn't have a few cards up his sleeve."

"He often does."

·29·

John Hutsell drove through what the locals called the Plaza on the way to Ashland's Lithia Park. He parked close to the park's entrance. He'd been cooped up in a vehicle for close to three days, and the crisp, cool air felt good. Hutsell led the way over a stone bridge. Amber walked behind him with Erin Laveau bringing up the rear. Amber stopped midway across the bridge.

"It's beautiful here, isn't it?" she said. "The trees, the rocks, the water."

"Good place to sit and reflect," said Laveau.

"Let's find the ducks," said Amber.

The trio followed a paved path till they came upon the park's playground.

"Just a minute," said Amber.

Laveau followed Amber as the young woman walked over and sat down on a wooden bench, while Hutsell remained on the path. The women watched several children at play.

"See the trees without leaves?" said Amber.

"Yes."

"Their leaves turned all different colors and were really pretty. Then they fell off. It made me sad, and Grandpa told me not to worry, they'd grow new ones." She watched for a few more minutes then stood and walked toward Hutsell.

The tour continued till Amber said, "There they are."

An older couple occupied the nearest bench, so Amber sat on a small rock wall to watch the ducks. "The pond is kind of yucky, isn't it?" she said.

She watched the ducks for a while, then turned her attention to the rest of the scenery. "There's the nasty water fountain my Grandpa wouldn't let me get a drink from."

The man heard Amber, turned, and said, "The water here has a lot of minerals, and it does smell 'nasty,' but it also contains barium, which is toxic. Your Grandpa was just looking out for you."

"He used to bring water with us, 'cos I'd get thirsty."

"Smart man."

Amber looked at the bag Laveau'd set between them. Laveau nodded and Amber pulled a bottle of water from the side pouch. She opened it, took several drinks, and said, "I'm ready to go."

On the way back to the SUV, Amber stopped at the playground a second time. There was a young couple sitting on the bench Amber and Erin had sat on earlier. The couple was arguing. Amber walked over to them.

"You should shut-up and watch your kids."

"Who the hell do you think you are telling us what to do?" the man said.

"Whoa, let's all take a breath," Laveau said as she made a move to place her body between Amber and the man. Amber side-stepped her.

"A man took me when I was six, and you ain't strong enough to handle what he and others did to me. So, shut the fuck up and watch your kids!"

"What do you say, we move on," said Hutsell.

The man opened his mouth to say something. He saw the set of John Hutsell's jaw along with the no-nonsense look in his eyes, and closed his mouth. Hutsell held out his hand to Amber as if to say, "After you." He waited behind to make sure the man didn't follow.

"What's wrong with her?" the man asked.

"She's right. You couldn't handle it. Watch your kids."

Amber and Laveau were standing by the Nissan when Hutsell arrived and clicked the doors open.

"What'd he say?" asked Amber.

"He wanted to know why you said what you did. I ignored his question and said you were right; he should be watching his kids."

"Guess Rick wouldn't like me using that word," she said.

"What makes you say that?" asked Hutsell.

"Miss Wyatt says he doesn't use words like that—he likes bigger ones instead."

Hutsell laughed. "Yeah, he likes to tell people off in a different way. It *is* fun to watch when he uses a big word that some punk doesn't know the meaning of. Hard for a guy to come up with a comeback, if he doesn't know what Rick said."

"I want to be smart like that," said Amber.

"Just need to get the tools of the trade," Laveau said. "You can do it. We talked about it the other night, remember?"

Amber nodded.

"Emigrant Lake next?" asked Hutsell.

"No. I want to drive my grandpa's house."

"All right. Hop in, and let's go."

Hutsell consulted the GPS directions he's stored the night before. Fifteen minutes later, the SUV turned onto an outer road. One more turn, and they were headed out of the small town of Talent, Oregon. They'd traveled a half-mile when Hutsell slowed down.

He pulled off the right side of the road. "That's it on the left."

The Mark Baylor house sat on a two-acre plot of land. It was a two-story frame house with a small porch that ran along the front. The house was slate-blue in color with white-bordered windows. An area was fenced off to the left that appeared to be a garden— though it was mostly barren now. A detached garage sat to the right, and a little behind the house. The structure was big enough to hold two cars plus a workshop. There was a gated wire fence around the perimeter.

Hutsell caught movement in the SUV's left-side window.

"A truck is coming up behind us. Just sit still. He's got plenty of room to pass."

The truck's left blinker came on and pulled into the driveway leading to Baylor's house. A man got out and waved as a dog watched from the truck's rear window. Baylor took a few steps toward the Nissan. He had an easy smile, his dark hair showing hints of the gray to come. Hutsell partially lowered his window.

"Everything all right, buddy?" the man asked.

"Yep, just checking my GPS."

"Ah, you got it covered then," the man said. "Have a good one."

"You, too, sir," replied Hutsell.

John Hutsell put the vehicle in drive and pulled back on the road. He drove a few miles and turned around at a crossroad. They passed the Baylor house for a second time and were soon at the outer road intersection. Hutsell stopped. He was checking traffic when Amber spoke.

"I want to meet him."

· 30 ·

Rick Hadley thanked Todd Jayson for his help and headed to his loft. It was 6:00 P.M., and he had one hour to get his act together before visiting hours began at the Fillan Center. First on the agenda: shave. He'd made only two passes with his razor when his phone rang. Chelle Thomas's name popped up on the screen. He hit the speaker so he could talk hands-free.

"Jean called me," said Chelle. "What happened?"

Rick told Chelle the full story of Elle's breakdown, then added, "Don't know what I was thinking. I knew she'd had a rough couple of days."

"Damn Rick, it wasn't you," said Chelle. "I screwed up Thursday at lunch."

"What do you mean?"

"She asked about wedding plans. One thing led to another, and the 'you-in-a-flowered-shirt-running' gag got in the mix. I teased her and said I could see her doing the eloping bit. Normally, she throws it right back in my face. But she didn't this time. The conversation ended with her saying everyone wished she'd get her act together where you were concerned—said you deserved more." She paused. "Flowered shirts, eloping, and . . .."

"If her relationship with me is causing her anxiety, why did she come back so soon? Chelle, she was gone only twenty-four hours? And why did she come here? I don't get it?"

"The truth? She knows she often heads down the wrong road. She wants someone to set her straight. So, she comes to me to bitch. I don't pull any punches and tell it like it is. And Cal, he does the same thing, only with finesse. You, on the other hand, do it with love. Whether she wants to admit it or not, she's drawn to the love nobody but you can give her. It's a tug of war—wanting that love, and thinking she can't return it." Chelle paused. "Rick, I

144

don't know if you've noticed, but some people shake their heads and make comments when the they see the two of you together. To some degree, I think she fears at some point you will agree with them and be gone."

"I've told her——."

"Yeah, that fear is unfounded, but in reality Rick, it's not about you. It's about *her* doubts and fears. Let's say she believes you— that you'll never leave. Who was the most important person in her life as a child? Her mother, right? Her mother loved her. Her mother wouldn't leave her. Yet, her mother is gone."

"How do I help her then?"

"In the same way we always have," said Chelle. "We can support her, but we *can't* make it better. She has to be the one to do that."

Rick rinsed and dried his face.

"When it comes to you and Elle, what's the best way to get a smile or a point across?" asked Chelle.

"Song lyrics or movie quotes."

"Hell, it's like you two speak in code sometimes. You know the answer. Remember the Wyatt Summer Fling last year?"

"Yes."

"What's the best way to handle a woman, Rick?"

Chelle disconnected the call. Rick looked at his image in the mirror.

"Love her . . . simply love her . . .."

Rick Hadley arrived at the Fillan Center at 6:55. He called John Hutsell.

"Heard from Deputy Mitch Brenner of Multnomah County today. He has confirmation of Amber's DNA. He's on his way to Talent to talk to Mark Baylor. The Sheriff's Department is holding off on the announcement for now."

"We drove by Baylor's place today. Amber's decided she wants a face-to-face meeting with him."

"I want to hear the story John, but visiting hours are starting— ."

"Call when you get home."

Rick got out of his truck. Pat and Jean Wyatt had been waiting in the parking lot and joined him at the entrance.

'Hope she'll see us," Jean said after they were inside the vestibule.

"She may not want to see any of us," said Rick.

"Right now, she's safe and that's what really matters," said Pat.

They were all going through the motions. and each one knew it.

The receptionist relayed the visitor's guidelines, the first being only two visitors allowed at a time.

"Rick, you go first," said Pat.

Rick nodded.

The desk clerk said, "Sir, you'll need to sign in, empty your pockets into a locker over there, lock it, and take the key."

Rick did as instructed and was directed to a large room. Several patients were seated around tables, visiting with friends and relatives.

Rick put his hands in his pockets and waited by the room's entrance. A few minutes later, Elle appeared.

"Hi," he said.

"Hi."

Elle chose a table on the left as far back from the entrance as possible. They sat in silence. Finally, Elle spoke.

"What did you do with the shirt?"

"It's in a drawer. I'll get rid of it."

"Don't. Keep it"

"Elle—."

"It was funny, Rick." She gave a half-smile. "In fact, I want a picture of you wearing it."

Rick shook his head. "You want to use it as blackmail, don't you?"

Her smile widened for a moment, then silence fell between them again.

Elle's left foot began tapping. She leaned forward and started rubbing her palms on her legs. "I'm back on the meds."

"That's good, isn't it?"

"I thought things were going great," she said, "so I stopped taking them. I can't think as well when I'm on them. But I guess being without them is worse, huh?"

"Have you asked Dr. Chandra about changing to a different type?"

"He did change them, and it was better. But . . .." She hugged herself at the waist.

"Ask him again. There are lots of meds out there. Dosage is a factor, too."

"Okay," she said, then changing the subject, asked, "Have you heard from John?"

"Yes. They made it to Medford last night. I don't know the full story yet, but Amber said she wants to meet her grandfather. Her DNA did match his, so, hopefully, they will get together soon."

"And what about you?"

"I worked in the lab most of the day, processing evidence from the case in Bolivar. The authorities think it's an attempted murder case. D'Orsey thinks it's attempted suicide." Rick looked around the room, then leaned over and in a low voice, asked, "What're you doing for entertainment?"

"Filling out a workbook about my feelings."

Rick reached down and scratched his ankle. "Put your hand under the table."

Elle gave him a questioning look.

"Just do it," he said.

Her hand went down and rested on her knee.

"Turn your palm up."

Rick placed the audio player in her hand. She quickly closed her fingers.

"What is it?"

"An MP3 player," he said. "It's in a case with earbuds and a charging cord, but you've got to be sneaky."

"What will they do if they catch you?" she asked.

"Tell me not to do it again."

"Shelby?"

"Yes. And Wheeler." He smiled, showing his one dimple. "And a little British Invasion topped off with some Motown."

"What—no Beach Boys?" Her attempt at humor failed, and she started to withdraw again.

"Elle . . .."

She shook her head, signaling for him to stop. Elle leaned back in her chair and brought both hands to her waist. As Rick used his body as cover, she slipped the player in her shirt.

"Jean and Pat are in the waiting room," he said. "Jean brought you a change of clothes."

Rick saw the same look in Elle's eyes he'd seen the night before.

"You don't have to see them Elle. You don't have to do anything you don't want to do."

"I've got to go."

Elle stood. Rick followed suit and watched her walk away

Deputy Mitch Brenner was on the road when John Hutsell's call came.

"Got some good news for you Deputy," said Hutsell. "Marissa Baylor has requested a meeting with her grandfather."

"Not that I'm looking a gift-horse in the mouth, but what brought about her change of heart?"

"She visited Lithia Park in Ashland today and reminisced. An older man heard her talking about a specific memory and told her that her grandfather was 'looking out for her.' She asked to drive by his home. We pulled off to the side of the road, so she could get a feel for the place. Baylor came up behind us and pulled into his drive He got out and asked if we needed help. Nice guy. Not long after, she said she wanted to meet him."

"Any ideas concerning a time and place for them to meet?"

"No, but Baylor needs to be aware of a few things. She wants to be called Amber, not Marissa. And for the most part, don't bring up her mother."

"You know the state got an anonymous tip on Kristina Baylor Revelle in 2005 for child abuse, right?"

"I do, but she doesn't. She's got a lot of anger where her mother is concerned, and I didn't want to add to it at this time."

"Anything else?"

"Just the usual cautions law enforcement gives in cases like this," said Hutsell. "She has seen the Facebook page Baylor and Lechay set up, so she knows he's never given up hope of finding her. And you can go ahead and tell him we were there today. It was after she saw and heard him that she decided on a meeting."

"Do you want him to contact you or the other way around . . . or do you want to come with me tonight?"

Hutsell hesitated.

"Look, Hutsell. I've talked with the Greene County Sheriff's Department and Lieutenant Gail Vashon in St. Louis. You check out. I'm not a glory hog. You're welcome to come along."

"Okay. Where and when do you want to meet?"

"You're in Medford, right?"

"Yes."

"The Medford Police Department lobby will work. Baylor's expecting me at 7:00 so let's meet at 6:30."

·31·

Mark Baylor leaned on the kitchen counter and wondered what 'news' Multnomah County Deputy Mitch Brenner had about his granddaughter. It had been almost a year since the last update—a phone call saying a review of Marissa's case had taken place and that no new leads had been developed. He listened to the hiss of the coffee maker as the few remaining drops left the reservoir. Somewhat nervous, he stuck his hands halfway in the pockets of his jeans and stared blankly at the refrigerator across the room.

His dog, Maxwell, walked through the kitchen and over to the dining room door that led out to the deck.

"Gotta go, boy?"

Baylor switched on the outside lights and opened the door of the small dining room. Maxwell took off. He jumped off the deck and ran around the fenced-in yard until he found the right spot.

Baylor returned to the kitchen and filled a mug with fresh coffee. He carried it to the dining table and set it down. He slipped on a heavy jacket and stepped out onto the deck. Baylor sipped coffee as he watched his dog make the rounds. He recalled the day he'd taken Marissa to a shelter where a similar dog had brought a rare smile to his granddaughter's face. He'd adopted the Irish Setter/Collie mix, and, on the way home, asked Marissa what would be a good name for the puppy.

"Bibi."

"That is a good name. How'd you think of it?"

"She's one of Clifford's friends."

That was two weeks before Marissa had gone missing. On the tenth anniversary of that day, Baylor had boxed up his granddaughter's DVDs, including *Clifford's Puppy Days* and stored them in the attic.

In a few months, it would be thirteen years since she'd disappeared.

Mark Baylor's phone sounded.

"Mr. Baylor, Deputy Brennen here. We're at the gate."

"One moment," said Baylor. *"We're"? There's two of them . . . not a good sign.* "Come on Maxwell, time to go in."

Mark Baylor held the door open for his dog, then made his way to the security panel and remotely opened the gate leading to his property. He moved to the front door, turned on the porch light and watched the Multnomah County Sheriff's Department vehicle come up the drive. Sensor lights illuminated the way for Deputy Brenner and his companion as they neared the house. Baylor held the door open as an invitation for his visitors to enter.

"Mr. Baylor, this is John Hutsell. He's a private investigator from Missouri."

"Mr. Hutsell," Baylor said extending his hand.

"Sir."

As Baylor shook Hutsell's hand, he realized the man looked familiar. "You were parked on the road across from my property today."

"Yes, sir, I was."

"You weren't lost then. You had the place you were looking for."

"This is true."

"Mr. Baylor," Brenner interrupted. "Is there somewhere we could sit and talk?"

"Sure," said an apprehensive Baylor. He held out his hand in the direction of the dining table.

Maxwell tagged along and lay down at his human's feet.

"Mr. Baylor," Brenner began, "Mr. Hutsell and his partner Rick Hadley, came across Marissa in southwest Missouri." Baylor steadied himself for the deputy's next line. "Mr. Hutsell and a female operative brought Marissa to Oregon last night. She is alive and well and in a Medford hotel at this very moment."

Mark Baylor had a million questions, but couldn't bring one to the surface.

"At the time she was found, Marissa was unsure of who she was. She agreed to have her DNA tested. Hadley ran the test and submitted results to various genetic genealogy sites. Both your DNA and that of Susanne Lechay's matched. It's her."

Mark Baylor's eyes began to water. "When can I see her?"

"I'll let Mr. Hutsell answer that," Brenner said.

"Mr. Baylor, your granddaughter is very distrusting of people and would like a public meeting that offers some privacy, but also allows for my colleague, Erin Laveau and me to be nearby," Hutsell said.

"How did you find her? Where's she been all these years?"

"Mr. Baylor, it's up to her to provide those answers—if she so chooses. But I must caution you on a few things before you meet with her."

"Okay."

"The first thing you need to know is that she has chosen to go by the name of Amber Lawrence. It will be up to her to tell you why," Hutsell said. "And keep in mind, she's been gone almost thirteen years—she's not the little girl you knew." He paused. "Let any discussion about the time she's been away originate with her. What's important right now is that she is alive and willing to meet with you."

"I can do those things. What else?"

"Don't initiate any physical contact," Hutsell said. "In some ways she is very strong, but she is also fragile. She *is* going to test you, so don't engage if she becomes confrontational. Remain calm, give her some time. She will cool down. She has seen her poster from the missing and exploited children's site and the Facebook page you and Ms. Lechay set up. She is also aware of her mother's death."

Mark Baylor closed his eyes and lowered his head. John Hutsell allowed time for the man to be with his thoughts. Finally, Baylor looked up, and Hutsell continued.

"Mr. Baylor, if at all possible, do not bring up her mother. She has fond memories of you, but there's a lot of anger where her mother's concerned."

"Okay. When can I meet her?"

"The meeting can take place as early as tomorrow if we can determine a suitable site. Any place in Talent that you can think of?"

"The Grotto, maybe," Baylor said. "It's a pizzeria with an elevated outside patio. It's unlikely people will chose to sit outside this time of year, and it's open till 9:00 P.M. The place usually clears out after the dinner crowd on a Sunday night."

"I'll present your idea to Amber and give you a call tomorrow."

"Thank you."

"Mr. Baylor?" Deputy Brenner said.

"Yes?"

"The Sheriff's Department will hold off till Tuesday to make an announcement that Marissa Baylor has been found."

The look on Baylor's face went from apprehension to alarm.

"The media will be on your doorstep almost immediately. I would suggest you prepare a statement ahead of time. You might even want a friend or family member to read it when the cameras show up."

"Any suggestions on what the statement should say?"

"Short and to the point—'Words cannot describe how thankful we are. We ask that you respect our privacy at this time,' " Brenner suggested. "Our office will inform local and state law enforcement agencies ahead of time. Call them if you need to."

Brenner stood to go. Hutsell and Baylor followed.

"Thank you, gentlemen," Baylor said.

John Hutsell pulled a Gambit Investigations card from his wallet. "My personal cell number is on the back. Amber does not want any undo publicity, and neither do we, so I would appreciate it if you would keep our involvement under wraps."

"That won't be a problem Mr. Hutsell. I'm thankful for all you've done."

"You'll be hearing from me soon," Hutsell said.

Baylor watched the Multnomah County Sheriff's Department vehicle clear his gate. He hit a button on the security panel, then pulled his cell from his pocket. His niece was in a Medford movie theatre with her fiancé. He knew her phone was turned off, so he texted, "They found her! She's safe! Call me!"

·32·

Sunday evening found John Hutsell and Erin Laveau sitting at a table just above the steps leading to The Grotto's patio. Amber and her grandfather were at a table on the far end. The body language of grandfather and granddaughter reminded Hutsell of the first time he'd seen his cousin Elle after the murder of her mother and the attempt on her own life. He knew from experience that the Baylors had a long road ahead of them.

"John?" Laveau said.

"Yes."

"Tuesday's when the headlines hit, right?"

"That's what Brenner said."

"It might be a good idea if Amber and Mark Baylor left town for a few days."

"What're you thinking?"

"The Oregon coast," Laveau said. "Off-season, so not a lot of tourists. Beauty and serenity—a time to reflect and get to know each other away from the spotlight."

"Not a bad idea. I'll see what accommodations are available when we get back to our rooms."

It was a quiet ride to the hotel. Hutsell had just turned on his blinker to exit I-5 when Rick Hadley's call came.

"We're almost to our hotel," Hutsell said. "I'll call you back in a bit."

"Okay," Hadley said.

Hutsell was waiting for a red light to turn green when Amber said, "Guess you'll be heading back to Missouri soon."

"We've got a little leeway, but not much," Hutsell replied. "There are a few items needing my attention in Springfield."

Like the identity of Mr. Rich, Laveau thought.

"He said I could move in with him," Amber said of her grandfather. "Said I could have the whole upstairs loft to myself. It has its own bathroom and everything."

"Is that what you want?"

"I don't know. He is a nice man, but he seems sad."

"Why do you think that is?" Hutsell said.

"I don't know. He says his niece wants to meet me. I guess she used to help take care of me some when I was little. He said she teaches at a college in Medford—something having to do with kids."

"She could probably help you get started with your education," Laveau said.

"Yeah, I guess so," Amber said, and paused before continuing. "Did you tell him to call me Amber?"

"I told him Amber is the name you preferred to go by," Hutsell said as he pulled into the hotel parking lot.

"What else did you tell him?"

"I told him you were a private person, and it was best he not ask questions."

"Well, he didn't. He told me about himself mostly. He said he built most of his house by himself—that he traded work with other guys for the rest."

"Smart way to go about it," Hutsell said. Amber went quiet. "You ready to go inside?" he asked.

"Yeah."

Hutsell disappeared into his room and called Rick Hadley and asked, "How's it going?"

"Elle's better. Extended visiting hours on Sunday, but Elle's allowing only short visits for now. Chelle was there for a while—so were Pat and Jean. On the business side, I want to remind you of my upcoming trip to Eagle Ridge."

"Second weekend in March, right?"

"Yep."

"I'll be back long before that," Hutsell said. "Things went well today with Amber and Baylor. He's offered her the second floor of his home."

"Gives her another option," Rick said. "I'll spend most of tomorrow in the lab or the office, then the evening with Elle. Any news from Carver about a Zimbeck meeting?"

"Not yet. Multnomah County's press conference on Tuesday may actually be the catalyst we need. Short on substance, it will reinforce my claim that Marissa Baylor's been found, but isn't talking. I've got enough info to prove his involvement, so it's in his best interest to deal with me. If not, I go to both Multnomah County and the FBI."

"You might be able to heat things up by giving Zimbeck an expiration date on your offer. Force him to make a decision now."

"True. Carver could tell them I'm only going to be in Oregon through Wednesday. The news conference is Tuesday—defecate or get off the pot."

"Cleaning up your language, John—substituting an eight-letter word for one with four?"

"Amber used a four-letter one yesterday, then mentioned she wanted to be smart like you and learn big words to use instead," Hutsell said. "I'm just trying it on for size."

"How does it feel?"

"Like shit."

John Hutsell turned on his computer and did a search for Oregon coastal vacation homes. He found one in Depoe Bay that was less than a two-hour drive to Salem . . . and the Oregon State Prison.

·33·

John Hutsell drove the rented Nissan down a short dirt driveway on the ocean side of a three-story vacation rental near Depoe Bay, Oregon. Mark Baylor followed in his dark blue GMC pickup. The two men parked side by side. Baylor got out, turned, and said, "Come on boy." Maxwell immediately took a flying leap out of the Sierra and started investigating.

Everyone, except Baylor, made their way to the entrance of the walk-out basement.

"I'll meet you inside as soon as Maxwell gets rid of some energy," he said

Erin Laveau and Amber were unloading groceries when Baylor walked to the nook and told Maxwell to stay. He filled a water dish and set it next to his dog.

"Anything I can do to help?" he asked.

"How good are you in the kitchen?" Laveau asked with a smile.

Baylor smiled back and said, "I've lived by myself for sixteen years, so scoot over and let me have at it."

Baylor began washing his hands.

Amber stood where she could see her grandfather's dog. "Does he bite?" she asked.

"No. He likes people—especially if they rub his ears."

"Is it okay if I go sit by him?"

"Sure. You can give him a treat if you want."

Baylor went to Maxwell's supply bag stored in the small pantry and returned with two dog treats.

"He can do a lot of things like shake hands, beg, and take a bow. Let me show you."

Amber followed her grandfather into the nook. Maxwell sat up when his owner entered.

"Maxwell, come," Baylor said. The dog walked over. "Sit." Maxwell did, and Baylor held out a treat. The dog gently took the biscuit from Baylor's fingers.

"Would you like to try?" he asked Amber.

"What should I tell him to do?"

"He can wave." Baylor handed Amber a doggie biscuit.

"Do I just say 'wave'?" Maxwell raised his right paw in the air.

"Yep. See it worked."

Amber stuck out the treat. Maxwell eased the treat into his mouth. Amber looked her grandfather. "Can I pet him now?"

"He's hoping you will."

Amber sat down and started petting Maxwell. Baylor sat in the chair next to her.

"Why did you name him Maxwell?"

"He's named for James Clerk Maxwell—the scientist who came up with electromagnetic theory of light."

"You know a lot about science, don't you?"

"My job depends on it, so I better. But I think if I did something else, I'd still learn as much about science as I could. Do you like science?"

"I like learning about things in space, like the planets."

"Electromagnetic waves are actually light waves and most of what we know about planets comes from studying the light waves that come from them."

"I'd like to learn more about them. John's cousin asked me what I wanted to do most. I told her I wanted to go to school. Miss Laveau said there were classes I could take that could help me get a diploma. Do you know about those kinds of classes? Are there any in the town where you live?"

"Yes, I know about them. I'm sure there are some in Medford. Would you like me to check and see where and when they meet?"

"I guess," Amber said. "She said some were free."

"I'm sure that's true, but if there are some you want to take that cost money, there's money available to pay for them."

"I don't know . . .."

"Amber, when you were born, your grandmother and I started a college fund. Every month we put money in the bank so you could go to college or a trade school. I still have money put in that fund every month. It's yours. If you want to go to school, you can."

Amber looked down. "I think I'll go unpack now."

By 10:00 P.M., all had retired to their rooms. Baylor and Maxell stayed in the room downstairs for easy outside access for Maxwell. Hutsell and Laveau occupied the two bedrooms on the main floor; Amber stayed in the third-floor loft. All but Amber spent their private time making phone calls.

Hutsell learned that Elle was still making progress. Jay told Erin he had a surprise for her to which she said, "It better be a Klingon bat'leth, or my first night back will be a lonely one for you." Mark Baylor placed a call to his niece.

"Susanne, I can tell she hasn't had much education, but she has a natural curiosity, and it's at the top of her priority list. Would you mind checking into classes for her?"

"Sure, Uncle Mark." Susanne paused, then said, "What does she look like? Describe her to me."

"She reminds me of her grandmother Roselyn in a lot of ways. Her dark, long hair and her eyes are like her grandma's. But her face has a different shape—more oval than heart-shaped. She's very thin, and I'd like to get her a complete physical. I can carry her on my insurance for several years, so if there are any medical problems, we can get them taken care of."

"I hope I get to meet her soon," Lechay said. "I've made arrangements to be off tomorrow. Andrew and I will be at your place when the press comes calling."

"Have you had time to check out John Hutsell and Gambit Investigations?" Baylor asked. "I've never been what you would call cynical, but he's putting out a lot of money and I can't help but wonder why."

"Well, he's got the money to put out. He inherited a big chunk of his grandfather's estate. Hutsell has been involved in some high-profile cases, but he doesn't seek the limelight. I emailed you a link to a cable TV show about him. Along with his Gambit Investigations partner Rick Hadley and a St. Louis detective, he's credited for helping solve the Anniversary Killer case a year ago. And his mother is a Missouri State senator. He had two years of pre-law at Notre Dame, but later transferred to John Jay College of Criminal Justice. He could have done anything with his money and connections, yet he chose a career in law enforcement. Maybe he was raised to give back to the community."

"Could be, but I've got a feeling he gets a charge out of the chase and putting bad guys away. And that's okay—the world needs men that will do what it takes. I just don't want my granddaughter getting caught in the crossfire."

Early Tuesday morning, John Hutsell carried his coffee cup into the great room of the beach home. Erin Laveau soon joined him. They stood in front of the curved panoramic window and sipped coffee. Mark Baylor and Maxwell were out for their morning walk. Hutsell and Laveau watched as Baylor tossed a piece of driftwood along the coastline. Maxwell immediately took out after it.

"Things went well yesterday, don't you think?" Laveau said.

"On the surface, yes."

"I know," she said. "He's seen only one side of her."

Amber, a floor above, watched the same scene from a picture window. She thought about the conversations she'd had with the man the past few days. Mark Baylor seemed to be welcoming her with open arms, but then again, he didn't know the whole story. Would he feel the same after he knew the true nature of what her life had been like the past twelve years? Would his offer of money and a place to stay still be there once he knew the truth? Maybe she should just take the money and run?

She watched Baylor jog toward the house, his dog running circles around him all the way. Amber got dressed and headed downstairs.

John Hutsell was in the kitchen, cooking bacon and eggs. Where meals were concerned, he handled breakfast, and Laveau took care of dinner. Lunch was do-it-yourself with cold cuts and veggie trays for the next few days.

At 10:00 A.M. Pacific Time, the head of Multnomah County Sheriff's public relations department walked in front of the cameras in Portland, Oregon. John Hutsell received a text from Rick Hadley five minutes later with a link to the broadcast. Hutsell motioned for Baylor to join him on the deck.

"Multnomah County just held their press conference. What time is Ms. Lechay making her announcement?"

"Two."

Amber opened the sliding glass doors, stepped into the cool air and said, "What are you talking about?"

Baylor looked at Hutsell.

"Multnomah County just had a press conference. They've announced that you've been found."

Amber's lips tightened. A furrow appeared across her forehead as her eyes narrowed.

"I told you I didn't want anybody to know what happened to me."

"Nobody does know," Hutsell said. "Come inside and you can watch the press conference."

Laveau had witnessed the scene unfold from the main room. Not knowing what had been said, she gave Hutsell a questioning look as he came inside.

"I'll be right back," he said.

Hutsell carried his computer to the dining table. He clicked the power button and pulled up the press conference. He positioned his computer so all could see, then hit play:

On May 21, 2006, Marissa Baylor of Medford, Oregon, went missing from the Multnomah Falls scenic overlook in the Columbia River Gorge. Despite an extensive search, including an FBI investigation, the only trace of Marissa ever found was a pink teddy bear given to her by her grandfather.

This morning we are happy to announce, Marissa Baylor has been found and reunited with her grandfather in southern Oregon. No other details are currently available. Miss Baylor and her family have requested the media respect their privacy and not contact them at this time. A link has been provided on the Multnomah County Sheriff's Department website for those wanting to send well wishes to Marissa and her family. Thank you.

After the video ended, Baylor's eyes moved from the computer screen to his granddaughter. Amber looked at her grandfather and, in a harsh tone, asked, "What are you looking at?"

Mark Baylor dropped his head. "I went about it all wrong."

Silence.

Baylor raised his head and looked at his granddaughter. "I wanted to stop her, but she threatened to keep you from me if I did anything. I didn't want to wait till she hit you again so I had Susanne call Child Protective Services and report her for child abuse. They investigated, but didn't find any evidence. So, Susanne and I came up with a plan for me to get custody of you."

Maxwell placed his chin on his owner's knee. Baylor stroked the dog's head.

"There was evidence that your mother took drugs, but I needed to prove I could take care of you," he continued. "The house was almost complete. Susanne was living in a studio apartment and working in Medford, trying to save money for junior college. We decided she'd move into the loft and become your nanny. She would have room and board and could get a student loan for tuition. As a college student, she'd be available all summer and after school once the fall term started."

Mark Baylor looked into his dog's gentle eyes.

"I talked to a lawyer. Somehow she got wind of it. The next thing I knew, you were missing. I'm so sorry . . . ."

Amber stood, walked over to the glass doors and out onto the deck. She ran down the stairs and took the trail that led to the beach.

"She doesn't have her coat," Laveau said. She went upstairs, got Amber's parka and headed to the door. She'd just taken hold of the handle when Hutsell said, "Let her grandfather take it."

Mark Baylor took Amber's coat, went downstairs, and grabbed his own. He motioned for his dog to follow and made his way to the beach. He held out his granddaughter's coat. Amber put it on, picked up a branch lying in the sand, and threw it as hard as she could. Maxwell chased after it. He returned and dropped the stick at Amber's feet. She threw it again. Baylor walked fifty feet to his right and sat down.

John Hutsell's phone rang. It was Carver D'Orsey.

"Any news?" he asked.

"You are set to meet Zimbeck and his lawyer at Oregon's State Correctional Institution in Salem tomorrow at 2:00 P.M. You'll have half an hour. Arrive ninety minutes early, as there may be check-in delays."

"Thanks, Carver."

Carver laughed. "Wait till you get my bill and see if you still feel the same."

·35·

Early Wednesday morning Elle Wyatt called Rick Hadley and said she was being discharged from the Fillan Center. He picked her up and drove back to the Gambit Investigations building. Rick paused at the outside stairs to let Elle go ahead of him.

"I'm going to go home, Rick."

"I'll go upstairs and get your key."

Rick returned and dropped the fob in Elle's outstretched hand. She got into her car and was soon heading south on Boonville Avenue. Elle stopped at a red light at the intersection of North Boonville and Chestnut Expressway.

Which way to go? Running didn't work anymore. The light turned green and a car sounded its horn. Forced to decide, Elle turned right.

From the top of the stairs Rick whispered, "Godspeed, Elle."

John Hutsell passed through security at the Oregon State Correctional Institution and waited to be called for his meeting with Dominic Serra and his client, Devin Zimbeck. Hutsell was taken to an interview room at 1:55. Serra stood and extended his hand.

"Save it," Hutsell said, dismissing the lawyer. "Let's get to it."

Serra sat down, Hutsell leaned against the wall.

"She was about to lose her meal ticket, wasn't she?" Hutsell asked Zimbeck.

"Who?"

"Sissy." No response. "Baylor was going for custody. If he was successful, Sissy would lose her government-assistance checks."

Serra tapped his pen a few times on the writing tablet in front of him.

"So, you talk her into going for one last big payout. How much did she get for a six-year old girl? How big was your cut?"

"Sissy left her alone by the falls. I don't know who took the kid," Zimbeck said.

"The fact that I'm here says you do," Hutsell said. "You know she's been found, and you know the guys in Portland don't have any details . . . but I do."

Silence again. Hutsell pulled out a chair and sat down.

"You showed up at Sissy's place that morning and drove her and Marissa to Multnomah Falls."

"The cops already know that," Serra said.

Hutsell didn't take his eyes of Zimbeck as he responded to the lawyer. "Yeah, but they don't know it was your client who took her by the hand and said, 'Your mommy sent me to get you.' And it was your client who walked her to a 'stranger's' car."

Serra glanced at Zimbeck.

Hutsell continued, "Marissa asked, 'Where's my mom?' You said she'd gone to get something to eat. You put her in the back seat of the car and strapped her in. The stranger got in the driver's seat and took off. And as she told me, 'That's when the real nightmare began'."

"What do you want?" Serra asked.

"His Midwest connection."

"I don't know who that is," Zimbeck said.

"Fine," Hutsell said and stood. "It just doesn't seem quite fair, does it?"

"What doesn't seem fair?" Zimbeck said.

"You good at visualization?" Hutsell said. "'Cause this is how I see it: you're about to get out of here. But instead of walking out of a minimum-security prison a free man, you get transferred to a maximum-security facility five miles down the road—big difference between the Oregon State Correctional Institution and the Oregon State Penitentiary. And to top it off, the population there will not take kindly to having a sorry son a of-a bitch in their midst that sold a six-year-old g—."

"You'll keep all this to yourself if he gives you the connection?" Serra asked.

"I won't say a word to the authorities," said Hutsell. "I don't give a rat's ass about your client. I want the guys in Missouri, Illinois, and Oklahoma."

"What guarantee do we have of your continued silence?"

"If your client's involvement is brought to light, the situation changes. The network will shut down to some extent. Leads will dry up. Hell, there's already been a murder in St. Louis connected to this case."

Zimbeck sat straight up. "What are you talking about?"

"Marissa Baylor escaped from a guy named Burleson almost two weeks ago. His body was found behind a truck stop last Thursday. Right now, nobody in the Midwest—except me—knows the Baylor connection. But hey, you don't want to deal . . . .."

Serra leaned over and talked with his client in hushed tones. He soon sat back in his chair. Zimbeck looked at Hutsell.

"I've been in here a long time. I don't know if things have changed or not."

"Cut the crap. What do you know?"

"The guy hired out to legitimate trucking companies, but on occasion, he hauled 'freight' for a 'firm' out of St. Louis."

Burleson—CDL. Pay dirt!

"Name of the guy and the firm."

"I don't know his real name. He went by Warden," Zimbeck said. "Truck had no markings, no signage."

"Describe him."

"Tall guy—six-three, maybe. He had a small mole at his temple. It was kind of raised up, know what I mean? I only saw it a couple of times—when he changed his regular glasses for prescription sunglasses."

"Was it brown like the one on Robert De Niro's face?"

"No. It was the same color as his skin."

"White guy?"

"Yeah."

"What else?"

"Dark hair, some gray. Maybe forty-five."

"Type of hair cut?"

"Kind of like Bruce Willis before he went bald. Combed back. Starting to thin. Hairline looked like a 'W.'

"Body type?"

"A little skinny, but knew how to handle himself."

"Accent?"

"No, but got a kick out of talking like he was Clint Eastwood."

"You mean just above a whisper?"

"Yeah, like that," Zimbeck said, "but you wanted him to talk, 'cos when he stopped talking things got bad."

"In what way?"

"He'd beat the shit out of ya."

"With his fists?"

"Nah, he carried one of those ASP batons," Zimbeck said. "He was a mean son-of-a-bitch. But he could come across nice when he needed to."

"Anything else?"

"No."

Hutsell rose to his feet.

"Why isn't Marissa Baylor talking?" Serra asked.

"None of your fucking business," Hutsell said and signaled for the guard.

John Hutsell made two calls from the Nissan on his way back to the Oregon coast. The first was to Erin Laveau to say he was on his way back. He asked about the 'atmosphere' in Depoe Bay and was told it was cordial. The second was to Rick Hadley.

Hutsell relayed what he'd learned from the Zimbeck interview. He ended the conversation by saying, "I'm no longer the anonymous source in this situation, partner. It's up to you when the time comes."

"Not a problem."

"How's Elle?"

"She's home. I haven't talked to her since early this morning."

"When will you see her again?"

"Don't know," said Hadley. "Do you have an idea when you and Erin will be starting for home?"

"Erin said things went well today between Amber and her grandfather, so I hope we can head back tomorrow," said Hutsell.

Rick thought about having dinner at Earhart's but knew people would ask about Elle, so he went home and ordered pizza delivery instead. After several slices and a couple of beers, he went into his bedroom and pulled the flowered shirt from its hiding place. He put it on over his plain white tee. Next, he stood in front of the mirror and took a selfie. He attached it to a message and sent it to Elle, "As per your request." Elle replied, "Looking good." He followed with a bitmoji Elle had created of him doing a John Travolta dance move. She countered with one of her, break dancing.

Rick pulled the movie, *Gravity,* from the multimedia storage cabinet in the corner and popped it in his DVD player. He woke up on the sofa at 2:00 A.M., picked up his phone, and read over the last few texts from Elle. He typed, "Miss you," then erased it before going to bed.

·36·

Amber and her grandfather were sitting on the deck, watching the waves recede from the Oregon coastline. Maxwell lay between them. The glass door slid open. John Hutsell and Erin Laveau stepped onto the deck.

"I understand you've decided to take your grandfather up on his offer and will be moving in once you get back to Talent," Hutsell said.

"That's right," Amber replied.

"Erin and I will be heading back to Missouri in a few hours," Hutsell said. "This place is booked through Sunday. You two are welcome to stay till then."

Amber continued to stare at the ocean. "Did you get what you came for?" she asked, with attitude in voice.

"I got enough."

"Going to see the nurse when you get back?"

Hutsell turned and walked inside.

"Damn Amber," Laveau said. "You should know by now the shock treatment doesn't work on him."

"Got a rise out of him about Tennessee."

"That had to do with Elle," Laveau said, "not him. And it didn't take him ten seconds to take control of the situation. You haven't given him much, but your little morsels here and there are all he needs. He'll make it work. And know, John Hutsell is true to his word. When things go down, you won't be in the mix."

"Who's he protecting in the big house?"

"You know how you want to keep things private?"

"Yeah."

"It would be nice if you would afford him the same courtesy?"

Amber remained quiet.

"I get it," Laveau said. "Information is your biggest weapon, and you've had to use it to gain advantage when and wherever you can." Laveau paused for effect. "I know it's hard to believe from your standpoint, but there are good men in this world. John Hutsell is one of them."

Laveau followed her boss inside.

Mark Baylor waited for the door to completely slide shut, then asked, "You okay?"

"Yeah." Amber stared straight ahead and asked, "You sure you want me to move in with you?"

"Is the sky blue? Is water wet? Does Maxwell like treats?"

Amber didn't answer.

"I've waited almost thirteen years to have you back. You want to be a smart-ass every now and then, have at it. I've got a thick skin." Baylor stood. "I'm going to take Maxwell for a walk on the beach. You want to come?"

"Maybe later. I've got something to do first."

Amber walked into the bedroom John Hutsell had occupied since Monday night. She shut the door behind her. John interrupted his packing and walked over to the door and opened it again.

"You need something?" he asked.

Amber made her way to the bed and sat down. Hutsell walked to the dresser and leaned against it.

"How're you going to keep me out of it when you find them? What evidence do you have against them if you don't have me?"

"We already know the two that held you captive that night. Burleson is dead, but eyes and ears in St. Louis, and throughout Missouri, are already tracking Kastner. We'll find his associates through surveillance—physical and electronic. We'll catch them in the act. It'll take time, but sooner or later, they'll pull a 'Burleson' and get sloppy. Then they'll go down."

Hutsell shifted most of his weight to his left foot.

"Mr. Rich is another story though," he said.

"Why?"

"General location and a scant description of his home is not much to go on."

"What do you want to know?"

171

"What he looks like."

"Short and mostly bald. Couldn't get it up till I put on a white blouse and plaid skirt. He made me sit on his lap. Then he combed my hair and put it in a ponytail."

"Coloring—as in hair, eyes, skin?"

"White guy. Short gray hair on the sides. Little nose, little eyes, little everything. Eyes kinda brown—looked green at times."

"Distinguishing marks—tattoos, moles, scars?" Hutsell asked.

"Tattoo. A naked girl all curled up on the floor—crying or praying—I don't know which."

"Was she lying on her side?"

"No, it's kinda like she was bowing at somebody's feet. 'Daddy' written at the bottom of the tattoo."

"Where was it located on his body?"

"Just above his 'sugar stick,' as he called it."

"What was his voice like? What kind of words did he use?"

"Kinda high at times, then it would go lower. That happened a lot. He talked to me like I was a kid, not a grown-up. He'd do something and ask if I liked it. I always nodded yes; I really didn't want to talk to him."

"And he was okay with that?"

"Yeah."

"Anything about the house or the room you were in?"

"Don't know anything more about the house than what I've already told you. The room had books on shelves. There were a couple of desks with computers. The desks were separated by a little wall. It reminded me of when I lived at the farm house and would go to my friend's place where we had school. There was a map on the wall and a couple of what Teena called bulletin boards."

"Any other furniture?"

"A couch and two chairs. He raped me on the couch." Amber stood. "I don't want to talk anymore."

"Okay. Can I give you some advice before you go?"

Amber nodded.

"The plan is that everything we learn will go to law enforcement by way of anonymous tips. But when authorities start their own investigation, there's the possibility they will learn about you. If so, they might come calling. Be prepared for that day, and if it comes, make sure you have a good lawyer."

It was 11:30 A.M. when John Hutsell turned over the Nissan's key to the rental agency's representative at Portland International Airport. He and Erin Laveau had fast and easy access to the terminal from the rental car area, and made it through the check-in line fairly quickly. On the way to their gate, a digital sign caught Laveau's eye. She stopped and said, "Look."

Hutsell followed Laveau's line of sight. The display was asking for travelers' help in identifying sex-trafficking victims. A list of warning signs was provided.

"Education is the key to identifying victims, but after that . . .," Hutsell trailed off.

"What do you mean?"

"Not easy getting the evidence on those at the top. Then there're the deals their lawyers make. They've got money, so until there's a conviction, many get house arrest in their mansions. If convicted, it's usually in a minimum-security facility with a minimum sentence."

Hutsell started walking, Laveau fell in step.

"Not going to change until the public stops sticking their collective head in the sand and demand action," Laveau said.

"Don't kid yourself. These guys have money—who are they hobnobbing with on the golf course and making deals with in the back rooms? Whose campaigns do they contribute to, and who makes calls to prosecutors on their behalf?"

"Those people will make any deal possible to keep from being labeled a 'friend' of a sex-trafficker, John."

"Yeah, forget helping victims and putting culprits away. Just cover your damn ass and keep the money flowing."

"True, but that's kind of out of your hands don't you think? Sounds more like the job for your mom and her colleagues who are willing to put forth the fight."

"Oh, I don't know," Hutsell said. "Burleson won't be forcing any more women and children to become sex slaves. Maybe that kind of attitude needs to make its way to the top."

Laveau came to a stop.

"John, just what are you saying?"

"Nothing . . . just talking out of school. Let's go. We don't want to miss our flight."

37

John Hutsell and Erin Laveau arrived in St. Louis at 9:30 P.M. Laveau passed on a connecting flight to Springfield. She could drive the distance in less time than the lay-over wait. Hutsell had plans to meet his former partner, Trish Rankin, in a downtown St. Louis bar frequented by law enforcement. He called up her contact info and sent a text.

"Just got the rental. On my way."

"Gabe and I are here. See you in a few."

Hutsell walked into the basement bar and immediately heard his name. He looked around and saw Rankin waving him over to a booth she shared with Fenske.

"Some people just get better looking with time," Rankin said before Hutsell sat down.

He smiled, moved his index finger from Rankin to Fenske and back again, and said, "When did this happen?"

"Remember the day of Anniversary Killer press conference?" Rankin said. Hutsell nodded. "That night."

"Finally took my advice, huh?"

Fenske smiled and said, "Didn't know I was a topic of conversation between you two."

"She was almost there. Just needed a little push," Hutsell said.

The waitress showed up, and Hutsell ordered dinner for himself and drink refills for his friends.

Rankin picked up the conversation and asked, "What about you, John? You still a manslut?"

All three laughed at Rankin's characterization of her former partner.

"By all means, Trish, don't pull any punches," Hutsell said.

"What the hell, John? How many times did I have to listen to talk about some woman you knew from some town . . . yada, yada, yada . . .?"

"Kept you from setting me up, didn't it?"

Rankin nodded in the direction of a blonde at the bar who had been checking out Hutsell since he'd walked through the door.

"Yeah, but the reputation you cultivated didn't have the effect you wanted on the female population of St. Louis. They still wanted your sorry ass. So, how 'bout it? Any woman getting close enough to perform a 'wingectomy'?"

"Nah, but Rick's wings definitely got clipped," Hutsell said.

"Your cousin do the honor?" Rankin said.

"No, he did it himself."

"Was that before or after Tennessee?"

"Really got started in August. Elle ran like the wind. But, they were definitely an item when they returned from Tennessee in early October."

"How is your cousin?" Gabe asked.

"A few bad days here and there, but with Rick there's stability––whether she wants to admit or not." Hutsell changed the subject. "How're Josh and Sophie?"

"Growing like weeds," Rankin said. "Gabe's coaching Josh's basketball team this year, and he has Sophie building her own computer."

"It's a well-developed computer kit for kids. She's actually learning to code," Fenske added.

"Speaking of the kids, we better get home and relieve the baby-sitter," Rankin said. "See you tomorrow, John?"

"I'll be by mid-morning to see Kleeman. We can have lunch before I head to Springfield."

Rankin saw a familiar face walk through the door. She nodded in direction of the pretty brunette. "And there's our cue, Gabe." Rankin and Fenske stood. Hutsell did likewise. Rankin smiled at Hutsell. "Have a good night, John."

Rankin and Fenske walked away as Hutsell picked up his glass and moved to the bar. At the exit, Rankin paused and caught the brunette's attention and said. "He's all yours."

The brunette hovered in the background and observed the blonde at the bar. The blonde's eyes moved up and down John

Hutsell's body. A man walked to the bar to place an order and blocked her view. His order arrived, and he headed toward the back of the bar. The brunette moved to the space he'd vacated, placed her elbows on the bar from behind and leaned back. The blonde moved her head to better see Hutsell. The brunette smiled.

"One thing you've got to understand about John Hutsell," she said. "For the time he's with you—an hour or two, maybe all night—he'll give you everything he's got. He'll make you feel like every man before him didn't know one damn thing about satisfying a woman. But keep in mind, that's all you're ever going to get."

The brunette took a step away from the bar and walked toward Hutsell.

"Hello, sailor," she said as she came up behind him.

Hutsell turned. "Hi, Stacy."

Stacy Parisi leaned in close. She whispered in his ear as she slid something in his right hip pocket, then made her way to the exit.

Hutsell took his time finishing his beer before leaving the bar. Thirty minutes later, he was in the parking lot of an apartment complex. He climbed the stairs to a second-floor unit and knocked on the door.

Stacy Parisi opened the door wearing her familiar tight camisole and panties.

"New place?" Hutsell asked.

"Yeah. Come on in, and I'll show you around."

Erin Laveau arrived home to an empty house. Jay Randall had volunteered to take the shift of a trooper who'd been injured in a car accident, and it would be several hours before he'd be home. She didn't take time to unpack—just grabbed a quick shower, brushed her teeth, and headed to bed.

Randall quietly walked in around 3:00 A.M. and crawled in bed next to her. She stirred.

"Where's my present?"

"In the morning."

"Is it a bat'leth?"

"It's better."

"I want a bat'leth."

177

"Go back to sleep, or I'll make you wait till the middle of next week."

"PetaQ."

"Now Marie, no need to go all Klingon on me," he teased.

"QamuSHa."

"I unhate you, too."

38

Friday morning, the first day of March, found Elle Wyatt working the *New Your Time*s Crossword Puzzle at the bar that separated her kitchen from the living area. She'd had little contact with friends and family since leaving the Fillan Center—preferring to spend her time sleeping and playing word games instead.

Her cell vibrated on the counter, causing her to cringe. Elle gave the phone a nudge and said, "Give it a couple of weeks people—anti-depressants don't work overnight."

Elle went to her bedroom, crawled into bed, and went to asleep. She woke four hours later and headed to the bathroom.

Elle turned on the water, raised her head and looked in the mirror. The woman staring back hadn't brushed her hair in several days. She thought about taking a shower, then told herself she'd take one at bedtime. A chuckle escaped. "Which bedtime, Elle? 4:00 P.M.? 8:00 P.M.? 1:00 A.M.?"

Kind of funny, but not really.

She felt dizzy and grabbed the edge of the vanity to steady herself. Her hands were shaking and she knew she had to get something in her stomach.

Elle opened the refrigerator door and checked the shelves. Nothing looked good. She moved to a nearby cabinet and pulled out a trail-mix blend of cranberries, raisins, almonds, and pepitas.

Pepitas—hell, call a pumpkin seed a pumpkin seed.

She decided on hot tea instead of coffee, and put the kettle on. She turned to reach for her tablet on the bar and saw her cell.

Damn. Check that text or someone'll be knocking on the door—
—"Are you all right?"

Elle picked up her phone and hit the message icon. She dropped her head when she saw the sender's name. She steadied herself and read the message.

"'Do you use a bow, or do you just pluck it?'"

She knew the answer, but hesitated typing the response. The sound of escaping steam momentarily distracted her. She held her phone in one hand and moved the kettle to a chrome trivet with the other.

Elle read the message again, then typed, "'Most of the time, I slap it.'"

She was putting a few ice cubes in her mug to cool the tea when another text arrived.

"Congratulations! You've won a ticket to a private screening of *Some Like it Hot* — released sixty years ago this month."

She started down a list of lame excuses in her head and settled on the weather.

"They're calling for ice tonight."

"The offer includes delivery of the critically acclaimed DVD and dinner—all before the temperature drops below freezing."

Buy some time.

She typed, "You watch movies with your spats on?"

"'I sleep with my spats on.'"

It might be fun . . . it was AFI's number one comedy . . ..

"What's on the menu?"

"Steak, salad, steamed broccoli, and cauliflower with cheese sauce."

She did need to eat . . ..

"Okay, but your place, not here," she typed.

"What time would you like your ride to arrive?"

"Before dark.

"See you at 5:15."

She had two hours before the Silverado would make its appearance in her drive.

Elle's body language said it all; keep a minimum distance. So, Rick opened the passenger door of his truck, but didn't offer a hand.

The conversation on the drive to Boonville was superficial; the lab had some new equipment, John and Erin were back from Oregon. They were two blocks from Rick's loft when he brought up another classic movie.

"*The Day the Earth Stood Still* will be at The Moxie in a couple of weeks," he said.

"Rennie or Reeves?"

"Rennie."

"Good to know," Elle said.

Rick followed Elle into his apartment and dropped his keys in the catch-all by the door. He took her coat and hung it with his in the closet.

"How about some Quincy Jones?" he asked.

Good choice, Elle thought. No mushy lyrics—in fact, no lyrics at all, except two words—watermelon man.

"Sounds good," she said.

Elle set her purse on one of four stools at the kitchen bar and sat down on another. Rick moved behind the bar and opened the refrigerator.

"Beer or raspberry lemonade?" he asked.

"Beer."

"You hungry?"

"Yeah. Haven't had much to eat today."

"Would you like an appetizer?" he asked.

"What you got?"

"The perfect thing to take the edge off before dinner."

Rick opened the cabinet and pulled out a package. He tossed it in the air and caught it behind his back before setting it on the bar.

Elle couldn't help herself—she laughed at the packet in front of her.

"Beer *and* peanut butter crackers," she said. "You sure know the way to a girl's heart, Hadley."

"Well . . . it's not pineapple," he said, teasing about her favorite pizza topping.

After leftovers were stored, and dishes were in the dishwasher, Rick and Elle moved to the living area. He sat on the edge of the sofa and picked up the remote. Elle sat next to him, her legs underneath her body.

"Ready?" he asked.

"Yep . . . nothing like Chicago in 1929 . . .."

Two hours later, Joe E. Brown told Jack Lemmon, "Nobody's perfect," and Rick turned so he faced Elle. He put his right elbow on the back of the sofa and leaned his check against his hand.

"It's Friday night. Neither one of us has to get up early," he said. "What next? How about a Billy Wilder double feature? I've got *Sunset Boulevard*?"

"Don't know that I'll last another two hours."

"Well, *Star Trek: Enterprise* is on in fifteen minutes on H&I."

Elle smiled. "Ah, the pink skins."

"Yep," said Rick. "Would you like to 'freshen up'?"

Another smile, "Yeah, I could use a potty break."

Elle returned from the bathroom and said, "Your turn." She made her way to a window that overlooked North Boonville Avenue. The fog blurred the street lights. Elle saw a lone car heading south. Her upper body shivered at the cold air filtering in. Rick entered the room and found Elle hugging herself. He took the quilted throw from the back of the sofa, walked over, and wrapped it around her shoulders.

"Better?" he asked.

Elle nodded. They resumed their positions on the sofa. Elle was asleep twenty minutes later. Rick turned off the TV and gently shook her arm. She opened her eyes.

"You'll be more comfortable in the bed," he said.

"You take the bed. I'll sleep here."

"My mother would have my hide if I made you sleep on the couch."

"Rick, you're six-four. Take the bed. I won't tell if you won't."

"Ain't happening."

Elle was too tired to argue. She went to the kitchen, got a cold bottle of water and her purse.

"Good night," she said.

"See you in the morning."

Elle walked in the bedroom and saw that Rick had laid out one of his shirts for her. She took her meds, put on his shirt, and got into bed. She closed her eyes and was thankful he had played her best friend tonight instead of her lover.

Elle awoke and checked the clock on the nightstand: 2:20 A.M. *That's what you get for sleeping all day.*

She'd left her tablet at home, so she picked up her phone and started to work a crossword puzzle. Upright or sideways, it didn't matter, the screen was too small.

Elle walked over to the doorway and looked into the living room. Rick was lying on his back; his head on a throw pillow, his hands at his waist. She watched him for several minutes, turned around and looked at his bed. It was big enough to get lost in. Most of her life she'd spent running, trying to do exactly that—get lost. But she'd learned the past year that being lonely was different from being alone.

"You know the preacher like the cold, he knows I'm gonna stay."

Maybe it was for the wrong reason, but Elle went to the sofa, knelt down and tapped Rick on the shoulder.

"Scoot over."

Rick adjusted his body so he was lying on his side. Elle slid in next to him. He offered half the pillow.

"It's cold," she said.

Rick pulled the quilt from the back of the sofa and spread it over both of them. He slipped his right arm under the blanket and pulled her close.

"Better?"

"Yes."

"Bacon, eggs, and toast okay?" Rick asked the next morning.

"What, no pancakes?"

"That's John's specialty, Ms. Wyatt."

With breakfast almost over, Elle stood and asked if Rick would like more coffee. Rick nodded, put the last bite of toast in his mouth, and leaned back in his chair. She refilled both their cups and returned to her seat beside him.

"How much time and effort did you put into planning last night?"

"Not that much. The steaks were in the freezer—."

"How did you know *Some Like It Hot* was released sixty years ago this month?"

"It's your favorite movie. I did a trivia search."

"I can't give anything back right now, Rick. Don't know if I'll—."

"Elle, what's important right now is that you concentrate on taking care of you."

"And where does that leave you?"

"Not your concern," Rick said. "Get rid of that guilt, Elle. You're not responsible for me or my happiness. I am."

"You went out of your way for mine."

Rick smiled. "No . . . the way you looked at me and smiled before your favorite lines, the crack about the peanut butter crackers—all those things made *me* happy. I'm a selfish son-of-a-gun."

Rick's phone vibrated in his pocket. He pulled it out and read a text from his brother, Chris. He held it up so Elle could see the message.

"Need a head count for Mom's birthday. How many coming from Missouri?"

Elle took the phone from Rick's hand, typed a reply and handed it back. Rick looked at her response. "Two." He put his fingers on the keys and added, "We'll see you Friday."

·39·

John Hutsell's BMW needed new tags, so Tuesday morning, he drove to Fabbiano's Auto in the small town of Battlefield to get the car inspected. The left bay garage door raised as Hutsell drove onto the lot. The owner, Anthony Fabbiano, acknowledged Hutsell with his index finger, then backed a truck out of the bay. He parked it two vehicles down from John.

"Anthony," Hutsell said by way of a greeting.

"Still driving it, huh?" Fabbiano nodded toward the BMW.

"Well, I've been meaning to talk to you about that," Hutsell said. "I need a low-profile, high-performance vehicle for the business. Suggestions?"

"That's easy. The Chevy Tahoe," Anthony said. "They're popular, so there's plenty of them on the road. If needed, the Tahoe's easy to work on . . . unlike . . .." Anthony nodded in the direction of John's sports car. "Four-wheel drive for back-roading, and there's enough room for a mattress in the back."

Hutsell laughed. "Now just what would I need with a mattress, Anthony?"

"Just thinking of those overnight stake-outs, John." Fabbiano smiled. He headed toward the garage. "Go ahead and check-in. Won't be long till you're back on the road."

Hutsell was at the office bulletin board, checking out local business cards when his phone sounded.

"Hello, Mom. How are things in Jeff City?"

"About to head to a meeting on mental illness health coverage, but that's not the reason I called," Senator Hutsell said. "I've given a lot of thought to the description of 'Mr. Rich.' It reminds me of Stephen Marens."

"CEO of Liberty Tours?"

185

"Yes. Besides the similarity in appearance, the voice component fits. His voice breaks all the time. It's like he's still going through puberty. That's why his wife was the official voice for the business. She divorced him last year, so don't know who the spokesperson is now. And John, get this . . . he lives in a gated subdivision on River Birch Road."

"Prairie Rose Estates?"

"Yes."

"Mom, that's not even five miles from your place."

"I know. Gotta go—talk to you later."

Hutsell's next stop was Carine Velardi's office in mid-Springfield. He walked into the reception area of the remodeled two-story home and gave the receptionist his name.

The woman checked her computer, made a few clicks, and said, "Have a seat Mr. Hutsell. I'll let Ms. Velardi know you're here."

Carine Velardi entered a few minutes later in a fitted black sheath accented with a white notched collar and matching cuffs. The realtor, with her blonde hair styled in a short-layered bob, was a strikingly pretty woman. Hutsell stood as she walked toward him.

"Good to see you again, Mr. Hutsell. If you'll follow me . . . .."

Hutsell looked around Velardi's office. The corners of his mouth slightly turned upward. "I like what you've done with the place."

She gave him a quizzical look accompanied with a smile.

"The former owners were good friends of my grandparents," he explained.

"The Lowes?"

Hutsell nodded. "In fact, one of their granddaughters was in my graduating class."

"Speaking of grandparents, I checked on your family's former home in Phelps Grove. The present owners are not interested in selling."

"It was a long shot."

"But there are several homes available you might like." Velardi gestured to small conference table below a mounted LED widescreen television. "Have a seat, and we'll take a virtual tour of a few."

Hutsell viewed several homes, then sat back in his chair and said, "I like the stone exteriors on the Portland and National properties. But the interior of the National home has changed too much from its original design to suit me. How soon can you arrange a tour for the one on Portland?"

"It's vacant and has a key lock box, so as early as this afternoon."

"1:00?"

"I'll meet you there," Velardi said.

"Well, what do you think?" Velardi asked as she and Hutsell stepped down the stone steps outside the Portland home.

"It's in great shape. I like the white kitchen cabinets and the arched doorways. And that curved Florida room . . .."

"To tell the truth, I'm surprised it's still on the market."

"About the only changes I'd make would be in the decor," Hutsell said.

Velardi leaned against her car and smiled. "I know a great interior designer . . .."

"Yeah, my Aunt Jean would love to get her hands on this one," Hutsell said, as he leaned on his own vehicle and loosely crossed his arms across his chest.

"What do you think of the asking price?" the realtor asked.

"Go ahead and give it to them with the stipulation they replace the blue carpet upstairs, and strip and paint the back porch and storage building."

"About the easiest sell I've ever made."

"It needs a little work, but I'd prefer to do that on my own."

"Well, you've definitely got the background," Velardi said. "You could be running Nelson Construction—what made you decide to go into law enforcement instead?"

"Good question." Hutsell smiled again. "Maybe I just don't like routine."

"Nah, it's more than that detective. But that's okay. That answer will satisfy a portion of the donne molto belle in town who aren't interested in your brain."

"When do you have to be back at the office?"

"Whenever I want—I'm the boss."

"Can you get me into the Prairie Rose Division near Battlefield."

"Business or pleasure?"

Hutsell continued to grin. "Ever thought about doing a little detective work on the side?" Velardi's eyes twinkled. "Follow me to my office," he said. "We'll drop off my car and take yours. I'll explain on the way."

Hutsell called Rick Hadley on his way to Gambit Investigations.

"Find everything you can on Stephen Marens, CEO of Liberty Tours."

"And we're interested in him because . . .?" Hadley asked.

"I think he's Mr. Rich. On my way to check out his house. Later."

Hutsell parked his car behind the Gambit building and got in Carine Velardi's SUV. Without giving much detail, he explained about the house he wanted to check out. Velardi came to a stop at a red light at the intersection of Fremont and Bradford Parkway. Hutsell noticed the Cherokee to his right. He recognized the driver as she made a left turn. He checked the clock on the dash and guessed Jenise was running an errand after work.

Jenise Alexander parked her Cherokee and walked to the office that housed her psychotherapist and three other mental health professionals. She was checking in at the desk when the door leading to the interior rooms opened. She turned around and saw Elle Wyatt.

The two women nodded at each other. Jenise sat down to wait for her appointment. Elle walked out the door.

John Hutsell was in his office at the end of the work day, when Rick Hadley walked in.

"The house checks out. It fits Amber's description," Hutsell said. "What did you find on Marens?"

"Forty years old. B.S. in business administration from Mizzo. Started out with bus tours to Oklahoma casinos in 2007—called Blackjack Tours. Changed the name to Liberty Tours in 2010 when he began offering nationwide excursions."

"Family?"

"Father immigrated to the U.S. from the United Kingdom. He's third generation American. Married Dana Schofield in 2002. Has two daughters, Leah, fourteen and Lily, eleven. Wife divorced him in October last year. She and the girls now live in Joplin."

"The girls go to private or public school?"

"Private."

"When will the oldest be fifteen?" Hutsell asked.

"July."

Hutsell recalled the Daddy tattoo Amber described, and the school uniform she was forced to wear.

"Castration's not enough for the son-of-a-bitch."

Hutsell pulled out his phone and dialed Mark Baylor. He tapped the speaker icon.

"Mr. Baylor, may I speak with Amber?"

"I'll see."

A few minutes later, Amber came on the line.

"What is it?"

"Remember when you said you didn't want anyone else to have to pretend to be a fourteen-year-old girl?"

"Yes."

"I found him . . . and I believe you were acting as a substitute for his fourteen-year-old daughter. What else can you tell me?"

"Such as?"

"Did he call you by a specific name? Did he ask you to call him by one?"

"Hold on."

Hutsell heard a door close, then a slight wind in the background. He knew she'd stepped outside for some privacy.

"No, but he did have a video camera. He filmed everything, forced me watch it with him then made me have sex with him again."

"Can you describe the camera?"

"It was on a stand."

"So, the video is of both you and him?"

"Yeah."

"Did he play any music?"

"Yeah. A girl singing about kissing it, making it better—something like that. I tried not to think about it. Just wanted him to get done."

"Anything else?"

"There were names on the bulletin boards, but don't remember what they were. Just that both started with the letter 'L'."

"Thank you, Amber."

"Is Miss Wyatt there?"

"No."

"I know what happened in Tennessee," said Amber. She paused. "I wish I could be like her."

Hutsell and Hadley exchanged looks.

"Amber, this is Rick Hadley. You are like her. She did what she had to do to survive, and so did you."

"Yeah, but that guy will never bother her or anyone else again."

"Give it some time," Hadley said. "We're working on it."

"Whatever."

The line went dead.

·40·

"What's for breakfast?" asked John Hutsell.

"You buying?" Rick asked.

"I was thinking you could treat me. I'm in the office, and I smell bacon. I could be up the stairs lickety-split."

Hadley laughed. "You're in rare form today. Come on up."

John checked his messages while Hadley put butter and orange marmalade on the bar. "Breakfast is served," he announced.

John put away his phone.

"How's Elle—I haven't seen here since I got back from Oregon."

"She's doing better," Rick said. "Dr. Chandra changed her meds and she's taking them as prescribed. Elle and I have decided to leave tomorrow for Eagle Ridge instead of Friday. It's a long trip, so we're going to break it up and spend a night in Nashville."

"Elle will like that," John said. He took a sip of coffee. "As for our next move, I'd like to devote more time to Marens, Kastner, and finding the Warden connection. What do you think of putting Erin on full-time?"

"I think it's a good idea. She's insightful and listens well. I like how she gives people enough rope to hang themselves." Rick chuckled. "You lead them down the path, then step aside so they fall in the hole. Erin follows them down that same path, and when they get to the hole, she pushes them in."

"Yeah, she does," Hutsell agreed. "Are the terms we set up for bringing in operatives still agreeable, or do you want to make any changes?"

"I'm good with the original plan. What about an office?"

"I called Pat, and he'll have a crew out here tomorrow. We have space for two more. Might as well go ahead and get a state-of-the-art conference room set up as well. How's the lab coming?"

"Waiting on a few more pieces of equipment," Hadley said. "We should start interviews for lab techs soon. I'll be concentrating on crime scene investigations. We really need a director for the day-to-day running of the lab. Todd Jayson is retiring from the army in June. He plans to stay in the area, and I doubt we could find a better person."

"He teaches forensic science at Fort Wood, right?"

"Yes. He's a few years older than me, has an advanced degree in forensic science and easy to work with. John, I've known him since middle school. He's solid."

"Go ahead and talk to him."

Hutsell's phone sounded.

"It's Kleeman," he said before answering the call. "Hi Joe. Rick's here. You're on speaker."

"Got a call yesterday from Mary Estes."

"Celia's mother—from your kidnapping case two years ago?"

"Yes. A lady contacted Mary for advice. The lady's daughter was being groomed online like Celia had been. Mary contacted me, and I put the cyber guys on it. One guess whose name came up?"

"Layne Kastner."

"Yep. Found him at the mall yesterday, grooming a young girl in the food court. I walked over, pulled up a chair and sat down. Showed my badge and asked her, 'Does he make you feel special?' She nodded. I said, 'Yeah, he learned from the best" and tossed the department's sex-trafficking brochure on the table. The picture on the cover definitely got her attention."

"What's the picture of?" Hadley asked.

"A girl looking out the back window of a car. 'Help' is printed on her palm," Hutsell said.

"Kastner was on his way out when I told him, 'You know, the postman always rings twice.' Went way over his head," Kleeman said, "but I got a large charge out of it. He's a 'loverboy,' John—a Romeo pimp. I had her call her parents and waited till they got there."

"Thanks, Joe," Hutsell said.

"Will be in touch," Kleeman said. "Sayonara,"

"Sayonara? That's new."

"Yeah, I'm going multicultural. Dating this cute Asian chick. Trying out the lingo."

"Hope she's into degenerates," Hutsell said.

Kleeman laughed. "Guess we'll find out. Anyway, adios—can't leave Hispanics out of the loop. Right partner?"

Luis Mendoza's reply was loud and clear, "Que te jodan."

"Bye, Joe," said Hutsell, a smile on his face. He set his phone on the bar and looked at his partner. "You're driving back to Springfield on Monday, right?"

"Really don't know. Elle and I had talked several weeks ago of taking a few extra days. But we haven't mentioned it since. I'll let you know when we decide."

John Hutsell needed to accomplish a lot before sundown. He headed downstairs, stepped into the front office, and told Gambit's secretary, Mia Guthrie, to hold all calls.

Hutsell called Erin Laveau to schedule a meeting where he would make an offer of full-time employment. He then did a search of Chevy Tahoes. He settled on a medium gray color instead of black, so he'd present as John Q. Public and not as a government official. He checked pricing and availability of his chosen model in Springfield, then sat back in his chair.

Hutsell checked the clock on the wall. Figuring she'd had enough time to drop her kids off at school, he picked up his phone and dialed Dana Schofield Marens in Joplin, Missouri.

The day was just getting started in Portland, Oregon. Multnomah County Deputy Mitch Brennen was getting a cup of coffee when a partial headline from a folded newspaper caught his eye. He picked it up and read, "Marissa Baylor: Home at last."

Brenner looked at a candid shot of Marissa and Mark Baylor on the porch of his home. It was obvious the two were unaware they were being photographed. Halfway through the article, his blood started to boil.

According to an anonymous source within the Multnomah County Sheriff's Department Ms. Baylor was found last month by a private detective operating in the Midwest. The detective verified Ms. Baylor's identity by submitting her DNA to a genetic genealogy site and then arranged for a reunion with her grandfather in Talent, Oregon.

Brenner slapped the paper on a table and said, "Somebody's head is going to roll."

A man in Springfield, Missouri was on his coffee break when his phone rang.

"Did you hear the latest out of Multnomah County?" the caller asked.

"I guess not," the man said. "Enlighten me."

"An unnamed Midwest detective is being credited with finding Marissa Baylor."

"Damn!" said the man.

"The article said Midwest, not Southwest Missouri."

"Don't give me that shit. She got away in Southwest Missouri, and soon after, Burleson and Kastner were in law enforcement's sights. It's him all right. Get the word out—minimum activity in Springfield until further notice."

"Yes sir."

John Hutsell drove to his apartment to drop off his BMW. Rick Hadley pulled in behind him. Hutsell jumped in Hadley's truck, and the two were soon pulling into a car dealership in south Springfield. Hutsell told the salesman what vehicle he wanted and what he was willing to pay, then said, "Make it happen." Paying in cash had its advantages where time and red tape were concerned, and Hutsell was on his way to Joplin in a new Tahoe before noon.

He'd just passed Mt. Vernon on I-44 when he got a call from Mitch Brenner. The deputy laid out the morning's developments.

"We've started an internal investigation," Brenner said, "but you know how these things go. I'm sorry."

"Yeah," said Hutsell. "Thanks for letting me know."

Hutsell thought of the implications of what he'd just learned. The world had no clue which Midwest private detective had found Marissa Baylor, but the people who'd lost her in Springfield had a pretty good idea. His connection to Joe Kleeman would reinforce their suspicions. Hutsell kept his eye on his rearview mirror more often than he normally would for the seventy-mile trip to Joplin. He didn't pull off I-44 till he was sure he was alone.

Hutsell pulled into the driveway of the rented home of Dana Schofield Marens. He walked up the front steps and rang the bell. The door opened.

"Mrs. Marens, I'm John Hutsell."

"I recognize you from media reports."

Marens stood aside for Hutsell to enter, then led him to the living area. She sat in one of two chairs and indicated he take the other.

"Thank you for seeing me," Hutsell said.

"I really don't think I can help you, Mr. Hutsell. But go ahead, have your say. Just keep in mind, the minute you mention my daughters, you will be shown the door."

Hutsell didn't mince words. "I have information your ex-husband is involved in sex-trafficking. I believe he is not only arranging for sessions with victims but is also videotaping them."

"And how does this involve me?" Marens asked.

"I'm not interested in anything prior to February fifteenth, but if Stephen Marens had any such tapes, where would they be?"

"What do you have in mind, Mr. Hutsell?"

"To put him away, and maybe take a few others along with him."

The woman across from Hutsell remained silent.

"He has to be stopped, Mrs. Marens."

"God, I hate that name." She stood and walked over to the French doors and looked out onto the court yard. "Okay Mr. Hutsell, I'll give you what you want—but only after spring break." She turned to face her visitor. "I filed for a name change for my daughters and myself the day after the divorce was finalized. The request was granted last month, and we're moving out of State. I'll call you the morning of March eighteenth, and tell you where he keeps his smut."

Hutsell stood. "Thank you."

He turned to leave.

"Mr. Hutsell."

He did an about face.

"You are to never contact me again. Do you understand?"

"Yes ma'am.

·41·

Elle spent Wednesday night at Rick's in order to get an early start on their trip to Tennessee the next morning. They shared his bed but only in terms of its true purpose—to sleep.

Conversation was light, mostly centered upon the Tennessee Hadleys and plans for the weekend. They stopped for a break at a fast food restaurant in Poplar Bluff, Missouri. Elle exited the restroom and found Rick looking at a collage of buildings on the city's National Register of Historic Places. She walked over and stood next to him. He pointed to a picture of an old movie theatre.

"Pretty neat, huh?" he said.

"Yeah, it is."

"Want to take a drive?"

"Sure."

Rick parked in a small parking lot across the street from the Rodgers Theatre. He walked around to meet Elle, then leaned on the truck next to her.

"Imagine you and I are in that theatre back in the day," he said. "We're sitting in the last row. The lights dim. The score begins. What movie title appears on the screen?"

"Hmmm, 1949 or after . . . ." Rick saw a sly grin cross her face—a hint of the playful Elle he hadn't seen much of during the past two weeks. "Let's go with lust and murder. *Niagara.*"

Rick moved so his body was between Elle and the theatre.

"Good choice," he said. "Monroe sang a song—how'd it go?"

"'Kiss . . . kiss me.'"

Rick placed his hands on Elle's waist, pulled her to him and kissed her.

"You're something else, Hadley."

"You mean like the cat's pajamas?"

"More like a fox in sheep's clothing," she said with a smile. "You started planning this little side trip before I got out of the restroom, didn't you?"

"Sort of. Didn't know what the outcome would be. It all depended on the movie you chose."

"Aren't you lucky I didn't go with *Kiss Me Deadly*."

"We could stream it tonight . . .."

John Hutsell welcomed Erin Laveau into his office Friday morning. He took a chair next to her instead of sitting behind his desk.

"Got anything going on?" he asked.

"Just finished a catfish case."

"A fake veteran on Facebook?"

"Close. Instagram," Laveau said. "Hot pictures of himself. Lifting weights, hugging 'his' dog—the standard profile for these guys.

"'I believe in God and country'?"

"Yeah, he did throw in a few religious memes," Laveau said. "Chit-chatting's not your thing, John. So why am I here?"

Hutsell grinned. "Cases are beginning to back up. Rick and I feel that we need another full-time investigator. You're our first choice."

"Terms, benefits, conditions?"

John reached over and picked up a manila envelope lying his desk. "All in here," he said.

"When do you need to know?"

"The end of next week," he said. "I've identified Mr. Rich and have some information about him coming on the eighteenth. I want to be able to give it my full attention."

Hutsell filled in Laveau about Stephen Marens and the promise made by his ex-wife.

Laveau smiled and said, "Lucky for her you showed up."

"Yeah, I had the same thought," Hutsell said. "It's not a coincidence that she'd arranged for a name change and a move out of State. I definitely think she had plans to start the ball rolling. It's better this way. She and the girls will be in the clear when he goes down."

"Anything new out of St. Louis?"

"Kastner's keeping a low profile since Kleeman identified him as a loverboy. Wouldn't be surprised if they sent him to Kansas City or Tulsa to hawk his wares for the time being."

"So, what's next?"

"As time allows, I'll work on the Sidemore connection till I hear from Mrs. Marens."

"What cases does Gambit have that need attention right away?"

"Personal injury, identity theft, judgement recovery—and Rick's out of town till at least Monday. Maybe longer."

"And Greg?"

"He's giving flight lessons to a husband-and-wife team. He doesn't have the time right now."

Laveau rose to her feet. "I'll give your proposal serious thought, John."

Hutsell stood and said, "If you have any questions, give me a call."

Laveau's phone rang. She pulled it out of her pocket and declined the call.

"Whoa," Hutsell said. "Fancy new phone case."

"It's the Klingon Order of The Bat'leth Badge. Jay got it while you and I were in Oregon. I think he missed me." She smiled. "Hey, this Gambit thing could really work for me. Along with a steady pay-check, if you send me away long enough, I could end up getting a real, full-size bat'leth."

Hutsell smiled. "Always good to have a goal."

After Laveau's departure, Hutsell engaged in several hours of cyber-sleuthing. Finally, his stomach protested enough that he called Garbo's Pizzeria and placed an order to go. He parked in the rear and entered Garbo's through the side door. He walked to the end of the bar and gave his name to the waitress.

"Well, look what the cat dragged in."

Hutsell turned and looked at the woman behind the voice. He smiled. "Good to see you too, Erika."

"Join me for lunch, and tell me what's new in the world of Springfield, Missouri's most eligible bachelor."

Hutsell took the pizza box containing his order and walked over to the table occupied by Erika León. Quid pro quo, he thought and smiled.

"You married yet?" he asked.

"Now why would I want to do a fool thing like that?" She held up her beer glass and signaled the waitress to bring two more.

"Are you at least staying out of trouble?"

"Define trouble."

"Making the powers that be cringe," Hutsell said. "Damn Erika, you were the only student the administration wished *wouldn't* show up for school every day."

"Served 'em right." She laughed. "Like Judge Judy said, 'Don't Pee on My Leg and Tell Me It's Raining'."

"They were on the verge of suspending you, then all of sudden they left you alone. How did you pull that off?"

"The truth?" she asked. "Mr. Azzano,"

"What could he do? They were after him, too."

"But they never forced him out, did they?" Hutsell shook his head no. "Let's put it this way," she continued, "Mr. Azzano knew where the bodies were buried. He shared the information with my parents, who, by the way, raised me to be an independent thinker, and that was the end of it."

"Were you the one behind Ms. Quinn's sudden departure?"

"She flew too close to the flame, John."

Hutsell laughed. "Well then, thanks to you, they brought Mr. Nichols out of retirement, and critical thinking became part of the curriculum again."

Hutsell sat up straight, moved his head from side to side and rolled his shoulders.

"Still bothering you?" she asked of his wrestling injury.

"At times."

León moved behind Hutsell and, in a gentle circular motion, rubbed his left shoulder. He was surprised she remembered which shoulder had been injured.

"You always were good with your hands," he said.

"Still am."

Hutsell smiled.

"Why don't you stop by the shop and get a massage?" she asked. "I'm in the office most of the time now, but I've got several good therapists working for me."

"Maybe I will."

"Oh hell, John. None of this maybe crap." León pulled her cell from her purse and phoned her receptionist. "When is Rylee's earliest opening?" She listened, then said, "Book it for John Hutsell." León disconnected the call. "You're in luck. Rylee had a cancellation and can take you at 9 A.M. Monday. You're your own boss, John. Get your butt up Monday morning and take care of business. And get there fifteen minutes early."

"Yes ma'am."

"I've got to head back," she said. "Don't be a stranger."

Erika looked at the check, then reached for her purse.

"Go on," Hutsell said. "I got it."

A man walked in the door as León was on her way out. They stopped to talk. John placed his credit card in the check tray and noticed Erika had left her key. He picked it up and looked at the items dangling from the metal ring: a margarita-filled cocktail glass, a blue flip-flop, and an engraved metal bar that read, "I am the woman to blame." He smiled and shook his head.

He called out, "Hey Erika."

She turned to see John holding her key. He gave the chain a shake and said, "I don't doubt it." She held out her palm and he tossed it to her. "By the way, how is Jimmy doing these days?" he asked.

"Still living on sponge cake."

·42·

Elle looked at the two queen size beds where normally there would have been one—a reminder of how things had changed in the past two weeks. Rick hung two shirts in the closet, turned and asked, "Dinner on the Honky Tonk Highway, or downstairs, then back up here for a movie?"

"We're in Nashville. No way are we spending the evening in a hotel room. The Highway. Dinner and dancing."

"You want to head out now or wait till later?"

"Let's freshen up; you change your white shirt for a blue one, and we're a go."

He walked up behind her and put his arms around her waist.

"And what will you be wearing Ms. Wyatt?"

"Will the peach Henley do?"

"How many buttons?"

"Two . . . to begin with."

Rick and Elle arrived back in their hotel room just before midnight. Elle slipped out of her shoes and flopped on the bed nearest the window. Rick took one of his white shirts from the closet and carried it over to her. She tossed it on the other bed, took his hand and gently pulled him down.

"Now where were we?" she asked. "One, two . . . .."

Rick put his fingers on the third button of her top. "Three . . . four . . . .."

Rick was the man who had shown Elle the difference between sex and making love. But with the total giving of one's self came vulnerability and fear. They were still together when he slightly moved, and her eyes flew open.

Almost pleadingly, she said, "No. Not yet."

Rick knew what she meant. She'd made the same request their first night together. But it was the look in her eyes this night that made him finally realize why. To her, if his body left hers, it was like he was abandoning her. In so many ways she kept him at arm's length, not allowing him to tell her how he felt. So, Rick did as he always did and showed her instead. He waited until she was asleep before he withdrew.

Elle got on the elevator. She was followed by a man in a tweed jacket and a lady in a 1920s flapper dress. The door closed, and the elevator operator asked, "What floor ma'am?" Before she could answer, tweed jacket said, "I'm Osgood Fielding the third." The woman's shoe slipped off. The man bent down and slipped the shoe back on the woman's foot. "I'm Cinderella the second," said the woman. A tall man in the back spoke to a little boy standing next to him, "A boy's best friend is his mother." The boy looked up at him and said, "I see dead people." Elle's skin began to crawl. The elevator stopped and Elle said, "Open the door." The operator replied, "I'm sorry Dave. I'm afraid I can't do that." Someone started banging on the elevator from the outside. The doors finally opened, but they stuck half way. A man with scraggly hair and beard stuck his head in and said, "Heeeeere's Johnny!"

Elle jumped. The motion of the bed jostled Rick awake.

"Everything okay?" he asked.

"Bad dream," she said.

Elle lay in the dark for several minutes, then asked, "What happens when I stop laughing?"

"What?"

"You said making me laugh is what makes you happy. What happens when I stop laughing? It happened once; it can happen again."

Rick raised up on his elbow. "Elle, think of everything that happened prior to that moment. It was a perfect storm. Your meds have been straightened out for two weeks now. The chances of it happening again are slim. Things *are* better. If they weren't, I wouldn't have done what I did yesterday."

Elle didn't respond. After a few minutes she asked, "Will you play some music?"

"Sure. What do you want to hear?"

"*Trio II.*"

Elle found comfort in the three-part harmony of Parton, Ronstadt and Harris and with Rick's arm around her, fell into a restful sleep.

·43·

Rick and Elle checked into an Eagle Ridge hotel a little before noon on Friday. They had forty minutes till they were due for lunch at the rural home that Rick owned. His parents had moved into the house after the incident in the Hadley family home six months ago. The entire Hadley family would be in attendance, including Alex Cline, Chris' former secretary, now law student and out-in-the-open girlfriend.

After a meal of Muffuletta sandwiches accompanied with veggies and dip, Rick's dad, Mike Hadley, headed downtown to fulfill his duties as Shannon County's sheriff. Those left behind settled in the great room.

"You've made the place your own, Mom," Rick said. "Looks a lot better than when I lived here."

"You moved your measly possessions from an apartment in Knoxville into this house when you bought it, Rick. You never added to them—let alone put any pictures on the wall."

"I know. Just couldn't get into it."

"It's a beautiful home, Rick," Alex said.

"That it is," he agreed, "but I like where I live now. Not as much to take care of."

"I've seen only pictures," Sylvia said, "but it seems pretty inviting—thanks to Elle's help."

"My adoptive mother's an interior designer, something had to rub off," Elle said.

"Still can't believe the place was big enough for a pool table," Sylvia said.

Chris changed the conversation. "Rick, Alex and I need to be heading back to the office. Can I see you for a minute before we go?"

"Sure."

The two Hadley brothers stepped outside. Elle excused herself to the restroom. The living room was empty when she returned. She could see Rick and Chris still talking on the wrap-around porch so she went in search of their mother and Alex. She heard voices as she approached the kitchen.

"Has Chris set up a time?" Sylvia asked.

"No, he feels that should be Rick's call. After all, he might not even agree to the meeting."

"There's no need for this," Sylvia said. "She got her pound of flesh years ago. I wish Chris and his dad had never decided to tell him."

'She,' 'Pound of flesh.' There was only one woman they could be talking about, Elle thought, Meredith Embry. Embrey and Rick had been engaged at one time

"He would have found out anyway," Alex said.

Elle headed back to the living room and bumped into a small hairpin side table on the way. Alex looked around the corner. She turned and faced Sylvia, her expression showing their fear to be real; Elle had overhead their conversation.

"I wonder how much she heard?" Alex asked. "We didn't mention Embrey. Does Elle even know about her?"

"Knowing my son, I'll bet she does. He's not one to keep secrets from those he loves."

"Then the question is, how much does she know?" Alex added. "If she puts two and two together . . .."

"I know," said a concerned Sylvia "One thing we know from experience is that Elle will never let anyone hurt Rick. One of us needs to talk to her, Alex."

"Rick's going to the department to visit with friends. Elle won't have a chance to talk with him till tonight. Let me see how Chris feels is the best way to handle it."

"I'm not worried about her telling Rick. I'm worried about . . .." Sylvia didn't complete the sentence. "Elle and I have had poignant conversations before, I'll explain the—."

Rick entered the room; Elle following behind.

"Mom, I'm going to drive Elle to the hotel on my way downtown. We'll see you tomorrow."

Rick kissed his mom, then turned and walked away. Elle lagged behind and said, "Thank you for lunch Mrs. Hadley."

Chris appeared at the entry and asked Alex if she was ready to head to his law office."

"We need to talk first," she said.

Rick and Elle had plans to meet Chris and Alex for dinner in a brewpub in a neighboring town. They were halfway through a pitcher of beer when Chris and Alex arrived. As soon as their orders were taken, Rick put a smile on his face and leaned back in his chair.

"So, when did you two finally go public?" he asked.

Chris gave him a questioning look.

Rick laughed. "Feign ignorance all you want, but the family's known since last summer."

Chris shook his head. "Mom should put out her shingle: Psychic. But to answer your question, when Alex resigned as my secretary and moved to Knoxville at the beginning of the spring term. You know how people's minds work, Rick. 'Who's using who?' The fact that we're a bi-racial couple would've just added fuel to the fire."

"Do you get much flack?" Rick asked.

"A few looks here and there, but I'm telling you, they ain't seen nothing yet."

"Yeah, I heard," Rick said. He turned to Alex and said, "The Honorable Alexandra Cline."

"First black female Supreme Court Justice. Mark my words," Chris said.

"Gentlemen, can we please change the subject?" Alex asked.

"And modest, too," Rick added.

Alex saw the server approaching with their order. "Thank goodness," she said and moved her napkin to her lap.

Alex and Elle headed to the restroom fifteen minutes before the house band was scheduled to take the stage. Elle quickly determined they were alone and got right to the point.

"What's Embrey trying to do?"

"She's got audio of J. Evan Litle from several years ago planning to take down Sheriff Mike Hadley and his sons. But she won't turn it over to anyone but Rick."

"Is it genuine?" Elle asked.

"Chris heard part of it and believes it is."

"That bitch."

"Well, supposedly she's changed and wants to make amends," Alex said. Elle sneered. "Yeah, I know," Alex continued. "No way in hell could that ever happen. But that's what Chance Middleton said."

"Who's he?"

"He heads up the property room at the sheriff's department. He and Rick have been friends since high school. They hung around together when Rick was a Shannon County deputy."

"How does *he* know she's changed?"

A lady walked in, interrupting their conversation.

"How was the weather on your drive from Missouri?" Alex asked Elle.

"Cold and overcast yesterday. We stayed in Nashville last night."

"Bet that was fun," Alex said.

The lady exited a stall and began washing her hands.

"Yeah, we hit the Honky Tonk Highway," Elle said.

The woman left the bathroom. Alex picked up their previous conversation.

"Middleton and Embrey have been an item since January. He kept it quiet till a few weeks ago because of her history with Rick and Litle."

"She's using him to get to Rick," Elle said.

"I agree."

"She still live in Hays County?"

"Elle, leave it alone. Let Rick handle it."

"That's the same thing your boyfriend told me last fall."

"Well, you do tend to shoot from the hip." Alex immediately regretted her idiom of choice. "Elle, I didn't mean—."

"Why shouldn't I? Bullets are cheap," Elle said. She turned and walked out of the restroom.

Elle exited the bathroom in their hotel room and found Rick sitting on the bed.

"I need to tell you something," he said, and patted the space next to him.

Elle walked over and sat down.

"Meredith Embrey has some evidence concerning J. Evan that she's willing to turn over, but there's a hitch."

"She'll only turn it over to you," Elle said. Rick gave her a questioning look. "I overheard your mom and Alex talking about it. Then Alex filled in some of the details tonight. I think she was worried I'd do something."

He kissed her forehead. "Well, you are protective at times."

"Do you believe she's changed?" Elle asked.

"No. But the evidence could get him disbarred, so I'm going to meet with her." Elle looked down. "I know Elle, but it's best if I do. Litle's used the DA's office to further his personal vendetta, by declining requests for search warrants and refusing to prosecute cases—all moves to make Dad look incompetent."

Not to mention what she did to you. A broken engagement was nothing compared to . . ..

"When?" Elle asked.

"Monday morning, before we leave town," he said.

"What about the short vacation we talked about?" she asked.

"How about a few extra days in a cabin near Fall Creek Falls? It's between here and Nashville—just a different route than we came in on."

Elle smiled. "Define cabin."

Rick knew her well. "Nothing *too* rustic. And by all means, no bear or deer comforters on the bed."

"There's hope for you yet, Hadley."

·44·

The weekend in Eagle Ridge was enjoyable for members of the Hadley family and their guests. All gathered at what was now the Hadley home for family movie night Saturday evening.

"Well birthday girl," Mike Hadley asked his wife, "what one did you finally decide on?"

"The one with the best kiss in movie history."

"Give us another hint please," Chris said.

"Directed by the Master of Suspense."

"*Rear Window*," Rick suggested.

"Nope. Starred Archibald Leach, better known as . . .."

"Cary Grant," said Rick's dad.

Rick tried again. "*North by Northwest*."

His mom shook her head no.

"*Notorious*," Elle said.

"Oh my god, Elle!" Alex said. "You're one of them."

Sunday afternoon, friends and family attended Sylvia Hadley's sixtieth birthday at a favorite Eagle Ridge restaurant. Aunt Cora excused herself early and went to the Hadley home to prepare for a small gathering of the Hadley clan that evening. When Sylvia Hadley arrived home, she found her coffee table covered with several gifts. She saved the biggest one for last. She opened the card and found it signed by both Rick and Elle. It contained a small quilt.

"Elle, did you make this?" Mrs. Hadley asked.

"Rick picked the colors. He even went with me to select the fabric. I pieced it together, but due to time, we had it machine quilted."

"It's beautiful," Sylvia said.

"Elle said you could use it a couple of ways," Rick said, "a throw or maybe a wall hanging."

"Thank you—both of you," Sylvia said.

Chris and Alex were gathering up wrapping paper when Chris found an unopened package.

"Wait a minute, Mom. You forgot one."

Sylvia Hadley opened the box and pulled out a distressed blue barnwood picture frame. A huge smile spread across her face.

"Is there a picture in it?" Chris asked.

"Oh, yes . . . .." Sylvia said. "Elle, this had to come from you."

The clues finally registered. "Elle you didn't?" Rick said.

Elle just smiled as Sylvia Hadley turned the frame around so all could see Rick Hadley wearing a flowered shirt as he took a selphie.

"Elle Wyatt, I swear, one of these days . . . .."

"'One of these days,' what?" Elle said. She leaned over and whispered in his ear, "I'll make it up to you later."

Rick took her hand and escorted her across the room. He opened the left French door, and she stepped outside. He turned back and said, "Excuse us." He smiled and added, "Don't wait up."

He joined her on the porch. "You'll make it up to me now," he said.

"Hadley, are you taking control?"

"Yes, Wyatt, I am."

He lifted her up on the railing and moved his body between her legs.

"You see that shed over there?" he said.

She nodded.

"It's not for storage."

"It's not?"

"No."

"What's it for then?"

"It's a sauna, and you and I are about to get real sweaty."

"One can always hope," she said.

"I'll show you hope."

"Please do."

"Elle Wyatt?"

"Yes."

"Shut up."

·45·

Monday morning, Elle sat in a bakery/café across the street from Chris Hadley's law firm, and waited on Rick. He finally emerged from the office at 9:15 A.M.

"How'd it go?" she asked.

"We got what we needed."

"Did she try to touch you?"

"She didn't get a chance to. Why?"

"I would have."

"What do you mean?"

"There was a time when I was—."

Rick interrupted, his demeaner curt. "I'm not interested in who you used to be Elle. You know that." He let out a deep breath. "I'm sorry; I'm going to the restroom, then get some coffee for the road."

Elle glanced out the window and saw Meredith Embrey crossing the street. She was headed toward the restaurant. The woman wasn't going to give up, so Elle pulled up a photo she'd sent to herself in an email and met Embrey on the sidewalk.

"You want to play?" Elle asked.

"I'm sure I don't know what you mean?"

"What did you do before you became a lawyer?"

"I modeled."

"Don't know if I'd call it that." Elle showed Embrey a still from a porn video. "Forget you ever knew him."

Embrey turned and walked away. Elle looked across the street and saw Alex Cline in the law office window. She waved, then went inside the café. She was ordering Rick's coffee when he stepped up beside her. They walked to the coffee urns where she filled his cup and said, "Fall Creek Falls, right?"

"Yep. You, me, and a place with a view."

212

"Is there a sauna?"

Rick smiled. "Who's making who laugh now?"

They were halfway to their destination when Elle said, "Pull into that abandoned farm house up ahead?"

"Why?"

"For some unlawful carnal knowledge."

"You've got one too many words in there, Wyatt."

"Okay. *F*or *U*nlawful *C*arnal *K*nowledge then — if that makes you happy."

It made him very happy.

John Hutsell handed his credit card to Erika León's receptionist.

"Standing a little taller there, Hutsell," León said as she walked up behind him.

"Finally have some relief."

"Did you make another appointment?"

"Next week."

"Good." León smiled. "You never know when you're going to need full range mobility, John."

"True." He smiled back.

"See you at Democrat Days."

John Hutsell nodded and headed out the door. The three women in the office watched as he walked to his vehicle.

"Is he dating anyone?" the receptionist asked her employer. León laughed. "John Hutsell doesn't date. He barely has relationships."

"How long have you known him?" Rylee asked.

"Since kindergarten."

"How *well* do you know him?"

"Hmm . . . let's just say the summer of 2005 was one of the hottest on record."

Across town, Free Stylin' Day at Rita's Rose was off to a good start. Heather Heinrichs from Mojo Pie Salon welcomed her third client of the morning—a young woman with long, dark hair.

"Are you just wanting a trim?" Heather asked.

A man accompanying the woman spoke up. "We were watching one of those beach movies last night—Beach Blanket Bingo, I think. Anyway, she liked the style of the main character. Here's a picture." He held up his cell phone.

"A medium length bouffant swept up on the right," Heather said. She looked at the young woman. "Is that what you want?" The woman nodded yes. "Okay, follow me, and we'll get started."

Heinrichs tried to engage the woman in conversation as she washed her hair, but all she got for her efforts were nods of yes or no with occasional shrugs thrown in. The stylist finally understood, when she caught a glimpse of a tattoo just below the woman's neck.

"Excuse me for a minute, I need to get my detangling comb."

Heinrichs caught Jenise Alexander in the hall and said, "I need to see you now."

"I think we've got a sex-trafficking victim."

"Signs?"

"She doesn't talk—a man answers questions for her. She's very submissive, avoids eye contact. And she's got a tattoo on her upper chest, chains surrounding the figure eight. The number eight is sexting for oral sex."

"Where is the man who brought her?"

"Sitting in the lobby."

"Take me to her."

Rick Hadley and Elle Wyatt were sitting on a porch swing when Elle received a call from Jenise Alexander.

"Elle, I need Rick's number. We've got a sex-trafficking victim at the clinic. She's twenty years old and willing to accept help, if it's not from law enforcement. Could Rick arrange something?"

"Rick is sitting next to me. I'll put you on speaker."

Alexander explained the situation and repeated the request for Hadley's help.

"Jenise, Elle and I are in Tennessee. But I'm sure John will help. Let me call him. Does he have your number?"

Alexander went silent.

Elle took over. "Jenise?"

"I don't know if he has it or not."

"We'll call him and make sure he's got it," Rick said. "I'm sure he'll call you immediately."

Alexander disconnected the call.

"Her number's the same as it was when she and John were dating," Elle said. "It was still in my contact list, but who knows if it's still in his."

Rick called John and related the substance of Alexander's call.

"Text me the number," was all John said.

The man who had accompanied the young woman into Rita's Rose came looking for her. He found Heinrichs styling a boy's hair and asked, "Where's my daughter?"

"She had a sore throat so she's in with the doctor."

"Okay, thanks," said the man. He headed back to the lobby but didn't stop till he was in the parking lot. He jumped in the passenger seat of a Hyundai Sonata.

"Let's get out of here," he told the driver.

"What a—?"

"Drive! Now!"

The driver had driven five blocks north when his passenger said, "Pull over in the parking lot of that bank." He placed a call and said, "Got a problem."

"What's going on?"

"Not sure how, but they made her, so we got out as quick as we could. She's not talking yet, or Kastner and I would be making our one phone call right now."

"Can anyone identify you or Kastner?"

"Just me. Layne stayed in the car."

"Okay. I'll be there in five minutes to pick up Layne. You get on the horn and set things in motion. If the girl decides to talk and they move on the place in Rogersville . . .."

"I know."

215

The caller signed off and dialed a second number. Two minutes later Layne Kastner was in the passenger seat of a white pick-up. The driver parked in a lot across from Rita's Rose.

"Pay attention boy," the driver said. "Tell me what you see."

"Two lanes leading to the clinic. One in front and another down the alley behind."

"Good. Lepke will be watching the back. You're watching the front. What are you looking for?"

"Most people going in and out of the clinic will be mothers with kids, or poor and/or homeless adults," he said. "Anyone not fitting those descriptions could be there for her."

"Yep. She's got to come out. The person who shows up to get her will determine our next move."

Kastner and his accomplice watched a gray SUV drive into the alley.

"It's Hutsell," Lepke said on speaker.

"Damn," the driver said. "That's two he's taken from us."

"So, how do we stop him?" Kastner asked.

"What do you suggest?" the driver said.

"He could disappear."

"And if he did, what would happen?"

"They'd look for him, but never find him."

"You've got a lot to learn kid," Lepke said over the speaker. "Don't mess with someone with his connections."

The driver took over the conversation. "Hutsell goes missing. The question is asked, 'What was he working on when he disappeared?' Your name will come up, so who will they come after? Then, where do you think you'll end up? It won't be the same dumpster, but it will be one just like it. You've got promise kid. I'd hate to lose you."

"So we do nothing?" Kastner asked.

"No, we pick up and move, then lay low. You've got to know when to cut your losses, and, as they say, 'live to fight another day.'"

"I still don't get it," Kastner said. "If Hutsell goes missing, why can't I go work somewhere else till things die down?"

"Because with that fucker, things will never die down," the driver said. Look at the places he's worked, his friends and associates: Greene County Sheriff's Department, Columbia PD, St.

Louis PD, the Highway Patrol. His mother's a state senator, and his best friend was Secret Service—and I'm warning you here and now, that friend figures in from over thirty years ago. And all this because Burleson wanted a little extra pocket money. Wish I could kill that son-of-a-bitch all over again."

"I'm heading out," Lepke said. "Warden is going to be pissed."

"We followed procedure, that's in our favor, but yeah I'm not looking forward to that conversation."

John Hutsell drove behind Rita's Rose and entered the building through Kyle Jeffries' office.

"Kyle," he said by way of a greeting.

"John," followed Jeffries.

Jenise Alexander was standing by Jeffries desk. "She's had a shower and a change of clothes, but she's still not talking. If you're ready, I'll get her."

"Did anyone get a look at the vehicle she arrived in?"

"No, and the man with her disappeared as soon as he learned she was with the doctor," Alexander said.

"We do have video, John," Jeffries said.

"I'd appreciate it if you'd send me a copy."

"Policy won't allow that, but I can arrange for you to view it. Just let me know when."

There was a knock on Jeffries back door.

"That will be Erin Laveau," Hutsell said.

Jeffries opened the door, and Laveau walked in.

Introductions were made, and Alexander left the room. She soon returned with a young woman and said, "This is Dani."

"Hello Dani, "I'm John Hutsell. This is my associate, Erin Laveau. We're going to take you to a woman's shelter in Joplin, if that's okay with you."

Dani nodded her approval.

Hutsell opened the door, and the three walked out. "Erin, I'll meet you at Gambit in a few minutes." Laveau nodded.

Hutsell watched till both women were in Laveau's vehicle, then turned and asked, "Where are the clothes Dani was wearing when she arrived? I'd like Rick to take a look at them."

"I'll get them," Jenise said.

Jeffries phone rang. Hutsell shut the door to afford the director privacy while he waited outside for Jenise. Alexander soon appeared and handed him a plastic bag.

"Thanks," Hutsell said.

Alexander's only response was a nod. She turned and walked back inside. Jeffries ended his call and watched Hutsell from a window.

"There's something there, Jenise," Jeffries said.

"What do you mean?"

"He's got a 'tell'." Jenise gave a questioning look. "He paused and looked down for a moment before he reached for the car door."

"Guilt?"

"Don't know that John feels guilt. He's got a reason for everything he does, so in his mind he's justified.

"What is it then?"

"Regret, maybe. But then he remembers his reasons, puts it out of his head, and moves on." He changed the subject. "Are you still planning to help man the table for Democrat Days?"

"Yes. It's always been a great venue for signing up volunteers."

Brett Gilson stuck her head in the door. "Kyle, you're needed out front."

"On my way."

Jenise watched him walk toward the lobby.

"You'll never find a better man," Gilson said.

"I know."

"So what's the problem?"

"An old wound festered."

"You're a nurse. Treat it before it goes septic."

Erin Laveau officially joined Gambit's investigative team on Wednesday, March thirteenth. On the following Friday, a small get-together was held in a private room at a tavern in south Springfield. After dinner, the investigators in the group engaged in shop-talk, so Elle Wyatt and Chelle Thomas peeled away for a conversation of their own.

"I'm glad you decided to dig a little deeper into Meredith Embrey's background," Elle said. "The info came in handy."

"Her attempt to engage Rick at the Hays County Sherriff's Department the day you two left Tennessee last fall just didn't sit right. So what did she do this time?"

"She'd been working on the plan for months, timing it for the weekend of his mom's sixtieth birthday. And when it didn't go the way she wanted, she made a second attempt to draw him back."

"How?"

"She followed Rick to a café. He was in the restroom, so I met her at the door. A few words were exchanged. She feigned ignorance. I showed her the photo. She left."

"Well played, Elle."

"I was as subtle as you can be with a photo of a porn star."

"Fine use of juxtaposition, Elle," Chelle said. "So how did the other photo go over?"

Elle smiled. "Jettisoned him off the couch. You know his approach with me has always been slow, building to a climax. Like he's testing the water before moving on to the next step?"

Chelle smiled. "You mean he's a considerate lover?"

"Yeah, he is pretty cute with it—and he was cute this time too, only he told me what he wanted instead of making it about me."

Chelle was smiling from ear to ear when Greg walked up and said it was time to go.

"Later," she told Elle.

Elle walked over to Rick and asked for his keys. He stepped away from the group.

"Please put the seat back in its original position."

"And if I don't?"

"Don't ask the question unless you really want to know the answer."

"You're playing with fire, Hadley."

"I have been for a long time now," he said. He put one arm around her waist, pulled her close and whispered, "And I like it."

"Hey, Rick," John called.

"Be right there." Rick slipped his key into Elle's hip pocket. "Text me."

Rick returned to the group.

"Anything new on Dani's clothes?"

"Nothing useful," Rick said. "What are your thoughts, John? Do you think she's part of the same network Amber was in?"

"Jay, you're more familiar with sex-trafficking in Missouri as a whole, what do you think?"

"I think the key here is both Amber and Dani seemed to be 'special' orders. The man who contracted for Amber wanted a fourteen-year-old girl in a school uniform. The one who ordered Dani was looking for Annette Funicello. I think these guys probably have an internet site where they sell men's sexual fantasies. Problem is, these sites are in operation only for a short time, then shut down and resurface on a different site later."

"Maybe the Southwest Missouri Cyber Crimes Task Force out of Joplin could offer some insight," Laveau said.

"Good point, Erin," John said.

"Even though the SMCCTF concentrates on internet sex crimes involving children, its members collaborate with the FBI, Homeland Security, and U.S. Marshals. There's a wealth of information and contacts at their fingertips," Jay added.

"Okay, let's put next week in order," Hutsell said. "I'll talk with Dana Marens on Monday, then delve into Sidemore's background. Erin, you work the personal injury case. And Rick, you talk to Lieutenant Colonel Jayson—make a trip to Fort Wood if you need to."

"What about Stephen Marens?" Rick asked. "I'm betting his pipeline has dried up for the time being, with the activity brought about by the loss of Amber and Dani. He won't be able to stop. He'll go somewhere else. Probably local."

"Guess we could all take turns doing surveillance on him. Concentrate on his after-work activities."

"Could," Rick said, "but he wanted Amber on a Friday night, no matter the icy roads. Chances are, that's his night of choice."

Rick's cell signaled a text. "I'm in your bed. Come home."

John said, "I'll pose the question to his ex-wife Monday. Anything else?"

"Not that I can think of," Rick said, and added as Laveau and Randall shook their heads no, "John, I need a ride home."

"Let's go then. See you Monday, Erin. Night, Jay."

Once inside Gambit's business vehicle, Rick pulled out his cell and typed a message, "On my way."

Hutsell put the SUV in gear and said, "You know, you two are on the verge of sickening."

"And how sweet it is."

·47·

Dana Schofield Marens called John Hutsell at 10:00 A.M. Monday. Hutsell learned that Stephen Marens had in his den a safe that he thought his wife ignorant of. He'd installed it in March 2015, when Mrs. Marens and their daughters had been out of State visiting her parents. Mrs. Marens learned about the safe from workers when she'd added a sunroom off the master bedroom that summer. Two years later, she became suspicious that her husband was engaged in illegal activities when his pornography searches started involving the word 'teen.' Hutsell surmised there was also a change in her eldest daughter as it would have been during that time that the daughter would have started developing into a woman.

"Was there any particular day of the week he engaged in these activities?"

"In February 2017, my father passed away, and I went to Virginia to stay with my mom for a month. When I returned home, he was very attentive and suggested I take more time for myself— girl's night out, movies with friends. He said Fridays were mine to do with as I wanted."

"Have you seen the contents of the safe?"

"My lawyer has. I did not want to see any of it."

"Where are those items now?"

"Mr. Hutsell, you said you were not interested in anything prior to February fifteenth. I know I brought up the date the safe was installed, but anything before last month is off limits."

"I understand."

"And if you contact me again, it will be considered harassment."

"Yes, ma'am."

By Wednesday, Hutsell had learned that Brenda Sidemore and her deceased husband had owned a small trucking company in St. Louis. They had local customers, but contracted out to larger transportation companies on an as-need basis. The company had since been sold. Mrs. Sidemore was now in retirement—at least from the trucking business. Hutsell confirmed that Burleson had been an employee of the company. It would take further digging to see if the man named Warden, mentioned by Zimbeck in Oregon, had worked for Sidemore Transportation.

Friday night was the beginning of Democrat Days, an important night for Hutsell's mother. The entire Gambit staff and their friends would be in attendance, so Hutsell contacted Harlan Price to see if the retired Greene County deputy would like a surveillance job. Price agreed.

The event got off to a start with dinner, live music and a silent auction at 5:00 P.M. in a hotel convention center in north Springfield. Rita's Rose was one of the charities that had set up tables in adjoining rooms.

Erika León was on her way to the restroom when she witnessed a near collision between Jenise Alexander and John Hutsell at the entrance to the restrooms. The tension between the two was palpable and prompted León to seek out Hutsell a few minutes later. She found him on a circular upholstered sofa in the lobby. She walked over and sat down beside him.

"So, when did you know?"

"Know what?"

"Was it a conscious decision, or was it a nagging feeling you had when friends started pairing off in high school?"

John gave a knowing 'huff.' "Both, but the term 'girlfriend' didn't appeal to me in high school."

"Well there were several who wanted to be yours. Some actually campaigned for the title."

"What about you?"

"I couldn't understand how some girls fell into the trap of defining themselves as somebody's girlfriend."

"You sound like Elle."

"I had things I wanted to do: goals, an education, a career. A full-time relationship didn't figure in. And if I 'settled down' there would be expectations of a family, and frankly, I never wanted to be more than anyone's Aunt Erika." She paused. "But there was a time, John, when you took a different route—around the time of the Cross Timbers Murder Case."

"That was the conscious decision part," John said. "I couldn't be two places at once. and realized then I'd never be in the one people most expected me to be."

León's date appeared across the room, held up his hand, and tapped his watch.

"What about him?" John asked.

"He's got his talents," she said. John laughed. "Speaking of which, see you around, as the best part of my evening is about to begin."

León stood, placed her palms on her ample hips and shimmied her dress back in place. She turned her head and looked at a smiling John Hutsell. "Rubenesque," she said.

"Yeah, I know. I first noticed the resemblance in our art history class."

At 8:35 P.M., Harlan Price called John Hutsell.

"Marens just picked up a young girl at a truck stop in north Springfield."

"What direction is he headed?"

"West on I-44."

"I'll make the call."

Twenty minutes later, working on an anonymous tip, a Greene County deputy pulled over Marens' Lexus as it crossed Republic Road into Battlefield. Marens was fiddling with his pants when Deputy Overton walked up to the window.

"Place your hands on the wheel," Deputy Overton said. Marens did as he was told. Now, please step out of the car."

A second Greene County Sheriff's vehicle, lights flashing, pulled up behind Overton's cruiser.

"Pull up your shirt," Overton said as Deputy Loniker made his way to the passenger side of the Lexus.

Marens pants were partially unzipped.

"No ID on the girl," Loniker reported.

He escorted the girl to his vehicle, then searched runaway and missing children bulletins on his computer.

"Are you Savannah Trager?" No answer. "Our only goal is to make sure you are safe, then get you home."

"If you really want me safe," the girl said, "don't take me home."

Loniker stepped out of his vehicle and told Overton, "She's a fifteen-year-old runaway from Walnut Grove." Loniker got back in his cruiser and picked up his mic. "The first part of the anonymous call checks out. Start the ball rolling on a search warrant for child pornography at Marens' residence. And get in touch with Child Protective Services."

Overton cuffed Marens. "Looks like we've got kidnapping and endangering the welfare of a minor for starters." He read Marens his rights.

The charges of kidnapping and the sexual exploitation of a child filed against Stephen Marens on Friday, March twenty-second, didn't hold as Savannah Trager had willingly entered Marens vehicle. Acting on a tip, a search warrant had been issued Saturday whereby investigators found evidence that resulted in a charge of possession of child pornography on Monday, March twenty-fifth. Southwest Missouri learned about Liberty Tours CEO on the evening news Monday night.

John Hutsell sent a text to Mark Baylor.

"I have some information for Amber. Please ask her if would be okay for me to send it to her in a personal text or email?"

The reply came a few minutes later. "She'll contact you,"

Hutsell soon received a message from Amber. "What do you have?"

Hutsell sent the news report link then typed, "Two down, counting Burleson."

"So they have the video of me?"

"Yes, but they don't have a name. It's my understanding there is enough for a conviction without its use."

"You kept your word. Thank you."

·48·

John Hutsell had been in his new home for five days when he had the gang over for a cookout. The group included Elle Wyatt, Rick Hadley, Greg Baptiste, and Chelle Thomas. They gathered in the main living area after dinner.

"How's the remodeling coming along?" Chelle asked.

"Just getting started. Ordered new wallpaper for the dining room, and these drapes have got to go."

"Yeah, the 'garden flowers' motif doesn't really fit your 'playboy' image," Greg joked.

John smiled. "I'm more what you'd call a loner. Besides I work a lot more than I play."

"Who are you *playing* with these days, John?" Elle asked. Laughter filled the room.

"You're about to drop a stitch, cousin."

Elle smiled. "Are you telling me to mind my own business?"

Greg jumped back in. "You don't like the playboy description, we can always go back to 'Hut-one Hut-two Hutsell.'"

"It's a good thing we've been friends since kindergarten, Baptiste," John said.

"Or . . .?" Greg said.

"Just keep it up. I *am* the best man at your upcoming wedding . . .."

"John Hutsell, you will rue the day you tamper with my wedding," Chelle warned.

"Don't you love the way she says 'my' wedding, instead of 'our' wedding?" Greg said.

"Don't mess with it, John" Rick said. "We've gone from a Bahama Beach to New Orleans Jazz wedding, which means I don't have to wear a flowered shirt."

"White or blue still the only colors in your closet, Rick?" Chelle teased.

Elle and Chelle exchanged glances.

"They still make up his 'signature' wardrobe," Elle said. She put up her hands as if framing a camera shot. "What do you think Chelle? Could he carry off a dusty green?"

"I think you'd be the only one wearing it, if one magically appeared."

"I look good in dusty green," Elle said.

"You look good in anything," Rick said.

"Oh, brother," John said.

A song playing in the background caught Greg's attention. He started laughing.

"What's so funny?" John asked.

"Too bad that song wasn't around when Angie was chasing you in high school," Greg said. "Listen to the chorus."

The singer's words were strong and clear. "I don't need a mother, I don't need another lover, I don't need another life-long friend."

Elle nudged Chelle and whispered, "It gets even better."

"I need a woman that'll listen when I tell her what's going down. I need a woman that won't follow me all over town. I need a girl that knows that a man's got to have his space."

"I handled the situation just fine," John said. "After our 'talk,' Angie left me alone."

"You may think your words did the trick, John, but I think the real reason Angie quit dogging you had more to do with Elle standing behind you giving her the eye."

John looked at his cousin. "So that's why Angie's mother hates you?"

Elle shrugged her shoulders and smiled.

"Hut-one, Hut-two," Greg said and turned his attention back to the music." This guy's good. Who is he?"

"Will Tucker. Two of his CDs appeared in my stocking last Christmas."

"Autographed CDs," Elle added with a smile. "Cal and I caught him in Memphis last year at BB King's place. That's him on lead guitar. I knew John would appreciate his music."

Forty minutes after his guests had departed, John Hutsell was on his way to the minibar for a cold beer when his doorbell rang. Hutsell opened the door and saw Carine Velardi holding a gift basket.

"Thought you could use a few items for entertaining," she said.

"Come in and we'll put them to use."

Hutsell carried the basket to the minibar and removed a bottle of wine from its contents as Velardi took off her jacket. He filled two wine glasses and looked up to see Velardi walking toward him. Her normal business attire had been replaced with tight-fitting jeans and a white shirt with vertical see-through lace inserts. Only one button, midway down, was in use. She took the offered glass of wine.

"Is the new carpet in the master bedroom to your liking?" she asked.

"Yes. Would you like to see it?"

"Very much."

The next morning, Elle Wyatt had an early breakfast with Jean and Pat. As Elle was carrying dirty dishes to the sink, Jean asked if she would drop off samples of drapery fabric to John on the way to her doctor's appointment. Elle agreed as John's new home was several blocks from the mid-town medical complex that housed her doctor's office.

Elle entered Portland Avenue from the west. She was three houses away, when she saw a woman emerge from her cousin's front door. She pulled to the side of the road and waited for the woman to get in her SUV and back out. She watched as the woman drove past.

Well, I'll be damned.

Elle rang John's doorbell a few minutes later. Hutsell answered wearing navy sleep bottoms and a gray tee-shirt.

"Thought you'd already signed the final papers on the house?" Elle said with a smile on her face.

"I did over a week ago."

"Must have been a social call then."

"Would you like a cup of coffee, Elle?" Hutsell asked, dismissing his cousin's inquires as he turned toward the kitchen.

"Sure."

John filled a cup for his cousin, then leaned against the counter.

"Smart move," Elle said. "An older woman knows what she likes in the bedroom and doesn't want to have your babies."

"Don't you have some place to be?"

"I've got a few minutes, yet."

"Then make yourself comfortable. I'm going to take a shower."

Elle carried her cup to the enclosed lanai and noticed a gift basket on the bar. She walked over and picked up a hand-written note.

"It was truly a pleasure working with you. Wishing you many years of happiness in your new home. Carine."

"Well, it's definitely off to a good start," Elle thought. "You've been all work and no play for a long time, John Hutsell. You need a little diversion, and if Carine Velardi can provide that, then good for you."

·49·

Silver Dollar City was on Rick and Elle's schedule the morning of April thirteenth. Rick was making good on his word to entertain Cooper and Caroline Jayson while their parents enjoyed a few days alone. Elle hadn't been comfortable with the idea of being in attendance but had been persuaded from the position that two sets of eyes was preferable to one in a large theme park. They met the Jaysons for breakfast that morning at Gailey's Breakfast Café in downtown Springfield before the day got into full swing.

Caroline was mesmerized by the glass blowers and bakers at Sullivan's Mill. She used her own money to purchase a glass swan for her mother and wanted to buy a loaf of fresh bread for her father. Elle was reminded of the term her Grandpa Stafford used for the park, "Steal Your Dollar City."

"How much money do I have left, Uncle Rick?"

"Why don't you let me get it," Rick said as he pulled out his wallet.

Elle was apprehensive about the rest of the weekend, as she wasn't what you could call a 'kid person,' but she saw an opportunity and interrupted the conversation.

"Caroline, have you ever made bread?"

"No. Cookies and cupcakes only."

"Do you know how to braid hair?" Elle asked.

"Yes."

"Would you like to make your dad bread instead of buying it? We could make it look like a braid?"

"You know how?"

"Yes. We can do it tomorrow."

Caroline hugged Elle and said, "Oh thank you, Miss Wyatt." She ran over to her brother and said, "I'm going to make bread just like that man over there."

230

Rick leaned in and whispered in Elle's ear, "And you said you weren't good with kids."

Elle didn't respond. She felt she might be able to stumble through a couple of days with kids, but any more than that would be a crap shoot.

Caroline fell asleep on the way back to Springfield, while Cooper and Rick talked basketball, pool and video games. Elle kept to herself.

Rick stopped at a grocery store in Ozark for flour and yeast, then drove through Kentucky Fried Chicken for a sixteen-piece bucket meal. Rick and Cooper played pool for most of the evening, while Elle and Caroline colored. At 10:30, Rick said it was time for bed. He set up the two twin mattresses from the safe house on the floor in his bedroom. Once the kids were settled, he returned to the front room and sat on the sofa next to Elle.

"They had fun today," he said. "Thanks for going with us."

Elle didn't respond.

"You okay?" he asked.

"Yeah, I'm fine."

"You want to watch a movie?"

"I don't know," Elle said. They sat in silence for several seconds before Elle said, "How about the Best of Little Willie John?"

Rick keyed up the CD, and after the first three lines of the first song, said, "You know that song took on a whole new meaning for me in 2010."

"How so?"

"Little Willie John is trying to tell a woman how much he loves her, right?"

"Yeah."

"To get to her, he'd 'fight lions with a switch' and says, 'If I don't love you baby, grits ain't groceries, eggs ain't poultry, and Mona Lisa was a man."

Elle laughed, "Oh, I know where you're going? You're talking about the theory that the Mona Lisa was a self-portrait."

"Yeah, and if it is, then Mona Lisa *was* a man."

"You've got too much time on your hands, Hadley."

"No, it's just that I'm a critical thinker." *And it got you smiling again.*

Elle leaned into Rick and got comfortable. She closed her eyes and said, "Hush. I want to listen to the blues."

Several hours later, Rick slipped out from under her. She stirred. "Time for you to go to bed, too?" he said.

"I'm fine right here."

"You'll have a sore neck in the morning."

"I don't care."

"You're going one way or the other." He gently picked her up.

"Rick, I want to stay out here."

"Okay." He laid her on the couch and covered her with a throw. "I'll see you in the morning."

Rick was aware baking bread was a time-consuming undertaking but it did allow for a few breaks in order for the yeast to do its job. So, he came up with a plan to alleviate the pressure Elle had put on herself to 'perform' where Cooper and Caroline were concerned. After all ingredients were mixed and Elle had shown Caroline how to knead the dough, he suggested a short outing to the Springfield Conservation Nature Center.

As they neared the building that housed the visitor's center, Cooper hurried ahead and opened the door for the other three. He continued to hold it open for an elderly couple and a young boy also walking toward the center.

They viewed various exhibits and came upon the grandparents and grandchild again in the children's reading area. The little boy was carrying a book to his grandfather when he fell on his bottom, dropping the book. Caroline picked it up, waited till the boy was back on his feet, then handed it to him.

"You sure have a nice family," the grandmother said to Rick and Elle. "You don't see many young'uns these days that go out of their way to help others."

Neither Rick nor Elle set her straight. After walking the short Savanna Ridge Trail, the foursome headed back to Rick's loft.

"Ready to punch it down?" Elle asked Caroline once they were inside.

"How do I do that?"

"Make a fist and punch down into the dough."

Caroline smiled and did as instructed.

"Now we divide the dough into three parts and use our hands to make each part look like a rope." When the task was completed, Elle demonstrated how to braid the stands together and let Caroline take over.

"Now do we put it in the oven?" Caroline asked.

"No, the dough has to rise again."

"Okay." Caroline jumped down off the kitchen stool. "Uncle Rick, can I watch one of the movies I have in my back pack?"

"After lunch."

"Okay."

Rick and Elle laid out the makings for deli sandwiches along with vegetables and dip. After she'd eaten, Caroline asked, "Now?"

"Yes," Rick said. "Come on and hop onto my big bed and pick one out."

With Caroline watching a movie in Rick's bedroom and Cooper playing video games with a friend on the living room TV, Rick refilled Elle's coffee cup, poured himself one, then sat down by her at the bar.

"Did you two make enough bread for two loaves?" he asked.

"Yes. One for us to have with dinner tonight, and one for Caroline to give to her father." Elle took a few sips, then said, "You're a natural, you know?"

Figuring she was going for a laugh, he smiled and said, "Natural what? And careful, children are present."

"A natural when it comes to kids."

He swiveled his chair, put his arm on the one Elle occupied, leaned in and whispered, "Elle—."

"I feel out of place, Rick."

"Do you want to leave?"

"In a way, yes."

"I can make sure the bread gets in and out of the oven on time," he said.

"You sure?"

"Yes. Will you be back for dinner?"

"I'll try."

Elle collected her purse. He followed her out the door. Standing on the landing, he put his arms around her. She didn't return the hug, an indication she probably wouldn't be back, so Rick Hadley held her till she pulled away.

The Jaysons returned to Springfield Monday morning at 9:45 A.M. Rick took the family on a tour of the facility that was to become the Leland C. Nelson Crime Laboratory. For lunch, he suggested Casper's, a historic Springfield diner housed in a Quonset hut in central Springfield. After consuming classic hamburgers and fries akin to those his grandmother Hadley had made, the Jaysons headed to the parking lot while Rick paid the bill. He stepped outside and found that Natalie Jayson had lagged behind her husband and kids.

"I'm sorry Elle couldn't join us today," she said.

"Natalie, from your own experience, you will understand how important this time is for her. The signs are there. She's on the verge of a breakthrough. Problem is, I don't know which way she'll go before or after it happens."

"What do you mean?"

"She has to figure out where I fit in. She'll either embrace what we have, or she'll turn me away. But whatever the outcome, it has to take place."

"She is in love with you, Rick. It showed in her eyes Saturday morning."

"My mom thinks the same thing. But I know if she admits that right now, she'll leave."

"I understand. She thinks she'll hold you back in some unfounded way or another," Natalie said. "Tell me this, does she realize she's leaning on you?"

"She does. And though supporting and caring for the one you love is important in a relationship, she doesn't see it that way. To her, leaning on me, no matter what the reason, is a sign of weakness." Rick shifted his weight, so he was standing solidly on both feet. "Elle doesn't trust herself. But she does trust me. She's let me see a side of her no one else has seen. Elle's never leaned emotionally on anyone. The fact that she is now is a step in the right direction, however bittersweet the outcome may be."

"Are you prepared for the possibility she might leave?"

"Here's how I'm looking at it. She's got a few more hurdles. I have faith she'll cross them."

"That doesn't answer my question?"

"What would Todd's answer be if asked the same thing?"

"Enough said."

Rick walked Natalie across the parking lot, then watched as the Jaysons drove off. He got in his truck, and even though he wanted to drive to the Wyatt Estate, he set his course for Gambit Investigations.

·50·

Jenise Alexander was leaving work on Wednesday, April seventeenth, when co-worker, Chad Kerwin caught up with her.

"Jenise, you got a minute?"

"Sure. What's up?"

Kerwin, his demeaner grave, looked around at the numerous hospital employees making their way to the parking lot. He nodded in the opposite direction and said, "Over there."

"Why all the secrecy? You organizing a surprise party or something?" she joked.

Kerwin remained deadly serious.

"Jenise, I saw a picture of you online last night that I'm pretty sure you have no idea is out there."

"What do you mean?"

"It was a picture of you and a man having sex."

"You must be mistaken."

"I wish I was. The picture was on an adult sex site. It was part of a profile for 'Nurse Jenise' in southwest Missouri. How many Jenises do you know in southwest Missouri who are nurses?"

"Oh my god." Jenise's knees weakened forcing her to lean into Kerwin for support.

"Do you know who might have set up the profile?" he asked.

"I think so," she said. "How long was my hair?"

"It was like you wore it maybe . . . four or five years ago."

"I was a mess back then."

Kerwin saw the panic in Alexander's eyes and tried to make her feel better by saying, "It just went up last night, so there's probably not a lot of people who've seen it yet."

"I've got to go," Alexander said. She turned and ran to her car.

236

On Friday, Jenise Alexander texted Elle Wyatt on her lunch break, "I need to talk to you as soon as possible. Can we meet after I get off work?"

"Sure, where?"

"Your place. About 3:45."

"See you then."

Alexander pulled into Elle's circle drive at 3:50 P.M. She watched through the gallery of windows as Elle made her way to the front door. The door opened, and Alexander walked in.

"Would you like some coffee?" Elle asked.

"You got anything stronger?"

"Beer?" Jenise shook her head. "Rum and Coke?"

"Yes."

Elle fixed Alexander's drink and handed it to her across the bar. Jenise took a few drinks, then stared at the half-empty glass. She finally looked up at Elle.

"When you're ready," Elle said.

Jenise finished the drink and held her glass out for another. Elle filled the glass a second time. Several moments later, Jenise began to speak.

"You remember when John left Springfield in October 2013?"

"Yes."

"Do you know why?"

"No. Nobody knows except you and John, as far as I know."

"Not true. John's the only one who knows. It might have to do with ...." She couldn't finish the sentence. "All I know is I fell off the deep end, and now . . .."

Alexander went silent a second time.

"Jenise, what is it?"

"I got involved with some pretty revolting people."

Going on her own experience, Elle asked, "People, as in men?"

Alexander nodded. "Several days ago, one of them created a profile on an adult sex site with my name and . . . pictures."

"Are you sure the pictures are of you?"

"I've seen them. It's me. The pictures were taken without my permission." Jenise took another drink, then folded her hands tightly in her lap. "My lawyer got the profile removed, but what if this guy does it again somewhere else? If I take him to court it all becomes public knowledge. Then, what happens to my job? What about my work at Rita' Rose? Elle, my mom . . .."

Elle poured herself a drink.

"Elle, how do I stop him? If a man did this to you—."

Elle interrupted and finished the thought. "What I would do? Jenise, what I'd do would get you arrested or killed." Alexander hung her head. "You have to call John."

"No. I can't call John. What about Rick?"

"Rick likes to play by the rules. He'd get it done, but it would take too long. If you call John, it will be over and done with tonight." Alexander turned away. She placed her elbows on the bar for support then dipped her head between her forearms.

Elle waited a few moments, then tried again. "Jenise, you don't have to make the call. I will." Then seeking permission, she asked, "Okay?"

Alexander's reply was barely above a whisper. "Go ahead."

Elle pulled her phone from her pocket and moved to the living room. John Hutsell answered on the second ring.

"John, Jenise is at my place. She's in trouble. Get here as soon as you can."

"What's going on?"

"I'll meet you at the door and tell you then."

Hutsell arrived twenty minutes later. Elle explained the situation in the entryway.

"Where is she?"

"At the bar."

Elle put on a light jacket and stepped outside.

Hutsell walked past the windows and rounded the corner and saw Jenise sitting at the bar. She was leaning on the surface with her head on her arms. He slowed his step, then made his way to the stool Elle had previously occupied. Hutsell noticed Alexander's empty glass and the bottle of rum on the kitchen counter.

"What's his name?"

Without looking at John, Jenise answered, "Rob Kolmyer."

"Where does he live?"

"He lived on South Scenic in April 2014. I don't know where he lives now?"

"Stay here with Elle till you hear from me, okay?"

She didn't answer. He tried again, "Jenise?"

She raised up, hugged herself at the waist, and nodded. John headed outside where he found Elle sitting on the native stone steps that led off the path to the main house of the Wyatt Estate.

"How many drinks has she had?"

"Three," Elle said.

"Steer her clear of anymore if you can. And make sure she stays with you till I get back."

"Got it."

Elle placed a call to Rick as her cousin drove away.

"Something's come up. Don't know when I'll be there."

"Need any help?"

"No. It concerns Jenise. I'll explain later."

"I'll work at the lab a while longer then. Text when you're on your way, and I'll meet you at my place."

"It'll probably be late before I can leave."

"You've got a key, Ms. Wyatt. Use it."

"You're getting kind of bossy, you know?"

"I can go from assertive to meek as a lamb in seconds if you need me to."

"Remember what you told me on the porch in Eagle Ridge?" Elle said.

"The part about getting sweaty?"

"No, the part where you told me to shut up."

Rick laughed. "And as I recall, you did."

"Time for you to take your own advice, Mr. Hadley."

Elle heard him laugh again before she hung up.

John Hutsell turned on his office computer and did a search for Rob Kolmyer. Luckily, the man was a home-owner, and, in a matter of minutes, Hutsell had his address, along with a link to his Facebook account. Kolmyer's cover photo, posted two months prior, showed him leaning against a new black Honda Civic. Hutsell clicked on the picture to get a better view of the man's face, then walked over to the closet and opened his gun safe. He pulled out a Wilson Combat 1911 pistol and inserted a full magazine. Hutsell then racked the slide, loading a round into the chamber. He activated the safety, shoved the pistol in his waistband and headed out the door.

It was a Friday night, so after work, Rob Kolmyer hit happy-hour before heading home. It was close to 9:30 when he parked his car in the driveway. He unlocked his front door and hit the light switch by the wall. The light failed to come on.

"Damn," he said. He took two steps before he tripped on something and ended up on the floor. Hutsell's knee was immediately in his back.

"What the f—!"

Hutsell leaned down to Kolmyer's ear and said, "Listen carefully."

Kolmyer felt cold steel on his cheek. He heard a distinct click as Hutsell released the safety of the 1911. Kolmyer knew that single click meant the pistol was ready to fire. Hutsell detected the unmistakable smell of urine.

"You have some pictures of a friend of mine you posted Tuesday night in a false profile. I don't know how many pictures you have or where you have them, but you will get rid of them. Do you understand?"

Kolmyer shook his head yes.

"If any pictures surface again, or if you cause her a moment's grief . . . well, let's just say, you didn't see me coming this time and you won't see me coming the next."

Kolmyer nodded again.

Hutsell placed the clock from Kolmyer's bedroom in front of the man's face. It had a lighted dial.

"Wait fifteen minutes before you head to the bathroom to clean yourself up."

It had started raining by the time Elle Wyatt saw the headlights of her cousin's vehicle pull in and park behind Jenise's Cherokee. She met him at the door, and with the overhang providing cover, stepped outside to allow Jenise and John some privacy.

John found Jenise staring out the front window watching the rain. He walked up to her, and in a gentle voice, said her name. She crossed her arms over her chest and placed opposite hands over opposite shoulders, leaving no doubt as to what body part she was protecting.

"He won't bother you again," John said."

She searched his face for something—anything. Solemn she thought, except for his eyes. Kyle was right, there was something there. Was it concern, or was it regret as Kyle had suggested? What did it matter? Nothing was ever going to change. She turned to leave.

"Do you have someone you can stay with tonight?" he asked.

"Why? Are you offering?" she asked, her voice hard and cold.

"Jenise—."

"Let me put it in a way a grandchild of Jenny Nelson will understand," she said. "'A legend's only a lonely boy when he goes home alone.'"

She walked past him and out the door. She paused on the way to her car and looked at Elle. Elle knew what Jenise was feeling. And though she felt her cousin would never intentionally cause so much pain, she addressed him as they watched Jenise drive away.

"I don't know what happened in 2013, and I don't want to know," Elle said. "But John, you have to make it right."

"I can't make it right. No one can."

Elle watched John's vehicle pull out of the driveway. He lingered at the gate and sent a text, "I know it's late, but would you like some company?"

Carine Velardi typed back, "Unlocking the door now."

Back inside her living room, Elle pulled up *Revelation Road* by Shelby Lynne. She was making herself a drink when her cell dinged. It was a message from Rick.

"I'm in my bed. Come home."

Home. Whose home? Where's home?

Lynne sang in the background, "Remember when the black veil falls, we all stand alone. Bare feet on the gravel man, we're on Revelation Road."

Elle threw her glass across the room, grabbed her purse and headed out the door. She drove the backroads to Clever, then to Nixa and Ozark as Rick tried several times to contact her. She finally ended up in the parking lot across from Gambit Investigations at 4:30 A.M. She sat there for fifteen minutes, turned on the wipers, and saw Rick crossing the street in the rain. She lowered her window.

"Come inside, Elle."

She clicked the passenger door open and said, "Get in." She drove to the back of Gambit, exited the car, and ran up the steps. Rick followed behind.

"I'll get some towels," he said.

She grabbed him by the shirt and said, "No. Shove me against the wall and fuck me."

Elle's hands went to unbutton Rick's jeans. He stopped her.

"What's going on?"

"I'm tired of this 'making love' shit. Fuck me like a man fucks a woman."

"You want hunger, Elle. I can give you hunger. I'll lift you up and press you against the wall, and love you as fast and hard as I can. But I will never shove you anywhere. You want passion, I'll give that, too. I'll lead you to the bed. I'll carry you to the bed. But I will never throw you to the bed and have my way with you. If I did, I would be betraying you and . . .."

He didn't have to finish. Elle knew who he was talking about, and she knew he was right.

When she spoke again, the contempt was gone from her voice "Why are you so damned perfect?"

Rick moved in close and brought his arms up to put around her. She pushed him away.

"Don't," she said. She backed away from him. "What in the hell are you doing with me?" she asked. "Why don't you find some nice—."

"Nice girl, Elle? Find some nice and *safe* girl, settle down, and have babies? Is that what you want me to do?"

Rick knew she was close to breaking, he continued to push.

"You want me to live a lie, Elle? Convince some nice, safe girl I love her, when it's you I want. Now that's the ultimate betrayal. I lo—."

Almost pleadingly, she said, "Don't say it Rick."

"You're cutting me loose," he said. "You're not going to cheat me out of saying it this time. I not only love you, I'm *in* love with you."

Elle picked her bag off the floor. She reached into the side pocket and pulled out the University of Tennessee at Martin chain that held the key to his apartment. She gently placed it on the kitchen bar and walked out the door.

Rick waited till 7:30 A.M. before calling Chelle Thomas and Cal Davies to request they check on Elle from time to time. The only information he provided was that she had returned his key.

Cal Davies stopped by Panera, picked up two coffees and two bagels, then drove to Elle's home. Elle hated the doorbell, so he knocked on the door.

"He called you, didn't he?" Elle asked.

"Yep."

"What did he say?"

"You returned his key," Cal said. "So, you going to make me stand out here and eat my bagel alone, or are you going to invite me in."

"By all means," she said and stepped aside for him to enter.

Cal took in the broken glass in the front room and the bottle of rum on the counter. "Must have been an interesting night," he said.

"An enlightening one maybe."

"Who got enlightened?"

"Me."

"In what way?"

"Oh hell, Cal. Do we have to do this?"

"How far back in the past are we going?" he asked.

"Cal . . . .."

"Just trying to save myself a trip to Memphis to set your sorry self straight."

"I'm not going to Memphis."

"Nashville?"

"Nope."

"Where to then?"

"Don't know. I'm on Revelation Road."

"Pretty cryptic, Elle."

"I understand and that's all that matters."

"And what about Rick?"

"He told me a month ago I wasn't responsible for his happiness," she said. "So, you can report to him I'm doing just fine."

"There you have it then."

"You don't sound convinced."

"Let's just say, where Rick Hadley is concerned, I have hope that my dear friend Elle Wyatt will come to her senses."

Cal Davies drove home and called Rick Hadley.

"She seems good, Rick. I asked her if she planned to go to Memphis or Nashville. She said no, that she was on Revelation Road, whatever that means."

"I know what it means," Rick said. "Thanks, Cal."

Forty-five minutes after talking to Cal, Rick Hadley got a call from the downtown YMCA. Their scheduled interpreter for the hearing-impaired had called in sick, and they hoped Rick could fill in. He agreed.

Elle got a text from Chelle Thomas just before noon. "Can you talk?"

"Yes."

Elle's cell rang. She picked up and asked, "Did Rick call you?"

"And good morning to you, too," Chelle said. "He's just concerned, Elle."

"He needs to follow his own advice," said Elle, and repeated Rick's words about responsibility.

"You want to go to a movie tonight?"

"No, I'm going to Galena."

"Your cousin's honky-tonk?" Chelle said.

"Yep. Good music and dancing."

"Have fun," Chelle said. "Lunch next week?"

"Sure. Call me."

Elle didn't go to Galena. She stayed home and tried to convince herself she'd done the right thing by recalling a scene from a week ago. It was a street play at Silver Dollar City.

Caroline Jayson was too short to see the action, so Rick had lifted her onto his shoulders.

Rick would eventually find someone else. Someone who deserved his love. Someone who could love him back. Sure, it would take time, but . . ..

Before going to bed, Rick picked up the shirt he had laid out for Elle the previous night and hung it in the wardrobe. Funny, Elle wasn't thinking of running, but he sure was—straight to her. He got in bed and thought about *Revelation Road*. Rick picked up his charging phone in the headboard cubby and brought up Lynne's CD. He skipped to track five and listened as Lynne sang about the lengths she'd go to in the hope of reclaiming a lost love.

"Say the word and I'll be come a thief . . .."

·51·

Claire Nelson Hutsell carried the Book of the Gospels during the entrance procession of her parish's 11:30 A.M. Mass. On her way from the alter, she noticed Jenise Alexander in a center pew. Jenise's head was bowed, and she was alone. There were any number of reasons why Kyle Jeffries was not with Jenise on this Sunday, but Senator Hutsell feared that it had more to do with her son rather than a scheduling conflict. Later, she caught Jenise in the parking lot and invited her to lunch at the Hutsell Estate.

After the table had been cleared, the two women remained in the dining room and sipped coffee.

"Amber is living with her grandfather in Oregon," the senator said. "She's actually been helpful in the investigation. The arrest of Stephen Marens was a direct result of clues she provided."

"That's good to know."

"How about you, Jenise? How are you doing?"

"Fine. Work keeps me busy, but I still have time for one day a week at Rita's Rose."

"Sorry I didn't get a chance to speak with you at Democrat Days. I was visiting with those at the Harmony House table, and when I got to the one for Rita's Rose, you weren't there. I did speak to Kyle for a few minutes. He's one of those rare finds, isn't he?"

"Yes," Jenise agreed.

Senator Hutsell took a few moments before she changed the subject.

"I don't know if you are aware that I was the one who suggested you be called that night in February."

"I never gave it much thought," Jenise lied. "I'm glad I could help."

"Jenise, there's something you need to know about John."

Jenise was hesitant in her reply.

"Okay."

Senator Hutsell moved her cup aside and placed her arms on the table.

"The day after Elle's mother was killed, and she was lying in a West Plains hospital bed, I sat down with John and told him what had happened. Both he and Elle were eleven years old at the time, and even though she lived several hours away, the two were close.

"He knew Elle was going to be adopted by Jean and Pat. That night, he asked to sleep in my room. We made a pallet near the window. He was still sleeping when I got up the next morning. I went to check on him, and beside him was the card Elle had sent for his last birthday. On the return address, John had marked out West Plains and written Battlefield underneath. What I came to understand in the coming months was that John wanted to make things better for his cousin, but there wasn't much he could do as an eleven-year-old boy."

Jenise looked down at the folded hands in her lap.

"John became a fixer in the full sense of the word when he dropped out of law school to pursue a degree in law enforcement," Claire said. "He couldn't make things right for Elle, so he went to work for other victims. First came the Cross Timbers case with Josenda Waters, then a coed in Columbia, Lydia Janssen in St. Louis a year ago, and Amber in February. He won't stop—he can't stop. There's always going to be another case—another person who needs him to make it better—to see that those responsible pay."

Senator Hutsell uncrossed her arms and leaned forward. She covered Jenise's hand with her own.

"John will never settle down in terms of a wife and family, Jenise. And if I were in your place, I know I couldn't keep from asking, 'what if.' I truly feel *if* things had been different—*if* he didn't have this obsession—you would have been the one."

Jenise closed her eyes as a tear fell.

"There's an ache, Mrs. Hutsell. It's like a piece is missing. John has that piece."

"The piece doesn't fit anymore, Jenise. He's placed it on the table in full view so you can see it doesn't fit," Claire said. She pulled back her hand. "I hope this answers any questions you still have about John."

Jenise nodded. *All but one.*

She stood and said, "Thank you for lunch, Mrs. Hutsell. I appreciate your candor."

Jenise walked to the buffet table, picked up her bag and headed out the front door.

Erin Laveau's car was in the shop, so Jay Randall dropped her off at Gambit Investigations the morning of April twenty-fifth. That evening, having completed a big corporate investigation case, the three investigators enjoyed a leisurely dinner at a restaurant in north Springfield. They were halfway through the meal when John Hutsell's phone rang.

"Be on the northside of the I-44 westbound exit ramp in twenty minutes. Watch for a silver Hyundai Sonata exiting from I-44 onto North MO-13. It will be worth your while."

Hutsell jumped to his feet. "We've got to go." He threw several bills on the table. He explained the situation in the parking lot.

"A silver Hyundai Sonata. That's the car that brought Dani to Rita's Rose on March eleventh."

"The exit ramp is just south of the turnoff to the zoo," Laveau said. "There's a stop light at the intersection of MO-13 and West Norton Road."

"Erin, you're familiar with that part of town, so you ride with Rick and wait there. I'll set up on the exit ramp and pick up the Sonata. You two fall in behind, and we'll switch off lead cars as needed."

John Hutsell spotted the Sonata as it came up the ramp.

"It's too dark to make out the driver," he informed the others as the car passed.

Both vehicles stopped for a red light at West Norton Road. A car turned in front of the Sonata and illuminated its interior.

"It's Kastner," Laveau said.

"Is he alone?" Hutsell asked.

"Nobody else in the front seat. I can't see in the back."

They followed Kastner for two miles before he put on his blinker to turn left onto West Farm Road 94. The trip was uneventful, until they reached Ritter Springs Park, where Kastner increased his speed, and without signaling, made a fast right.

"He's made me," John said.

A mile down the road, Kastner made another hard right. Hutsell followed.

"Keep straight, Rick," Laveau said. "John, he just made a crucial mistake. That road runs up against McCauley Ranch where the black top turns to gravel. The only way out is to turn left at the fence and then take another left to bring him back to the road Rick and I are on."

"We got him," Hutsell said.

With Hutsell following close behind, Kastner turned left at the fence as predicted. He had covered only a short distance before he saw headlights coming toward him. Hutsell swerved the Tahoe so it sat perpendicular in the road behind the Sonata. Hadley did the same on the other end. Kastner was trapped.

Hutsell exited the vehicle and ran to the driver's side. His eyes fell on a terrified young boy strapped in the back seat. John pulled his weapon.

"He's not alone," he yelled to his partners. "He's got the St. Louis boy from the Amber Alert yesterday." He lowered his voice and spoke to Kastner, "Open the door."

Kastner did as ordered. Hutsell yanked him from the car and punched him in the face. Rick retrieved the boy from the back seat and handed him to Laveau as Hutsell continued to hit Kastner.

"John, you gotta stop," Hadley said.

"He needs killing, Rick."

"Maybe he does, but it's not your call. We need to contact Greene County immediately for the boy's sake."

"So he fell," Hutsell said as he punched Kastner a fourth time. "And I think he's about to fall again."

Hutsell drew back his fist for a fifth blow when Kastner spoke. "Marteen."

Hutsell stopped. "What did you say?"

"Marteen."

Hutsell threw Kastner to the gravel and said, "Call Greg."

"Why? Who's Marteen?" Rick asked.

"Greg's mother."

"Erin, call Greene County," Rick said.

Hutsell only had so much time before Greene County deputies were on the scene. He pulled Kastner to his feet.

"What do you know about Marteen?"

"Warden took her."

"Where is she?"

"I don't know."

"Who's Warden?"

"I don't know."

Hutsell drew back his fist.

"Royce knows."

"Who's Royce?"

"He works for Warden."

Hutsell heard sirens. Rick yelled, "Greg's on the line."

"Is Royce a first or last name?"

"First."

"Last name?" demanded Hutsell. Kastner hesitated. "Now!"

"Parmer."

Hutsell shoved the man against the Sonata.

"When they get here, your story is you jumped out of the car and started running. You fell to the gravel, got up, ran for the woods. You tripped on something and fell face-first against the fence. Got it?"

Kastner nodded. Hutsell turned and took Rick's phone.

"Your mom didn't leave thirty-two years ago, Greg. She was abducted. We have to move quickly. Call your contacts in D.C. Have them find everything they can on a Royce Parmer. We have to get to him first. Once law enforcement picks him up—."

"I know," Greg said. "No access."

·53·

John Hutsell headed to his office to meet Greg Baptiste, while Rick Hadley and Erin Laveau handled the situation with Greene County deputies. Greg was parked at Gambit's back entrance when he arrived.

Inside, Hutsell asked, "Strategy?"

"Head to Parmer's place as soon as we have an address," Greg said. "You handle the questioning. I'll look menacing in the background. Make him think you're trying to keep me from beating the crap out of him—that all you're interested in is answers."

"Got it."

Greg's phone rang. "It's Donavan with the FBI."

Hutsell handed him paper and pen. Baptiste made notes, then said, "We've got an address and a photo. Let's go."

Parmer lived in an upscale subdivision in southeast Springfield. Hutsell drove into Parmer's driveway as the garage door began to rise. Both men exited the Tahoe, and hanging back along the edges of the driveway, approached the garage from opposite sides.

Parmer started to back out when his vehicle signaled something in his path. He recognized the gray SUV blocking his exit as belonging to Hutsell. He pulled a gun from under the seat, got out and took cover behind the vehicle's door.

"He's armed," Hutsell told Baptiste. Then said to Parmer, "So, the word's already out that Kastner got picked up, huh?"

"Don't know what you mean," Parmer said.

"I'd be in a big hurry too, if I were you," Hutsell said. "It's just a matter of time. You can talk to us or Greene County. But if you want a head start, I suggest you talk before they get here."

"I don't know anything."

"Let me at him, John," Baptiste said.

252

"Hold back, Greg," Hutsell said. "Parmer, put the gun on the floor and kick it across the garage."

Parmer did nothing.

"Tick, tock," Hutsell said.

The weapon went sliding. Hutsell and Baptiste entered the garage.

"Where's my mother?" Baptiste asked.

"Last I knew she was in central Illinois. But that was back in 2000."

"Warden took her in '87, right?" Hutsell asked.

"Yeah. Can I go now?"

"Circumstances?"

"She fell for his, 'going to make you a model' bit. He prostituted her for years, until a man he worked with wanted to buy her. She was about thirty then, and Warden liked to deal with young girls, so he sold her."

"And the man took her to central Illinois?"

"That's what Warden said."

"What was the man's name?"

"Warden called him Tate."

Tate. Farm houses. Corn fields.

"What else do you know?"

"Nothing. I never saw her again."

"Who's Warden?"

"If I tell you, I'm a dead man. I'd rather take my chances with the law than give you info on him."

"Can I go now?"

"Two questions? Is he local, and is Warden his real name?"

"Yes, to the first. No, to the second." Parmer started to plead. "Come on Hutsell, everyone says you're true to your word. Let me go."

Hutsell and Baptiste returned to the Tahoe and backed out. Parmer headed north and turned west at the intersection. Hutsell followed Parmer to US-65, where Baptiste pulled an untraceable cell from the console and phoned in a tip to Greene County Crime Stoppers.

"A man involved in the abduction of Elijah Jacobson is heading north on US-65. His name is Royce Parmer and he's driving a black, two-door Audi A6."

Hutsell dialed Rick Hadley. "Status report."

"Kastner lawyered up. Deputy Eastmon wants to talk with you."

"Are you and Erin free to leave?"

"We can leave any time."

"Meet Greg and me at the office as soon as you can."

The three Gambit investigators, along with Greg Baptiste, gathered in John Hutsell's office to share information.

"Okay, let's put it together," Hutsell said. "What do we know?"

"Concerning sex-trafficking, Warden moved from abducting victims in 1987 to transporting them in 2006. It looks like he's now in-charge of a sex-trafficking network in southwest Missouri. And his associates would rather go to prison than cross him," Hadley said."

"Warden abducted Greg's mother in 1987," Laveau said.

"He sold her to a central Illinois man named Tate in in 2000," Greg added.

"Warden brought Amber from Oregon to southwest Missouri in 2006," Laveau continued. "Amber was purchased around 2010 by a man named Tate to be his daughter's friend and study partner, among other things. She lived in a farmhouse down the road from Tate and his family. There were corn fields between the houses."

"Tate could be a first or last name. Amber thought it was a first," Hutsell said.

"From previous conversations with Amber, we know Tate's wife, Evonne, is disabled and may be bi-racial," Laveau said. "Evonne had an African American live-in helper named Teena."

"Marteen. Teena," Hutsell said. He looked at Greg, then to Laveau, "We need to talk with Amber. Erin, she opened up to you about these people. You want to make the call."

"Sure."

"Use my phone. She'll recognize the number," Hutsell said.

Amber answered on the third ring.

"Hello, John," Amber said.

"Amber, it's Erin Laveau. You're on speaker."

"Who's listening?"

"John, Rick, and Greg Baptiste."

"Why are you calling?"

"We caught up with Layne Kastner tonight. He had a young boy with him. The boy is safe, and Kastner is in the Greene County jail."

"Thanks for letting me know."

"There's more," Laveau said. "During the time we were in Oregon, John learned that Warden was the name of the man who brought you to Missouri. Through information John elicited from Kastner a few hours ago, we know Warden now occupies a high position in the network."

"Okay."

"We also learned that Warden abducted a Springfield woman in 1987," Laveau said. "In 2000, he sold her to a man from central Illinois named Tate. The woman's name is Marteen Baker, and she is Greg Baptiste's mother. You had a friend when you lived on a farm. Her father's name was Tate. There was an African American woman named Teena who took care of his wife. We'd like to send you a picture of Marteen Baker to see if she and Teena are one in the same."

"Go ahead."

Hutsell took his phone, called up a picture Greg had sent, and forwarded it to Amber. All waited anxiously for Amber's reply."

"It looks like her."

Greg Baptiste closed his eyes and tried to put his mind around the fact that his mother hadn't abandoned him, and that she might still be alive.

"Amber, would you mind answering a few questions to help us find her?" Hutsell asked.

"You've taken two of them off the street, and you did it without giving me up, John. I'll tell you what I can."

"Was the farm you lived on in central Illinois?"

"I think so. I spent three years there, but I hardly ever got to go anywhere, except for the house my friend Hannah lived in."

"Do you remember anything that might help us pinpoint where the farmhouse was? The name of a town, landmarks, names, conversations."

"One night, Tate and his friend, Terry—the guy who kept me all the time—were talking about a rich man who'd disappeared in the 1950s."

"Do you remember the name of the rich man?" Hutsell asked.

"No, but he had a new green Cadillac. Terry told Tate the rich man was married and liked running around on his wife. He also liked to gamble. Terry said a lot of people thought the rich guy'd been killed by a jealous husband, or maybe someone he owed money to. A sheriff figured the guy and his car had been dumped in a mine shaft and then covered up. The guy was never found. They laughed about another man who said he could find the body and car by using a stick. That all he had to do was walk around the mine till the stick started shaking. He said the stick would point to the place where the man was buried."

"Do you know what kind of mine it was?" Hutsell asked.

"Coal, I think."

"Anything else?"

"Terry told Tate he drove by the rich guy's house all the time. That it was just before the big corner on the road to town."

"What can you tell us about Tate and Terry? Race, features like eye and hair color."

"Both men are white. Tate is short and really strong. Dark hair, mean looking. Terry's taller. His eyes are brown. He's bald, except for some gray on the sides. Tate's wife Evonne had light brown skin."

"And Teena?"

"She hardly spoke. She was nice to me. She took care of everything 'cos Evonne was in a wheelchair most of the time. Teena tried to keep Tate from hurting Hannah when Evonne was sleeping—at least that's what Hannah told me."

"How did Tate want to hurt Hannah?" Hutsell asked.

"Hannah never said, but he was always telling Terry how Hannah wasn't a little girl anymore, and it was about time she learned what life was all about. I thought it meant he wanted to have sex with her. It wasn't long after that, that Terry took me back to St. Louis."

"Have you ever heard the name Warden?"

"No."

"How about Royce Parmer?"

"When Burleson put me in the car that night in Springfield, Kastner said Royce would really be mad if he found out."

"Amber, is there anything else you can tell us that would help us find Marteen?"

"Not that I can think of."

"Will you call us if you do?"

"Yes."

"One more thing," Hadley said. "Do you remember why Evonne was in a wheelchair?"

"Hannah told me it had to do with her muscles."

"Multiple Sclerosis or Muscular dystrophy sound familiar?" Hadley asked.

"The first one."

"Thank you, Amber," Hutsell said.

Hutsell, Hadley, and Laveau began online searches for a man from central Illinois who had gone missing in the 1950s, while Baptiste called Chelle Thomas to tell what they'd learned. Within ten minutes, Laveau struck pay dirt.

"Fay Rawley," she yelled out. The three men hurriedly walked to her office. "Fulton County in central Illinois. Town of Summum."

They gathered behind Laveau and her computer to read an article titled, "Where Is Fay Rawley (and His Cadillac)?" It was written by Charlie Parkinson and published in *The Zephyr* out of Galesburg, Illinois, in 1998.

"It's got all the elements Amber gave us," Laveau said. "Rich farmer, green Cadillac, womanizer, coal mine, and a 'divining rod'."

"How big is Summum?" Hadley asked.

A few clicks later Laveau said, "About 200."

"Closest airport in a town we can rent a car?" Baptiste asked.

"Looks like Macomb," Laveau said. "About thirty-five miles from Summum."

Baptiste pulled up his android assistant and asked for the flying time between Springfield, Missouri, and Macomb, Illinois. "One hour, two minutes."

"John, wheels up at 7:00 A.M.," Baptiste said.

"See you then," Hutsell replied. "Rick, you want to take Erin home? I'm going to arrange for a rental for tomorrow morning in Macomb, then go home and pack."

"Sure thing."

With Laveau in the passenger seat, Hadley headed to north Springfield. He'd driven two blocks when he asked if Jay Randall would be home when they got there.

"No, he's on patrol tonight. Can't wait to update him on Kastner, though."

"Yeah, it's been an eventful night," Hadley said. "What's the full story on Greg's mother? I know he was raised by his grandmother, but not much more."

"I really don't know, but Elle will. Why don't you give her a call?"

"We aren't seeing each other anymore."

"What?" a stunned Laveau said.

"She returned my key last Friday."

"Dang, Rick. Did she give a reason why?"

"Supposedly I deserve better."

"That's bullshit."

"I know, but . . .?"

"Oh hell, Rick. I'm sorry," Laveau said. "You think it's permanent?"

"I don't know. Could be. She did this once before," he said. "Of course the circumstances were different then."

"Tennessee?"

"Yeah."

"You could tell her how you feel."

"I told her Friday, just before she put my key on the counter. It has to come from her now."

They pulled up in Laveau's driveway.

"Take it easy, Rick," she said.

"Yep. See you tomorrow."

·54·

Greg Baptiste and John Hutsell set down in Macomb, Illinois, a little after 8:00 A.M. A rental car was waiting for them at the airport. The only information Hutsell had gleaned from an online search of Summum, Illinois, was its elevation and township. So the two men settled on the town of Astoria, five miles from Summum, to begin their investigation. They discussed strategy on the way.

"Astoria's demographics listed the black population at a little less than three percent, right?" Greg said.

"Yes," Hutsell said. "Evonne and 'Teena' would definitely stand out."

"Hope the citizens are the friendly type."

"Small town people usually are."

"Well, they might not take kindly to someone asking about their neighbors," Greg said, "and I'm not exactly the kind of man they are used to seeing."

"White, black, or in-between Greg, it's your eyes and that half-smile of yours that put people at ease. How is it that Chelle describes your eye color?"

"Pale aqua green."

"We've got a good approach," Hutsell said. "I'm sure we'll develop a lead or two."

Hutsell parked in front of Astoria's State Street Grill. "Time for breakfast and a little conversation."

Hutsell and Baptiste were halfway through their meal, when the waitress stopped to top off Hutsell's coffee. He sat back in his chair and assumed his open-body pose—hands on his upper thighs, elbows out.

"You lived around here long?" he asked the waitress.

"All my life."

"I'm John Hutsell from Springfield, Missouri, and this is my friend, Greg Baptiste. Mind if we ask you a few questions?"

"No, go ahead."

"We're looking for Greg's aunt. Her name is Evonne. She was married to a man named Tate, and we know they lived in a farmhouse near Summum from 2000 to 2013."

"You don't know their last name?"

"My Aunt Evonne met him online. Tate is the only name we knew him by. We don't even know if they ever really married," Greg explained. "She received a monthly stipend from a trust set up by her father. Aunt Evonne has MS. Tate convinced her he loved her and would take care of her. After she moved to Peoria to be with him, he began cutting her off from family and friends. We got a letter every now and then, but there was never a return address. The last letter we got was in 2013 where she mentioned living in a farmhouse in a town named Summum. My mom is Evonne's sister. She's terminal and wants to see Evonne one more time."

"Just a minute," said the waitress. She made her way over to another customer and talked with him for a few minutes. The man rose and walked toward Hutsell and Baptiste.

"Mind if I have a seat?" he asked.

"Please do," Hutsell said.

"I understand you're looking for a man named Tate."

"Yes, sir, we are," Hutsell answered.

Hutsell introduced himself and Baptiste, then let Greg give his spiel.

"His full name is Tate Slinkard, and I own the home he rented and the farm it stood on," said the man. "I'm Don Fortner."

"Rented?" Hutsell asked.

"Yeah. He ran off six years ago."

"Do you know where he went?" Baptiste asked.

"How bad do you want him?"

Hutsell needed more information. "Sir?"

"He cabbaged parts from my farm equipment before he ran off. I'm willing to trade information. I'll tell you what I know, and you get in touch with me when you find him."

"Deal," Hutsell said.

"Slinkard was a friend of my foreman, Terry Nagler. He lived in the house down the road from the one I rented to Slinkard. I own that place, too. Can't shake the idea that Terry was somehow involved in the whole thing."

"Did Tate work for you, too?"

"No. He drove a truck for a living," Fortner said. "Anyway, Slinkard was an ass, but he kept the place up and paid his rent on time. He was a good tenant right up until the night he stole my stuff and disappeared."

"When was that?"

"Spring of 2013. I had a lot of equipment out there—some of it mine and some I'd rented 'cos we were running ditches to cut down on erosion," Fortner said. "Along with parts from my tractor and combine, the son-of-a bitch took parts from a bulldozer and backhoe."

"I assume you tried to find him," Hutsell said.

"Yeah, best we came up with was an address for his wife in Peoria. She said he'd run off and left her, and she had no idea where he was."

"Is her name Evonne?"

"Yep. She and her daughter were living with relatives."

"Was it just the three of them living in your house?" Baptiste asked.

"No, Mrs. Slinkard was in a wheelchair, and there was a black woman that stayed with them and took care of things."

"Do you know her name?" Baptiste asked.

"Nope."

"How about Nagler? Would he know?"

"Terry committed suicide two weeks after Slinkard left."

"Was the black lady still with Mrs. Slinkard when you found her?"

"No, guess she didn't need her anymore, since she had relatives taking care of her," Fortner said. "When you've finished eating, come on over to the hardware store across the street, and I'll give you the contact info for Slinkard's wife."

"Will do," Hutsell said.

Fortner left the restaurant as Hutsell signaled the waitress for the bill.

"What do you think?" he asked Baptiste.

"I wonder what the true situation was in that house, and what caused Slinkard to leave like he did."

"At least we've got a lead," Hutsell replied. "You ready?"

Baptiste nodded.

Hutsell drove the rental across the street to free up parking space for the restaurant. Fortner met them at the counter and led them to his office.

"You guys law enforcement?" Fortner asked.

Hutsell smiled. "That evident, huh?"

"Too many questions about the black lady."

"I used to be," Hutsell said.

"So, she's the one you're really looking for?" Fortner asked.

"Yes. Can you tell us anything more about her?"

"I rarely saw her."

Baptiste pulled his phone and showed Fortner the same picture Hutsell had sent Amber. "Is this her?"

"Could be. The lady I saw was older. Who's the kid?"

"Me," Baptiste answered.

"I see."

Fortner went to his filing cabinet and pulled out a piece of paper. He made a copy and handed it to Hutsell.

"I expect to hear from you guys in a day or two," he said.

"You will," Hutsell said. "We can count on your discretion till then, right?"

"Yep. Terry's relatives still live around here. I don't want word getting out just yet."

"Thank you," Hutsell said. "We'll be in touch."

Hutsell drove to another part of town and parked. He powered up his tablet and searched public records for Tate Slinkard but found nothing after 2013. A similar search for his wife showed Evonne no longer lived at the address given by Fortner. Hutsell found a current address for Evonne on the outskirts of Peoria. Records indicated Hannah had lived with her mother up until July 2017, but there was nothing on the young woman after that date.

Baptiste pulled up the driving directions from Astoria to Peoria. "It's an hour and ten-minute drive."

"Hutsell handed the tablet to his friend. "See what you can find on Evonne's relatives on the way."

Five minutes into the drive, Baptiste spoke up.

"Looks like Evonne and Hanna lived with Cheryl and Derek Brown for about five months before moving into their own apartment. In 2015, Evonne purchased a small home in a gentrified section of Peoria. Two years later, she sold it and moved to her present address."

Baptiste used his finger to navigate the site for more information. "The Browns sold their home in February 2017 and moved to Davenport, Iowa."

"Wonder what prompted Tate to change his ways the night he disappeared from Summum," Hutsell said. "As far as anyone knew, he wasn't involved in any illegal activity for the time he was there."

"Whatever the reason, he's definitely been flying under the radar since," Greg said. "How do you want to present to Evonne?"

"Could go with the truth—at least some form of it. You're looking for your mother," Hutsell said.

"Might not be a bad idea. It would help if we knew the status of the relationship between Evonne and her daughter."

"We'll just have to play it by ear."

Hutsell's phone rang. He answered and told Rick Hadley he was on speaker.

"Deputy Eastmon came by to get a statement from you," Hadley said. "I told him you were out of town. He asked if your timely departure was related to Kastner. I said the reason could have anything to do with several cases Gambit was working. He wasn't convinced."

"Well, he did his duty," Hutsell said. "He tried to interview me; I just wasn't available."

"Assault, John," Hadley said. "Not good for you, the business, or your mom."

"Did Kastner talk?"

"No, but that's not the point."

"Did he lose any teeth? Has he got a broken jaw?" Hutsell asked.

"No."

"So even if he had talked, we'd only be looking at a misdemeanor," Hutsell said. "Big deal."

"You were out of control, John. And that's not like you," Rick said.

"It was worth it," Hutsell countered. "We wouldn't know about Greg's mother if I—."

"And how far would you have gone if Kastner hadn't had something to bargain with?" Hadley asked.

Hutsell remained silent.

"Think about taking some time away from the business when you get back, John."

"We'll see," Hutsell said and disconnected the call.

"Rick's got a point, John," Greg said. "Anything else going on besides this case—something personal maybe?"

"Just tired of playing by the rules."

"When did that become a problem? And are you talking about the rules of law or society or both?"

"Expectations, Greg. Tired of living by other people's expectations."

"Sounds like something Elle would've said a year ago. You were about done with her at the time as I recall."

Hutsell didn't respond.

"Hadley's the one who called you on that one, too," Greg said. "Eyes on the prize, John. You're no good to yourself or anybody else if you step over that line."

It was a few minutes before Hutsell spoke, and when he did, it had nothing to do with the subject at hand.

"How much farther?"

"We've just left Pekin, so about eleven miles," Greg said.

"You take lead on this one," Hutsell said.

"Will do."

"Your destination is on your left," came the voice from Baptiste's cell.

Hutsell and Baptiste looked at the building that housed Evonne Brown Slinkard.

"It's an assisted living facility," Hutsell said. "Changes things a bit."

"Yeah. Gotta pass the front desk test."

"You ready?"

"No time like the present."

Hutsell followed Baptiste inside the building.

"May I help you?" asked one of two receptionists behind a window.

"Hi. I'm Greg Baptiste, and I would like to visit with Evonne Slinkard."

"Is she expecting you?"

"No. My mother used to work for her. Mom was Mrs. Slinkard's care giver for thirteen years. She also helped take care of Mrs. Slinkard's daughter, Hannah."

"I thought you were going to say you were a relative. From pictures I've seen, you and Hannah look so much alike—especially in the eyes."

Baptiste smiled. "People often remarked how my mom and Mrs. Slinkard resembled each other. Would you tell her Teena's son is here to see her?"

"Have a seat and I'll be right back."

Baptiste and Hutsell sat in the reception area and waited for the lady to return. Baptiste paged through a six-month old *Time* magazine.

"Greg, I'm going to throw a scenario out there."

"Okay."

"Evonne has MS. She wants a child. Tate thinks a pregnancy could have an adverse effect on his wife's health, so he won't agree to getting Evonne pregnant."

Baptiste set the magazine down.

Hutsell continued. "He wants her happy, so he finds someone who resembles his wife."

"You think my mom is Hannah's mother?"

"What's striking about your eyes? The color. How many bi-racial kids are born with pale aqua green eyes?" Hutsell asked. "Just a thought . . . .."

"That's pretty farfetched."

The receptionist returned. "Mrs. Slinkard will see you in the Meditation Room, just off the Chapel. When I buzz you in, turn left and go all the way to the end of the hall."

"Thank you," Greg said.

Evonne Slinkard was sitting in her wheelchair, looking out onto the courtyard when Hutsell and Baptiste entered. Hutsell hung back as Greg walked over and took a chair beside her. Evonne adjusted her wheelchair for a better view of his face. Greg looked at Evonne Slinkard and saw a very unhappy woman. Her mouth was downturned, forcing the wrinkles around her mouth to take center stage. Clips held her soft dark brown hair in place behind her ears. Baptiste stared into her blue eyes and wondered if they'd always been as cold as they were now.

"You look a lot like your mother," Evonne said.

"I look a lot like Hannah, too."

"How much do you know?"

"Not nearly enough. Where is my mother?"

"Who's your friend?"

"A man I've known since I was five years old."

"How did you find me?"

Greg motioned for John to join him and take part.

"You remember Maddie?" Hutsell asked.

"Yes."

"You know your husband and his friend sexually abused her the entire time she was in Summum, right?"

Slinkard didn't answer.

"Maddie was sex-trafficked from the age of six until she escaped her captors two months ago. She knew Tate was about to do to his little girl what he'd been doing to her. She wants to make sure Hannah's safe so she gave me clues that led to you."

"How does Teena fit in that story?"

"Teena's real name is Marteen Baker. She was abducted by a sex-trafficker in Springfield, Missouri, when she was nineteen," Hutsell said. "But you already knew that, didn't you?"

Slinkard remained silent.

"It's all going to come out," Hutsell said. "Do you want to be on the cooperating end or the other side of prison bars? It's up to you."

"How long do I have before they come for me?"

"Depends on what you do right now."

"I won't talk to you until I see Hannah."

"Fine," Hutsell said. "Give her a call."

"Not that easy. She won't talk to me."

"Why?" Hutsell asked.

"Because of what she found out about Teena."

"Is Hannah my sister?" Baptiste asked.

"Yes."

"Where is my mother?"

"Bring Hannah to me, and I'll tell you."

"Where can we find Hannah?" Hutsell asked.

"She works in the gift shop at Tea Room at the Depot in Mackinaw. It's about twenty miles from here."

Conversation was sparse, as Hutsell drove to the only tea room in Mackinaw, Illinois. The building that housed the restaurant was originally a train depot that had been built in 1910. Hutsell parked in the adjoining lot.

"When you're ready," he said.

"Wished I'd asked to see a picture of Hannah before we left," Baptiste said.

"I'll snap a few while we're inside."

Baptiste reached for the door handle. "Okay. Let's go."

It was a little after noon, and the place was busy. Hutsell and Baptiste sauntered through the gift shop trying to get a peek at the person at the cash register. Near the tea room entrance, a lady asked if they had reservations. Baptiste explained that lunch wasn't on the schedule, but that he was looking for a unique gift for his grandmother.

"I'm sure you'll find something," said the hostess.

The crowd finally thinned enough that Greg got a good look at the sales clerk. Her name tag said Hannah. Baptiste was astounded at the resemblance of the woman in front of him and pictures of his mom in her late teens. He selected a large paisley print silk shawl and walked to the sales counter. Hutsell followed and held back as if in line, keeping other customers at a distance.

"Will this be all?" Hannah asked.

"Yes," Greg answered. "It's for my Mom-Mom."

"Mom-Mom?"

"Mom-Mom is what I call my grandmother. She raised me, so she was kind of like two moms: Mom-Mom."

Hannah smiled. "I get it," she said. "That's a pretty cool name."

"My mother went missing when I was two. Her name was Marteen, but some people called her Teena. You look a lot like her." Greg held up his phone and showed Hannah the same picture he'd shown Fortner that morning.

Hannah was visibly shaken.

"I heard she had a daughter who would be about eighteen now. Sure wish I could find her to tell her she's got a grandmother and brother."

Hannah was brought back to the present when a customer excused herself as she squeezed between Hutsell and the counter on her way to the exit.

"Will you be paying with a credit card, sir?"

"No, I have cash."

Baptiste handed over several bills. In the middle of the bills was his business card with his cell number hand-printed on the back. Hannah organized the bills as she put them in the register. She pocketed the card. She handed Baptiste his change and the register receipt.

"Thank you, sir."

"What time do you close?"

"At 2:00."

"Thank you for your help, Hannah."

Hannah Slinkard was relieved at 12:45 for a short break. She stepped outside and walked to the far end of the old depot. She entered Baptiste's number into her cell and hit the phone icon.

"Hello, Hannah. I'm sitting in a white Infiniti in the second row," Greg said, his phone on speaker.

"Please stay where you are. I have only a few minutes before I have to go back to work. I can't talk with you today. My boyfriend will be here at 3:00 to pick me up and I don't want him to know about any of this yet."

"Is there a time and place we can meet?"

"Tomorrow. I'm off and will be going to the grocery store in the morning. The store has a restaurant attached. I can meet you there at 10:00 A.M. The restaurant won't be busy then."

"What's the name of the restaurant?"

"The Hy-Vee Market Grill on North Orange Prairie Road in Peoria. Enter through the outside door instead of going through the grocery store entrance."

"I'll see you in the morning at ten," Greg said. He hung up and turned to Hutsell. "Looks like there's nothing more we can do today. Let's go to Peoria and get a room for the night."

The two life-long friends checked into a hotel close to the Hy-Vee Market Grill. Once they were settled, Hutsell sent Amber a link about Kastner's arrest with the caption, "Three down." He then went to swim laps in the indoor pool.

Baptiste sent Chelle the pictures Hutsell had taken of his half-sister. He then called her.

"When are you going to tell your grandmother?" Chelle asked.

"I'm going to call her after we hang up. All she knows at this point is that her daughter didn't run off because she wanted the drug life more than she wanted her son. I'm not going to tell her about Hannah until I have more information."

"Probably a good idea."

"Chelle, I'm worried about her. Would you mind—?"

"I'm ready to walk out the door, now. I'm going to take her to St. Agnes."

"Adoration Chapel?"

"Yes."

"All I'm going to tell her right now is that John and I are pursuing a lead we developed in Peoria," Greg said. "Call me when you get back home."

"I will."

"I love you, Chelle."

"I love you, too. Please take care."

"I will. There's two of us. Things will be fine."

"I hope so." Chelle paused before addressing her concerns. "John's changing, Greg. He's distancing himself from family and friends."

"I know. I think he's trying to decide who he really is."

"That puts both Nelson cousins in the same boat."

"So, while you're in the chapel . . .."

"I'll say a prayer for John and Elle, too."

After dinner, Hutsell found an article in a Lewiston, Illinois, paper about Terry Nagler's suicide. Hutsell knew where the town was, as he had driven through Lewistown on the way to Peoria. He made a few more clicks for background info and found that Astoria and Summum were in Fulton County; Lewistown was the county seat. As he'd done previously with those who had abused and imprisoned Amber, he sent the link and typed, "Four down."

At 6:00 P.M., Chelle kneeled by her future mother-in-law under the skylight in St. Agnes Cathedral's Adoration Chapel. She thought of her friends and silently drew words from a Catholic prayer, "Our friends are struggling with difficult trials. I can see their strength faltering, Lord. Let them feel an extra portion of your strength that will help them get through this time. Amen."

·55·

Hutsell and Baptiste arrived at the Hy-Vee Market Grille an hour early. From their standpoint, Hannah had made a wise choice for their meeting. The restaurant's seating offered privacy with high-backed booths and even higher partitions between sections. The men selected a wide circular booth facing the outside entrance. They sat down and ordered breakfast. The table had been cleared of everything except their coffee cups when Hannah walked in the door. They stood as she approached.

"Have you had breakfast?" Greg. asked

"Yes."

"Would you like some coffee?"

"Tea would be nice."

Baptiste signaled the waitress and placed Hanna's order. He waited till she'd taken a sip before speaking.

"Let me start by telling you a little about myself," he said.

"I looked you up online so I know some of it. You're thirty-four and a pilot. You have a chartering business in Springfield, Missouri."

"Yes."

"You have a degree in criminology from George Mason University, and you were in the Secret Service for about ten years."

"All true," Greg confirmed.

"Why did you leave the Secret Service?" Hannah asked.

"I wanted to marry my high school sweetheart."

"Did you?"

"We're getting married in August."

"Tell me about Teena," Hannah said.

"Her full name is Marteen Deandra Baker. She was born in November 1968. She got involved with drugs when she was

271

fifteen. She cleaned up when she found out she was pregnant with me. She was seventeen when I was born."

Greg took a drink of coffee. Hannah waited patiently for him to continue.

"My grandmother took care of me while my mom took classes to get her GED. I was two when some of her old friends started coming around. Grandmother protested, but my mom said she was trying to help them go straight. Then she went missing. There wasn't much police could do. There was no sign of foul play, and she was of age. A missing person report was filed, posters went up, but nothing came of them. Most people felt that the lure of drugs had been too much, and she'd chosen them above all else."

"You haven't heard from her since then?"

"No."

"I don't understand," Hannah said. "She had pictures of you."

Greg and John exchanged glances.

"She told you about me?" Greg asked.

"Yes. She said she'd messed up and lost you. She had a small box that had several pictures of you. Some of them were just of you, others with your grandmother. And there was one with Tate."

"Do you know how she got them?" Greg asked.

"No, but she looked at them all the time."

"Hannah, what do you know about my mother?"

"She lived with us until the night Evonne told me Teena was taking me on a trip. We were on the road by the house when Tate ran into us with his truck and pushed us into a field. He told me to run home, and I never saw her again."

"Do you know what happened to her?"

"No. I ran in the house, and Evonne told me not to tell Tate about the trip. Tate was real mean at times, so I didn't say anything. He told me the next day that Teena had tried to kidnap me, and she wouldn't be back. A week later, Evonne and I moved to her cousin's house in Peoria."

"Tate didn't go with you?"

"No, he had to stay and work, so we'd have money."

"Hannah, when did you find out Evonne wasn't your real mother?" Greg asked.

Hannah closed her eyes. Greg and John could see she was trying to compose herself.

"Tate would show up every now and then. He and Evonne always fought when he did. I was scared of him. One day I came home from visiting a friend, and he was there. I came through the back door and heard them yelling, so I listened."

Hannah went quiet. Moments passed before Greg prompted her.

"What were they fighting about?"

"Me. He said he wanted to see me. She said no, that he was a pervert, and he was never going to get his hands on me. Tate said he wouldn't give her any more money. She said he was going to give her as much as she wanted, or she'd tell on him. He said he'd tell me about Teena. My phone rang, and then they knew I was home."

Hannah moved her empty cup aside and said, "May I have some chocolate milk?"

"Sure," Greg answered.

John rose to his feet, "I'll get it."

"He's your best friend, isn't he?" Hannah asked Greg.

"Yes."

"I had a best friend once."

"Maddie?"

Hannah's eyes went wide. "How do you know about Maddie?"

"John and I have a lot to tell you, Hannah. When he gets back, you can finish telling us about the fight, and then we'll tell you what we know. Is that okay?"

Hannah nodded. Hutsell returned and placed a glass of chocolate milk on the table. After he was seated, Hannah picked up where she'd left off.

"Tate yelled, 'You want to know about Teena, don't you Hannah? Come on in, and I'll tell you all about her.' Evonne told him to shut up, but he wouldn't. 'I'm your father, but Teena was your real mother.'"

Tate's words registered with both Greg and John. "*was* your real mother."

"Evonne told him again to shut up. He asked if I wanted to hear more, and Evonne pulled a gun from under the blanket she had on her lap."

"Did she have a gun with her all the time?" Hutsell asked.

"He hit her the last time he was there, so she bought one to be ready for the next time he showed up," Hannah said. "He said, 'Ask your 'mother' where all the money comes from.'"

Evonne told me to go to my room. I did, but didn't go in. I shut the door from the outside and snuck back to listen. Evonne said she'd written everything down about Tate and his 'business,' and that she'd sent copies to three people in case anything happened to her. Then she told him to give her enough money to take care of her the rest of her life and to never come back, or she'd tell the people to give the letters to the police."

"Did you ever learn where the money came from?" Hutsell asked.

"She wouldn't tell me. I told her I'd ask her cousins, and she said, 'I wouldn't do that if I were you.' Mr. Baptiste, I'd never seen that part of her before. My whole world was turned upside down, and I left home. I moved in with my boyfriend and his mother, and I haven't seen her since. I can't bear to call them my mom and dad anymore."

"She wants to see you," Greg said.

"No," Hannah said.

"She won't tell us what happened to our mother unless you do."

Big tears welled up in Hannah's aqua blue eyes.

Greg's voice was soft and gentle when he asked, "Hannah, do you want to know the whole story?"

She nodded as the tears ran down her cheek. John Hutsell handed her the handkerchief he always carried with him. She wiped away the tears as she listened to her half-brother tell of the appearance of 'Maddie' on the Hutsell Estate in February to the conversation with Evonne Slinkard the previous day.

"Mr. Baptiste, what am I going to do?"

"Hannah, I'm your brother. Start by calling me Greg."

Feeling like Greg and Hannah needed time alone, John asked, "Do you have a grocery list?" Hannah nodded. "Give it to me. I'll do your shopping while you and Greg work things out."

She handed him the list.

Thirty minutes later, John texted Greg he'd completed Hannah's shopping. Greg replied that he and Hannah would meet him outside the restaurant. Hutsell met Baptiste on the sidewalk.

"Hannah went to get her car," Greg said.

"What's the verdict? Is she willing to meet with Evonne?"

"She's leery on two fronts. One: does Evonne have an ulterior motive? Two: she's trying to decide how much to tell her boyfriend and his mother. She said she'd call tonight and let me know her decision."

Hannah drove up in a blue 2014 Honda Civic and popped the trunk from inside the car. Hutsell and Baptiste loaded the groceries as she made her way to the rear of the Civic.

"What was the total?" she asked Hutsell.

"Don't worry about it," he said. "Hannah, your brakes are screeching. It's probably just the pads, but you need to see a mechanic."

She turned away from him.

"I'm sure there's a place close by—."

She interrupted. "How much will it cost?"

"Nothing."

"Mr. Hutsell—."

"You can pay me back a little at a time, say five dollars every paycheck. Will that work?"

"Thank you."

That evening, Hannah called her half-brother and agreed to meet with Evonne. They decided on a meeting the next day at 1:00 P.M. Since it was a Sunday, Baptiste knew there would be a lot of visitors at Silverwalk Manor. If Slinkard had a roommate, finding private accommodations might not be easy. He decided to give her a call. It took a few minutes for the call to be routed to her room.

"Did you talk to Hannah?"

"Yes," Baptiste said. "She's agreed to see you tomorrow. Is there a room available for a private meeting?"

"I want to see her alone."

"Not going to happen," Baptiste said. To make his point he asked, "You still got your gun?"

No answer.

"Fine," Baptiste said. "Instead of a meeting with Hannah tomorrow afternoon, expect a visit from law enforcement."

"I have my own room. The meeting can take place here."

"Okay. This is how it's going to be; my friend and I will do a search of your room and your person before Hannah ever walks in. We will be in attendance for the entire meeting. Any questions?"

"Time?"

"1:00."

"I'll leave word at the desk," Slinkard said.

Baptiste placed a second call and informed Hannah the meeting was a go.

56

Greg Baptiste and John Hutsell met Hannah in the parking lot of Silverwalk Manor. Hannah stored her purse in her trunk.

"Hannah, we need you to stay in the reception room while John and I conduct a search of Evonne and her room."

The trio entered the facility. Baptiste checked in at the counter and remained standing while the receptionist informed Evonne Slinkard her visitors had arrived.

Baptiste and Hutsell were directed toward Slinkard's room.

Baptiste entered and asked, "Where's your gun?"

"In a gun safe in the closet."

"Is it the only weapon you have?"

"Does that include kitchen knives and scissors?" she asked in a mocking voice."

Unphased, Baptiste said, "Yes ma'am."

"Oh hell, do your search and get it over with."

"John, you want to search Mrs. Slinkard and her chair, while I start with the bathroom?"

"Sure thing."

After the search was completed, Hutsell went to the lobby and motioned for Hannah to follow him to Slinkard's room. Hannah paused at Slinkard's door. She steadied herself, then nodded her readiness to proceed. Hutsell opened the door.

Evonne's wheelchair was positioned so her back limited the view outside a small picture window. To her left was an end table and another chair. A circular glass table sat in the center of the small living area. Hannah chose to sit on the small sofa that separated the room from the kitchen. Hutsell leaned on a partial wall on Slinkard's right. Baptiste sat next to Hannah.

"How are you doing, Hannah?" Slinkard asked.

"Well," Hannah said. "I have people who take good care of me."

"I cared for you."

"If you say so."

"I protected you from your father."

"But you didn't protect Maddie from him, did you?"

"I did the best I could."

"You knew what business Tate was in, yet you used that business to your own ends," Hannah said. "I'm the product of a rape you instigated. Do you really think I want to be here? Do you honestly think I want anything to do with you?" Hannah was struck by her own word choice. "'Honest'. You don't know the meaning of the word."

"I've made mistakes——."

"Evonne, quit," Hannah said. "Just tell me about my mother."

Hannah's words hit home. For sixteen years, the young woman in front of Evonne Slinkard had called her 'mother.' Evonne knew she would never hear her daughter call her "Mom" again.

Hannah prompted, "From the beginning, please."

"I wanted a child," Slinkard said. "Doctors said I could carry a baby full-term—that it was unlikely a pregnancy would make my condition worse. Tate said no, but that he'd get me what I wanted anyway. Why he treated me differently than other women, I'll never know. He said it was because he loved me, and at the time, I believed him. Looking back, I don't think he was ever capable of loving anyone but himself. With him, it was all about power and control." She paused. "Would someone get me a bottle of water?"

Hutsell moved to the refrigerator, grabbed a bottle, and brought it to her.

"Tate was a transporter for a sex-trafficking network based in St. Louis. He put out the word he wanted a sex-slave, then gave physical requirements. Another transporter, from Springfield, Missouri, offered Teena. He bought Teena and got her pregnant. When she went to the hospital, Tate gave them my ID. She was registered under my name, and that is why my name is on your birth certificate."

"Why didn't Teena tell the doctors or nurses who she was, and that she'd been forced to be a surrogate?" Hutsell asked.

"Tate used her son to keep her in line. Tate said her son would be killed if she ever tried to escape." She looked at Greg. "To prove his point, he would bring pictures of you to her every so often. In one of them, Tate was sitting by you watching a ballgame. Teena knew what he was capable of, so she toed the line. That is until she heard Tate and Terry talking about how you, Hannah, needed to become a woman. She begged me to give her money and let her take you away. I did. I was thinking of you, Hannah."

"What happened that night?" Hutsell asked.

"Tate left for work. I gave Teena fifteen thousand dollars. I thought it was safe after he'd been gone twenty minutes. But I was wrong."

Slinkard took a drink of water.

"He went by Terry's on his way to work. He told me later it was because Maddie needed to earn her keep. But she vomited on him so he came home to get cleaned up. He saw our car on the road. I couldn't drive, so he knew it had to be Teena. He used his truck to slam the car into the field. You came running in, scared to death. I told you to keep quiet, and I'd handle it."

"I don't remember Maddie being sick," Hannah said.

Slinkard ignored Hannah's statement and set the water bottle on the table. Hutsell's instincts clicked—there was something she wasn't saying.

"Did she have the flu or food poisoning?"

"No."

Hutsell continued to push. "Why was she sick?"

Slinkard turned her head and addressed him directly. "What would cause a sexually active woman to vomit on a regular basis?"

Everyone in the room understood the implication.

"She wasn't a woman," Hutsell said. "What happened to the baby?"

"There never was one. Maddie 'fell' down the stairs two days later."

"What kind of person are you?" Hannah asked. "How could you let him do the things he did? And what does all this make me? The only person who really cared for me was my real mother, and you both led me to believe she was a kidnapper and thief. Tell me Evonne, what did Tate do to her?"

"He killed her."

Hannah rose and ran from the room; Baptiste followed.

Hutsell walked over and shut the door. He turned, and referring to Marteen Baker, said, "Where is she?"

"I don't know. Tate had to go to work. There was earth moving equipment on the farm at the time. I heard one of the machines start in the middle of the night and figured it was Terry. She's on that farm, but exactly where, I don't know."

"Did you really send letters to people to be opened upon your death?"

"No, but he believed me, and that was enough."

"Where is he?"

"I don't know."

"Is he still involved in sex-trafficking?"

"I don't know."

"What skills does he have besides driving?"

"He's good with computers."

"They'll be coming soon," Hutsell said. "Get yourself a lawyer, and tell the prosecutor everything you know. Hope you look good in orange."

He opened the door and walked out.

Hutsell stopped at the front desk and tapped the window.

"Ma'am, the meeting with Mrs. Slinkard and her daughter didn't go well. You might want to put her on suicide watch."

The woman immediately ran out while the second receptionist got on the phone.

Hutsell found Hannah in her brother's arms. Her face streaked with tears.

Hannah looked up at Greg. "Our mother was the only true innocent in all of this."

"That's not true, Hannah. You are, too."

"I don't want to go home, Greg. They'll be full of questions I don't know how to answer."

"We've got a hotel suite. You can stay with us for the time being," Greg said.

"Hannah, give me your keys, and I'll follow you and Greg to the hotel," said Hutsell.

Hannah did as requested. Neither she nor Greg spoke during the ride. Greg showed her to his room and told her he'd be nearby if she needed anything. He pulled the door to, but stopped shy of closing it. He joined Hutsell in the sitting room.

"What else did Slinkard give up?"

"Your mom is buried on the farm—just where, she doesn't know. She heard one of machines on the farm start up in the middle of the night. Tate was gone, so it had to have been Nagler. He probably used the backhoe to dig a grave."

"How did you leave things?"

"Told her to expect law enforcement, then stopped at the desk and suggested Slinkard be put on suicide watch."

Greg placed his elbow on the chair's arm, raised his hand and rubbed it across the lower part of his face.

"You okay?" John asked.

"We both knew there was a good chance she was gone—especially after Tate's comment that Teena 'was' Hannah's mother. But it's still a lot to take in. We need to find her, John."

"I know. I'll go in the other room and get things rolling."

Hutsell began by calling the Illinois State Police, as the murder of Marteen Baker had taken place in Fulton County, yet Slinkard lived in Peoria County. Next, he called Don Fortner and informed him that law enforcement had been apprised that a murder had been committed on his property in the spring of 2013. His final call was to Rick Hadley.

"Long story short," he said. "We found Evonne Slinkard. Amber's friend Hannah, is Greg's half-sister. His mother was murdered in 2013 and is buried somewhere on a farm in Summum, Illinois. Nobody knows where Tate is."

"How's Greg doing?"

"Hard to say," Hutsell said, "but you and I both know it will hit hard in the coming days. I don't envy him having to tell his grandmother. She'll finally have some answers, but for victims of violent crimes, the pain is never over. How are things on your end?"

"Todd Jayson has accepted our offer," Hadley said. "I think we can have the Leland C. Nelson Crime Lab open for business by the end of July. Guess I'll have to dust off my suit jacket."

"Anything changed with Elle?"

"It's been over a week since I've seen her. Chelle and Cal say she's doing okay."

"And you?"

"Keeping busy," Hadley said. "What's next for you and Greg?"

"I've contacted the Illinois State Police and Don Fortner. He owns the farm in Summum. I've got a meeting with him tomorrow. He said he'll give permission for a search on his property. I'll foot the bill if it means we don't have to wait for governmental red tape to start digging."

"What about Tate?"

"He's dropped off the grid," Hutsell said. "The case crosses state lines. Greg's friends at the federal level will pull out all the stops to find Tate. It's in their hands, now."

"Well, don't worry about things in Springfield. Erin and I have it under control."

"Good to know," Hutsell said. "I think I'll go with your suggestion and take some time off when I get back. I'll talk to you when I have something new to report."

Greg Baptiste accompanied Hannah home and sat with her as she told her boyfriend and his mother the whole story.

"It's going to be on TV and in the papers," Hannah said. "I'm so sorry I brought this on."

"Hannah, you're a victim just as much as your real mother was. We'll deal with it," Mrs. Griffin said.

"If only I didn't have the Slinkard name."

"You can change it," Greg said. "Your mother's name was Baker. I think she'd want you to have it."

57

Greg flew back to Springfield Monday morning. He spent the day with his grandmother and was again amazed at the woman's strength.

John Hutsell returned to Astoria to meet with Don Fortner. Fortner was disappointed to learn that Tate Slinkard's whereabouts were unknown, but encouraged at Hutsell's assertion that law enforcement at the federal level would work to find him. To facilitate the investigation, the two men set out to find the body of Marteen Deandra Baker.

They left Astoria in Fortner's pick-up and drove seven and a half miles to his farm on the outskirts of Summum. They'd just passed the city limit sign when Hutsell asked, "Don, if you wanted to hide a body on your farm, where would it be?"

"Me? Well, I wouldn't put it in an erosion ditch or field. There would always be the chance the bones could be discovered due to the nature of farming. The soil's always being turned one way or another throughout the season. I'd go for the wooded area behind the house. No one really goes back there."

"Okay, let's start there," Hutsell said. "We'll be looking at the topography first. Keep your eyes open for a depressed circle in the earth. It's been several years, but check for vegetation that is different from the surrounding area. This is known as 'vegetation of opportunity.' You're a farmer; you know what happens when you disturb the soil."

"Plant growth is encouraged."

Fortner turned off US-24 and followed a gravel road until they came to a large, white two-story house. He drove around to the back of the house and behind several out buildings before coming to a stop. The two men searched on foot for most of the afternoon with nothing to show. They had just crested a small hill when Fortner came to a standstill.

"Damn, I don't know why I didn't think of it before," he said. "In 2012, a couple was writing a book about their family's history. They thought one of their ancestors had been buried in a Civil war cemetery back here and asked permission to look for his grave. What better place to hide a body than a cemetery?"

Fortner turned to his left and led the way as he continued to talk.

"Of course, the cemetery was overgrown, but they cleaned it up. They took pictures of the entire area, along with close-ups of some headstones. They included several of the photos in their book."

Hutsell and Fortner surveyed the area. Some graves were marked with engraved stones; others had only a rock implanted in the ground to mark a fallen soldier's remains.

"I don't see anything indicating that Baker's here," Fortner said.

"You got a copy of that book?" Hutsell asked.

"Yeah, back at the store."

"I'm going to take some pictures. We can compare them to the ones in the book. Maybe we'll see something."

Hutsell took in the scenery once they were back on the blacktop. A curve was coming up on the left. He looked at the house they were about to pass and asked, "Is that Fay Rawley's place?"

"Yeah. Hell, he disappeared about the time I was born. How do you know about Fay Rawley?"

"A memory from a little girl," Hutsell said. "It's what led us to Summum in the first place."

"Was she one of Tate's victims, too?"

"Yes."

"Inmates don't take kindly to those who rape kids, do they?"

"One way or another, Tate is going to pay," Hutsell said. "And it won't be pretty."

Hutsell placed a call to Greg Baptiste from his hotel room in Peoria at 6:30 P.M.

"I think we found your mom's grave."

"Where?"

"In a Civil War cemetery on Fortner's farm. We compared pictures taken of the site with some taken in 2012. There's a thin, irregular shaped rock, standing on end in-between two headstones that doesn't appear in the 2012 pictures. It has no markings, and it's obvious the rock wasn't placed there by nature."

"Why would he call attention to the grave by marking it?"

"The 2012 pictures were published in a book. Doubt Tate knew about them since Fortner's the one who dealt with the authors. There are similar stones in the cemetery, so the stone would dispel any curiosity if someone came snooping and saw a depression."

"When is the excavation planned?" Greg asked.

"Wednesday. Both state and county law enforcement will be there. Chain of evidence and all that."

"Okay, I'll fly up tomorrow. I'll text my arrival time."

"How's your grandmother?"

"Amazing woman—one who truly lives her faith. She's worried about me, but also for the granddaughter she didn't know she had until today. I've shown her the pictures you took in Mackinaw. They took her back thirty-two years. She's hoping to meet Hannah soon."

"Do you think Hannah will agree to a meeting?"

"I'm hopeful," Greg said. "When you think of it, we're the only *real* family she has. I'll try to see her tomorrow. She needs to know about the excavation. I doubt she'll attend. She feels she can't take off work right now, as paychecks in the Griffin household are more or less month-to-month."

"I can help financially," Hutsell said.

"I've already offered. She doesn't want to be 'beholding,' as our grandmother would say. And she's afraid she'll jeopardize her job by asking off right now."

"Is she that committed to her job?"

"She's eighteen. She could always work fast food, but her present job allows for evenings and Sundays off. And she only has to work every other Saturday."

"Find out what she's interested in? Springfield has a lot of educational opportunities in addition to four-year institutions."

"I'll bring it up."

Wednesday, May 1, 2019, a body, along with a box containing pictures of Greg Baptiste, was unearthed on Don Fortner's farm in Summum, Illinois. It would take several weeks for official DNA confirmation, but the photos gave credence to the theory the body was that of Marteen Deandra Baker. The story was covered by a Peoria TV station. The only details given were that a body had been found on a farm outside Summum, Illinois, and investigators were pursuing clues in order to identify the body and the cause of death.

Marilyn Baker contacted her priest about a memorial service to be held after Illinois released the DNA results.

Hannah Slinkard worked her normal Wednesday schedule. It was late afternoon when she met with Greg Baptiste on the porch of the Griffin home.

"Our grandmother would like you to have a part in planning the memorial service for our mother."

"In what way?" Hannah asked.

"Flowers, hymns, personal remembrances."

"She liked yellow violets. They grew wild in the woods behind the farm."

"Hannah, your grandmother wants very much to meet you."

"I know."

"Your next full weekend off is the eleventh. The twelfth is Mother's Day. It takes only an hour and ten minutes to fly from Peoria to Springfield. I could pick you up after work on the tenth, fly to Springfield that evening and have you back Sunday."

"I'll think about it."

Baptiste and Hutsell left Peoria for Springfield an hour later.

Jenise Alexander visited her mother on Springfield's southside. After dinner, she spoke of her April twenty-first conversation with Senator Hutsell.

"Well, he has 'settled down' to some extent," Mrs. Alexander said.

"What do you mean?"

"He no longer lives in an apartment. He bought a house on Portland. Remember when I used to take you trick-or-treating in Phelps Grove?"

"Yes. You said it was a safe neighborhood."

"It also had the best candy," Mrs. Alexander said. "There was a house on a corner lot that always took top honors in Halloween decorations. Do you know which one I'm talking about?"

"Yes. One year, their front yard looked like a real graveyard."

"John lives in the house next door."

"Mom, how did you find out about this?"

"Jody Simpkins. Her daughter works for Velardi Real Estate."

Jenise left her mother's house and headed home. She turned down the road that led to her apartment complex. She was about to enter the parking lot when she changed her mind. Jenise turned off her blinker and drove to the Phelps Grove subdivision in central Springfield instead.

No more. It ends tonight.

Hutsell and Baptiste touched down at a downtown airport in Springfield at 9:15 P.M. Greg and Chelle met at his grandmother's house. An hour latter, Greg walked Chelle to her car, kissed her goodnight, and went back inside to stay the night with his grandmother.

John Hutsell saw the outline of a vehicle sitting in his driveway as he approached his home from the east. He was in front of his neighbor's house when he recognized the red Cherokee. The car had been backed into Hutsell's drive. He parked the Tahoe beside the Cherokee. John and Jenise exited their vehicles at the same time. Hutsell spoke first.

"Hello, Je—."

She interrupted and said, "I just have one question, John."

"Okay," he said in a matter of fact tone.

"Would you have left if we hadn't lost our baby?"

John Hutsell looked at Jenise for several moments, then turned and walked away. And with that action, Jenise no longer cared. She was done.

John Hutsell walked into his home and went upstairs to the master bedroom. He deposited his wallet and keys on the dresser, and changed clothes. He headed to the main floor and grabbed a beer from the fridge behind the bar. As he listened to Will Tucker, he sent a text to Rick Hadley, "Going out of town for a while. Not sure where or for how long. Will be in touch." He sent the same message to Erin, Greg, and his mother.

·58·

John Hutsell had a hunch, so Thursday morning, he went to his safe and pulled out five thousand dollars in cash. His plan for the next week did not include leaving a trail—paper or electronic.

Hutsell believed that Jay Randall was correct about the sex-trafficking network that Warden operated. He was confident that the organization had moved from the wholesale transportation of victims in its early years to a mostly online business today. Brenda Sidemore might have sold her trucking company a few years back, but her 'friendship' with Kastner told him she was still in the mix. Factor in Tate Slinkard's computer skills, and the path became clear.

Hutsell wanted Tate, and Sidemore was going to lead him to the bastard.

Brenda Sidemore owned a million-dollar home in the St. Louis County city of Wildwood. Hutsell navigated the wooded two-lane blacktop that led to her driveway. He drove past, taking note of the surroundings, then circled back an hour later and pulled into a small park across the street from Sidemore's home. It was the perfect spot for surveillance, as the park featured both hiking and equestrian trails.

The two-story stone house sat on a small hill, which allowed Hutsell a good view over the tree-lined forefront of Sidemore's lane. At 1:15 P.M., a maroon Lincoln Continental made its way down the small incline and stopped. A petite woman exited the car and checked the mailbox. Using his binoculars, and a picture from a file he'd compiled during the last two months, Hutsell confirmed the woman to be Brenda Sidemore.

He followed the Lincoln as it headed in the direction of Wildwood's business district. Hutsell immediately looked for items that set Sidemore's car apart from other maroon Continentals that might be on the road. He made note of the Lincoln's red and white St Louis Cardinals License Plate holder and the Malloy Ford dealership sticker on the left side of the trunk. Once on main street, he moved in closer so as not to lose her at a stop light. He followed Sidemore to a small business complex and watched as she entered a dentist's office.

Hutsell settled in and had a lunch of protein bars and cold water from an ice chest. Ninety minutes later, he followed Sidemore home. As she drove up the lane, he parked and walked behind a copse of trees and relieved himself. The park closed at dusk. Hutsell had noticed throughout the day that there'd been a steady stream of police officers patrolling the area, so with the sun low in the sky, he drove to a bar and grill between Sidemore's home and Wildwood city proper. He entered and chose a seat next to a window that provided a view of a main intersection, had dinner, and used the facilities. At 9:30, Hutsell drove to an all-night truck stop, set his alarm for 5:30 A.M. and went to sleep.

·59·

Hutsell's alarm sounded. He grabbed a back pack from the cargo area and went into the truck stop where he took a shower and donned a clean set of clothes. He purchased two breakfast rolls and coffee before he left.

Hutsell listened to a local radio station as he drove to the park to set up surveillance for a second day. He was pleased to hear forecasters calling for a day of partial clouds and a high of seventy-three.

At 10:18, Hutsell spotted Sidemore's car moving down the lane that led to the road between the park and her home. He started his vehicle and followed. She drove to the intersection he'd kept his eye on the previous night as he'd had dinner. The Lincoln made a right turn. It was a three-way stop, so Hutsell had to wait for a car to pass before he could pull onto the main road. He looked ahead to a succession of traffic lights. The first two were in close proximity to each other. With a car between him and the Lincoln, Hutsell concentrated on the second light, as that was the one that could cause him trouble.

The first light turned green. Sidemore put on her left blinker and pulled into the left lane. The car behind her continued straight through the light. Hutsell moved in behind the Lincoln. The second light turned green. Sidemore waited for traffic to clear. A break finally came, and the Lincoln turned left. Hutsell stared at the light and waited for an oncoming car to pass. The light turned yellow as the car went by, allowing Hutsell enough time to make a legal turn.

Sidemore turned into a bank parking lot. The size of the building and the fact that the Lincoln hadn't headed for the drive-thru suggested that Sizemore had important business. Hutsell figured she might be making a huge cash transaction as it was the first of the month. It also crossed his mind that she might want to access a safety deposit box. After all, what better place to hide large amounts of cash gained from an illegal enterprise?

Twenty minutes later, Sidemore was back on the road. She headed east on MO-100. Fourteen miles later she turned right onto Historic US-66. She was now in Kirkwood.

Hutsell maintained a safe distance as Sidemore drove to the southern part of town and pulled into an apartment complex just north of the I-270 entrance ramp. She drove past the office, rounded a corner and parked in front of building 5A. Hutsell watched as Sidemore took the outside stairs to the second-floor landing. She knocked on the door to the right. The door opened and Sidemore walked inside.

Hutsell parked and picked up the file sitting in the passenger seat. Two pages in he confirmed he was sitting in the parking lot of the apartment complex Layne Kastner lived in at the time of Trey Burleson's death.

Sidemore emerged from the apartment forty-five minutes later. John Hutsell did not follow her out of the complex. He waited, and at 2:30 P.M., watched Tate Slinkard walk to the bottom of the stairs outside 5A, get into a black Mustang and drive away.

Hutsell waited fifteen minutes, climbed the stairs and used his skills to enter apartment 202. He did a preliminary search, then positioned himself where he couldn't be seen by anyone entering the apartment. He was sitting at the bar in Tate's apartment at 4:15 when he heard a key in the door.

Slinkard entered, but before he could close the door, he was pushed to the floor from behind. The door slammed shut. Hutsell rounded a corner and saw Don Fortner standing over Tate Slinkard.

Shit.

"Back off Hutsell," Fortner said. "He's mine."

Hutsell realized he was now faced with two threats instead of one.

"You should have been watching your 'six,'" Fortner said. "If you'd been covering your ass John, you wouldn't be in this situation. Now you're going to have to justify two kills. You up to it?"

"Won't have to justify anything," Hutsell said.

"To yourself you will."

"Convince me you deserve the privilege."

"He raped my niece. I'm avenging a family wrong."

"So you're going to take care of this asshole?" Hutsell asked.

"Yep."

"He's all yours."

John Hutsell got in the Tahoe and headed south on US-67. He knew he'd lost his edge, and he had to make sure it wouldn't happen again. He spent the time on the road reevaluating the steps that had brought him to this point. Where had he lost his 'six.'

You stop watching your back, and you got trouble.

Three hours out of St. Louis, he pulled into a store in Poplar Bluff and paid cash for a new computer. He drove six more hours before exiting at Texarkana, Texas, where he spent a second night in a truck stop parking lot.

Hutsell arrived in Galveston, Texas, at 1:45 Saturday afternoon. He located a Panera restaurant and hooked up to the internet. Two hours later, he walked into a Gulf Coast beach cottage, deposited the few items he had, and went for a swim.

·60·

It had been over two weeks since Elle had returned Rick's key. On Monday, May sixth, Elle walked into Chelle's office and shut the door. She took a seat and looked at her friend.

"Is he getting out?" she asked.

"Not much," Chelle said as she sifted through her unopened mail. "He's become a workaholic. He's gone out a few—."

"Who with?" Elle interrupted.

"No one in particular. It's always been in a group situation. People trying to set him up—that kind of thing."

"How is he?"

"What do you want me to say, Elle? He's burning the candle at both ends." Chelle threw the remaining envelopes in her hand onto her desk. "Why the hell do you care, anyway? You're the one who shoved him off the cliff."

Elle rested her elbows on Chelle's desk. She placed her forehead in her palms and took a deep breath.

"There is *one* positive thing," Chelle said.

Elle raised her head, looked at her friend.

"Being in the lab instead of out in the field is giving him time to volunteer at the 'Y.'"

"Interpreting for the deaf?"

"Yes. Otherwise, I'd say he's about as miserable as you are."

Elle got up and walked to the door. With her back to Chelle she asked, "Does he hate me?"

"You really don't have a clue, do you?" Chelle said. "No Elle. He doesn't hate you. He never will."

294

On Tuesday, in an attempt to gain some normalcy, Rick accepted a dinner invitation from Erin Laveau and Jay Randall at Dublin's Pass in downtown Springfield.

Laveau and Randall were enjoying a beer as they waited for Rick. A tall blonde with a form-fitting red dress walked by and winked at Jay.

Randall put up his hands, palms out and said, "Don't know her. Don't want to know her."

Laveau smiled. "I see a bat'leth on my office wall in the near future."

Randall checked his watch and then the entrance as the blonde continued to try to get his attention.

"Jay, no need to worry," Erin said. "She's more or less an open book. Narcissistic as the day is long." She signaled for another beer. "Our friends on the other hand . . . ."

"What about them?"

"Well, Elle's issues are just below the surface. Rick's got his own secrets and John . . . well you're going to have to dig through layers and layers to get to his."

At that moment, Rick entered the pub.

Erin and Jay had selected a table midway between the small stage and an elevated booth he and Elle had shared numerous times. A solitary man occupied the booth on this night. The waitress arrived and took Rick's drink order with the promise to return once he'd had a chance to view the menu.

"No need," he said. "I'm ready."

Erin and Jay added their selections and the waitress left to place their orders. She soon returned with Rick's beer. He'd taken two drinks when a woman making her way from the restroom caught his eye. It was Elle, and a moment's hesitation in her stride let him know she'd seen him, too. She resumed her pace and joined the man in the booth.

Erin noticed that something, or someone, had captured Rick's attention. She followed his line of sight and saw Elle as she sat down across from a man Erin had never seen before.

"Do you know him?" she asked Rick.

"No."

Jay Randall turned in the direction of the booth and said, "We don't have to stay, Rick."

"Springfield's not that big," Rick said. "It was bound to happen sooner or later. It will happen again. Might as well get used to it."

A woman who'd been sitting at the bar walked over and took the empty chair next to Rick.

"How's the private detective business?" she asked.

Erin took the lead. "Busy," she answered. "What's new with you, Candace?"

"Nothing," she said, "Still holding down the fort at the center. We added another 911 operator last week, so we don't have to work overtime anymore. What about you, Rick?"

"We hired a man for director of the crime lab," Hadley said. "We're looking at a July opening."

"I thought you'd probably serve in that position," Candace said.

A loud crash silenced the conversation. Must of the bar's customers looked in the direction of the noise and saw a waitress staring at the back door as it closed. Rick's dinner lay amid the pieces of a broken dish on the floor.

Rick looked at the booth. Elle was gone. He jumped to his feet.

"Stay put. I'll go," Erin said. Rick started to protest. "Remember what you told me two weeks ago?"

Rick sat down.

Erin asked the waitress, "How many exits are back there?"

"Two. One through the Gillioz lobby and another to the alley.

Laveau headed out the front door and toward the intersection of St. Louis and Jefferson. She looked around and found Elle leaning against the wall of a building.

"Elle, you okay?"

"Of all people, why Candace Gorman?"

"What are you talking about?" Erin asked.

"Why would he take up with her?"

"He hasn't. Candace sat down uninvited," Erin said. "What's wrong with Candace?"

"She told him things about me when he first came to Springfield. Things no one . . . .."

Elle didn't finish the sentence. She looked away from Erin.

"If he means that much to you Elle, why did—?"

"I didn't want to end up like Jenise."

"Rick's nothing like John, and you know it," Laveau said. "Drop the bullshit."

With Erin's words, Elle's mask came down.

"I didn't know it would hurt this much."

Elle pushed Erin aside and said, "I have to go."

"Where to?" Laveau asked. Elle didn't answer. "He'll come after you, you know."

Elle stopped, but didn't turn around. "I'm going home. Check on me if it you have to, I don't care. Just keep him from doing it."

Laveau watched as Elle ran across the street to the parking lot of the Discovery Center. She returned to Dublin's Pass and told Candace Gorman theirs was a private party and Candace needed to leave.

"Did you see her?" Rick asked.

"Yes."

"How is she?"

"She's fine, Rick."

"Then why did she leave the way she did?"

"Candace."

Rick started to get up.

"She doesn't want you going after her, Rick."

"You don't understand. She—."

"You'll only make it worse."

"Did she say where she was going?"

"Home."

"Do you believe her?"

"Yes."

Rick put enough money on the table to cover his dinner and left. He drove the few blocks to his loft, walked inside and dropped his keys in the catch-all by the door. He pulled a long-neck from the refrigerator and because misery loves company, keyed up Tracy Lawrence.

"Don't tell me that she looks amazing . . .."

Twelve miles away in Battlefield, Elle sat in her living room and listened to a daily mix from a music streaming app. The effect of a third rum and Coke on an empty stomach was finally having the effect she wanted. Soon, she would be numb enough to fall asleep. She'd just mixed herself a fourth drink when she recognized the beginning of a Lady Antebellum song. Elle steadied herself as best she could before walking to the sofa. She sat down, put her arm on the back cushion, stared into the night sky and listened to the lyrics, "It's a quarter after one, I'm a little drunk, and I need you now . . .."

Elle finished her drink, and when the song ended, she picked up the remote and hit the repeat button.

· 61 ·

John Hutsell used the time in Galveston to find his center. The stilted house he'd rented gave an unobstructed view of the Gulf not only from the deck, but also from the master bedroom that jutted out from the main structure. Windows on three sides of the room had provided him with a seaside panoramic view the last three mornings.

Hutsell kept to himself. His activities centered upon runs along the beach and on ocean swims. The physical activity was good for him. The cold of the Gulf's water was invigorating, and the hard runs cleared his mind. He rented a boat on Tuesday and found even more solitude out on the ocean itself.

On Wednesday, Hutsell was ready to venture into town. He found a small dive with good food and even better music. That night, he went back on the grid. He checked upcoming appearances for the Will Tucker Band and found that they would be performing at BB King's Blues Club in Memphis Thursday night. He messaged Rick Hadley that he'd be back in Springfield on Friday.

Hutsell carried a beer onto the deck and sat in an Adirondack chair. He was contemplating heading back inside for a second beer when his phone signaled a call from Hadley.

"Any idea what time you'll make it in on Friday?"

"Depends on when I roll out of bed Friday morning. Will Tucker's in Memphis Thursday, and I plan to make a night of it. It's only a five-hour drive from there to Springfield, so mid-afternoon at the latest. How are things on your end?"

"Professionally good."

"Personally?" Hutsell said.

"I'll tell you when you get here. Did you catch the news today?" Hadley asked.

"Nope."

"Kirkwood PD found the body of Tate Slinkard this morning."

"Details?"

"Manner of death: homicide. Cause: traumatic asphyxia. Not much info for the public yet, but word from Kleeman is they found several USB drives with crucial information about the sex-trafficking network he was part of. Slinkard was going by the name Oscar Dimming. No clue as to who's responsible for his death."

"Probably the same people who took care of Burleson."

"Could be. See you Friday."

Hutsell went inside and watched the news report out of St. Louis, then sent the link to Amber. "Five down." As soon as the body of Marteen Baker was identified, he would contact her again. He wouldn't include information on Hannah, unless the young woman gave her permission.

Hutsell decided to watch a Springfield evening news report to see what had taken place during his absence. He learned of the death of Springfield icon Ralph Manley, who'd parachuted into Normandy with the 101st Airborne Screaming Eagles on D-Day. The next news item dealt with the opening of an addition to Greene County's jail located just north of Gambit Investigations. A smile crossed his face when the camera panned the crowd, and he saw Rick Hadley and Erin Laveau. But it was the interview with the jail's operations captain that made him sit up and pay attention.

Hutsell did a quick search of Captain Ronald Inskeep, then called Erin Laveau.

"Saw you and Rick on the news. Glad to see Gambit was well represented."

"Hell John, only had to walk a couple of blocks—good for my girlish figure, don't you know?"

"You were with Greene County till 2016, right?"

"Yeah."

"I've got a few questions about Inskeep."

"Shoot," Laveau said.

"In what capacity did he start with the department?"

"As a substitute detention officer, I believe."

"When did he go full time?"

"Let's see. I was hired in 2007," Laveau said. "It was soon after. He worked his way up to sergeant a few years later."

"Then all the way to captain of operations of the jail in 2015?"

"I believe so."

"Erin, do you remember how Zimbeck described the guy he handed Amber off to in 2006?"

"The man he called Warden?" Laveau asked.

And with the name 'Warden,' Laveau understood what Hutsell was thinking. "Oh hell, John, he can't be Inskeep."

"Go over the description."

"Tall, receding hair line, mid-forties—oh and that raised mole."

"He'd be in his late fifties now," Hutsell said. "When did Inskeep stop wearing glasses?"

"Damn, John, maybe four years ago."

"Think he got Lasik surgery?"

"Could have. Doubt he would have waited till he was in his fifties to get contacts."

"Erin, pull up the video from the evening news, look at Inskeep closely, and tell me what you see."

Hutsell waited till Laveau came back on the line.

"Did you see it?" he asked.

"Yeah, right there on the temple as Zimbeck described."

"Even the name 'Warden' fits," Hutsell said.

"How do you want to handle this, John?"

"It's no telling who Inskeep's got working for him, but I'm willing to bet he's got people at all levels. I think the best thing is to tell Jay. Let the State guys conduct the investigation. They can start by checking to see if Inskeep held a CDL and worked for Sidemore Transportation around the time Amber was abducted."

"Okay. He's in the other room. I'll make a fresh pot of coffee and interrupt his reading binge."

"I'll be back in Springfield sometime Friday afternoon. You can fill me in on the situation then," Hutsell said. "Oh, and as far as the State guys are concerned, this 'tip' came from Jay's February nineteenth informant."

"Got it. But you know if this pans out, law enforcement in Springfield and St. Louis will figure out who the 'informant' is, right?"

"Could be, but it's the official line that counts, as far as I'm concerned."

"Got it. See you Friday."

Hutsell grabbed another beer from the fridge and went back outside. He placed his cell on a nearby table and listened to the soothing sounds of the ocean. He thought about his upcoming night in Memphis and reached for his phone. He hit the message icon and typed, "Want to meet in Memphis tomorrow night?"

"Yes," came the reply.

Hutsell finished his beer, set his alarm for 4:00 A.M. and went to bed.

In Battlefield, Missouri, Elle Wyatt was brushing her teeth while the theme from *Star Trek: Voyager* filtered in from the TV in her bedroom. In a few minutes, *Star Trek: Enterprise* would be starting. She looked at herself in the mirror. Elle pulled the tie from her hair, and watched her hair flow around her shoulders. She closed her eyes and thought of the last time Rick had pushed her hair behind her ears before he kissed her cheek. Without any warning, Sylvia Hadley's words from seven months ago came back to haunt her.

"He's not the one that sees you as damaged, Elle. You are."

She entered her bedroom as the Enterprise theme started. Elle had always liked the song, though some saw it as kind of hokey. She'd heard it dozens of times, but on this night, one of the lines made her stop and turn around.

" . . . they're not gonna hold me down no more . . .."

"He's not the one that sees you as damaged, Elle. You are."

And there it was, the cold naked truth. It wasn't her stepfather or memories of the numerous men she'd been involved with that were holding her back. It was Elle herself.

She watched the screen and saw the image of Alan Shepherd. Unassuming Alan Shepherd. Elle Wyatt slid down the side of her bed, finally let go of the past and cried.

62

Greg Baptiste was sitting in his office at Safety-Net Thursday morning when a local reporter entered the building and asked to see him. Baptiste agreed to speak to the woman.

"There's a story on the wire that the body of a murdered woman found in Illinois is that of your mother, Marteen Baker. Do you have any comment?"

"I haven't seen the story, so no comment at this time," Baptiste said. "Now, if you will excuse me, I have an appointment."

He walked to the door and opened it.

"You'll have to talk to one of us sooner or later," the reporter said.

"If the story is true, my family will make a statement. Good day."

Baptiste called his grandmother.

"There's supposedly a report out of Illinois about Mom. Do not answer the phone or go to the door. I'm on my way."

Baptiste walked to the reception desk.

"Ashley, is Chelle with a client?"

"No, but her next appointment is in ten minutes."

Greg tapped on Chelle's office door and walked in.

"A reporter was just here. Word is out about my mom. I'm going to my grandmother's. Hope I get there before the reporters do."

"Call me."

"Will do."

Greg sat with his grandmother and watched the developing story out of Peoria. According to the Illinois State Police, DNA results proved the body found on a Summum farm on April twenty-ninth was that of missing Marteen Deandra Baker from Springfield, Missouri. It was also reported that a Peoria woman had come forth to say Baker had been held captive by her husband and a Summum man for thirteen years. The woman informed authorities that her husband, Tate Slinkard, had murdered Baker in the spring of 2013.

Greg Baptiste copied the link to the news report and sent it to his half-sister and warned her to be wary of reporters. He again extended the invitation for her to come to Springfield the following weekend.

Hannah Slinkard wanted out of Illinois. She replied by asking if Greg could fly to Peoria that afternoon. Greg agreed and arranged to pick her up at the Griffin home at 4:00. Baptiste sent the same link to John Hutsell and told him he would be flying to Peoria to get Hannah and bring her to Springfield that night.

John Hutsell was on his way to Memphis. He exited the highway after receiving Greg's message. Hutsell ate lunch as he watched the news report. He then sent a text to Amber.

"Evonne Slinkard is turning State's evidence in an attempt to say out of prison. As for the other players, we have identified the man who took over for Tate at Multnomah Falls. From evidence taken from Tate's residence, I am confident that an investigation will lead to his arrest and the break up of the sex-trafficking network he operates in southwest Missouri."

Hutsell's phone rang.

"Thank you, John," Amber said.

"That only leaves Devin Zimbeck. He's due to be released from prison in three months. Amber. There's nothing more I can do on that front," Hutsell said. "If you want him to face charges concerning your abduction, you'll have to come forward. If you do, the man you need to contact is Multnomah County Deputy Mitch Brenner. He kept things quiet about you for as long as he could in February. He'll look out for your interests. I'll text you his number."

"Okay," Amber said. "I wanted you to know that I'm taking GED courses now, and I'm also in counseling. My therapist and I have talked about me going public—that my story might help others and would give me a 'purpose,' as she called it. Bringing Zimbeck to justice might be the beginning I need."

"That's good to hear."

"I've never thought of myself as being lucky," Amber said, "but if I hadn't found shelter in your mother's greenhouse that night, you wouldn't have been the one that found me. I could have ended up anywhere, but because of you, I feel—."

"I understand," Hutsell said of her unfinished sentence. "Take care, Amber."

"And John, if I do go public, I'll do my best to keep your name secret."

"I appreciate it. Goodbye."

Rick Hadley held the door open for Gambit's secretary as she left for the day. He locked up and headed to his office. He sat down to respond to an earlier email and noticed a new message in his inbox. He looked at the sender's name. There wasn't a subject heading. He checked its arrival time: 5:04 P.M. It was now 5:06. Rick leaned back in his chair and tapped his index fingers on the edge of his desk as he contemplated the repercussions of opening her message. He finally placed the curser on the entry and double clicked.

"Thought you would enjoy this singer/songwriter." A YouTube video address was included. Rick followed the link. A man named Eric Erdman was sitting in a chair. A sly grin crossed the man's face as he began playing a guitar. The tune was upbeat even though it told of a lovers' quarrel. Rick finally 'got it' when Erdman reached the chorus.

"We've been down this road before, but I didn't mind the drive. If two wrongs don't make a right, then how about three or four or five."

Rick listened till the end. He found himself smiling with Erdman as the artist sang the last few lines.

"I know back then we had a fight, but when it comes to me and you. If two wrongs don't make a right, come home with me tonight, and we'll find out how many do."

Rick typed a reply. "He's good. How'd you find him?"

As he waited for a response to his email, his cell vibrated. He picked up the phone and tapped the message icon. "A friend in Nashville."

"Thanks for passing on the link," he messaged back.

"Where's John?"

"In Memphis. Why? You need something?"

"Is the back door security code still the same?"

Rick put his cell in his pocket. He walked down the hall to the rear entrance and opened the door.

"How many times do you think it will take?" he asked, referring to Erdman's song.

"One."

Elle walked inside and Rick shut the door behind her.

"Rick—."

"Shhh."

Rick put his arms around Elle and held her close. When he broke their embrace, he took her hand and led her to his office. He stepped aside for her to enter first. He was standing behind her when she tried again.

"Rick."

"Yes." He moved in and encircled her waist. She placed her arms over his and leaned back against his chest.

"You want to get married, right?" she asked.

"Always thought marriage was somewhere in my future," he said.

She turned to face him. "That's not what I mean."

Rick sat on his desk and pulled her into the space between his legs. "Do you want to get married, Elle?" he asked as a matter of fact question, not as a proposal.

She put her arms around his neck. "Yeah . . . I'm thinking I do." She caressed his right ear between the fingers of her right hand.

"How long 'till you'll know for sure?" he asked as he brushed her cheek with his.

"Maybe another ten minutes."

"You got a time frame?"

"Yes," she said. Her nose kissed his. "No big announcements, though. No picking colors or anything like that."

"What're you thinking?"

"Driving to Nashville . . . .." She took an involuntary deep breath, as he lightly raked her ear lobe with his teeth. ". . . getting a license . . . and tying the knot."

"All in one day?"

"There's a female minister that will do the honors," she said just before he gently kissed her lips.

Rick's eyes went to the clock. "What about rings?"

"Lance can help in that department."

"Is he working tonight?" He lightly kissed her again.

"He's closing. But Rick . . .."

"Yes."

"I don't want to pick out my own ring," she said.

"Understood." He looked over her shoulder again. "So, do you want me to ask you, or do want to do the asking?"

"I'll 'let' you. We both know you're into that kind of thing." She slightly pulled away so she could see his face. "But please Rick, don't do the kneeling thing, okay?"

He smiled. The room went quiet as Rick watched the clock and mentally counted down the last few seconds. Finally, he brought his eyes back to hers.

"Elle Wyatt, will you marry me?"

Elle took a step back. She made a fist with her right hand and dipped it twice, American Sign Language for 'yes.' Rick's smile went full face. Then, using four distinct hand motions, she signed, "Now, take me upstairs."

John Hutsell arrived at BB King's Blues Club in Memphis thirty minutes before the Will Tucker Band was set to take the stage. He passed a fifty-dollar bill to the hostess, gave the name of the woman he was expecting, and asked that she be directed to his table.

Will Tucker began his first set at 5:00. Fifteen minutes later, a woman walked up behind Hutsell and rubbed his left shoulder. He enjoyed the touch of her fingers for a few moments, then stood and pulled out the chair next to his.

"Did you have any trouble getting away?" he asked.

"No. I rearranged a few things on the schedule and walked out of the office at ten."

"Are your things at the hotel?"

"Yes," Erika León said. She smiled. "You'd think they were expecting me."

Rick Hadley walked up to the jewelry counter of a Battlefield Mall department store and found Lance Geraghty filling out paper work.

"Hello, Lance."

Well, if it isn't Gambit's very own crime scene investigator," Geraghty said. "Tell me, what brings you to the Battlefield Mall?"

"I need a ring."

"Our men's rings are in the back bay. Let me put this up, and I'll be right there."

"Not the kind of ring I'm interested in," Hadley said.

Geraghty looked up and smiled. "Oh, really. Well Mr. Hadley, pray tell, what kind of ring are you 'interested' in?"

"One that goes on a woman's left hand."

"So she finally came to her senses, huh?"

"Yeah, but she wants it quiet for now, Lance."

"Who wants what quiet?" Cal Davies asked as he walked up and stood beside Hadley.

"Hello, Cal," Rick said.

"Go ahead and tell him, Rick," Lance said, "Cal and I are both good at keeping secrets."

"I'm here to buy a ring," Rick said.

"An engagement ring," Lance added.

"It's about time," Cal said. "So, it's official? You asked, and she said yes?"

"Yeah, but you can't tell a soul until she makes the announcement."

"Have you set a date?"

"Yes, but—."

"Not until she makes the announcement," Cal said. "I get it." A huge smile crossed his face. "Chelle is going to be so mad I knew about this before she did."

"Let's get started," Lance said. "What do you have in mind, Rick?"

"Something special, unique."

Lance smiled. "You haven't a clue what you want, do you?"

"Not really."

"Lucky for you, I know what she likes. But I want you to look around for a few minutes before I show you the ring I think she will love."

Hadley did as instructed. He had Lance pull out a couple of pieces, but wasn't sold on either one.

"Okay Lance, dazzle me," he said.

Lance walked down to the side case, opened it, and brought out a white gold diamond ring.

"This is not an actual engagement ring, and the only way to get a matching band would be to have one custom made. But Rick, there's not another like it in southwest Missouri."

Rick took the ring and examined it while Lance continued to talk.

"First of all, it's a Le Vian vintage designer piece, which guarantees that it is unique. Elle already has two white gold Le Vian rings, so this will be a nice addition to her collection."

An associate walked up and told Lance there was a Diet Coke for him in the back.

"Andrea, come try on this ring so Mr. Hadley can see how it looks."

Andrea slid the ring on her finger.

"It's a little big on Andrea, but it will fit Elle perfectly since she's a size seven. It's a cluster setting of vanilla diamonds surrounding a center stone."

Andrea handed the ring back to Rick.

"It has an open halo," Lance said. "Guards are popular right now as wedding bands. The placement of the halo actually resembles a guard. So in essence, you have an engagement ring with a built-in wedding band. Then there's the two half-moon settings on a split shank sprinkled with diamonds to make it even more distinctive."

"It's perfect for her, Rick," Cal said.

"It is different from anything in the store," Rick said. He continued to study the ring. Finally he said, "Sold."

"Now to the men's wedding bands," Lance said. "Let's hope we have one in your size."

Rick selected a white gold band accented with a subtle milgrain border.

"Okay, Rick, now what about a wedding present since you got by with buying only one ring for the bride?"

Rick laughed. "By all means," he said. "Show me the second piece that is 'perfect' for Elle."

"Aquaprase is a new blue-green gem with a white-brown matrix. It was discovered by gemologist Yianni Melas in Africa a few years back. And it just so happens I have a Le Vian art deco aquaprase ring in stock."

Will Tucker fine-tuned his guitar, then began playing the last song of the evening. John immediately recognized the song as it was written in part by Dean Dillon, one of Elle's favorite songwriters. He stood and offered Erika his hand. They walked to the small dance floor as Tucker sang, "Tennessee Whiskey."

Halfway through the song, a lady at the bar nodded at John and Erika and said, "Now that's how you polish a belt buckle."

John settled the bill and arranged for a ride to the hotel. They entered the lobby.

"Quaint," Erika observed.

"Yeah, it's one of the few places in Memphis that hasn't been renovated to the point that it's just another hotel."

John opened the door to the room he'd rented for the night and stepped aside for Erika to enter first. She took a few steps forward, he followed. She turned around.

"Wish you'd recorded that last song," she said.

He pulled out his phone. "Who do you want? David Allen Coe, George Jones, or Chris Stapleton?"

"Stapleton."

They made it through the first chorus before the clothes started coming off.

Erika was lying on her stomach when she awoke several hours later.

Time for Round Two.

She slid her hand down John's inner thigh.

"John, wake up and take care of business."

She moved her hand slightly to his left and felt his body respond.

Hutsell raised up, leaned over her, and grabbed a condom from the night stand.

"Always loved the fact you weren't a raw dog rando," she said.

He laughed. "Don't hold back Erika, speak your mind."

He kissed her neck and slowly moved down her body.

"You're getting warmer," she said when he reached her breasts.

He stopped at her panty line and said, "Great tattoo."

"You like she dragons?"

"On you, it's very felicitous," he commented before advancing farther down.

"Word study always was one of your favorite classes."

"It's a Nelson thing."

He continued to please her until she climaxed. He raised up and said, "Roll over."

She did. He put his hands on her hips and pulled her to him. The headboard hit the wall with every thrust. Someone in the next room banged his annoyance. Hutsell didn't miss a beat as he grabbed a pillow, pulled back the headboard and stuffed the pillow between the headboard and the wall. He waited till she climaxed a second time before he allowed himself to release. They both fell to the bed.

"That's better," she said. "You can go back to sleep now."

63

Rick Hadley was in the bathroom when Elle awoke Saturday morning in their Nashville hotel room. She held up her left hand and admired the ring on her third finger.

"Sadie, Sadie, married lady. See what's on my hand."

Rick emerged from the bathroom, stark naked and whistling. He disappeared into the living area.

"Strutting your stuff there, Hadley," she said.

He held a paper at his side as he walked back into the bedroom. Rick jumped on the bed, landing on his knees and placed their marriage certificate in front of the Hadley family jewels.

"'Signed, Sealed, Delivered, I'm Yours'."

Elle burst out laughing.

"Can we tell everyone now?" he asked.

"Go ahead," she said. "Send the message you've been dying to send since yesterday afternoon."

Rick took a picture of their marriage certificate and sent it in a joint message to their friends and family members. Congratulations immediately started to arrive along with requests for details. Rick read several replies out loud before one made him chuckle.

"What?" asked Elle.

"Mom sent a picture of Joe Kenda saying, "Well, my, my, my.""

Elle smiled, then reached for his phone. Thinking Elle was going to send a message of her own, he handed it over. But instead of typing a text, she walked out of the room. She soon returned and said, "Send them this pic."

Rick looked at a picture of the Do Not Disturb sign from the door handle and smiled. He quickly typed, "Sorry everyone, but Elle says . . ." He then attached the picture and hit send. He showed it to Elle before placing his phone on the night stand.

"By the way, I liked that thing you did with my ear in the office on Thursday."

"I stole it," she said.

"I know. From the best love scene in movie history—according to my mom."

"Hard to beat Bergman and Grant." She smiled. "Unless it's Bergman and Bogart . . . or Bergman and Peck . . .."

Rick went serious, "Elle, what made you change your mind?"

"About us?"

"Yeah," he said.

"It's kind of sappy."

"I like sappy."

Elle turned from her back to her side so she was facing him and said, "Alan Shepherd."

Rick's face took on a puzzled look. "As in first-American-in-space Alan Shepherd?"

"Yep," confirmed Elle. "Combine the theme from *Star Trek: Enterprise* with something your mom told me last fall and . . .."

"And . . .?"

"I gave the past a Viking funeral," she said. "Then I started planning on how to get back into your life."

Rick took his wife in his arms. "I can't believe how much I love you," he said.

"Who's getting sappy now?"

Rick raised up and said, "'Woman, do you love me'?"

Elle smiled at the song lyric he'd just quoted. She changed the next line to a question.

"Do you need me to be your woman?"

"'I need you more than want you, and I want you for all time.'"

"Ooh, nice segue, Hadley," she said. "You just went from Bernard Webb to Jimmy Webb in one degree."

"Yep, with Paul McCartney in parenthesis," he added. "Top that one Mrs. Hadley."

"That's Wyatt–Hadley, thank you very much."

Rick laughed. "Whatever . . . a rose by any other name . . .."

Rick looked at the ring Elle had placed on his finger less than twenty-four hours ago.

"You don't have to come right out and say it, you know," he said.

"But you want to hear it, right?'

"For now, I'll settle for something else from *Notorious*."

"Like a Cary Grant line?" she asked.

Rick nodded.

"'When I don't love you, I'll let you know'," she said.

Rick smiled and pulled her close.

"Yeah, that's the one."

ACKNOWLEDGEMENTS

Special thanks to the following for their expertise, encouragement, suggestions and support in the writing of *On the Border*.

Sharolynne Barth, I can't count the many hats you have worn since our first meeting: mentor, muse, cohort in crime, but friend is my favorite.

Becky Stephenson, my Bridge Over Troubled Water.

Douglas Perret Starr PhD, for editing.

Rc for the better, "Click"

My Central Illinois Team: my Aunt Eulala Hoke, and cousins Judy Hoke White, Landa Skiles, Janet Skiles, Robin Skiles Shawgo, Mark T. Skiles

Sandy Walden Kircher in Talent, Oregon
Will and Shelby Tucker in Memphis
Frankie Sutherland in Memphis
Officer Fielding and St. Louis County PD
Kyle Davis
Bruce Patrick
Heather Heinrichs
Pat Berndt Mccollum
Karen Evans Eckert
Joe Skaggs
Don Ingrum
Hope Elaine Shock
Patty Edens Fielding
Marcy Ibrahim
Agnes Lemercier Stansbury
Jonathan Starr
Tori Hull
Dale Walden
Ginnie McLaughlin
Michael Hernandez
Ra-Chelle Johnson, Sarah Bennett and Alex Cline for donating their names for characters.

Songs of *On the Border*

"On the Border", The Eagles
https://www.youtube.com/watch?v=WeuaxvEI9Dw
"Walk Like an Egyptian", The Bangles
https://www.youtube.com/watch?v=gzeOWnnSNjg
"The Right Thing to Do", Carly Simon
https://www.youtube.com/watch?v=RwGyW17KE6s
"Let Them Talk", Harry Connick, Jr.
https://www.youtube.com/watch?v=mxS9Yfn7wb8
"Walkin' Thru the Park", Muddy Waters
https://www.youtube.com/watch?v=yuZgoFj79Mg
"Marie Laveau", Bobby Bare
https://www.youtube.com/watch?v=xpZzehuWdM4
"They Don't Know You", Lee Roy Parnell
https://www.youtube.com/watch?v=1VwrTE18D0g
"You Can Sleep While I Drive", Trisha Yearwood
https://www.youtube.com/watch?v=zLWtkB0s1qE
"Aces", Cheryl Wheeler
https://www.youtube.com/watch?v=W0gX47VB8P8
"Addicted", Cheryl Wheeler
https://www.youtube.com/watch?v=nMb5CgjK-E4
"Ain't Too Proud to Beg", The Temptations
https://www.youtube.com/watch?v=1NZkeB6D7Jw
"I Know Why (And So Do You", Manhattan Transfer
https://www.youtube.com/watch?v=xH8S5IJ043w
"You Turn Me on I'm a Radio", Gail Davies
https://www.youtube.com/watch?v=x1bIVoUbA58
"Raining on Sunday", Keith Urban
https://www.youtube.com/watch?v=HNaQc1L4gO0
"Hush", Billy Joe Royal
https://www.youtube.com/watch?v=KrtguJg8F-8
"Help!", The Beatles
https://www.youtube.com/watch?v=MKUex3fci5c
"That's How I Got to Memphis", Buddy Miller
https://www.youtube.com/watch?v=qL923gEd2qg
"I Am a Rock", Simon and Garfunkel
https://www.youtube.com/watch?v=JKlSVNxLB-A
"It's Five O'Clock Somewhere", Alan Jackson, Jimmy Buffet
https://www.youtube.com/watch?v=aqbVVYD3je8
"Something to Be Said", Shelby Lynne
https://www.youtube.com/watch?v=nhc8ofCkoh4

"How to Handle a Woman", Richard Harris (Camelot)
https://www.youtube.com/watch?v=ARWsdOyHUYU
"Watermelon Man", Quincy Jones
https://www.youtube.com/watch?v=FycJuQTXdqw
"California Dreamin'", The Mamas and the Papas
https://www.youtube.com/watch?v=qhZULM69DIw
"Kiss", Marilyn Monroe
https://www.youtube.com/watch?v=iBrTcgoZkeI
"Margaritaville", Jimmy Buffett
https://www.youtube.com/watch?v=CICf8xoLyG8
"You Can't Talk Me into Loving You", The Will Tucker Band
https://www.youtube.com/watch?v=0Rto0WIUguI
"All Around the World", Little Willie John
https://www.youtube.com/watch?v=0XHC-qZXOyI
"Legend in Your Own Time", Carly Simon
https://www.youtube.com/watch?v=sI68BcPjehg
"Revelation Road", Shelby Lynne
https://www.youtube.com/watch?v=vHnQPGDs0Ik
"The Thief", Shelby Lynne
https://www.youtube.com/watch?v=asYZD7O2XyM
"Lie", Tracy Lawrence
https://www.youtube.com/watch?v=KXcvo9GuZ68
"Need You Now", Lady Antebellum
https://www.youtube.com/watch?v=_LGEGEuBckU
"If Two Wrongs Don't Make a Right", Eric Erdman
https://www.youtube.com/watch?v=CXCHAr6oC8Q
"Tennessee Whiskey", Will Tucker Band
https://vimeo.com/363075272?fbclid=IwAR0MaAhchPgk4-
6WemwFIGsBONtoMjJdvCAcyTJYb9V6YFMuVgSZ_gO1U7g
"Tennessee Whiskey," Chris Stapleton
https://www.youtube.com/watch?v=4zAThXFOy2c&list=RD4zAThXF
Oy2c&start_radio=1
"Sadie, Sadie", Barbra Streisand (Funny Girl)
https://www.youtube.com/watch?v=ixr_IN8JalA
"Signed, Sealed, Delivered (I'm Yours)", Stevie Wonder
https://www.youtube.com/watch?v=6To0fvX_wFA
"Woman", Peter and Gordon
https://www.youtube.com/watch?v=XPqMlOQOfgo
"Wichita Lineman", Glen Campbell
https://www.youtube.com/watch?v=Q8P_xTBpAcY

Films of *On the Border*
The Simpsons Movie (2007)
Hope Floats (1998)
Sun Valley Serenade (1941)
Out of the Past (1947)
Angel Face (1953)
Macao (1952)
Gravity (2013)
Some Like it Hot (1959)
The Day the Earth Stood Still (1951)
Sunset Boulevard (1950)
"The Postman Always Rings Twice (1946)
Niagara (1953)
Kiss Me Deadly (1955)
Psycho (1960)
The Sixth Sense (1999)
2001: A Space Odyssey (1968)
The Shining (1980)
Rear Window (1954)
North by Northwest (1959)
Notorious (1946)
Beach Blanket Bingo (1965)
The Vikings (1958)

Television Shows of *On the Border*
The Simpsons
Sesame Street
Grey's Anatomy
The Red Green Show
I Love Lucy
Criminal Minds
Hogan's Heroes
Clifford's Puppy Days
Star Trek: Voyager
Star Trek: Enterprise
Homicide Hunter

Made in the USA
Monee, IL
20 July 2020

36761670R00194